CREEP

B.C. BLUES CRIME NOVELS

Cold Girl
Undertow

CREEP

A B.C. BLUES CRIME NOVEL

R.M. GREENAWAY

DUNDURN
TORONTO

Cover image: istock.com/Koshenyamka
Printer: Webcom

Library and Archives Canada Cataloguing in Publication

Greenaway, R. M., author
    Creep / R.M. Greenaway.

(A B.C. blues crime novel)
Issued in print and electronic formats.
ISBN 978-1-4597-3989-5 (softcover).--ISBN 978-1-4597-3990-1 (PDF).--
ISBN 978-1-4597-3991-8 (EPUB)

    I. Title. II. Series: Greenaway, R. M. B.C. blues crime novel.

PS8613.R4285C74 2018   C813'.6   C2017-905985-8
                                       C2017-905986-6

1 2 3 4 5   22 21 20 19 18

 Conseil des Arts du Canada   Canada Council for the Arts   Canada   ONTARIO ARTS COUNCIL CONSEIL DES ARTS DE L'ONTARIO an Ontario government agency un organisme du gouvernement de l'Ontario

We acknowledge the support of the **Canada Council for the Arts**, which last year invested $153 million to bring the arts to Canadians throughout the country, and the **Ontario Arts Council** for our publishing program. We also acknowledge the financial support of the **Government of Ontario**, through the **Ontario Book Publishing Tax Credit** and the **Ontario Media Development Corporation**, and the **Government of Canada**.

Nous remercions le **Conseil des arts du Canada** de son soutien. L'an dernier, le Conseil a investi 153 millions de dollars pour mettre de l'art dans la vie des Canadiennes et des Canadiens de tout le pays.

Care has been taken to trace the ownership of copyright material used in this book. The author and the publisher welcome any information enabling them to rectify any references or credits in subsequent editions.

— *J. Kirk Howard, President*

The publisher is not responsible for websites or their content unless they are owned by the publisher.

Printed and bound in Canada.

VISIT US AT

 dundurn.com | @dundurnpress | dundurnpress | dundurnpress

Dundurn
3 Church Street, Suite 500
Toronto, Ontario, Canada
M5E 1M2

For Dill, Modobenny, Bogie, Knighthawk, and Gem

One

SHAPE-SHIFTER

ONLY DISTANCE HAD shut up Jack Randall. After the footbridge over Lynn Creek had come boardwalks and rustic stairs, then tree roots, boulders, and now a steadily rising incline. The October rain was coming down — not the second flood Randall had predicted, palm out in the parking lot, but a meanish drizzle. In the time it took to pause, unzip his patrol jacket, and swear at the sky, Dion's new partner had gone charging ahead, invisible but for the reflective stripes on his uniform.

There was no hurry, in Dion's mind. Somewhere up the path a dead man waited, growing cold, but a minute here or there hardly mattered. It wasn't a crime, according to the dispatch. What it sounded like was an unfit man who had hiked himself to death. Happens.

But Randall was new at this, and ambitious — he'd even said so — and was probably hoping for a startling turn of events, a knife in the back or bullet hole in the temple. What he was going to find was everyday tragedy.

Dion had met Randall half an hour ago, their introductions made in the shadows of the parkade as they responded to the call-out, but already he knew more than he needed to about the man. Randall hadn't stopped talking from the moment he'd turned the key till — well, the distance now growing between them had put an end to it.

Randall was twenty-four, a few years younger than Dion. Born in Chilliwack, raised in Surrey, started his career in the central interior. Then, just days ago, he'd lucked into this North Shore posting, which he thought was great. He hoped he would get to stay a while. The plan was to work his way into the Serious Crimes Section, where he could put his brains to good use. He had good brains — he'd said that, too.

Dion pushed on. Rain spattered on his forage cap and his shoulders, on cedar boughs and the pathway, and before his eyes, the remaining daylight dimmed. There had been no second flashlight in the boot of the cruiser, and all he had was the penlight on his belt, so when a halo blossomed around Randall's silhouette ahead — the little bastard had finally switched on the truncheon-sized Maglite — Dion jogged to share the illuminated path.

Randall heard him huffing and turned to stare. "You okay there?"

Aside from this summer's trouble, which had landed him back on uniformed patrol with a loudmouth rookie like Jack Randall, much like when he'd left Depot ten years ago, yes, Dion was okay. "I'm fine," he said. "Why?"

"We're leaving the senior's path now," Randall said, grinning. He was short but fit. Round-faced, with ginger-gold bangs poking out from under his cap, wire-rimmed glasses, and easy enough in this spanking-new relationship to mock his partner. "Might get a little tougher from here on."

It did get tougher, but not for long. Their destination appeared between trees, a blot of light. In the distance, Dion counted three figures standing around a mound of shiny fabric. One of the figures appeared to have two heads, but as he caught up, he realized it was two people glommed together in the twilight.

Randall was talking to a medic when Dion arrived. The mound was a body lying on the ground, covered in a foil blanket. Rain thumped on the foil, danced, and splashed. The glommed-together couple resolved into two teenagers in a tight embrace, a boy and girl in rain gear, their hoods up. A second paramedic stood apart, talking on a satellite radio. Everybody winced against the falling rain.

The first medic was saying to Randall, "… Just time and place, you know, thought it'd be a good idea if you guys took a look."

"Sure," Randall said. "What's the story?"

"Probably heart gave out. Name is Aldobrandino Rosetti, fifty-two years old."

Randall asked to take a look.

"Yes. Just watch what you say. Those are his kids. They found him. Came looking for him when he didn't get home by dinnertime."

Dion heard the teenagers murmuring to each other. He heard the word *Mom* repeated. He looked up the path Aldobrandino Rosetti had apparently come down, a dark tunnel through a wall of old-growth trees. Crazy idea to hike alone, and so late in the day. The victim must have collapsed as daylight waned, when the path had cleared of other hikers. Otherwise someone would have come upon him, reported the find. Nobody had. He might have lain here all night, if his kids hadn't gone out searching.

Randall leaned over to pull back the blanket, using his flashlight to look up and down the dead man's body. He checked the pockets for a phone and found one. Dion leaned forward to see what he could of the dead man. He caught a flash of grey-green cargo shorts and a fat, pale elbow flopped to the dirt. Randall lowered the blanket and went to talk to the kids.

Randall introduced himself to the young Rosettis. He got their names, address, and contact information, while Dion configured penlight and notebook to take it down. Randall asked the teens about their father, what brought him here, how they'd come to find him. Wetness choked up Dion's pen, and he interrupted Randall, more with sign language than words, that this was all stuff they could ask later — in the patrol car, out of the rain — time not being of the essence here. He put away his notebook and asked what really mattered: "Does he have any history of heart trouble?"

"No, none," the boy said. "His doctor told him to get more exercise. Like everything else he does, he went at it too fast, too hard. I should've slowed him down. I should've gone with him. I should've seen this coming."

Randall said, "Shorts and a sweater. He doesn't seem so well prepared."

The boy and girl were silent a moment, looking at Randall, maybe thinking that criticizing their dad at a time like this was just nasty. Then the boy said, "He knew it was going to rain. His app told him. He loves his weather app."

"He loves all his apps," the girl said.

Imitating the deeper voice of an older man, the boy said, "Is there an app for that?"

The girl burst out laughing and the boy started crying. Dion shifted his boots on the uneven ground and looked into the woods. He heard the girl say, "He aimed to be home long before the rain started. He was going to be home for dinner."

Randall asked, "Any idea what else he took with him? Gear, packs, hat, camera?"

"He took his new pack, for sure. I guess his phone, wallet, keys. Lunch. Maybe extra clothes. Probably his camera. I don't know," the boy replied.

"Definitely his camera," the girl said.

"You tried calling him, of course?"

"Of course. Went to voice mail."

"Sure," Randall said. "No signal up here, for starters. I don't see a pack anywhere. Did you see it when you arrived?"

They shook their heads.

"Can you describe the pack?"

The boy described a cheapie from Bentley, black with grey detailing. Randall nodded at the kids, letting them go back to their private conversation. He shone his light at the ground near the dead man's feet. He looked under the foil blanket again, then spoke to Dion, not quietly enough. "No blood, eh. No wounds."

The distance between Randall's mouth and the kids' ears was too short, in Dion's opinion. He agreed with Randall that there was no obvious sign of injury and asked the kids to move away, please. They did as told, went to stand behind the paramedics.

Randall crouched to study the earth around Rosetti's body. The path was sodden now, pooling in places, and smothered in a reddish-brown carpet of conifer needles. The carpet appeared to be disturbed under Randall's probing light beam. "Looks like he gave the ground a good kicking. Must be hell when that thing gives up, eh? The heart." He scanned his light about, into the flashing rain, the woods, the undergrowth as far as the rays could reach, then along the path down which Rosetti must have come rushing before his collapse. "So where's this famous pack?"

He and Dion climbed some distance farther before they found the first piece of evidence, a small bulk picked up in the light beam, bright red. A bloody hunk of meat, Dion thought, shocked enough to gasp — until he saw it was not organic, but man-made. Not a carcass, and not a pack either, but a heap of red material. A man's hiking jacket. Up around the curve of the path lay the black nylon pack itself. Like the jacket, it looked brand new. In the dirt nearby, Dion found a small silver item. "Camera," he called out.

"Really?" Randall said. "Don't," he added sharply, as Dion bent to pick it up. "Take pictures of all this stuff *in situ*. Okay? Just in case."

"God," Dion said. He used his own camera to take shots of the three items where they lay, bright white flashes pricking the night, then picked up the dead man's camera by its strap and dropped it into one of the exhibit bags tucked in his utility belt. He stuck the thing in his jacket pocket, to be sealed and labelled back at the cruiser.

Now that they had what they were looking for, they would get going, he hoped, out of the wilds and back down to civilization. He watched the leafy underbrush swell and shudder on either side. Even armed, and even in the presence of another man who was also armed, the woods made him nervous. There were carnivores here on the upper reaches of the North Shore. Bears, for sure. Cougars weren't unheard of.

"How far d'you reckon we walked from the body?" Randall asked, chipper and sharp. He sounded young, almost girlish, like a teenaged boy whose voice had not yet broken. He stood looking down the path they had just climbed, gauging distance with his eyes.

Dion looked downhill, too. "A long way."

"Over a kilometre," Randall said. "What d'you think, my friend?" Without warning and without waiting for an answer he shut off his light, and the darkness was abruptly all over them, blacker than black. Dion stared at where Randall must still be standing, and Randall's voice hissed, "*Listen.*"

Dion tightened his fist on his unlit penlight and listened. His eyes adjusted, and his partner became visible to him: a ghostly glimmer, pinpricks of light marking the prescription lenses. He could hear what Randall was maybe wanting him to hear, what he had heard all along, now amplified by the darkness: the living rainforest. The ruckus. Creaking, whispering, pattering. Something moaned.

"Would be kind of scary if you were alone, hey?" Randall said.

"Sure."

"There would have been daylight still when Rosetti was here. But getting dim. What was he running from?"

"Rain in the forecast, maybe. Let's have some light."

"Rain?" Randall's laugh was a startling blast of gaiety in the darkness. "Get real. If he was scared of rain, he would put on his jacket, not drop it."

"An animal, then. Or his imagination."

"What animal? If something was in hot pursuit, it would have caught up."

"Imagination," Dion said, losing patience. "Saw a bear or a cougar, or thought he saw one. Ran like hell. Who wouldn't?"

Unlike Dion, Randall was enjoying the debate. "Ran too far for an imaginary fear," he said. "He's not an experienced hiker, but he's not green, either. If he saw an animal, he may have run, sure, or walked very fast for a while. But he would have realized soon enough that whatever it was, it was not coming after him. Natural human pride would have kicked in, if nothing else, and he would have slowed down. Right?"

Dion took a deep breath, let it out slowly.

"Made noise, waved his arms, took precautions," Randall continued. "Instead he ditched his belongings and ran for his life. Ran so hard his heart gave out."

"So he got tired. Stopped to take a break. Felt something wrong with his heart, got scared, took off trying to get back to the parking lot before he went into cardiac arrest." Dion switched his light on, to show he was done. "Obviously he didn't make it. Let's go."

He bent to gather the backpack, then the jacket, and started down the path, with or without Randall and the powerful light beam he had finally switched back on. Randall didn't follow immediately — fussing with rocks, by the sound of it, marking the spot — but soon joined him to continue the argument.

"Sure, feeling chest pain would have worried him, made him rush. But to drop everything and flee? Because that's what it feels like to me, like he was fleeing something."

Dion knew that if he let every what-if bother him, little would ever get done. He said nothing.

"It's that distance," Randall said. "A kilometre? How far can you run after a stroke? Think you can run a kilometre?"

Dion was thinking about the 9 mm at his side, about using it on Randall, when Randall stopped in his tracks. The light from his torch swung wildly into the trees as he reached out. "Hey, the camera! Let's see what's on it."

The darkness pressed at Dion's back and the rain hammered his cap. Whatever had pursued Rosetti was still out there, and it was high time to get out of this wilderness. "No chance. The water would have killed it."

"Won't know till we try, will we?"

Dion dug out the camera and handed it to Randall, who blotted the thing dry with a tissue, then pushed the review button. His round, pale face was lit greenish by the little screen — it wasn't dead after all. Dion forgot the shadows at his back and stepped closer, watching Randall for reaction.

"Tourist shots," Randall said, disappointed.

Dion took the camera, shielded it from the rain with a hand, and had a look. The last few photos were stock snapshots — quite nice, actually — the long rays of a dying day shooting between cedar trunks and lighting up endless miles of bush, and a patch of what looked like devil's club — leaves the size of manhole covers, yellowed now by winter, hiding their razor spikes. Pretty in a forest setting, but armed to the teeth.

He grinned at Randall. "What did you expect, monsters?"

"Would have been nice," Randall admitted.

* * *

"'Scuse me, nature calls." Randall parted ways with Dion in the corridor to head toward the staff washrooms. Dion watched him push at the wrong door, the one clearly marked *female*. Tempted to say nothing, but pleased the little go-getter wasn't perfect, he called out a warning. "Hey, Jack. You're not a lady."

Randall's response shocked him. "It's Jackie, not Jack. And yes, I am."

He disappeared into the ladies' room. She, not he. The door closed behind her.

Dion stared at the door. Presumption had built on presumption. He had misheard Randall introduce herself as *Jack*. Between her bulky uniform, her low cap brim, and poor lighting, *Jack* she had remained to him, a man, short and shrill. Now that she was Jackie, she was so clearly female that he burned with embarrassment. Well, at least she'd have a good guffaw with her buddies tonight.

In the big picture, it didn't matter. It was just laughter. If being laughed at was going to be his worst problem on the job, then he was one lucky cop who was apparently getting away with murder. He dropped into his chair before his computer, switched on the screen, and got on with his plan of being a good man for the rest of his life.

Two

THE WOLF

DIARY ENTRY OF STEFANO BOONE —
OCTOBER 23:

Humans are such mad deluded creatures all tiny whirring particles within the universe each believing they are the universe saying nothing seeing nothing being nothing so blind so dull so vain. I am not.

Stefano wasn't vain, and he wasn't the universe. He knew what he was, a *speckle* within it, but a major speckle, one with an important part to play, if only he could figure out what that part was. Right now in this world he was nothing but a really bad fit.

The pain didn't help. It spasmed in his calves, ran up his thighs, pinged in his scapulae, but not disabling, and in some ways reassuring. It told him he was developing, that he belonged elsewhere. Not here, chopping carrots.

He chopped like a machine, *bang bang bang bang bang bang bang*.

As if from above, he watched himself working. To escape the tedium of chopping carrots, he planned his next canvas. He would be his own subject, as always. Not a detailed self-portrait, but a streak of cheap acrylic lurking within the slashes of dark and light lines that could be lampposts, or faceless crowds, or trees, abstract verticals toppling like blowdown and blurring his outline to the viewer.

Except he had no viewers. Only Troy, the little blond boy with the goggle-like eyeglasses who lived down the street. Troy had taken to crawling through Stefano's window now and then to visit. He would look at the paintings and sometimes comment. He said they were "neat."

Stefano wanted real feedback, from grown-ups. His parents knew a lot about art and creativity, but they hadn't even tried to see the paintings he showed them. Showing them had been a mistake.

But worse was the time he had hauled his best pieces into the little gallery on Lonsdale. The gallery lady had gone out of her way to give him what she must have considered to be constructive criticism, but she didn't know a thing about him or what he was trying to say. And she needn't have bothered, because her first reaction said it all, that fleeting look of dismay, then pity. She may as well have stabbed him in the heart.

Now he showed no one, never, no more.

The restaurant had peaked at around nine and was quieter now. The wait staff and dishwashers were taking short breaks, flirting by the refrigerator, goofing around.

They ignored Stefano, and he knew why. He scared them all with his physical presence — or maybe lack of it. At twenty-two, he stood taller than the crowd. He was a looming invisibility. His body had grown long and concave from years of fussy, almost food-phobic eating. His hair was black and wiry, and his lashes were long. His beard had come in as wispy as the patch of hair on his chest. He would have liked a wild and messy beard, but people in the food industry should be well groomed, as Chef Jordan had told him, and he did everything he could to please Chef.

She talked about it sometimes on their shared commute, complimenting his haircut or his new shoes, whatever efforts he made to look nice. She said nothing, though, whenever a horrible, sleepless night had left him bristly or unkempt, like today.

He hadn't shaved today because of his parents' Scarlatti. It had kept him awake, that damned harpsichord tinkling through the floorboards — along with the endless groan of Anastasia's CPAP machine — down into his lair, glassy notes dripping on his head till he ducked under the blankets with a snarl. Head covered, he had stayed in bed till past noon and risen too late to get properly ready in time for pickup by Chef in her Rabbit.

What Stefano desperately needed was a place of his own, but the dream was fading, and worse than hopelessness is hopelessness that follows hope. Two years ago he had secured this job at the Taverna. After saving up for over a year, and after an excited month hunting for his own apartment — that was back in June — he understood that he could fill out rental applications till his fingers rotted off, and still nobody would accept him. He was too different. Anyway, he couldn't afford to move out, not on his wages. He was stuck in his parents' home with no escape.

Something had to give. And what would give, if not him?

Not them, Paul and Colette. They were dried out and timeless. They would live forever, and he would live below them for just as long. He was their burden, their disappointment, the boy who had destroyed the family, and as punishment they would play the cursed CD. Scarlatti in the morning, Scarlatti at night. Sometimes — just sometimes — they would break it up with Schubert.

A waitress shrieked a laugh, and a busboy shushed her, the two of them skidding like drunks on a dance-floor. Stefano squeezed his eyes shut. The din never stopped in the Greek Taverna. Chatter from the dining room, the whisking rush of the waitresses' nyloned legs, the banging from the dish pit. Chef and sous-chef were arguing about eggplant, and as always, the radio buzzed on its shelf, CKLG-FM, volume down so low that the DJs sounded like mosquito people.

He glanced at the clock and clamped his jaw. Almost quitting time. The tightness and tingling coursed down from rump to Achilles tendon. At just past 11:00 p.m. he heard the last diner belch his satisfaction, pay his bill, and go. Instantly the staff dropped their manners and became their normal vulgar selves. Hyenas.

Stefano cleaned his work surfaces and packed vege-tables, scowling as he thought about Anastasia. The pier-cing shriek of that waitress had done it. Shrieking girls always took him back to his sister's last laugh. Chairs were being pulled aside now, and the dishes were loaded into the bins. The staff moved down the narrow corridor past Stefano to the back exit, not looking at him. They filed out into the night, and the door eased shut with a thump. A hush fell over this steamy, smelly dungeon — except for the yapping radio.

He switched it off. Chef Jordan was nowhere in sight. She had sung out good night to the girls, done what she had to do, then disappeared. She would be outside, rewarding herself with a short toke as she waited.

Stefano pictured her there in the dark, sucking her poison, tall and slim, as dark as the night around her. Her mother was black and her father white, and she looked exotic, with her umber skin, grey-blue eyes, and deep gold curls. He loved the slow, soft lilt of her voice. He loved everything about her.

He threw his apron in the hamper and pulled on his ski jacket. The back door that opened onto the parking lot was steel plated like it was meant to keep out tanks instead of the briny portside chill. There was a patter of light rain as he stepped out, and the sharp drift of burning weed located her to him in the darkness — there she stood, almost invisible by the blue dumpster, with her woolly coat wrapped close. She smiled and nodded at him, and together they headed toward her car. A crackling series of bangs sounded off in the distance. Halloween was around the corner, and even in the drizzle kids were out getting a head start on the fun.

Chef was stuffed into her driver's seat now. Stefano took his place beside her. It was icy cold in here, and his fingers, linked on his lap, looked bony and blue. Chef twisted the key and started the car, her Rabbit, her Little Lemon, as she called it, and along with its uneven poop-poop, something in its workings chattered like windup teeth. Chef said, like she said so often, "Oh dear, there go the valves."

What could he say to that? "Oh dear," he murmured.

He knew she must wish him gone. She would prefer a small-talker like herself, what with all the hours they'd spent jammed together going to and fro since May, when she had moved in just down the block. How did it happen that he was so well read and not a bad writer, yet in her presence, the spoken word got stuck somewhere between his brain and his tongue?

His few attempts at rejoinder were always drowned out by something larger than himself. If it wasn't the drone of a truck, it was a passing siren. If not a siren, it was her exclaiming about the funny bumper sticker ahead. There was always something.

The Rabbit idled on the white line. Chef looked westward for a break in traffic. "Problem is, you take her in for the valves, and they say, 'Sorry, ma'am, looks like the whole tranny's gotta go.' You say, 'Ouch, how much is that gonna set me back?' They say, 'Ooh, well, this one's kind of a doozy.' It's always a doozy with cars, Stef. Trust me, you're better off with public transit."

He looked at her sidelong and bent his mouth into his sexiest practiced smile, but her eyes were on a passing bus. She pulled out so fast they nearly hit its rear end. Stefano seized the grab handle at his side. Chef was a menace on the road. It was a miracle they weren't both dead, with all the miles they put in between the harbourfront, where they worked, and upper Lynn Valley, where they lived.

Lonsdale to Keith, Keith to Grand Boulevard — always the same roads. Chef was telling him about the threat of coyotes to small pets. She had a cat named Radar, as he well knew by now. He didn't bother looking at her as she prattled on about cats and coyotes. His mind was on his own inner processes, his cold and airy nasal passages, the tightness of his face. His teeth ached, pushing against his jawbone. How odd that nobody noticed the changes coming over him. When would Chef look at him, finally, and gasp?

Someday, he would take her up into the wilds, where she would be the helpless one, and *he* would be in control. He smiled, and his mind went back to his next painting. It would be a self-portrait in vermillion. He would bring his long face out from the trees for a change, into the foreground. It was time to show his teeth.

Three

THE GHOSTS OF SUBURBIA

DAVE LEITH SAT ALONE in a haunted house. The house didn't belong to him, but to the people upstairs. He had been on the North Shore since April and in this place since August, with his wife Alison and young daughter Izzy — they were away this week visiting Alison's family in Parksville. He knew he was lucky to have landed the main floor of this sizeable home, even if the rent was hemorrhaging his bank account. He should be grateful.

Instead he was sulking. He sat on a dining room chair by the living room window, looking out at the rain splashing down on somebody else's rising equity.

The ghost in the walls groaned. He ignored it. This was a nearly new monster house in a nearly new neighbourhood, and as far as he knew, it had no gruesome history. He hadn't believed the warnings of the landlord's young daughter the day he and Alison moved in. The kid had watched as they carted things from the U-Haul down to the side entrance, and on one of his passes she had told him, "There are ghosts down there, you know."

He had thought it was cute. He'd smiled at the little girl like the big, brave man he was. But he had since heard the proof, usually late at night: the sighs and thuds of what could only be the residual angst of those who had passed on.

Leith was itching to leave this house. Not because of the ghosts, which he could take or leave, but because he wanted a place of his own, a place with property pins, a lawn, a concrete pad for his barbecue. All his life he had been a freehold landowner. Then he'd moved to North Vancouver and found himself out of his depth. Getting a house here was out of the question. A condo, maybe. Renting was just plain brutal. This was his third move this year, always on the lookout for a better deal.

His work cell rang, and he hoped it was the office wanting him to come in and do something. Anything. Sitting alone and listening to weird noises wasn't fun.

"Leith," he said to his phone.

The caller was Corporal Michelin Montgomery — known to staff as Monty. He was a silver-haired newcomer to the North Vancouver detachment, even newer than Leith. Unlike Leith, he had already made a ton of friends.

"Dave, sorry to spring this on you," Monty said. "Looks like we've got trouble in Lynn Valley. Up to you, really, but we're going to be all over this tomorrow, and I thought you might want to have a first-hand look."

Leith jotted down the address, agreed to be on scene in twenty minutes, and disconnected.

He was putting away his notebook when something moved along the floor toward him. He jumped to his feet, toppling his chair, and stared into the shadows of the haunted house.

He looked down. Nothing but a large house spider scuttling along the floorboards. The spider was as startled as Leith was and had frozen in its tracks, waiting for this hell to pass.

Leith killed the spider with the slap of a rolled-up *Westworld* magazine, knowing that for a big, brave man, he had leaped fairly high. Not a good start to a new homicide. He stuck the mess in the kitchen waste bin, then fetched his fleece-lined RCMP jacket off its hook and headed out the door.

* * *

The rain poured on Lynn Valley. On a little spur of road that jutted up into the trees, out of line with the well laid-out suburbs, stood the subject house — behind the high fence that hid it. The spur of road was named Greer. Lynn Valley Road, intersecting Greer, was jammed with police vehicles. A handful of concerned citizens were out in their raincoats, talking to RCMP members about what the heck was going on here.

Leith popped open his umbrella and made his way through an open gate and into a yard. The yard was big by North Vancouver standards, he saw. There were several ugly trees growing here, leafless and hairy, throwing spooky shadows. The branches seemed polka-dotted with withered apples hardly bigger than cherries. An old orchard, maybe, though North Van was anything but fruit-growing country.

Light dazzled his eyes. A heaved cement path led to a front porch, but the action seemed to be at the side of the house. He left the path and crossed a stretch of soggy turf to join Corporal Montgomery and others in their rain capes. JD Temple was present, he was glad to see. Her short dark hair was plastered to her head and framed her face so that her eyes seemed larger than usual.

LED torches cranked high and spiked into the turf directed splashy light onto the side of the house and all around, the beams fanning out to make rain and faces sparkle. The group was looking toward the house, not up at its boarded windows, but down at its foundations. Leith followed the general line of sight and saw that where concrete met dirt was a man-sized hole. It looked to him like a poorly installed access hatch had rotted out some years ago, allowing in the elements.

"Shabby," he said. He'd been in the construction trade for a few years before joining the force, and he knew everything there was to know about foundations.

"Looks like the hole was covered with that bit of ply-wood, but it's fallen down," JD said. She pointed out the piece of wood half-buried in mud and a scattering of largish rocks that had maybe propped it up.

"Or dogs smelled something fishy and got at it," Leith said. Dogs weren't supposed to run off leash in the city, but sometimes they got away.

He could see water pooling in the dirt around the hole, building up and spilling into the crawl space. From the blackness within, a vague light shifted and flickered.

"The cause of all this fuss is in a duffel bag," Monty said. "Ident's in there, just checking if it's human. In which case we got a problem, 'cause Dad sure isn't going to fit through that hole."

Dad, Leith interpreted — as he'd had to time and again since his arrival in North Vancouver — was Jack Dadd, the overweight coroner. Gauging the hole in the foundations now, he could see the problem. The wind shifted, and he could smell death.

"Freaky place," JD said. She was looking up into the stark branches of the trees, the unappetizing fruit that hung there. "What can you grow in this part of the world? Crab apples?"

Monty looked around, too, but with something like admiration. "One week to Halloween, what a setting for a zombie bash. Great whadyacallit, ambience. Which reminds me —"

A grunt from the base of the house interrupted whatever Monty was reminded of, and Leith watched a white-suited Ident tech squirm from the hole — like a weird birthing — and into the hard beam of the floodlight. The tech made it to his feet and approached the detectives, removing his mask and spitting into the grasses.

"Yeah, well," he said to Monty, "it's a body, all right. Been there a while. Lying in a puddle. We got some pictures, but didn't want to mess around too much. What d'you want us to do? Leave it as is, or haul it out?"

"How fragile is it?" asked JD. "Are we going to rearrange the anatomy if we move it?"

"I think we'll get it out pretty clean." The tech looked back at the foundations with a tradesman's squint. "Shift it onto a tarp, pull it out slow. We got a clear path, no obstacles. I don't see a problem."

"It's either that or a *Jack*-hammer," Monty said.

Both he and the tech chuckled. JD appeared to get the joke, but didn't seem to find it funny. A moment later, Leith got it, too. *Jack* Dadd. He obliged with a grin, briefly. Across the lawn the constables were toiling like concert roadies, setting up the polypropylene tent that would protect exhibits and equipment. Leith recognized one of them, a man who should be here next to him, in plainclothes, being a detective.

"So what do we know about who owns this place?" he asked Monty.

"JD's given me a little history on that," Monty said. "Eccentric dude named Harmon is on title, now living in Florida. We're trying to contact him. He built it in the sixties, but not to code, and a few years ago it was declared unlivable and closed up. But he refuses to sell or upgrade. As a result, he's blessed Lynn Valley with its first derelict mansion."

"Wow." Leith looked up at the house with interest. It was hardly a mansion, just a regular two-storey home, squat and graceless with a peculiar hip-roof construction and an odd wannabe-tower structure stuck at one corner. The roof was clad in dark metal, the siding in black-brown clapboards clustered with moss. In a neighbourhood of beautiful, bright homes, this one tucked back in the trees had the quality of a mould blemish.

Monty turned to the Ident tech. "Do we preserve the body *in situ* or do we preserve the hole? I guess we could rip up floorboards, approach it that way, but I'm not sure it's worth it."

Leith asked the tech how the ground in there was for prints.

"Lousy," the tech replied. "All grit. We stayed off the drag path as best as possible and got a bunch of shots of scuff marks that aren't going to tell us anything. Ripping up the floorboards will just drop a bunch of crap down, contaminate it all to hell unless we lay down some serious plastic. Again, not worth it. If there's anything in there, it's lost in the sand. We're going to have to sift it all out one way or another."

"Let's haul it out. What d'you think, get some good video footage as we go?" Leith asked Monty.

Monty agreed. "Let's do that." And to the tech, "Bag got a zip, or what?"

"Drawstring at the top. Knotted, like, a million times. We had to cut a flap in the fabric to see in. Could see the top of somebody's head and looked like part of a hand. I mean, if we cut the bag wide open, it'll be that much harder to get it out clean. Best just to bring it out in one piece, bag and all, extra careful."

"Go for it," Monty said.

The full team filtered in over the next hour. The rain tapered to a light drizzle. Beyond the fence, Leith knew, the neighbourhood was wide awake now. The more inquisitive neighbours would be hanging about, coats and gumboots over their pajamas, asking questions and trying to get a glimpse through the gates. Here in the yard, the night sky was blotted out by the glare of the LEDs. Jack Dadd arrived. The grisly sack was tugged into view. The army-green canvas was soaked at the bottom, dry on top. Inch by inch, it was transported on its tarpaulin-cum-sled to the shelter. Dadd gave the okay to open the bag.

Some of those present wagered on a Halloween prank even to the last moment, until the heavy canvas was peeled back and what lay within killed all conversation. The corpse was stiffened into a twisted huddle — male or female, it was impossible to say. The camera flashed as the body, released from its bondage, slouched into a gentler curl against the tarp.

Even uncurled, the head remained tucked into its chest, as if shying from their prying eyes. The internal organs would be soup, seeped into the duffel bag's fabric and the sand below, the rest gutted by bugs. No eyes visible, a mouldering nose, a fine gold chain around its neck.

"Female," Monty guessed.

"Male," JD said.

Leith was thinking male, too. The corpse had to have been a young man. Fair-sized in life, probably, but shrunken in death. The head was shaved almost to the scalp but for a bisecting flop of dark hair, flattened and brittle, the modernized Mohawk style. He wore faded black hipster jeans that were shredded in places, a mouldy-looking hoodie, also black, and one dark-blue running shoe. The body had brought with it that foul smell, dissipated by the open air, but unmistakeable. It was that odour that had caused the citizen's complaint that had brought out the uniforms. Those first responders had made some calls, cut the padlock, entered the lot. Their flashlights had picked out the hump of bag in the crawl space, and they had decided it was sinister enough to call in GIS. And here they all were.

"She was young," Monty said. "Time of death, Doc?"

Coroner Dadd was the only one present not huddling and grimacing at the rain, his grimace reserved for the fate of the victim before him. "It's John, actually, not Jane. I'd guess two months, three at most."

"Two to three months ago? How come we're only getting complaints now?" JD said.

"The big rains only started this month," Leith pointed out. "If the crawl space flooded recently, and the body was lying in water for the first time, it could have released the odours in a bigger way. A wet dead mouse smells a lot worse than a dry dead mouse, believe me. Also, we don't know when that hatch came down. If it was recently, that could be another reason."

JD looked at the house and the high fence that surrounded it. "October, September, August. Whoever dumped this guy knew the area, knew this place was sitting empty."

Leith had to agree. It wasn't a busy neighbourhood. Whoever had done this had lived close by long enough to observe that the house was up for grabs. Possible, too, that whoever had done it was an out-of-towner driving in random circles. That person might have driven by and noticed the *Do Not Enter* signs posted around and thought to himself — or herself — *Aha, nice.*

But what about the locks on the gate?

Looking around, he suspected the fence marched in an unbroken rectangle all around. Nothing but a shrubby lane ran along the side of the house and, maybe, continued around back. Must check for a weak link first thing. Or a weak board, in this case.

The concert roadie constable who should have been a detective — Cal Dion — approached from the area of the driveway. He looked both soaked and overheated, his cap removed and jacket unzipped. He skirted the corpse on its tarp, not even glancing down, as if to show how little he cared. He nodded briefly at JD and Leith and told Monty, "We're done here. Constable Randall wants to know if it's all right to go get a full statement from Mr. Lavender now."

"Mr. Who?" Monty said.

Dion pointed south. "Mr. Lavender. Lives across the road there. He reported the smell."

JD made a noise that Leith heard as a snort of laughter, while Dion clarified his request to Monty. "Jackie Randall and I were first on scene. We talked to Lavender and said we might be back. Randall wants to finish up with him. She also wants to start canvassing the neighbourhood. I told her we need permission." He looked at JD as if daring her to laugh again. "So I'm here."

Monty shrugged at Leith. "Want to weigh in?"

"Somebody else can deal with Lavender," Leith said. "And we're certainly not canvassing anybody this time of night. The body's been down here a while. Another few hours won't matter. Thanks, Cal."

Leith had first met Dion on a case in the Hazeltons earlier this year, but it was a complicated working relationship, the kind he felt was best left at a comfortable distance. He got the distinct sense that Dion felt the same, only more so.

Though Dion nodded a *yessir* without argument and walked away, the story didn't end there. A minute later, a shorter, stouter figure came squishing across the lawn to challenge Monty on the same issue, but with a lot more pepper. This was a constable Leith didn't recognize. Young, probably new to the job, but already taking charge. "Constable Jackie Randall, sir," she informed Monty. "Half the neighbourhood's out on the sidewalk, so it seems a good time to ask questions."

"Last I looked, the neighbours cleared out back home. Nothing to see," JD said.

"All the more urgent to get knocking on doors," Randall shot back at her. "Before lights out. And I do want to hand in a full report, which means completing my statement from the man who called in the complaint."

"Anybody can talk to the man who called in the complaint," JD said.

"I'm not anybody." Randall was a head shorter than JD, but a few decibels louder. "I was first on scene."

Leith opened his mouth to deliver his final no, but Monty beat him to it with a compromise. "If Mr. Lavender is willing, go talk to him, but leave the canvassing for now. As Dave here has just advised your partner, another few hours isn't going to change things. The first forty-eight is long gone."

Randall opened her mouth, but Monty made a motion like a magician sending his assistant up in smoke. She gave a brisk shake of the head that said, *Wow, I'm working amongst idiots*, and tramped away.

"What a little fireball." Monty grinned. "That girl's going places."

There came exclamations from the area of the tent, and JD jogged over to hear the news. Leith and Monty followed. The dead male had been shifted over to expose his bad side, and his body on display was now speaking out — or screaming, more like. The left arm had been amputated at the elbow, and the face was mostly gone. Not taken by rot, but like flesh had been ripped from bone. The mouth gaped as though whatever agonies the man had suffered still coursed through him, showing a set of teeth chipped and knocked from the gums.

"Here's the arm," somebody said.

The severed limb was lodged between the dead man's knees.

Leith wondered about the significance of the crude packaging. A deliberate insult, or a matter of disorganization? It didn't strike him as either symbolism or panic, but it did point to a certain spontaneity.

He turned away from the body and its attendants, taking a break from the view. He had been through some scary cases in Prince Rupert, and in other postings during his years in the service. Transferring down to the metropolis sure hadn't gotten him into a better class of crime. But whether in Prince Rupert or North Vancouver or Happy Valley, horror happens.

Some days ago he had told Alison — maybe trying to convince himself more than her — that down here in the big city, there was at least a better support system. The more mules, the lighter the load, right? He had told her as well that his North Van workmates seemed like an exceptional bunch. Broad-minded, empathetic, and smart.

Beside him, Monty said, "Hoo-boy, that's some bad mincemeat job. Almost enough to turn you vegan, eh, Dave?" and laughed.

Four

CHARMED

CONSIDERING THE LENGTH of Constable Randall's interrogation of Mr. Lavender, Dion wondered if she had eyeballed the man as her prime suspect, instead of a harmless retiree who had called the sanitation department to report a vague stink on the breeze. The sanitation department had told Lavender there wasn't much they could do about it, so Lavender had called 911.

On his climb up the front steps, Dion had predicted five minutes of conversation, at most. But five had turned to ten, and Randall was still harping at Lavender about wind direction, garbage removal days, troublesome neighbours.

Lavender seemed to enjoy having late-night visitors. He drew out every answer and ended it on a hook. Dion began to feel it was strategic. When Lavender invited them to move from the porch where they stood to somewhere more comfortable within, Dion decided he was one cop too many and told Randall he was going back to the vehicle to catch up on his notes. When she didn't object fast enough, he left.

Out in the rain, he looked back at the house, at Lavender's closed front door. Maybe Randall was right, and Lavender was now pulling out the machete and chasing her around the living room. But then there would be the sound of police-issued 9 mm gunfire — and a whoop of triumph, probably.

Jackie Randall could take care of herself. All Dion had to worry about was getting from here, under the covered archway at Lavender's front gate, to his parked cruiser down the road without getting soaked. The neighbourhood looked sound asleep. The sky had reneged on its ceasefire and was doubling its efforts to drown the planet. Water drummed down, hit the pavement under lamplight, and crawled toward Dion like a league of ghosts. Randall's flood had arrived with a vengeance.

It was probably her flood that had flushed the odours out from under the abandoned house and set the alarm bells ringing, leading to John Doe. He thought about the body lying on the tarp and reeking.

He hadn't stopped to look, because that death smell had a way of coating a person for days, and getting stuck with the smell was no longer part of his job description. All he could guess from what he had seen in passing was that the body had been there a long while.

Randall was more explicit. She had looked and listened, and then reported to Dion what she knew. The body was a young male, and far from fresh. Monty had told her the first forty-eight was long gone, but so what, she argued. In a way, it had just begun, now that there were police buzzing about the scene, advertising their presence in a big way. It changed the game, and somebody in one of these apparently sleeping houses could be hastily doing god knows what. Packing their bags, making a call, flushing the evidence.

Dion thought Randall had a good point, but he wasn't going to encourage her.

He walked down the road, assaulted by the pouring rain. On the other side of the bushy spur named Greer, a house facing Lynn Valley Road stood out like a beacon, and he stopped to look at it. Unlike its neighbours, this one was lit up. It was one of the older homes, a double A-frame, painted maroon with cream trim. Clapboard siding, conventional landscaping, but not so well maintained, as if the homeowner had lost the will to trim those laurels. There was a driveway and a carport off to the side, a little white car parked within. The gutter spouts drizzled noisily.

He could almost see into the main floor of the place, as the heavier drapes were hooked back, leaving only a gauzy screen to obscure the view. White-gold Christmas lights sparkled everywhere, strung across the window and sparkling like stars amongst the foliage. It looked like the kind of place he could walk into and never want to leave.

Somebody standing behind those drapes was returning his stare, he realized with a start. He turned to go, but the front door opened, and the woman who had been watching him called out. "Hey you, hello!"

He called hello back to her. She was oddly dressed for a cold October night in baggy shorts — maybe boxers — a plum-coloured cardigan, and tall rubber boots. She was a dark-skinned woman with a mass of goldish-black hair. She stood blurred behind rain falling from the eaves like a flickering bead curtain. Dion knew that from where she stood, he must be a human bead curtain himself.

"What's happened over there?" she asked. "Was somebody hurt?"

A reasonable assumption. The commotion of emergency vehicles, lights, and noise made it obvious enough. He pushed open the gate and walked to the bottom of the stairs so he wouldn't have to shout, but even here he had to project his voice over the din of rainfall. "There's an investigation underway."

"At the Greer house?"

"Yes, ma'am," he said, thinking she was more a hippy than a ma'am. She was around his own age, near the thirty mark. Her casual clothes and her tangly hair and her unkempt garden all pegged her in his mind as some kind of poet.

"Don't *ma'am* me," she said. "Or I'll *sir* you. Who got hurt? Is it serious?"

"There's been a death, so there's going to be some activity around. Just letting you know."

"A death? I'm sorry to hear that. How awful. I did wonder, a bit."

From the bottom of the stairs, he watched her. A follow-up question sprang to mind, but that would be somebody else's task. "If you've noticed anything out of the ordinary happening over there in the last few months, we'd appreciate hearing about it," he said. "Somebody will be around tomorrow to get your statement. Just let them know, if you could. Anything's helpful."

She didn't seize the opportunity to wish him good night and return inside, but stayed where she was and gazed down at him, as if she had something to add. He couldn't help wondering what it might be. "Unless there's anything you can tell me now, since I'm here?" he asked.

"Well, why don't you come in."

The golden lights twinkled all around her. He looked up and down the block as he radioed Randall, letting her know he was talking to a witness who had volunteered information. He gave the address and hoped Randall would not race over to join him.

Randall ten-foured him.

Dion ran his hands along his gun belt, just checking, then climbed the stairs and followed the hippy inside. She shut the door behind him as he glanced around the dark interior. Something strange about the place, a noise ...

But it was just the forced-air heating rumbling through the ducts and blasting out the vents. He needed the warmth that gusted down. He was an ice block after the hours he'd spent outside the Greer house, setting up lights and tents. It hadn't been smart, stripping down to his shirt sleeves in the October rain, but he hadn't seen this far ahead, didn't know Randall's overblown work ethic would have him canvassing the neighbourhood after hours.

Inside the house, the woman didn't wait for his name and ID, as she should have, but removed her rubber boots, slipped her feet into sandals, and went whisking down the dark corridor. She called back at him, "Holy moly, I'll make some tea, warm us both up."

She had disappeared to her right. He followed her into a brightly lit kitchen, where he saw nice appliances and expensive but unenthusiastic furniture, none of it matching up with the woman, somehow. She gestured at a clunky table to one side, next to a window. From here he could see a hallway leading to a living room, with more furniture that didn't seem to be hers. Here and there on the pale-grey walls were darker squares and rectangles where pictures must have once hung — for years, maybe decades.

"I know," she said, as if reading his mind, but missing the point. "This place needs a serious make-over, doesn't it?"

She put on a kettle and went about preparing cups. She moved with brisk energy, despite the hour. Dion sat at the table and unzipped his jacket halfway. He flattened his notebook and asked the woman for her name. "Farah Jordan," she said, and spelled it for him.

He occupied himself filling in the details of the interview. Then he glanced around, still trying to understand the disconnect. Centered on the table were porcelain salt and pepper shakers shaped like bell peppers, one red and one green. There was a jar containing chopsticks and teaspoons, a sugar bowl, a vase with assorted flowers that had died and dried some time ago. Unlike the rest of this place, they all seemed to belong to this woman. Maybe she was a boarder.

The window at his side was open a crack, and cold air seeped in. On the sill sat an ashtray, and in the centre of it was a single crushed-out roach. He glanced down and over at the woman's bare legs as she worked at the counter. "Who else lives here?" he asked.

It was a question that might have alarmed her, if she followed the news and realized the lengths to which some rapists would go to get past a woman's door. A phony police uniform was one of the oldest tricks in the book.

"Besides me, just Radar." She took the chair across from him. "My cat."

Just her was hardly the answer he expected. The furniture, the colour scheme, even the air — all seemed mannish to him, as though a middle-aged, cigarette-smoking bachelor occupied the space, not a hippy and her cat.

"Are you going to show me your ID?" she asked. She said it lightly, as if she was more curious about police ID in general than the bona fides of his presence.

He dug out his wallet and showed her his identification card. She inspected it with interest and handed it back. He explained again who he was and why he was here, then asked, "Have you lived here long, Ms. Jordan?"

"If you have any urge at all to call me Farah, I'd be more than happy if you gave in to it. I've been here since May."

Half a year, he thought. Then it clicked. She had inherited the house from an older male relative, a father or grandfather. One she had not been too fond of, if the first thing she did was to take down his favourite pictures. Her face was kind, so the male relative was probably unkind. She poured tea as if they had all the time in the world. He couldn't decide whether her overly relaxed manner was suspicious or nice. Probably it had something to do with the roach in the ashtray. "You had something to tell me?"

"Did I?" she said.

"I thought you did."

She poured tea into a second cup and smiled at him brightly. "No, I'm sorry. It's just you looked so cold out there. All I wanted to do was bring you inside, warm you up." Her teeth were white against her dark skin, and her blue-grey eyes were hypnotic. Suddenly he wasn't sure who was doing the luring.

"Here's sugar, if you like," she said, and he said no, thank you, worrying that this was more of a tea party than an interview. He had told Randall that he was speaking to a witness who had info to offer. He imagined Randall's inevitable question, *What was Ms. Jordan's intel?* and his inevitable answer, *Actually, she just wanted to warm me up.*

Must work at building a better foundation for this visit. "I'm wondering," he said, "do you know anything about the house across the road — who owns it, who lived there, anything like that?"

"No, I'm sorry, it's been vacant as long as I can remember. But will you tell me what happened there? Was it an accident?"

He told her he couldn't say anything more than that a body had been found, sorry.

"I understand," she said, but apparently didn't, as she added without pause, "Man or woman? Not a child, I hope. Children seem to like getting into places."

"Well, like I say."

"Sorry, yes," she exclaimed. "You just finished telling me you can't divulge anything, and then I go and ask for more details." She sipped her tea and looked wistful. "About how long would you say it's been there, though? Not long, I'm sure. I just started noticing this kind of bad smell last week, but I thought it was somebody's garbage. Oh rats, I've done it again, and you're starting to look exasperated. I'll just have to wait for the news, I guess."

Something banged. Dion looked around to see that a cat had just slipped through the cat flap in the back door. It walked into the room and studied Dion. It was slim, dusky grey, with bright-green eyes. It looked a bit like its owner.

Its owner seemed delighted to see the animal and enticed it over with a *ksk-ksk* noise so she could stroke it from ears to tail. "They're such snobs," she told Dion. "But you have to love them. And every time she comes home, I'm so grateful, as there are coyotes out there. They'll go for cats. Do you have any pets?"

When he had lived with Kate, she had a tabby. A fat cat that ate, slept, complained, and damaged furniture. He had never seen the point of it, himself. "No, I don't. I'd like to have a dog."

He blinked in surprise at his own words. He hadn't meant to say anything so personal.

"Me, too," Ms. Jordan said. "Not so big, not so small. A rescue mutt!"

And now they were talking about dogs. Dion described sitting in the park this fall and watching dogs and dog owners at play. It seemed like a good, safe, amiable relationship. He told her about the coal-black pup he'd seen at the SPCA the other day, in the course of his duties, how tempted he'd been to sign the adoption papers and bring it home. He had imagined the pup following along on his heels and curling up by his feet at night.

But having a pet wasn't practical, and neither was sitting here talking about it with a witness. He asked, "Do you recall what day you first noticed it, the bad odour you thought was garbage?"

"I couldn't give you a date. It came and went."

"That's fine." The other question that had cropped up meanwhile had somehow gotten away from him. He wondered if she could smell death on him. The tea scent pluming up from the cup in front of him was doing a good job of overriding the crime scene stench that lingered in his nostrils, but it didn't quite do it, and still the idea of eating or drinking made him queasy.

"It's nice, isn't it, the bergamot?" she asked.

"Bergamot?" he said.

"These weird hours," she said. "Do you always work this late?"

The solidity of the question brought him back to earth, and he picked up the cup and gulped the tea she had gone out of her way to make for him. It was nice, warm, comforting. "I'm on nights," he said. "Seven to seven."

"How awful."

"Not really. It's usually quiet in the shop. A good time to catch up."

Randall's voice came over the radio, saying she was done and at the car — did he need assistance? He replied no, he'd be out in a minute. He apologized to Ms. Jordan. "It's really late, and you must be wanting to get to bed. Thanks for thawing me out."

"It's okay. I work quite late myself. I'm used to the hours. I work at the Greek Taverna, down on Lonsdale."

"Really?" He was happy for an excuse to carry on the conversation. He didn't want to leave, go back to Jackie Randall and reality. "I've had dinner there. Quite a few times." Though not lately, and not in this life. "Great food. You're a waitress?"

"Head chef, actually," she said.

He watched her smile and wanted more. The low-grade lust he felt was nothing new. He was single, hungry, and easily infatuated. But of course nothing would happen. It was time to go, and he put his final question to her. "I know it's none of my business. But this house, is it an inheritance?"

"Yes, exactly. My mom died when I was little, and my dad's been here for the last fifteen years. He got ill in May, so I gave up my Lonsdale apartment and moved in to take care of him. Now it's just me. He passed away last month."

"Oh, I'm sorry," Dion said, and mentally kicked himself. What a completely unnecessary, insensitive question. "I'm sorry."

"Don't worry about it. And thank you. Yes, it's strange to hear him shuffling about upstairs, looking for something. We'll all end up like that to some degree, I guess. Looking for something."

An odd statement, and an odd woman. He had the feeling Ms. Jordan was a little mad. The wind wailed, the ducts roared, the house creaked, and out in the car, Constable Randall would be growling. As they walked to the front door, he told Jordan to call if she could pin down the dates any further of when she had first noticed the smell across the road. It could be helpful.

"Yes, I will," she said, opening the door. "What's your name again?"

"Dion," he said, and the question he had forgotten popped back into mind, a more particularized version of his first remarks while standing out in the rain. "You must have a pretty good view on the Greer house from here. Have you noticed any activity over there since you moved in?"

"It's got a high fence," she said. "Isn't there some kind of bylaw saying fences can't be more than five feet tall? That one's at least six."

He didn't like the question. She wasn't the kind of person who measured fences and lodged complaints, so what could it be but a deliberate diversion? He tried again. "I thought from upstairs, you might be able to look across, see if there's anyone moving around inside?"

She shook her head, shrugged an apology.

He could think of nothing else. Standing on the front porch, he searched his wallet, found a business card, and handed it over. "Well, if you do think of anything …"

She seemed to find the RCMP crest — gold and blue, with its honourable motto — funny. It turned out it wasn't the crest she was laughing at, but his name. "Calvin," she said. "That's so nice. Where's Hobbes?"

Calvin and Hobbes was a popular comic strip, he knew. He was still trying to think up a reply — though what could he say to that? — when she spoke again, more seriously. "I shouldn't laugh. This is obviously not the time for that. It's just, I feel like we're in a movie. You say, 'If you think of anything …' and now the bodies start piling up, and you save my life, or I save yours, and we end up falling in love. Isn't that how it goes?"

He said, "That's for sure. Good night."

Randall watched him drop in beside her. He was still swearing at himself. Farah Jordan had all but offered herself up nude, and his response had been *That's for sure.*

"What's the matter?" Randall said. She had ridden shotgun earlier, but was now behind the wheel, looking about ready to drive off without him.

"Nothing."

She started the engine. "Get anything good?"

"No. You?"

"Nope."

A lot of time and one big embarrassment for nothing, then. They headed back to the city lights, leaving Lynn Valley and its secrets behind.

Five

MESACHEE

IN THE LATE MORNING, Leith and JD accompanied Corporal Michelin Montgomery back to the crime
scene, the derelict house on Greer where a body had
been stuffed so unceremoniously some months ago
and removed so carefully last night. The Ident people
had been working the grounds since daybreak, and
the house now sat temporarily empty but for a small
crew and a rotation of auxiliary constables to guard
the scene.

On approach, Leith saw that daylight redeemed
the place. Stepping inside, he found that even with
the main floor windows boarded up, sunlight seeped
through enough cracks to expunge the horror. "Not so
spooky now," he remarked.

Monty cheerfully disagreed. "Still horrifying to me,
Dave. We're just in the day-before-all-hell-breaks-loose
scene. Lots of ominous music and the promise of things
to come. What d'you say, JD?"

JD said she found the place freaking scary, considering a faceless killer had been crawling around here not long ago, dragging a dismembered body into the blackness underfoot. If that wasn't spooky, what was?

Upstairs the windows were unboarded, but murky behind a buildup of wind-blown dirt. Leith stood in what once must have been the master bedroom. The floorboards were raw plywood, as someone had removed all the carpeting. The drywall was marred with nail holes and splotched with mould. All the fixtures were either gone or broken.

"If only I was a movie director." Monty was still on topic. He stood with arms crossed in the centre of the room, staring at the floor. "What a setting. Even my shadow looks creepy."

True, Monty's shadow was creepy, a stiff-shouldered, bullet-headed shape stretched across the rough flooring.

"I'm told there might have been squatters in here at some point," JD said.

"Squatters who left nothing interesting behind," Monty replied. "A huge make-work project for the lab folks, is what it is. Food wrappings, cigarette butts, liquor bottles, and other assorted necessities of living. Nothing recent. Probably just kids."

"And a girl's bracelet," JD told Leith. "On a windowsill. Fake gold, a dime a dozen."

"*Woo-hoo*," Monty called experimentally, maybe expecting an echo.

The results were oddly flat, Leith noticed. He moved to one of the two windows in this upstairs bedroom. From it he could see houses, mostly obscured by trees.

Only one home would have had a clear line of sight to this one, but for the branches of a large evergreen. One of its upstairs windows was clearly visible, and if someone stood at that window, they would be able to see him in this one. They would also be able to see down into the lot, if they craned. He studied the scraggly orchard below, and in his mind's eye he saw a figure dragging a heavy bag across to the foundations. Since this was his imagination at work, he made it a moonlight scene.

What a shock that would have been, if it had been spotted. It would surely have been reported. He put the question to JD, just to be sure. "That place has been canvassed?"

She peered across at the big maroon house behind the branches. "Of course. That whole block's been checked off. Nobody saw anything."

No surprise.

Monty left the room to explore the rest of the upstairs. Leith followed. On the west side was a child-sized room, also denuded of its carpeting. A peel-and-stick wallpaper border, *Shrek* motif, ran around its perimeter, unpeeling and unsticking. In a corner of the room Monty discovered a set of deep gouges in a small section of the plywood flooring. He squatted down for a closer look, pushing at the wood with his knuckles.

Leith crouched, too.

"If I didn't know better, I'd say these were the scratch marks of a large *Canis lupis familiaris*, better known as *dog*," Monty said, shooting back to his feet with an ease Leith envied more than the Latin. He rose, too, slowly and with a twinge of knee pain. Alison was right; it was time to get out the jogging gear, stop making excuses.

"But it's not," Monty went on. "Too aggressive, too acute. Some kind of tool, maybe. One of those gardening claws? Interesting. Get a picture, Dave. Somebody should check under that board, too. It's got flooring nails, but it's loose. Classic hidey-hole."

Ident would have gotten a shot of the gouges, or they would soon enough as they continued to scour the place, but Leith took the time to snap a few shots for reference. When he was finished making a note of the details, he looked around and found JD and Monty were gone.

Their silent departure was strange. Not so much for JD, who walked like a cat — but Monty was the noisy type. Whatever he did and wherever he went, he seemed to emit a whir of enthusiasm.

Leith was quite sure he liked Monty. He had been out for drinks with him and the crew a few times since Monty's arrival in September — because how do you say no to an invitation that comes with a hearty slap on the back?

The reasons for liking Monty were virtually endless. He had an impressive curriculum vitae and thrilling life stories that he seemed only too happy to share. Far from being self-centred, he was curious about his workmates and wanted to hear their life stories, too. If he found out you had kids, he wanted to see your wallet photos. If you were short of pocket change, he'd pay for your beer. He was also going places. With the force for thirty-plus years, he'd spent the past seven of those just over the bridge, in Surrey, the province's largest detachment. North Van was just a stopover, he had told the gang at Rainey's the other night, as the International Operations Branch would be taking him overseas within the year. Where exactly, he wouldn't or couldn't say, but it sure as hell wasn't going to be boring.

In short, everybody liked Monty. He had verve, and charisma, and brains. Unlike Leith, he lit up the room when he walked in.

Actually, correction: Leith didn't like Monty. Because how much verve can a person stand, in the long run?

Leith was working on banishing these uncharitable thoughts when he left the child's room, turned the corner, and froze. A corpse floated in the dim light at the end of the hallway, its head twisted, eyes rolled back, outstretched hands frozen into hooked claws.

Of course it wasn't a corpse, and it wasn't floating. It was standing on its toes and just kidding. Monty was whooping it up now, not a man in his fifties, but a teenager who had just pranked a buddy. Leith's arms had gone up in self-defence, and they came down now in fists of anger. "Jesus, Monty!"

JD climbed the stairs to see what the commotion was.

"Sorry, but I couldn't resist," Monty laughed. "I mean, look at this place. When will I ever get the chance again?"

He maybe saw something in Leith's face that said *not cool*, and his grin faded. "C'mon, man. It was a joke."

Leith brushed past him and stomped down the stairs. JD shadowed him. Out in the light of day, Monty's apologies took on a note of impatience. "No harm done, right? So what's the problem?"

The problem wasn't Monty's verve, really. Leith's problem was Leith. He was homesick for the prairies, the togetherness of his once-large extended family, now scattered across Canada. He was sick of the North

Vancouver traffic. He was sick of renting. He was socially awkward, mysteriously guilt-ridden, and on top of it all, inexplicably lonely.

"Better get used to it," he told Monty. "I'm a natural-born stick-in-the-mud."

"He is," JD confirmed.

But Leith wasn't done. "Frankly," he said to Monty, "if our ranks were reversed, I'd tell you a thing or two. I could have shot you. You know that, right?"

"You didn't reach for your gun, I noticed."

"I've seen enough movies. You can shoot a zombie full of holes, but you won't kill it."

"Sure you can kill it. You just gotta aim for the brain."

"*What* brain?"

Leith smiled at his own snappy repartee. Their nonsense had popped the tension, and the rift was mended. In a better mood, the three of them went on to explore the boundaries of the lot, looking up into the tree branches and down into the shrubbery. They went out the back gate into the alley — more of a weedy mule track running between woods and home — that had once provided a place for long-ago residents to store their junk, judging by what remained; old car parts and appliances sat heaped along the fence.

The gate at the back, like the one at the front, had been securely chained and locked against trespassers when the police had arrived on the night of the call-out. The chains on both gates had been cut and were now left unlocked for investigative purposes. Whoever had used the property for squatting had apparently gotten around the difficulty of chains and locks by stashing a shabby old stepladder in the woods behind the house. Inside the fence, shoved in amongst the lilacs, were a couple of plastic milk crates that had probably done the job for getting back out. Ident had seized ladders and crates and taken the lot of it in for analysis.

"Wasn't just one quick visit, then, was it?" JD said. "Or kids finding a hangout to smoke pot. Somebody was living here, coming and going, for a while. Same people who used it for a body dump?"

Leith walked along the back fence, looking along its top for wood scuffs and dents that might tell him where the ladder had leaned. "Here," he said. The marks looked relatively fresh and ladder-width apart. The story was starting to come together. But, as JD had said, did the squatters have anything to do with the murder?

Back at the side of the house, they had another look at the access hole in the foundations. The autopsy had not yet begun, but Jack Dadd had told Leith he believed their John Doe had died of blood loss. Mauled to death. Could have been a knifing, except the wounds were shallow and chaotic, more suggestive of an animal attack. Probably a large dog. Hard to say, as the flesh wounds were old and had lost definition. Post-mortem animal predation also had to be taken into account, of course.

"Even if dogs killed the poor guy, they sure didn't bag him up and drag him in there, did they?" Monty said.

Leith agreed that a dog probably couldn't work a decent half hitch. "The knots might tell us something."

Monty snorted. "They'll tell us what we already know. The guy didn't know when enough knots is enough knots."

"Like he was afraid the thing he'd bagged could get out if he didn't tie it up real good," JD suggested.

"Anyway, hopefully our experts will give us more," Leith said.

Like Corporal Hillary Stafford, for one, the toolmark specialist who also analyzed bite marks. She would look at the remains and try to determine the what, where, when — if not why. She might provide knot analysis advice as well, but it was the weapon Leith was mostly interested in. Hopefully, after her examination, she would give them the size of the dog, maybe even the breed, which could at least point them in the direction of the beast's owner.

Back in the car, its cab chilly and damp, Leith took the wheel, JD next to him in the passenger seat. Behind them, Monty said, "Guys, I did mention the party, right?"

Another thing to add to Monty's list of virtues was persistence. The party had been mentioned a few times, and Leith had worked hard at not giving a straight answer, hoping it would go away. "Yes," he said now. "A costume party, at your place, Sunday. Be there or be square. Sorry, one thing I don't do is costumes. But thanks for the invite." He turned the heater on full blast.

In the rear-view mirror he saw Monty's blue eyes surrounded by fine crinkles. Lines in aging faces could say a lot about character, and Monty's had nice-guy written all over them. "I tell you what it is, Dave," he said, relaxing back, his arms outstretched. "You're socially rusty. You're the Tin Man without an oil can. But it's not fatal. Sometimes you just got to push yourself, get out there. Have some fun. At best, you'll have a blast, make new friends. At worst, you come to my party, you say, *Fuck, this is lame*, you dodge out first chance you get. I won't stop you."

Leith looked at JD beside him. Her eyes said, *Don't ask me; I'm sure the hell not going.*

Of course she wasn't. Except for the occasional drinks night when she joined the crew at Rainey's, she was a confirmed loner. Even when she deigned to come out, she wouldn't stay long. She'd take a chair and join in the conversation for a bit, end up criticizing the music or the unhealthy snacks, and usually leave on a sour note. Sometimes Leith wondered if her attendances were some kind of self-imposed chore — like teeth-flossing.

Did he want to end up like JD? Hell no. Monty was right. Socializing is a lot like going for a walk; it's easier not to, and the longer you put it off, the harder it gets, but once you're out there, it feels great. "Okay, but no costume," he said.

"No costume, no candy."

Leith checked his colleague in the mirror. In this new-age world, *candy* had all kinds of meanings, some not so innocent. Monty read the glance and cried, "Oh, for Pete's sake, Dave! By *candy* I mean candy. Gummy Bears and such. You weren't kidding about the ol' stick-in-the-mud thing, were you?"

JD laughed aloud.

Leith drove back down Mountain Highway, and behind him Monty said, "Oh, look here." He was reading something off his phone, an email or text. "Looks like we have a lead. Couple of neighbourhood kids were up the Mesachee trail this summer and might have seen something of interest. Of interest to who, I'm not quite sure."

"Mesachee, where's that?"

"Don't ask me."

JD knew. "Above the Headwaters."

Leith told her that meant nothing to him. After six months he was still forever getting lost on the North Shore. Behind him a phone pinged again, and Monty chuckled. "This just in. My fiancée." He leaned to show JD. She took the phone in hand, looked at the little picture on display, then tilted it at Leith.

Leith glanced away from the road and squinted at the screen, which showed a pixie-like girl pulling a rude face at the camera. She looked about twelve. "She's pretty," he said, and it wasn't a lie.

"Pretty as a picture," Monty agreed, retrieving his phone. "She's not jailbait, if that's what you're thinking. She's twenty-eight."

Leith was more interested in where the Headwaters were than Monty's amazingly young-looking fiancée, and JD went on to fill him in. Around the bend from Greer, the neighbourhood they had just left, she told him, was the Lynn Headwaters Regional Park, bisected by Lynn Creek — which was more raging river than babbling brook — into formal and informal halves. On the far side of the river from the parking lot were the mapped trails, with walks that ranged from beginner to murderous, all clearly delineated on governmental signboards. No mountain bikes allowed. But on this side of the river lay the Mesachee, an unendorsed, uncharted swatch of forest created by mountain bikers, for mountain bikers. The Mesachee, as JD went on to de-scribe, was a crazy network of trails and death-defying obstacles, ramps, mud swamps, and switchbacks.

"Sounds like you've challenged these death-defying obstacles yourself," Leith said.

"No, but I've personally signed my niece's leg cast."

Monty had been busy reading emails. He tucked his phone away and set the agenda. "We'll have lunch, then go talk to these kids. Apparently they're out and about, mountain biking at this Mesachee place. But they're being rounded up for us as we speak."

"Good," Leith said. He had a feeling when Monty said, "We'll have lunch," he meant *together*. And Leith was right.

"So whereabouts for lunch?" Monty asked. "Ideas, anybody?"

JD said, "At my desk, out of my brown bag, if you want to join me. Otherwise, you can just go ahead and drop me off."

As she had told Leith once, she had given up on the whole team spirit, rank-climbing bullshit long ago. Maybe it was her disfigurement. Her mouth was scarred by a birth defect, which might have led to her being bullied, which might have led to loneliness, which had maybe left her with a defensiveness that was just a little over the top, as he'd told her. She had told him in reply to go fuck him-self, so she was definitely warming up to his charms.

But rank-climber was Leith's middle name. He looked at Monty and said, "I've always wanted to try the Tomahawk, if you're up for something new."

Six

HOWL

THOUGH IT WAS JUST PAST NOON, the forest seemed to be sinking into dusk. Dion and Jackie Randall were in the midst of the Mesachee Woods, looking for two young witnesses who were said to be mountain bike fanatics and were possibly hereabouts.

The trails on this side of the river were narrower and not so hiker-friendly as those woodsy corridors on the far side, the headwater trails where just this week, Aldobrandino Rosetti had lost his life. Muddier here, too, as the knobby treads of bikes were always chewing through the ground cover. Dion was sweating more than he had on the Rosetti hike; his thighs ached, and his boots were starting to look like shit, literally. "Five more minutes and we're going back," he called to Randall ahead of him. "Didn't I tell you we're better off ambushing them at the trail head? And it'd be a lot easier."

"Five more minutes," Randall agreed, over her shoulder. "The problem is, these kids have had their phone privileges revoked. And they're on bicycles, and we're not, and they could be anywhere from here to Mount Fromme."

Dion corrected her. "You can't get to Mount Fromme from here. You have to go around. Mountain Highway takes you up there, but you'd need a vehicle."

"You know your way around pretty good. You a biker?"

He had been, when younger. He had flashed down these very trails, in fact, coated in mud. He had thumped the tracks, done a couple of end-over-ends, earned his kudos. "I've done some biking in my time."

Randall grinned. "I'm a pretty hot biker myself. Got an old one-speed with a basket and a bell in my mom's basement. But, oh, right, I don't do hills."

They continued walking. Dion explained that this area was an old set of trails that had been refurbished by young freeriders some years back, because bikes weren't allowed on the main park trails, and the kids wanted somewhere more accessible than the Mount Fromme wheelie wonderland.

"It's kind of an outlaw route," he said. "Not even on the maps. We should go back. Hear me, Jackie? Enter at your own risk."

She turned to laugh at him. "You're such a wuss."

"*Watch out!*" he warned her.

They both stepped back as a cyclist charged by, telling them, "Get off the path, motherfuckers!"

Two more groups of bikers passed, and Randall yelled at them, "Hey, any of you James or Ronald? I'm looking for James Wong and Ronald Graham. Can you help me out?"

Her pushiness paid off, and they were directed to a patch of woods somewhat off the beaten trail. Gently sloped and fairly open, it had been built into a playground for bike gymnastics. Happy young voices echoed through the trees, and there were their witnesses, two mud-spattered teens taking turns tackling one archaic-looking wooden ramp.

Dion watched one of them land, skew, nearly lose it. He called out for them both to take five and come over and talk.

The boys laid down their bikes and approached. Introductions were made. The skinny white kid said he was Ronnie Graham. The heavier Asian kid said, "Wong … *James* Wong."

"You guys must be the only human beings on the planet without cellphones," Randall told them.

"Even if we had phones," Graham said, "there's no signal up here."

"And no phone is the new cool," Wong said.

"First I've heard of it." Randall's breath puffed out white in the chill. "You're not in trouble, but mind coming with us? Grapevine says you might have seen something up here that might be of interest to the police."

"We did," Graham said, and he would have said more, but Wong stopped him with an arm shot out sideways.

"There's a reward, right? If you catch it?"

"It?"

"*It*," Wong said.

"It," Randall said to Dion, and her eyes sparkled. "This is going to be interesting."

* * *

Dion decided he was not needed and stayed in the car when the GIS members arrived. The black sedan pulled in alongside. Leith and JD Temple, along with the corporal whose name Dion had forgotten, left the car and joined Randall and the boys in the gloom. Randall would promptly hand the kids over now, then join him, and they would return to their duties keeping North Vancouver safe from graffiti artists, jaywalkers, and shoplifters —at least that was how he saw it unfolding.

When things didn't unfold as he expected, he stepped out of the car and leaned against it. Introductions were made — Wong ... *James* Wong — and then some bonding talk about the sport, the park, the weather. Everybody was being chatty, including Randall. Dion signalled at her that they had to get back to work, but she ignored him. He stopped listening to the group and watched the sky, which was gathering itself into another great blue-black bank of rain clouds.

Yeti, he heard Ronnie Graham say.

"Wasn't a yeti," Wong said. "Don't listen to him. Yetis are a creamy white or a pale grey. This was black. It was a werewolf. Up on the bike path near the Rock. Near enough that we could see it."

A bogeyman was the hot tip, then. Dion waited for someone in the group to smarten up the tipsters with a warning and call the whole thing off, but nobody did. David Leith was doing the talking now, and Dion moved in closer to hear, as the air was heavy and voices were muted, even over short distances.

"Let's forget what it's called," Leith said. "What did this thing look like?"

"It was big and black and running along on all fours," Wong said.

"We looked for tracks," Graham added.

"Later, when we were sure it was gone."

"Didn't find any."

"Could it have been a dog?" Leith asked. He sounded tired.

"Way too big," Wong said. "It was like a really big man."

"Bigger," Graham said.

Leith asked for the circumstances: When was the sighting? What were the kids up to at the time? Wong said, "Two months ago, August. Last week of summer holidays. We were up on the trails. It was at night, like, ten o'clock or something. Dark, but we had headlights. Then we heard something, like this blood-curdling howl."

Graham failed to chime in to back up his friend's story of the howl, as he had backed up everything else, and Dion expected Leith would pick up on the boy's silence, challenge him on it. But Leith didn't catch it, and neither did the corporal who had introduced himself as Montgomery. They were focusing all their attention on Wong, the loudmouth, the squeaky wheel.

Wong said, "It was like this," and pitched his face upward so it caught the blue-black wash of coming storm, squeezed his eyes shut, and let loose a howl. He didn't do a bad job of it. Graham didn't contribute to the howling, and Wong went on with the story. "So we heard this howl, and couldn't tell where it was coming from really, up or down, so we kept going up, and then we saw it, this big dark shape, kind of crouched on the path, right? I think we scared it, 'cause soon as we showed up it took off."

"Running on all fours?" Corporal Montgomery asked.

"Yes. Not like a dog so much, but not like a man, like something in between."

"Like a yeti," Graham said.

"It was summer, you genius of the undead!" Wong bawled at his friend. "No snow, no Himalayas, no yeti. Altogether the wrong *country*. Okay?"

"Then a sasquatch. Same thing."

"Sasquatches are huge," Wong said. He looked up pleadingly at JD, Leith, and Corporal Montgomery. "If this was a sasquatch, it was a midget sasquatch. No, this isn't a joke. We saw a werewolf, and I'll swear my life on it." His palm went over his heart.

"Whatever it was," Leith asked, "was it running level, uphill, or downhill?"

"Up," Wong said.

Up. If it was a steep enough *up*, Dion thought, a man doubled over for balance could be seen as running on all fours.

JD must have been thinking along the same lines. "How steep uphill?" she demanded, dark brows angled dangerously.

The boys watched her blankly and didn't answer.

"You guys are making this up, hey?" she said. She began to describe what kind of serious trouble they could get into, telling stories to the police, but Wong interrupted, his teeth a flare of white in the dusk. "It's not stories. And what about that dead guy who came out of the woods and fell down with his hair white as snow? That's not stories."

Dion sighed.

"What dead guy?" Leith said.

"Heart attack fatality last week," Randall told him. "Name of Rosetti. He was found up on the Lynn Peak trail. Cal and I attended to assist. His hair was *not* white as snow."

For the first time, Corporal Montgomery spoke up, to scold the boys, "See here, this is how rumours get started. An acorn falls on your head, and next thing you know the sky is falling. How far up the path are we talking here, where you saw whatever you saw?"

"Maybe ten, fifteen minutes," Wong said. "By bike."

"If Dave and I brought our bikes around tomorrow, would you show us where you saw this werewolf?"

"Well, hang on," Leith said.

"What kind of compensation are we talking about?" Wong asked.

"*Compensation?*"

"I don't have a bike," Leith said. "And even if I had one, I only do paved roads. Count me out."

"And if you were thinking of counting me in, don't," JD added.

Dion looked at Jackie Randall, waiting for her to jump in and volunteer.

She did, but not how he expected. "Cal here knows the trails like the back of his hand, and he's an ace mountain biker."

Dion spoke up loud and clear, telling Montgomery, "I'm not on duty tomorrow, I don't have a bike, and I haven't been on these trails in years."

Montgomery smiled at him. "We'll work something out. We've got us a team, and that's a good starting point.

Okay guys," he told the young witnesses. "We'll be in touch first thing tomorrow, and you can take us to the spot and show us around. Sound good?"

The boys confirmed their contact information, promised to stay reachable tomorrow, strapped on their helmets, and cycled off. Once they were safely out of earshot, Leith exclaimed, "Werewolves? Yetis? Some mad survivalist in a fur coat is what they saw. You're not seriously thinking of biking up there to look for this guy?"

Dion put in his own objection. "I can tell you what you'll find. More trees, more skunk cabbage, more mud."

"What *we'll* find," Montgomery corrected him. "Guys, where's your sense of adventure? I believe these boys really saw something. If somebody's hanging around in the woods playing monster and scaring kids, even if it's got nothing to do with John Doe, we've got to check it out. Right? And it happens I'm a pretty badass off-roader myself." He was grinning at Dion. "Looks like it's you and me, Cal."

"I don't have a bike," Dion said again, but less loud and clear, knocked off guard by this stranger's friendliness.

"I've got a spare."

"It's been a while."

"C'mon. It's like riding a bike."

With record-breaking speed, Dion was starting to like Corporal Montgomery. Montgomery's friendliness seemed real, nothing put-on about it. His stare was direct and full of positive energy. His grin turned his face into a thousand creases and made Dion feel like grinning right back at him.

Montgomery reached out to shake on it, seal the deal. "You and me, Cal."

Dion reached and shook. The wind was beginning to buffet them all, and the trees were shushing ominously. Leith pulled cigarettes from his coat pocket and gave Dion a hard-to-read stare, maybe a warning. Leith didn't like Dion, didn't trust him, and was probably expecting trouble, but Dion was feeling too pleased with himself to care. There was nothing to worry about. It was just a field trip with a superior he admired. It was a break from routine.

Montgomery handed him a note he had scribbled out, an address and phone number. "Meet me at my place tomorrow, eleven a.m. No, make it ten thirty. We'll have coffee, exchange war stories, and you can meet Lady Victoria."

Leith exhaled a gust of smoke and turned to squint at Montgomery. "Meet *who*?"

"My fiancée, Tori." Montgomery was not so much answering Leith as informing Dion. "She's a real doll," he said, with a cheery wink. "You're gonna love her."

Seven

SHADOWLAND

CORPORAL MICHELIN MONTGOMERY had a nice house in the nice neighbourhood of Seymour Heights. Dion left his car in the driveway and followed the footpath to the front door. He wore cold-weather joggers, runners, a grey hoodie over a T-shirt, and his rainproof RCMP jacket. His optimism of last night had waned. He was anxious about this meeting, but resigned. Randall had volunteered his services, and what was done was done. He took a deep breath and rang the bell.

Corporal Montgomery welcomed him in with the same big grin as last night. Dion could sense the presence of a woman in the home instantly as he walked in. It was the look of the place, boldly decorated, but floral, with a sweetness in the air. And the music, which was too loud for comfort. Big-band kind of stuff.

"How're you doing?" Montgomery said.

"Good."

"You look nervous. Don't be. I won't bite."

"I'm not nervous." He followed Montgomery down a level into a living room space, where the music got louder. In the middle of the room a twiggy girl waited. Or not a girl, but a woman Dion guessed to be in her mid-twenties. Her cheeks were flushed, and her short blonde hair was coiled by wetness. Workout sweat, judging by her spandex joggers and damp T-shirt. The T-shirt seemed a couple sizes too small. She wore nothing on her feet.

"Tori, meet Cal," Montgomery said.

Her smile was generous, but her handshake was so limp and brief that Dion wondered if she was sick, maybe in a serious way. "So pleased to meet you," she said, and without a break, she went on nattering at him. She apologized for stinking, but she had just gotten back from a run, then she mentioned this awful weather, her tennis elbow, the sunroom she wanted installed to replace the open back deck, and somehow that led to a new pastry shop she had discovered that was run by Ukrainians and made excellent poppyseed rolls. Which reminded her of the snacks she had prepared — oh my god, what kind of a hostess was she?

She ran off, promising to be back soon, don't go away.

No, she wasn't sick at all.

"Isn't she great?" Montgomery said.

"She's, wow, yes, great."

They sat in armchairs and talked. Montgomery told Dion about his years in Surrey and his future overseas. "Hate to leave this place," he said. "Love the North Shore. Love the team here. Great people." Heading to the Middle East was a complication, but exciting, he said. The house, he explained, was a lease deal. All of his and Tori's things would have to go into long-term storage. The drawbacks of an exciting career. "But I wouldn't trade it for the world."

Dion asked how he and Tori had met, and Montgomery exclaimed, "I know, she's way too good looking for this ugly mug. We met at a fashion show fundraiser in Surrey. She's a model and was doing the runway bit for the cause, sashaying along in those filmy long sleeves, legs to here. But it was her smile that did it for me. Well, I fell head over heels in love, of course. Hell knows why she looked at me twice. But she did."

Tori was back with a loaded coffee tray. She set it down and sat herself on the sofa next to Montgomery. She had changed into skinny black slacks with flared cuffs, platform shoes, and a tiny sweater that looked even more shrunken than the T-shirt. Dion thought he had seen her somewhere, maybe on posters in a mall. He was going to ask her, but she was back in natter mode. "I just had a shower," she told him, explaining her hair, wet now in a clean way — he caught the sweet strawberry scent from where he sat. "I run every day," she said, "if only for the endorphins, which have become an absolute addiction. Excuse this gross thing, by the way. Just what I need, right? Cold sore barely hours before a big shoot. It's slathered in meds right now, because it has absolutely got to be gone by tomorrow. Do you run, too?"

He couldn't see the cold sore she was pointing to at the side of her mouth, nor any slathering of medication. She said, "I like to try out the different trails. You could live here all your life and run on a different trail every day. I love the canyon. There's the Baden-Powell, of course, which is about a million miles long. The Headwaters are great, too. I can't get enough of this place. Have you lived on the North Shore long? It's not really new to me, as I used to live across the water. I grew up in Surrey, mostly. That's where I met Monty. "

"My lucky day." Monty grinned.

"But I'm glad we're here now. It's such an awesome city," she said. "So diverse. And just steps away, you're in the middle of nowhere, where it's like you're the only person on the planet. You're in the middle of this amazing primeval forest. I keep thinking I'll run into a dinosaur around the bend. And the air! It's so therapeutic. You can just breathe it in, just kind of let go, give yourself to nature. Absorb its power, bring it inside, you know?"

Dion said he knew what a great place this was, though he was starting to wish he was anywhere but here. The music was skittering wildly, like the orchestra was on drugs. It went loud, louder, loudest, then crashed into silence. Tori cried, "Hoo-*wee*! Don't you love this? It's Gershwin. Incredibly complex, really. Multi-faceted. He's my latest discovery, and I'm playing him to death, as Monty can attest. Poor Monty. D'you like him, Gershwin?"

Dion didn't worry about answering. He had figured out by now how irrelevant he was to this conversation. Now Tori was asking her fiancé if he had remembered to invite their guest to the Halloween party.

"I did," Montgomery said. "Last I heard he was undecided."

Tori looked amazed and ordered Dion to make up his mind. He told her he probably wouldn't be able to attend. She flapped a hand at him and cried, "You don't have to wear a costume, if that's what you're afraid of! Or just put on a cowboy hat. You'd look nice in a cowboy hat."

She sat in a sexy slouch next to her fiancé, looking like a daughter he'd had too late in life. Sounding like one, too. But even with the age difference, they seemed to fit well enough together. Montgomery was good looking and likely as fit as she was. They were probably so madly in love that age meant nothing.

She seemed to be waiting for him to answer, for a change, so Dion said, "I'll try to make it over."

"Fabulous!" she cried. "With parties, you know, the bigger, the better — lots of people, all different kinds of interesting new people. Are you married?"

"No, I'm —"

"Gay!" she shrieked. She laughed, flapped a hand at him. "Just kidding. You're not gay. I have a gay-guy radar, and you're not, not that it would matter. Gay guys are the sweetest. There's tons of them in my line of work. You're gorgeously quiet and mysterious, by the way. Girlfriend? No? Even better, because there will be *scads* of beautiful girls for you to meet."

"She'll sort your life out for you, like it or not," Montgomery said, then stood and stated it was time to get on with the day. Dion silently thanked his lucky stars. Aloud, he told Tori it was really nice meeting her.

"See you later. Do come by for drinks after."

"Thanks. I'll try."

Dion followed Montgomery outside, past a carport sheltering a white Acura four-door, and into a garage that was being used for storage, by the looks of it, boxes stacked on boxes. This was where the bikes were kept.

"Here's my old fave." Montgomery wheeled out a black Maruishi. "Great bike for the trails, but kind of heavy. Check out this beauty. Just got it." He invited Dion into the garage to view a featherweight, brushed-gold bicycle on its hook. "I've already put a thousand klicks on it. Titanium. It's like balsa wood, man. But unbreakable."

"You're taking this on the trails? They'll demolish it."

"Oh god, no," Montgomery said. "This one's going with me today. My go-to off-roader." He pulled out a fat-wheeled bicycle with low bars and heavy duty shocks. He and Dion rolled the bikes out to the street, where a minivan sat parked. Montgomery hooked the bikes to a rack at the van's rear, and a moment later they were on the road to Lynn Valley.

It was a great day for a bike ride, cool and overcast, but not raining. Conversation came easy and, unlike with Tori, Dion was allowed to get a word in. Better yet, it seemed like a safe conversation that wouldn't go off the rails and threaten him with questions he couldn't answer.

Montgomery reminded him of somebody in some unlikely way, but he couldn't pinpoint who or why. He was still puzzling over the question and somehow afraid of the answer, when Montgomery took this perfectly safe conversation and rerouted it. "I'm actually glad we got this opportunity to talk," he said.

Damn.

"Yeah, and don't roll your eyes at me. This is important. I know who you are. I heard about your crash and the shit you've had to go through. Many others might have given up on the spot, but you made a comeback. You've had your ups and downs, but by all accounts you're no quitter, and I commend you for that."

Dion was flattered that Montgomery would care, but didn't like being commended for his comeback. Everything about the crash was a lie, and when the truth came out, he would be chucked in jail. He would disappoint everyone. "I'm getting by. I've also come to accept that I'm not what I used to be, which is fine. I'm okay."

The van pulled up to a red light and idled. "My boss tells me you're not what you used to be because you're a defeatist," Montgomery said.

Bosko, Dion thought. "Right," he said. "Which is the same as a quitter."

"Bit of a difference there. You're not living up to your potential, that's all. Which is a shame. So what are we going to do about it?"

The light turned green. The boss Montgomery referred, Mike Bosko, was a meddler whom Dion didn't trust. Leith was another meddler, but easier to take, because he didn't even try to be nice about it. So now Montgomery was joining in, probably at Bosko's urging.

Bosko was dangerous, because he was sharper than he looked. He knew there was something about the crash that didn't sit right. He was looking for a way to flip Dion over, make him talk, get at the truth from any angle he could. But Dion wasn't going to flip that easy. "I'll get by," he said, slightly tweaking what he'd said earlier, but with a cool finality.

Montgomery shrugged. "I'll lay off, but it's not over."

Even with its disappointing start, the day shaped up well. The Sunday traffic was loose knit, and they made good time up to the Headwaters parking lot. James Wong and Ronnie Graham were waiting impatiently by the little museum building that was shut down for the season. The group of four set off for the Mesachee, cycling single file up the soft, dark pathway that rose switchback style into the forest.

Wong pulled a wheelie and took the lead. Montgomery followed, keeping up effortlessly. Graham dawdled a bit, and Dion fell back, getting accustomed to the Maruishi. Looch — that's who Montgomery had reminded him of. Which made no sense, as the two men were nothing alike.

It took some experimenting with the gears and one near crash into the undergrowth before he felt comfortable on the bike, and by now he was alone in the woods. He geared down, stood on the pedals for thrust, and pushed to catch up with the others. It was coming back to him, the burning lungs and the exhilaration. Like riding a bike.

The trail curved upward, chilly in the shade of cedar and fir. He huffed and puffed and caught up with the group, which had reached its destination: a widening in the path, which was split by a large boulder. The Rock. Bikes abandoned, they were on their feet, and Wong was pointing out to Montgomery where he and Graham had seen the howling creature, then where the creature had fled.

"We were coming up the trail," he said, as Dion laid down his bike and joined them. "It was right about here. It saw us and went loping off, up that way." He pointed.

Montgomery and Dion looked up the slope of low brush into a vague shadowland atop the ridge. "Now it's loping," Montgomery said.

"Really fast. He was like half wolf."

Dion kicked at the brush through which the creature had supposedly run. The terrain was rough, sludgy, and snarled with tree roots and decaying logs. Even in the height of summer, when the ground would have been drier, he couldn't imagine any human loping through it. Must have been an animal, a large dog gone wild. Just as he had expected, there was nothing to be seen here except more of the same.

Montgomery was briskly saying to the boys, "Well, we'll keep this sighting of yours in mind for future reference. In the meantime, if you see anything else of interest, you can let us know. But my advice would be stay out of the woods till further notice, a'right?"

"No way," Graham said. "I'd rather die."

"What about that reward if you catch 'im?" Wong said.

"Sure you get a reward. A nice warm sense of accomplishment."

As they gathered their bikes for the return trip, Montgomery and James Wong discussed gear shifters at some length, so Dion found himself alone with Ronnie Graham. Graham had less to say than his friend and seemed comfortable speaking freely only while in tandem with Wong. Dion recalled yesterday, the challenge nobody had put to the kid. The howl. He thought about Mike Bosko calling him defeatist and said, "Question for you."

Graham, like Dion, didn't like questions set up like this, with a warning shot. He looked worried, resentful, and chilled. He glanced around Dion, searching for his pal. But Wong was still talking to Montgomery.

"You didn't seem so convinced about the howl you guys say you heard. What did you really hear?" Dion asked.

"We did hear it." Wong and Montgomery were looking this way. Graham said, almost under his breath, "Yes, there was something in the trees. Right over there. I'm not lying."

Montgomery joined them, but Dion halted Wong in his tracks, telling him to stay where he was just for a minute or two.

"What's up?" Montgomery asked.

"Nothing," Graham said. He was leaning against his bike frame, squeezing the brakes on and off, averting his eyes.

"He wants to tell us what they saw up here. He didn't hear a howl," Dion said.

"Is that right, Ronnie?" Montgomery said. "You want to say what really happened?"

Ganged up on, Graham confessed. "It wasn't blood curdling. It was just some stupid guy trying to scare us. He howled, but then he coughed, too. We weren't scared."

"Did you see him?"

"I saw him running away. He stumbled. And howled again just a bit. But it was dark, and he was all black-like. He wasn't running on all fours, but low, like this." Abandoning his bike, he bent his knees and leaned into a shuffling run for a few steps. "He was … weird."

Graham was flat out lying when he said he hadn't been scared, Dion thought. Of course he'd been scared. Who wouldn't be? James Wong had been scared, too, probably, but not scared enough, and he'd had to take the bizarre encounter and make it more spectacular. A tall tale that got taller with each telling.

"Could you describe this guy at all? Age, height, anything?" Montgomery asked.

"Just weird," Graham said. "Hairy."

Eight

MONSTERS

SINCE THEY WERE IN THE AREA, Montgomery swung by the Greer house to check up on progress. He parked behind an Ident van, and Dion stepped out and looked at the quiet neighbourhood. Nothing extraordinary about this block except the yellow crime scene tape over the gate. No signs of shock and horror, no trauma. Trees towered, crows cawed, and there was the gentle hum of distant traffic. Just another day in Lynn Valley.

He followed Montgomery through the gate and up the path, even into the house itself, which up to now he had seen only from the outside. Montgomery told him to go ahead and take a look around.

Upstairs, Dion talked to the techs, who were wrapping up loose ends, lifting, photographing, vaccing. The rooms were empty. The design of the place was generous, maybe eccentric, with broad and solid stairs and plenty of odd nooks, large rooms, and high ceilings alternating with low. He thought of his own cramped apartment with its thin walls through which he could hear the mumbling of neighbours and the banging of dishes.

He looked out a window at a moody skyline, a homey neighbourhood below, lights twinkling. Before the crash, he had lived in a high-rise just blocks from the waterfront. He could see all of Vancouver Harbour from there. Not so high — only the tenth floor — but with a good view of two bridges, the strait waters and, in the distance, layer upon layer of mountain ranges jutting into the skies.

There had been a good-sized balcony, too. He had hosted barbecues up there, stood necking with Kate there. Loved it there.

Compare that to this comeback, as Montgomery called it, living in the rear of a low-rise, its small balcony with a view of conifer needles too thick to let in even a strangled ray of sunlight. No Kate, no Looch, no nobody.

He pulled a face and studied the row of houses across the road. That would be Mr. Lavender's residence, the man who had called in the tip that launched the investigation. And that would be Farah Jordan's place, if he wasn't mistaken. He looked down at the lot below. Some old apple trees and lots of overgrown winter-dead grass.

He looked at the window on the top floor of her house; it was visible from here, just past the sweeping branches of a tall fir. Seemed like a pretty good vantage point. Hadn't she said she couldn't see anything from her place? Had he asked? Must check his notebook.

Must remember to check his notebook.

He couldn't make a note to check because he didn't have a notebook to write it in. He made a mental note instead.

Back out on the sidewalk, Montgomery was about to beep open his minivan, but had to stop to take a phone call. As Dion stood waiting, a figure appeared, coming along Lynn Valley Road, heading this way in a hesitant fashion. A curious neighbour, probably. Dion watched the figure draw closer and resolve itself into a small older man wearing dark work trousers and a woolly brown sweater. His hair was thinning on top, worked into a bit of a comb-over, messed up by the breeze. He had a lumpy nose and pitted skin. He didn't look happy, but called out, "Good day."

He had drawn to a stop at some distance and was speaking not to Dion, but past him to Montgomery, who had finished his call and was tucking away his phone.

"Hi there," Montgomery called back.

"You a policeman?" The man drifted closer.

"That I am." Montgomery smiled across the distance with a friendly squint. Dion watched the man close the distance between them: twenty feet, a dozen, ten, eight, six.

"I know 'cause I seen you before. From my window." The stranger pointed not so well down toward the road called Kilmer, his index finger curled like a bird's claw, and along a few houses. "That's my place, with the green roof."

Montgomery nodded, still smiling, doing the PR thing. "Yes, I'm afraid we've been making a bit of a hullabaloo around here lately. Things will soon get back to normal, promise."

"I seen *him*, too," the stranger said, looking at Dion. "Going into the Harmon place, middle of the night. Him and the other one, they was the first. He was dressed like a cop."

"I *am* a cop," Dion said.

How on earth could this man recognize him — especially now, in his civvies — as the cop who had come around the other night with Jackie Randall? From way over in that house with the green roof. Through rain and darkness. Must have eagle eyes. Or a good set of binoculars.

"Yes, well, it was quite a busy night for all of us." Montgomery was already losing his PR sparkle. The temperatures were dropping, and he looked ready to move on with his day.

"You guys came around my place, too." The stranger was still addressing Montgomery, still ignoring Dion.

Dion guessed that "you guys" didn't mean Montgomery and himself, or Montgomery and anybody. It meant the plainclothes constables who had gone canvassing the neighbourhood over the past two days, spreading the net wide, checking for leads on the John Doe murder.

"Asked if I seen anything. I said I seen him go into the Harmon place." The stranger gave Dion another fixed stare. "So what's up there, you mind me asking?" he added, not to Dion, but Montgomery.

"Up where, sir?"

"The woods back here." He indicated the air around them. The neighbourhood was closely embraced by forest, the same forest that fell away into the Lynn Headwaters Regional Park, where kids rode their bikes, and hikers hiked themselves to death, and werewolves were said to roam. "I seen you people looking about. What're you guys looking for, is all I's asking."

"Just scouting the area," Montgomery said. "Routine inquiries."

"The wolf," the stranger said. A statement, not a question.

Now Montgomery and Dion were both staring at him. Montgomery asked, "Wolf?"

"Like I told the cops who come around. The wolf. Maybe you didn't read their fings."

Things, Dion interpreted.

"Their reports there," the stranger clarified. He had a fast and muttery way of talking and kept his chin tucked low, which made him hard to understand. He seemed afraid, Dion thought. He looked like a man who lived with fear. Probably, he was nuts. "I know they reported it 'cause they wrote it all down, eh? Wrote down all what I said."

"You've seen a wolf, sir?" Montgomery spoke up, projecting his voice and being concise as a hint for the man to do the same.

"Hear it. Not see. Hear. Howls."

"Uh-huh? Could be dogs, right?"

"Dogs don't howl. Not like wolfs, they don't. Not like these kinda wolfs."

Dion had heard and seen domesticated dogs howling their hearts out, just like wolves. Sirens set them off, for one thing. Or loneliness. Watching this little man with the anxious eyes, he wondered if the community was already putting a surreal spin on the death at the Greer house. Like Wong and Graham and Jackie Randall, everyone was hoping for monsters.

Montgomery asked the stranger for his name.

"Ray," the man answered. His shoulders tightened, but there was a new shine in his eyes. Eagerness, maybe, and Dion thought he knew why. Ray was retired, single, and bored out of his idle skull. The fear was self-induced, to beat the boredom, and being asked his name by a cop was the year's biggest thrill. "Ray Starkey."

"And how often have you heard this howling, Ray?"

"Three, sir. Three times altogether. August twenty-fifth was the first time. That was around eleven at night. Then September thirteenth, at one-thirty in the morning. And October eighteenth, a little past midnight. That last one's just two weeks ago."

"Damn, I wish my constables kept such good notes," Montgomery said. Friendly still, but jingling his car keys.

August, Dion thought. From the glimpse he'd had of the body along with what he'd heard around the detachment, it seemed the body had been under the house since the summer, give or take a little.

"It chills the blood," Starkey went on. "I write stuff like that on my calendar. I like to keep track of fings." He beetled another suspicious stare toward Dion.

Dion had had enough of the little man and his silent accusations and climbed into the passenger seat of Montgomery's van to wait. With the door closed, the men's voices were now muffled. He flexed his arms, drummed his feet. His body felt wrecked from the exercise, but the ride had done wonders for his spirits. He would get a bike of his own to replace the one he had abandoned after the crash, with all the rest of his belongings, before riding the Greyhound northbound.

Montgomery climbed in behind the wheel, chuckling. "That's one loose screw. Finally shook him off. Wolves!"

"Still," Dion said. "I'll talk to Wildlife tomorrow."

"Somebody else will talk to Wildlife tomorrow," Montgomery said. "It's your weekend. Take it. Recreate. Want to take up Tori's offer, swing by for a drink? Brunch?"

Dion thanked him, but said he had a few things to take care of.

Once dropped off, he climbed into his car and drove home to his apartment. With the weekend and recreation in mind, he showered off the Mesachee mud, then looked over his wardrobe. He picked out his best clothes. It was getting on time for dinner, and for a change, he had plans.

Nine

FLIRTING 101

THE GREEK TAVERNA was close enough that he could walk down. Lonsdale was wide, six lanes including parking. Sometimes it was busy, and other times it stretched out empty like the main drag of a ghost town. Now it was busy, with cars, buses, taxis, delivery trucks, bicycles. A lot of people walking, too, as he approached the harbour. He saw the restaurant ahead. Hadn't changed a bit since his last visit, which wasn't as long ago as it seemed.

Could it have been only two years? Seemed more like a decade.

The young hostess gave him a dazzling smile, and he smiled back at her. She offered a small table for two, stuck in a nook shaded by palm fronds, and left him with the menu. A waitress came by soon after and took his order for a bottle of beer. She congratulated him on his choice of brew, said it was her favourite, too, and went off to place his order.

After studying the menu, he studied the restaurant. Warm and aromatic, the lights down low for ambience. Plucky traditional Greek folk music was playing, just like at every other Greek restaurant he knew. Not too busy, but it was early yet. If it was still as popular as it was when he used to come here with Kate, Looch, Looch's girl Brooke, and whoever else happened to be in his circle at the time, then by seven o'clock, there would be a lineup for seats.

When the waitress came around to take his order, he asked if Farah Jordan was the chef tonight.

"Yes, she is." The waitress was even more delighted than she had been at his choice of beer. "Are you a friend? Would you like me to pass on a message?"

In the space of a pause, he lost momentum, and his *yes* turned into "No, don't bother her. I was just wondering."

Probably it was best to chicken out, anyway. Farah Jordan was too offbeat for him, with her brazen attitude and her talk of ghosts. He smiled at the waitress, and the look she flashed at him was keen and interested. Maybe the message would get passed on, anyway.

He said, "I guess it would be Chef Jordan's souvlaki, then?"

"It *is*. And she makes a *spectacular* souvlaki."

When the dish arrived and he'd had a few bites, he decided it was good, if not the best he'd ever tasted. Looch had been fussy about food, an Italian snob. Himself, not so much. He ate diligently, ploughing through the dish, forking it in, chewing carefully, self-conscious, alone at this table for two. He ordered another beer to wash it down. The restaurant filled and became noisy, and he wished he had stayed home.

He pushed his plate aside, and a shadow fell over the table. He looked up. The woman gazing down at him wore the standard double-breasted white jacket, knots for buttons, no chef's hat. Her gold-black hair looked even golder under this light. It was neatly tied back, and there was nothing hippy about her now.

He stood to greet her and noticed the changes right away. Not just the uniform, but the way she averted her eyes from his. She was flustered, not the woman who had invited him into her house that blustery, rainy night. She said, "Jen told me a really cute guy was asking about me. Her words. So I had to come and check it out. I mean, I couldn't let that one go, could I?"

Dion read disappointment in her laugh. He was disappointed too, at her reaction and the underlying insult. He said, "I didn't mean for her to bother you."

"I know. You've just got a bunch more questions. No problem."

"Questions?" he asked. Then he got it, or at least part of her reaction, which made him grin. "No questions. Actually, I was just hungry."

Now they were both smiling broadly. Along with pleasure, Dion could read relief in her face. The relief vaguely worried him.

"Then you came to the right place, officer. I hope you were satisfied."

"Very. Can you have a coffee? Have time?"

"You're not rushing off?" Her eyes shone. "As it happens, I'm allowing myself a bit of a break. Hang on. I'll get it. Is decaf good?"

"Great."

She brought two cups and sat across from him. He asked how long she had been a chef, and she told him how as a teenager, she had worked in her dad's diner on a windblown byway in Richmond. "Just burgers and stuff," she said. She had a slow, velvety voice, with the faintest trace of an accent. "But one thing led to another, and I eventually went to college, got my learner's ticket, landed a real job, and have been working my way up since. I'm still a journeyman. No big hat!"

Just like that night at her house, she was almost supernaturally nice. She was inviting him to make a move, and this time he was going to do it right. It was something he should be good at, flirting. A little out of practice now, but still … "You're off at eleven tonight?"

Instantly he knew he had blown it, and her supernatural smile faded. He couldn't blame her. He had blurted it out like an amateur, putting her on the spot, leaving no graceful exit. He was worse than out of practice, he was back to Flirting 101.

He went babbling on, seeing it coming, but too late to pull out. "If you wanted to go for a beer or something. Only if you felt like it, of course, though I know it's late."

She reached out to almost touch his arm, but drew back. "It's not you. It's completely me. I didn't expect this really kind offer. You see, I've just gotten myself out of a few binds, and I've promised myself to take a year off, kind of thing."

Dion's only goal right now was to pay his bill and leave. "It was just beer," he assured her, wallet out. He could feel himself blushing, even as he smiled at her. "That's all. No strings."

"No strings? Is there any such thing?"

"No, I get it, sure," he said, knowing he sounded like a man who didn't get anything. "I understand. It's a messed-up world. Even one damn beer can turn into a custody battle, right?"

She nodded, but doubtfully.

"In fact, I'm the same. Strings make me nervous. So there we go. Lucky us."

"I'm sorry," she said.

"Don't be."

"And, of course, there's Stef."

Dion was wondering whether to pay with cash or credit, and if cash, how much to leave for a tip. He stopped calculating and looked at the woman who had given him all the wrong signals, who was now telling him about some boyfriend she'd all but forgotten, which just about tore it.

"He's the fellow I work with," she explained, pointing. "Him."

Part of the kitchen was visible to diners over a high counter, adding to the restaurant's pseudo-peasanty ambience, and there Dion could see a reedy man in a prep cook's kerchief, chopping viciously.

"He and I carpool," Farah said. "We work the same days, same hours, and he lives just a couple blocks from me, so we have this arrangement where I drive him to and from work. So I'm kind of committed, anyway. Don't worry about the bill, Calvin, honestly."

Her use of his first name startled him. He couldn't remember sharing it with her. But of course — she had looked at his RCMP card, laughed, and compared him to a comic book character. "Thanks, but you're kind of a witness," he said. He was trying to ease out of his tantrum, be at least a little bit funny, so she wouldn't think he was a total asshole. "Can't take any gifts. Might be seen as hush money."

Not a great joke, and she didn't seem to get it, anyway.

She said good night, self-consciously shifted the fit of her chef's jacket, and went back to her kitchen. Dion sighed and went to pay the bill, forgetting to return the hostess's dazzling smile.

Ten

BASH

MONTY'S HALLOWEEN PARTY had been billed as a casual thing, starting anytime in late afternoon and running to the wee hours, or as long as anybody cared to stay. Leith had lied to Monty when he said he never did costume parties. As a child he had leaped around the streets wearing superhero masks and capes. As a young adult he had once gone to a house party as a devil, prodding girls with his plastic pitchfork. Another time, in a more ambitious cliché, he had gone as a box of popcorn. As a devil and as popcorn, he had failed to pick up the vampiresses he had lusted after.

Even as a grownup, he had attended friends' costume parties wearing something or other, though his limited flair was pretty well shot. Tonight he was back to the devil standby. He had dug out a red T-shirt and, stepping into the dollar store, had bought a set of horns and a paste-on Mephisto-like moustache, thin and black. At home, the mirror told him he would convince nobody. His hair was lumpy and blond, his eyes were middle-aged and blue, and his middle name would never be "fun."

He bared his teeth at the glass and said, "*I am the devil.*"

He arrived at 7:30 with beer and potato chips. Walking in — the moustache already lost — he found the party well underway, music playing, people in costume eating, drinking, and milling. He stood amongst strangers and, just like on his first day in junior high, the sinking sensation in his gut told him he would never belong.

Monty seemed to have plenty of friends for a newcomer to the North Shore. But maybe some of these people were imports from Surrey, or friends through the fiancée. Leith was looking for a place to chill his beer when Monty spotted him and beckoned him over. He wore an elaboration of mismatched plaids: sports jacket, slacks, bow tie. "Go on," he told Leith, who was pretending to be blinded by the sheer ugliness of the ensemble. "Guess what I am."

Monty's friends fired off suggestions: a pervert, Don Cherry's cousin, an undercover narc.

"Cars!" Monty shouted. He was already half-crocked, Leith guessed, those ice-blue eyes paler than usual, as though diluted by whatever he was drinking. "You bunch of losers. I sell *cars*. Used cars, the used'er the better." He reached to hook an arm around Leith's throat, and together they staggered. "And what kind of costume is this?" he asked, scotch fumes blasting across Leith's face. "Can anybody guess what this guy's supposed to be?"

Someone in the crowd guessed right: a party-pooper.

Leith broke free and straightened his horns. "C'mon, man, I tried!"

Then Monty's inebriation was suddenly gone, to Leith's surprise; he was no longer crocked, but his normal, pleasant self, saying, "I'm happy to see you, believe me, but where's your better half and baby girl? I was hoping to meet 'em."

"Izzy's still a bit young for the hour. Where's *your* better half?"

"On her way," Monty said. "Promise. But what are you waiting for? Get yourself a damn drink and go compare battle scars, or whatever we cops do at parties."

Over the next hour, Leith lost the new-kid feeling, and even enjoyed some of the conversations he was pulled into. He wasn't the only party-pooper, it turned out, and with a generous rum and Coke inside, it was all pretty funny, anyway. Two drinks was his limit, maybe two and a half, as he planned to be dead sober by midnight.

Cal Dion showed up. Jeans, T-shirt, and a rather artsy cardigan with blocky patterns of various colours. No attempt at a costume, unless the cardigan was it. Leith braced himself, because conversations with Dion never went well, and made his way over. "Hey, how're you doing?"

"Hey," Dion said, looking pleasantly surprised. "I'm great. You?"

So far so good, Leith thought. "Fine," he said. "That's a cool sweater."

"Thanks. I like your costume. It's convincing."

"Huh," Leith said, and was stuck. Then he recalled certain pleasantries he could share. "Monty says you got some info out of the Mesachee biker kid, Ron Graham. Got him to admit they were just making stuff up."

"Not really making stuff up."

"Whatever. Point is, whoever's creeping about in the woods, he's of this earth."

"And probably nothing to do with anything, either. Just a dead end."

"Still, that was sharp of you, catching him out."

"It wasn't sharp," Dion said. "It was obvious. I was waiting for you to pin Graham down, 'cause he was practically shouting *I don't agree with my buddy James Bond here*. 'Cause up to then, they were backing each other up all the way. It came to the howl, and Graham went silent. It was written all over his face, if you'd looked over at him instead of focusing on the other clown. By saying nothing, he was saying everything: *There was no blood-curdling howl, and me and James are full of shit*."

"Huh," Leith said again.

Dion appeared to listen intently to something — maybe the echoes of his own nastiness. "Where's the beer?" he said. Leith pointed the way and was left blessedly alone. Joy.

Putting Dion out of his mind, he picked up where he had left off, sipping at his rationed cocktail and socializing. Along with police and civil servants were people from the outer world, friends of the famous fiancée that Leith was yet to meet. Tori was due soon, apparently. Off in Richmond on a modelling assignment.

He stood looking at a large black-and-white photograph of the woman on a wall, framed against simple black glass. It was a professional shot, and she was gorgeous. Sweetly so, pale and delicate, with a shy, sidelong smile that seemed to say she was clutching a bouquet of wildflowers behind her back, and was about to spring them on you. No wonder Monty was dizzy about her. Still studying the photo, Leith wondered if Tori was after Monty for his money. Which he would have plenty of, with that upwardly mobile career of his.

He wondered if he was jealous. Probably.

An hour later, still no Tori. Leith had seen a few partiers in theatrical makeup come and go. He kept an eye out for werewolves, but saw none, which was just fine with him. By the third hour, he was ready to leave. He saw Dion talking with Monty now, and not only smiling, but laughing. *Laughing*. That was a first. Laughter looked good on him. Yet another accomplishment by the amazing Michelin Montgomery, turning water into wine.

Maybe a little jealous, yes.

A beep at Leith's wrist told him it was time to push off. Tonight was Halloween, and mischief was afoot. More than likely, he would be contacted as the team got swamped with call-outs. He wouldn't be called about the little goblins blowing off their fingers with firecrackers or stealing each other's candy, or about the bush parties getting out of hand at the dam or the local parks. It was the bigger goblins he was concerned with. A few of those would be out and about as well, no doubt, taking advantage of Mask Day to get away with murder.

* * *

Dion stood in a small bay of solitude, away from the main crowd, and watched the action. Montgomery had roped him into conversation, calling him a fucking cheapskate — "Not even a Walmart set of hillbilly teeth?" When the conversation had gotten too fast and slippery, he had made his break. A side effect of head injury was an inability to deal with too much overlapping information, which was a good reason to avoid parties. Confusion led to panic, which led to bad choices. Turning, he saw David Leith in his red T-shirt setting down an empty glass and not picking up a refill.

Dion wished he had apologized to Leith on the spot. Even five minutes later wouldn't do it. An immediate and simple *Sorry, man, I was out of line*, would have been good enough. Or better yet, *Sorry, sir*. But *out of line* didn't sound natural — and wasn't completely true. Probably in clarifying, he would have only made things worse. Better to keep his mouth shut.

He saw a woman dressed as plush dice intercept Leith, pulling him into a chat. The star of the party, Tori, was still nowhere in sight. Why was he waiting for her? Because she was funny. Not that he would ever want to deal with her one on one, but in a safe environment like this, it could be quite a show.

Leith had broken free of the dice lady, and he headed for the door, collecting his jacket on his way out. Others left, too, and more arrived, bringing a fresh swell of party atmosphere and the din of conversation. Dion wove his way through bodies to Montgomery, waited for a gap in the conversation, and asked, "Will Tori be here anytime soon?"

"Just texted," Montgomery told him. "Still at her gig in Richmond. Photo shoot. Supposed to be back by now. Must have got held up. You're not running off, are you?"

Half an hour more, Dion decided. His beer was going warm in his hand. A new guest arrived, another who hadn't bothered with a costume. Constable Jackie Randall, off duty, wearing jeans and a heavy blue polo shirt under her parka. "Trick or treat!" she sang out, scraping her boots on the welcome mat.

He was glad to see a familiar face. He waved her over, and she plucked a can of Diet Pepsi from the cooler and joined him, saying, "Hello there. Fancy meeting you by the potato chips."

"I didn't expect to see you here!"

"I didn't either, frankly. But I decided I just had to come along. Bit of a class reunion. I went to school with Tori in Surrey."

Dion expressed polite surprise.

"Hung out some," she continued. "Played floor hockey together. Learned to drink and smoke together. But you know how things go. She went her way, I went mine. But when I heard who Corporal Montgomery is engaged to, I just had to come along tonight and see her again. Probably more out of curiosity than anything, but don't tell her that. Anyway, she's not here, so looks like it just might not happen, judging by that clock on the wall and considering my own ridiculously early bedtime. I'll just stick around an hour and then go."

Dion wasn't going to stick around that long. He would talk to Randall for a few minutes, then excuse himself and go.

"I know what you're thinking," she was saying. "Jackie Randall plays hockey? Yup, and I wasn't a bad goalie. Wide, you know." She grinned. She talked about hockey for a while, as Dion crunched on crackers, daydreamed, and counted down the minutes. "… And it was brutal," she said, having tacked off on another topic. "Regina doesn't make it easy for us short ones."

By Regina she meant Depot, where RCMP recruits were trained. "Must have been tough."

"Brutal," she said again. "What got me through was proof. Proving that I could do it to all those who doubted me. Which was everybody I know. And it was worth it. The parade, the ceremonies, the I-told-you-so's. I can still taste grad. I thought my heart would burst. Did you hear we got a name for John Doe?"

The body in the crawl space.

"Benjamin Clifford Stirling," she went on. "Ben. Changes things in your own heart, doesn't it? Knowing his name, seeing his picture. He was a nice-looking boy."

Randall gazed around at the room decorated in orange and black streamers, large fake spiders climbing up and down fake webs, and said more cheerfully, "I'm surprised she's so late. Her audience is waiting. She should be table-dancing by now."

"I heard she's working in Richmond," Dion said. "I also heard she's always late for everything."

Randall snorted. "You can say that again. She's like the opposite of a team player. On Tori's priority list, Tori always comes first. If she's having too much fun wherever she is, she probably won't show up at all. Don't repeat this to anybody, but Tori and Monty — it's going to be the marriage from hell."

It was a depressing prediction. Dion not only liked Montgomery, he would have liked to have had him for a father. He wanted the upcoming Montgomery marriage to be made in heaven, not hell. "Who's Benjamin Stirling? Where's he from?"

"Saskatchewan. He's a nobody, at this point. Not even certified yet it's him, but blood type's a match, facial structure looks promising. Dental records look okay, too, but yet to be confirmed. They're having trouble with that because Ben's last dental X-ray was when he was ten. They've located his brother, Sam, a CP yardman who lives in Rush Lake, which is near Swift Current. He says he last heard from Ben in April and reported him missing in May. Like a lot of young people, Ben left the prairies and came west looking for work and all the rest of it — thrills, malls, new social circles."

"And an ocean," Dion added.

"And that. Sam says Ben was a good kid. Deep, he says. Never been incarcerated, but kind of a misfit. He was twenty-three when he took off, would be twenty-four now. Nobody took the missing report too seriously, he says, because Ben wasn't great at staying in touch. But he wouldn't have dropped off the map, either, Sam says."

"And you picked up all this how?"

"Eyes and ears open," she said. "As you know, I'm not in GIS — yet — but every chance I get, I'm up there. They've even got me helping with some real grungy, bottom-of-the-barrel tasks."

"Congratulations."

"Thank you. Sadly, there won't be much for Sam to ID when he gets here, but he's flying over, anyway, to see how he can help out. We expect him tomorrow at four o'clock."

Dion watched a heavy man dressed as a bumble-bee buzz in tight circles around Montgomery. A tinfoil crown flew like a Frisbee. The loop of Halloween music was getting tiresome — "Monster Mash" again. Still no sign of Tori.

No more guests were arriving, and a few were leaving. Trick-or-treaters still rang the bell, but no more little kids at this hour. Only teens with painted faces. Drunken fairies handed out more insults than candies. In a gap of silence between songs, somebody's cellphone went off, and every vampire, bumblebee, and go-go dancer in the room checked their device. So did Jackie Randall. So did Dion.

But it was Michelin Montgomery's phone that was ringing. Dion saw him answer and saw a range of emotions that were, maybe, just the effects of liquor: surprise, then something like alarm, then a smile of recognition. Montgomery plugged an ear and spun a finger at his guests to carry on, then walked away — not so steady on his feet — to find a quieter place to talk.

A little blonde woman with a wired-on halo shouted after him, "That better be Tori with a big fat apology."

On Montgomery's return, he let the partiers know it was Tori, and she was going to be here any minute now, and she was sorry for the delay. *Any minute now* was not good enough for Dion. He wished Jackie Randall good night, told her to go easy on the Pepsi, and made his way over to say goodbye to his host. "Thanks for inviting me. It was great. I had a good time."

Montgomery turned around, a look of surprise on his face. He clamped Dion on the shoulder with a hand,

and slurred, "Seriously, so soon? My girl, didn't she explicitly tell you to be here?"

No drunk should ever try to say *explicitly*. Dion apologized and said to give Tori his regards.

Montgomery unhanded him with a slight shove. "'Kay. Well, glad you could make it anyway, buddy." He turned back to his more faithful guests, and Dion looked toward the front foyer. It was so packed and noisy that he decided to find another way out.

From the living room, he stepped into a kitchen. A few oddly dressed adults stood about in serious conversation, ignoring him as he slipped by. He found a door leading to a veranda, and from there went outside to what turned out to be a large, open deck, where he was suddenly and refreshingly alone. The yard below was dark, and with the door behind him pulled shut, the noise seemed capped off and distant.

The tension seeped out of his muscles. The sky stretching east to west was dense with clouds, and the rain came down in long arcs, fine but steady. It always rained on Halloween. He had only one precious Halloween memory, fainter every time he called it up and threatening to fade altogether. He must have been four or five. He wore an eye patch, and his mother had knelt to paint a moustache under his nose, then shown him the results in a hand mirror. He could feel and hear that plastic sword scraping along the sidewalk behind him. It was a big adventure — not so much the costume as being outside at night, holding her hand and walking with her into the mysterious darkness. The rain had been light, like it was now; all the way down the block the drops were lit like falling stars, and he had thought — mistakenly as it turned out — that they were leaving forever.

The faint click of the motion-sensor lights snapped his thoughts back to present. He stared down at the backyard, washed in electric white, and blinked. Midway along the path leading from what must be a back lane stood an angel.

Eleven

AZRAEL

EXCEPT SHE WASN'T an angel. She was a slight young woman in platform shoes and a long gown that rippled with sequins. Her feathery wings confused him, until he recalled this was dress-up night. She looked as shocked as he felt, and he realized he was backlit, probably unrecognizable, and might be seen as a threat. He started forward into the light, but she had come alive and was moving along the cement path toward the stairs at a good clip, her gown gathered up in her fists. From her shoulder swung a little bag as twinkly as her clothes. There was no twinkle in her expression.

"What the *hell* are you doing?" She was clumping up toward him. "Standing there in the freezing-cold dark! Trying to scare me to death?"

He told her he was sorry for scaring her, that he was just leaving, but mid-apology, saw that he was wrong — she wasn't angry at all. She had climbed the stairs and was smiling at him. "Aha," she said. "Just having a smoke? Well, that's all right, then. You'd never guess, but I'm Azrael!" She laughed, swinging side to side to flap her wings. Her teeth were perfectly straight and white, and her green eyes glittered.

Her wings were a little uneven, Dion saw. They seemed to be made of real feathers — not white, but black or grey blue. He lifted his hands to show he wasn't smoking, actually, but too late, as the motion sensor flicked off and he and she were once more in near darkness, only faintly lit by the home's ambient glow.

"*Whew*," she said. "What a night. Shall we go in now, before my feathers get wet? I must make my grand entrance, and you must be part of it. When I squeeze your arm, you lean over and kiss me, okay? Together we shall make my Monty *insanely* jealous."

She had hooked his arm to guide him back through the door, but he resisted the pull. "Like I said, I'm just leaving. I'm sorry I missed you, but I arrived quite early, so —"

"Just leaving," she echoed, with a blurt of laughter. "How can you be just leaving? *I* just *got* here!"

She hooked him tighter and pulled harder, so now he had to plant his shoes and physically unhook her hand with his own. Freed, he moved away from her and toward the stairs, hoping it was all just her idea of good fun. "'Night, Tori."

"Wait!" she cried. He stopped, one foot on the top step. She seemed to float toward him through the darkness. Her body blocked the misty rays of light from the windows behind her, and her face was in shadow, so all he could see of her were the whites of her eyes and the pearly gleam of her teeth. "So sorry," she whispered. "I'm terrible with names, which is extra nasty of me, because you remembered mine. It's Edwin, isn't it? Or Edward?"

"Cal," he said.

"Can you do me a big favour, Cal, and stop acting like a complete idiot? I want you to come inside with me and meet my friends." She took his hand, to his surprise, and brought it to her mouth, gazing up at him as she pulled her lower lip along his knuckles. It was a good performance, and if he wasn't so baffled, it might have done wonders for his morale. "One friend es*pecially*," she said. "She's gorgeous, and newly single, and ooh, what a coincidence, you're single, too! C'mon then, let me introduce you!"

He stared into her flushed face, saw her chest rising and falling, and wondered if she was climbing or crashing from whatever she was on. "I have to get going. I'm sorry."

She whipped out a hand to grab his arm. "You don't understand," she hissed. Her hand was fine-boned, but had an iron grip, and her pretty face had grown ugly with fear. "It's just, I screwed up," she told him. Her voice had transformed, like her face, and was now low and urgent. "I should have been home hours ago, and Monty, you don't know him when he's drunk. And he *is* drunk. I could hear it on the phone. Please, Cal. I'd feel so much better if we went in together. You can just hang around for a few minutes, make sure everything's cool, then you can go."

"What are you saying? You're saying he's violent toward you?"

"He can be … emotional. I just need you to be there, that's all. Please?"

Emotional? He looked at the lit windows of her comfortable home flickering with silhouettes. "There's a house full of people, most of them cops. Take your pick."

"Cal —"

He had run out of patience and was no good at head games. He lifted his arm to break her grip, and before she could latch on again, started down the stairs. It was all so silly, and he expected her to laugh, but she didn't. Instead, her words shot after him in a sudden, explosive rage: "You know what, Cal? You know what your problem is?"

He paused to look back at her.

"You're a fucking ass-banging *queer*," she called.

So gay guys weren't the sweetest, after all. He kept walking, down the path and into the floodlight zone. The motion-sensor lamp came on again, showing the pavement leading two ways: straight ahead to the back lane, and off to the side, which he supposed would take him to the front of the house. Out to the street, to his car, to escape. He stood still as he heard a shriek and whistle — not the woman, but fireworks. Looking to the west, he saw a green-and-gold explosion of whirling sparks, then another, and another. Below the flickering sky, he saw the back alley, the roofs of houses, the gleam of a parked vehicle.

Montgomery's fiancée was still shouting at him. "You don't even know where you're going." Her voice cracked in anger, the snap of a whip. "It's that way, you blind sonovabitch. That way."

Her rage rattled him. He had committed no crime, and didn't deserve this kind of abuse. *It's not me, it's her*, he told himself. She'd had a bad night, maybe. Was high, or low, or bitten by a mad dog. But for sure, whatever was interfering with her reason, she sure as hell shouldn't have been driving.

He didn't look at her again, but walked around the side of the house, through the carport, past Montgomery's van, and out onto the street.

He was at his car, rummaging his pocket for keys. A few oversized late-night trick-or-treaters, drunk on sugar — or something stronger — torpedoed past in the rain, making their way to the Montgomery front door with its strobing lights and recorded spooky noises looped and broadcast, a soundtrack of witches cackling, ghosts wailing, demons laughing. There were synthetic cracks of thunder, too, a pale imitation of the real thing.

"Trick or treat, smell my feet," one monster who could have been his own age bellowed after him.

"Fuck off," he bellowed back.

He eased his Honda Civic from the curb, where it sat tightly packed amongst many, and drove back to his apartment. Soon he was in his neat bathroom, stripped down to his shorts and vigorously brushing his teeth in the dark. He crawled across his mattress to crash into the pillow, and reached out to press *play* on his stereo. Didn't matter what was on — in this case it was an ambient track that sounded like an approaching train. Ever since the crash, noise had helped him sleep. Pan pipes or trash can lids or newscasts, it didn't matter. Anything to break up disturbing thought patterns. Tonight he needed it more than ever. The woman with the dark wings had cranked his depression level back up to ten out of ten. Eleven.

By the third track, he was dozing. Not that it lasted. Moments later, it seemed, the jangle of his cellphone dragged him back to the surface. The clock's red numerals read 1:02, and the caller was a dispatcher, trying to round up extra manpower. There were problems out there in the night, which was nothing new to the North Shore, but it was always worse on Halloween. And this involved a young teen, a trick-or-treater gone missing in the Edgemont Village neighbourhood. Could he pitch in?

"Yes, of course," he rasped, and he was sitting up already, reaching for his clothes. "Right away."

Twelve

CREEP

IN THE EARLY-MORNING hours of Stefano's second day off, he finished his thirty-third painting. His bare arms were smudged black and blue, and his hands were cold and cramped. He breathed hard, inhaling the pleasant stink of acrylic paint, sweating like a long-distance runner in front of his canvas propped on its makeshift easel, still wet. Forest at dusk, lines of dark through mottled light. His self-portrait had failed, and he had receded once more behind gobs of ochre and onyx.

But though he had painted trees over his ghastly form, with its lowering face and bloody ribs showing through torn fur, it didn't matter, because it was there all the same, inside the canvas, staring out. Good, he thought. The best so far. But good *enough*? Never.

He went to wash the paint off himself, and when he returned, excited to see the masterpiece afresh, he saw instead a mess. It happened every time; the best became the worst upon the moment of completion, and no extra strokes would fix it.

He could not look at it now. He would let it dry, then place it with the other thirty-two, facing the wall, and try again only once he had built up new courage.

But for now, he was stuck. He had run out of both inspiration and stretchers. He needed to make more as soon as possible.

Paul had a woodwork shop in the basement, on the far side from Stefano's suite. There were lathes and sanders and chisels, a mitre saw, everything Stefano needed to make his stretchers. The shop had been set up so Paul could make mouldings and spindles to finish the house nicely. He no longer used it much, but Stefano did, whenever Paul and Colette were out. He would listen for the front door upstairs to thump shut, then for the long process of getting the wheelchair strapped into the van. As soon as the vehicle purred out of the driveway and was gone, he would set up the equipment and bang together a frame or two. In his room he would stretch the cheapest canvas he could find, staple it into place, slather on the gesso.

Midnight struck. The music was off upstairs. Stefano looked at his skin folded up in the corner. There had been technical problems with fit and flexibility, so last week he had torn it apart and was now putting it back together. It was almost ready for another test run, but for now, he was only a man.

He picked up his running shoes and padded up in stockinged feet, avoiding the squeaky risers. At Anastasia's door, he paused to listen, wondering if his father was in there with her. Paul spent a lot of time in there, too much time. He could do anything to her, and Anastasia couldn't complain.

But no, he could hear Paul snoring from the master bedroom, and from Anastasia's little cell, there was only the wheeze of her breathing machine.

On the back steps he sat and tied on his scruffy runners, then proceeded down through the woods, giving the neighbourhood a wide berth. He emerged close to Chef's house and craned to look across a couple of lawns to see if her windows were lit. They should be. At this hour she would still be awake, maybe visible moving around inside. He would slide into her garden, creep around the foundations, urinate on the decorative shrubs. He would press against her back door in case it was open, as she had left it once, on that night he had broken in.

Tonight he would not only break in, but break through, confront her.

He dropped to a crouch, crawled across a dip in the dark lawn, avoiding the motion sensors. By the back hedge, he stood tall and stared.

Her windows were dark, the lights off. Her car wasn't in the carport.

She was out. At 1:00 a.m. Doing what? With who?

He clambered up the back porch, heaving with rage, and rattled the doorknob. The handle turned without resistance. He paused, breathed on the glass for a moment, then pushed. The door swung inward.

Thirteen

THIRTEEN

AT 1:30 IN THE MORNING on November 1 the rain had stopped, leaving only gusty winds to sweep the North Shore, and Dion was out looking for a missing trick-or-treater. Alone in his cruiser, he tracked over an unlikely stretch that had already been searched: the loop of Sunset Boulevard that would take him around Eldon Park.

His reason for checking out Eldon was a complaint from earlier on in the evening, teens getting rowdy behind the baseball field. The party had long since been disbanded, but the missing girl was also a young teen, and it might be worth it to take another run through the area.

He entered the MacKay Creek Greenbelt and was slowing for the curve when something caught his eye to his right, cropping up in his high beams and falling away again. A flutter that could be leaves or grasses flaring in the sweep of his headlights.

He pulled over and set the hazards flashing, and since he was parked in a place with poor visibility, he switched on the emergency lights to warn oncoming cars. He stared into the rear-view mirror, at the road and trees flickering red and blue. The road was a two-laner and poorly lit, but now he could see something glittering on the asphalt, maybe broken glass.

He called it in, putting the dispatcher on notice that he might have a situation and would check it out and confirm. Outside, the night was a medley of smells. Wet earth, mostly, car exhaust lying low in the cold, and maybe a whiff of gunpowder, as firecrackers were still sounding off from the direction of the ball field. Far away, a chorus of sirens raced to an alarm. The glittering objects picked out in his light beam, he discovered, were not glass shards, but wrapped candies, two on the road and three in the grass, a good forewarning of what his Maglite beam was going to find next.

She lay partly hidden behind the concrete barrier, downslope, sprawled in the weeds. If not for the flutter of fabric that lifted and fell from her clothing, he would have missed her altogether. He crossed the barrier and blasted his light square in her shockingly chalk-white face. Her lids were sooty black, crimson blood streamed from a gash in her cheek, and crude black stitches radiated from the corners of her mouth and across her forehead.

Halloween paint, all of it. The only real blood that Dion could see was a creek of darkness tracing a jagged line from her nostrils, down her cheek and into her hair. She was a zombie in grey rags, the theatrical effect spoiled by a dark-blue ski jacket with lime-green accents. He knew she was dead before he crouched at her side and felt for a pulse at her throat. No pulse, and her skin was cool to the touch — but not cold.

He jogged back to the car to give the dispatcher his location, asking for ambulance, traffic control, GIS.

After the call, he returned to the child, nothing to do but stand watch over her. She lay as thrown, he believed. Dead on impact or abandoned to die. There was no question who she was, as she fit the description of the missing teen, Breanna Ferris, to a T: small stature, pink hair, zombie duds.

The rags seemed to be made of bedsheets and cheap gauze cut ragged. It was a gauze strip unravelling from her hips that had flagged his attention. Black tights covered her slim calves, and on one foot was a clumpy high-heeled boot. She looked younger than thirteen to him. She looked too young to be out and about on this dark forested road all alone.

From one ski jacket pocket spilled more wrapped candies.

He walked up to the road. The spill of candy would mark the point of impact. His flashlight beam picked out skid marks, the burn of a hard braking. Whoever had hit her had seen her too late and tried to stop. A simple, violent story.

The other boot lay in the grass, on its side. To a passing driver it would look like just another rock. And now something else appeared on the asphalt some distance away — a tall pointy hat, tumbled there by the wind. Did zombies wear witch hats? Was there another victim hereabouts? As he watched, the tall hat tipped over in slow motion, scuttled farther down the road, and tried to take flight. Instead, it spun once and lay still.

He was searching for a second person, dead or alive, on the off chance, when the ambulance arrived. The paramedics confirmed what he already knew, that there was nothing they could do for the girl. He stood with them and waited for the ultimate confirmation of the coroner.

Between idle conversation with the EHS crew, he thought about the dead girl's pink hair. Colourful hair was all the rage these days — purple, pink, green, or rainbow. But it hadn't been, as far as he could recall, back when he'd spun his Charger out of the gravel pit last year, pedal to the metal, trying to catch her, and instead gotten T-boned by the red sports car at the intersection. Pow, his best pal dead, his world torn to smithereens, and the mystery girl with the pink hair, the witness who had seen god knows what, had escaped into the night.

"Rough, eh," the paramedic was saying. "Just glad it's not me breaking the news."

Dion nodded at him. "Just hoping it's not going to be me."

Next out, a big gun arrived, putting in a rare appearance in the field. Inspector Hope was a heavy bull who had been with the North Shore for years. He came tonight wrapped in a dark coat over a dark suit. He wanted the details in broad strokes, and Dion described how he had come to be checking the area, taking a final sweep of some known teen hangouts that had caused a bit of trouble earlier in the evening.

More members arrived. David Leith piled out of one of the unmarked cars. He was lead on the search, and Hope began to harangue him for a job not well done. "Constable Dion here came out on his own initiative, and he found her. This area's been gone over, Leith. Don't your people have eyes?"

"She was hard to spot," Dion offered. "She's lying out of sight down there. In fact —"

"There's candy all over the fucking road," Hope said, not to Dion, but to Leith.

"Yessir," Leith said. "I don't think —"

"Which I spotted a mile away myself, without my glasses. Candy. And what's that?"

Leith, along with everyone else in the vicinity, looked in the direction of the man's pointing thumb at the witch's hat seated at the road's shoulder like a soggy black pylon. Hope wasn't looking at the witch's hat, because he was looking at Leith.

"That actually blew onto the road just now." Dion said it more forcefully, not to be talked over again. "And I came out on his instructions," he added, indicating Leith with a glance. "There was a party at Eldon that got dispersed earlier. David said to follow up."

He had Hope's attention now — and Leith's — and went on. "I almost missed her. Driving past in the dark, I didn't see the candy on the road. The hat wasn't there when I arrived, and she lay out of sight completely. If that fabric she's wrapped in hadn't fluttered, I would have driven right by."

"If it fluttered for you, it fluttered for everyone else," Hope said, and went back to snarling at Leith. "What it is, is we've got a bunch of guys out here moping over last night's hockey scores instead of keeping a lookout. How much time have we wasted? At whose expense? I'm not impressed."

Leith said, "Yessir. We were focusing on Edgemont and the Highlands, because —"

"Struck by a car," Inspector Hope interrupted, but more pleasantly, to Dion. "Hit and run."

Dion had to agree. He guessed the driver hadn't stopped for longer than a heartbeat before running. When Hope went to speak to the coroner, Dion asked Leith about the mystery of the witch's hat. "Was she supposed to be wearing one? There was no hat in the description I got."

Leith was looking pale, tired, and disgusted. Probably smarting from Hope's bellowing, which still left angry ripples in the air. "I don't know," he said. "Good point." And went to make arrangements to have the entire park searched for a possible second victim.

* * *

In the refuge of his car, Leith sat looking at his map of the North Shore. He felt shredded. He was disgusted with anyone who would mow down a child and flee. Also with his inobservant crew, whom he personally had assigned to run all roads in the area, even on the periphery, like this one. He hadn't told them to keep a sharp eye out, because that went without saying, didn't it?

The disgust he felt for the parents who had let their daughter out at night, dressed all in darks — no reflective clothing that he could see — was complicated by a searing pity.

The map was a blur, even with the overhead light on, and he couldn't find his reading glasses. He could see Dion outside, talking to one of the Ident techs, a guy from traffic. They were looking at the road surface. Leith rolled down his driver's window, letting in the cold, and gave a sharp whistle.

Dion got in on the passenger side, and they looked at each other. The lateness of the hour, the horror of the girl's death, and their mutual weariness seemed to have sapped the antagonism out of both of them. "Thanks for the lie," Leith said. "Didn't put a plug in his fat mouth, but you tried, and I appreciate it."

"It wasn't a lie," Dion said. "You mentioned Eldon in the briefing."

"Did I?"

"The bush-party angle. You said check it out."

Leith decided not to pursue this gross rubberizing of the truth, and Dion seemed happy to do the same. "I can't read this fucking map. Can you show me where we are?"

Dion found their location and marked it with a pen. He then checked his notes and was able to place an X where Breanna Ferris lived, too. Or *had* lived. "Highland Boulevard, just down from Tudor," he said.

"But she was trick-or-treating down here, in Edgemont Village, with a friend," Leith said. "Grace something or other."

"What did Grace say?"

"Nothing much. Says she and Breanna split up about eight thirty, still in the village." He squinted at the map. "Down here. Grace went home, which is here, not far from where they split up, and she says she thought Breanna was going to do the same."

Dion looked at all the points of interest, tracing them along with his finger. "If they split up here, and she wanted to head home, she would have beelined up Highland, like this. Why come out this way, if not for the party at the Eldon ball field."

"Doesn't look like easy walking distance to all points," Leith said.

"Quite a hike, but doable."

Leith had found his glasses, and he was able to locate yet another spot on the map to mark with an X on Ridgewood, close to Edgemont Village. "We found her phone about here," he said. "So we thought she might have boarded a bus. There's a stop close by. Transit's been questioned, but nothing from that. Can't unlock the phone without her code, and her parents don't know it, so it'll be up to the techs to crack." He folded the map, not so neatly. "Now, I've got to get on with it, deliver the news to the parents."

"I'll go with you," Dion said.

And he did.

* * *

Judging by how Leith navigated to the Ferris home, Dion could tell he didn't know his way around the North Shore so well yet. If the GPS said to go this way, he went this way, instead of a sleeker alternate route. But best to keep his mouth shut, he decided. It didn't matter, anyway. The streets were silent and empty at

3:00 a.m. out here in the suburbs. Even the late-night revellers had gone silent.

The lights were blaring at the Ferris house.

"You never get used to this," Leith said, as he parked the car and pushed open the driver's door. Dion waited a moment, wondering why he had volunteered to do this. Because Leith shouldn't have to do it alone, he supposed. Nobody should.

Fourteen

LOST

ONCE HE HAD CONFIRMED his daughter's identity and composed himself enough to leave her side, Roy Ferris followed Leith to one of the small meeting rooms reserved for tough talks like this. Dion went to get coffee from the machine. Caffeine wasn't a good idea, he realized as he fed the coins and pressed the button. But it would go untouched, anyway. It was a formality, and a familiarity, a pale comfort in an unreal situation.

He returned to the room and closed the door. Ferris sat in a daze. He said thanks for the coffee and clutched the paper cup. He went on to relate how he had dropped his daughter at Edgemont Village earlier this evening, where she was going to meet a school friend, whom she was going trick-or-treating with. The friend's name was … Grace. "Now it seems so … vague," he said. "It was her first year out on her own. For Halloween, I mean. She really wanted to go without chaperones. How … how could we have let her? But how could we not?"

"It's something all parents have to struggle with," Leith said. "Kids have been fighting for their independence from the dawn of time. You can't blame yourself."

The grieving man shook his head. "I'll always blame myself." At a little after 9:00, the agreed-upon curfew, he had phoned Breanna. She had answered her cell, said she was still out with Grace and they were having fun, could she have another hour? He had given her till 9:30, then he would pick her up. Yes, she'd call, she had promised.

"At nine thirty I called again," he said. "She didn't answer."

Immediately the worry set in, hard. He had phoned Grace. "I gave you guys her contact info, didn't I? She said she and Brea split up around eight thirty. So Brea had lied to me. She wasn't with Grace. Grace said she thought Brea had headed straight home, or was going to call to be picked up." He looked at Leith, at Dion. "Why was she on that road? Who took her there?"

By 9:45 he was driving around Edgemont, up and down the avenues, peering into the patches of shadow and light for a familiar little figure, but the area was too big and he had no clue where to begin looking. At 9:55 he phoned the police, who immediately started an effort to triangulate the phone Breanna had been carrying. The phone had been located in the grass on Ridgewood, and its discovery only compounded concerns. And while mother and father waited for good news, Leith had shown up on the doorstep with just the opposite.

The interview was done. Ferris was dropped off at his residence, and Dion returned with Leith to the detachment. They sat at Leith's station in GIS with plans of drafting out their combined observations and recall of all that had transpired that night.

Leith was left-handed, Dion saw. The pen hooked over the words as they formed, the writing oddly sloped — but neat. Leith gave a broken running commentary as he worked, more a thinking aloud than a sharing. Kids and independence, the worrisome age when babies think they're grown-ups. He would be talking to Grace first thing tomorrow, see if he could get some clue as to why Breanna had lied, then made her way up Sunset Boulevard instead of heading home. Possible there was something even more sinister at work here than an accident, he said, then corrected himself with a growl. "As if leaving the scene of an accident isn't sinister enough."

Dion looked at his watch. He didn't think anything would surface beyond a child struck by a speeder who didn't have the guts to stop. Their inquiries would show the young teen was breaking the rules, heading out to party. A meet up with others at the ball field, maybe a boy. Could be she'd already been and was heading home, or had changed her mind en route. Or realized she couldn't find her phone and was retracing her steps. Maybe she was lost. He didn't believe she had been picked up and murdered.

Leith had shifted in his chair to stare gloomily at the black windows. "I lied when I told him he can't blame himself, though," he said. "He *should* bloody blame himself. Thirteen is way too young to be out on her own.

So what that she's got a cellphone. It's the new security blanket. False faith. Makes parents lazy."

He was on a rant because he had a small daughter of his own, Dion guessed. Once up north he had seen them together, father and child. She was small, just a baby riding on her dad's shoulders. She was still a few years away from trick-or-treating age, but it was going to happen, and Leith would be facing his own tough decisions, how and when to let her head out on her own.

The moment was melting into a dream. Dion blinked to wake himself and struggled to his feet. "If there's nothing else —"

Leith was still writing out his awkward notes. He dismissed Dion with a wave of a hand. "Sure. Get lost. I mean, don't. Not literally."

Only while driving the short distance back to his apartment minutes later did the insult sink in. *Don't get lost.* Dion snorted, thinking if anyone was going to get lost — *literally* — it would be Leith, relying on his GPS to find the easiest of addresses. Watching the road ahead, he thought of Leith's anger at the Ferris parents, and about young girls walking alone in the dark. He wasn't as shocked as Leith was at how parents could make bad decisions. *Faith.* As he saw it, unless a man has been through some kind of personal hell, faith is the default approach to life.

Mr. Ferris would lose faith now. He had been hit by reality too late, and his newfound wisdom would go to waste. Dion had been hit by reality early in life, which gave him a head start on wisdom. Until the crash set him back to zero.

Why was he so disturbed? Why was he gripping the wheel like he wanted to kill it?

With a whump of fear he understood what had been nagging at him. It was Breanna's pink hair. It had set his mind on a near-forgotten loop, thinking about that girl on the ridge of an old gravel pit, her looking down, him looking up. He didn't know her name, age, anything. She was a giant X. About all he knew of her was the unusual sheen of her hair as she turned to flee, that she rode a dirt bike, and that in his pursuit, he had gotten his good friend Luciano Ferraro killed.

He had gotten barely a glimpse of her standing up there, but she had been watching him. Watching as he stood sweating over a shallow grave, his heart hammering. How long she had been watching and what she had seen, he didn't know. Had she actually seen his face from that distance, in that dim light? Would she be able to identify him? And the kicker: why had she never gone to the police?

He forced his hands to loosen their grip on the wheel. He thought of more immediate problems, of Breanna Ferris walking alone, up or down the road to or from Eldon Park, in the dark.

Even with her pink hair she would have been nothing but a shifting sliver of night moving along that creekside road. Easy enough to miss, if a driver was even slightly distracted, reaching to adjust the stereo, lighting a cigarette. He went back subconsciously to superimposing Breanna's face over the mystery girl's, trying to fill in the blanks, when he realized that in his abstraction he had just passed 13th Street, meaning he had missed the turnoff toward his apartment block.

Turning back around wasn't as easy as it should have been. One street was closed for repair and another re-organized into a one-way, trapping him in a temporary cul-de-sac. *Lost.* He thumped the steering wheel. It wasn't just the few minutes wasted trying to get turned around, when he desperately needed sleep. It was the way he kept blundering about since the crash. Time was ticking and his chances of becoming anything were slipping away, and no matter how he tried to convince himself he didn't care, he did.

What were his chances of getting back on top when something as silly as a girl's pink hair sent him into a tailspin of panic?

Then panic would beget anger. Anything, anytime, could set him off. New office furniture, rearranged roads, strangers in the halls. An updated operating system on his phone. He no longer had a heart beating in his chest; it was a pounding fist.

He pulled into the parking lot below his apartment block, only to find a boat-sized Buick had taken his reserved spot. He reversed out with a triple-chirp of tires, swearing, forced to find parallel parking on the street. The only option was a narrow slot, and it took some tries before he could winkle his way in. He stepped out of his car, breathing hard, and slammed the door shut. Above him, the night skies were giving way to the first light of dawn, and within he seemed to be giving way to darkness.

Fifteen

SEIZE THE DAY

AT THE NOVEMBER 1 afternoon general-duties briefing, Dion learned what progress had been made on the
Breanna Ferris case, not from the slow-speaking sergeant
conducting the meeting, but from Jackie Randall sitting
next to him in her trousers and blazer. The hit and run was
being handled upstairs in Serious Crimes, but Randall had
been helping out with background checks on the case, and
she gave Dion the gist. "We're getting there, slowly but surely," she said, flapping her plainclothes lapels at him proudly.

He smirked at her use of *we*. "You're head of the unit
already, are you?"

"I might as well be." In a low voice and in bits and
pieces while the briefing went on, she told him what
the accident reconstructionist had reported so far, and
what Leith and JD Temple had extracted from Breanna's
friend Grace. Under pressure, Grace had added to her
story, filling in at least part of the puzzle.

Brea had a top-secret boyfriend, was the bombshell confession.

"That's what I figured," Dion said.

So secret that Brea had only told Grace the boy's avatar name, something that sounded like *Bonfire*. Last night, when Grace and Brea had parted ways, an hour earlier than Brea had told her parents, Brea had gone to the north end of Edgemont Village to meet Bonfire.

The boy had a car, but Grace didn't know its make or model, or whether the two had planned to go anywhere.

Lastly, Grace revealed that Brea and Bonfire had probably broken up that night. At least going by the last text she received from Brea. *BF is a creep. Going home.* Grace had written back, asking for details, but there was no answer.

"BF is a creep," Randall repeated. "One little line that says it all. Bonfire kicked her out of his car, or she got out on her own. Maybe he ran her down. Maybe on purpose."

"What's her phone doing on Ridgeway?"

"I was thinking about that. She was in contact with Grace just after nine, had been with her boyfriend up till then. Only thing I can think of is she left the phone in his car, or he took it from her. Then he chucked it out the window as he headed wherever he was heading. It would be the kind of thing a creep like Bonfire would do."

Finding Bonfire was going to be a hell of a job, she added. The meeting was finished, other members were leaving, and Randall was no longer talking like a spy sharing secrets in a church pew. "But we'll get him."

"I don't think the boyfriend mowed her down," Dion said. He grabbed a piece of paper to diagram out his reasoning. "The driver was coming around this corner too fast, saw Breanna too late, slammed on his brakes, and contacted her about here. She flew like this, landed here." He drew a stick figure. "If the boyfriend hit her on purpose, it would look different. Unless he drove off, then came back gunning for her, but changed his mind at the last second. I don't think so. This driver skidded and, by the looks of it, almost avoided a hit. I've seen a lot of MVA victims, and on that scale, Breanna looked to be in pretty good shape. It was an accident, Jackie."

Far more interesting than the boyfriend angle would be the trace evidence, he thought. Debris on the road, paint in the girl's wounds, bits of glass in her hair. Or it would have been interesting, if he was on the case. He crumpled the diagram.

"Where were you last night while we were all out working double time?" he asked Randall. "I had my eye out for you. I thought you'd be right in there, leading the troops."

She pulled a face. "I slept through the call, would you believe?"

So she wasn't perfect. He was glad, and told her so. He described Inspector Hope showing up and yelling at everyone. Randall said now she *really* regretted sleeping through the call. The last mystery of the night was solved when he told Randall about the odd witch's hat blowing onto the road. It didn't fit with the girl's costume. Randall had a suggestion for that, too. It wasn't a witch's hat, but a warlock's. And if Bonfire had been a warlock that night, he had just given himself away. Hats made great repositories for DNA.

Before the meeting finally broke, the team watched various recorded news clips. On the Ferris hit and run, a reporter standing close to the deadly corner on Sunset Boulevard told of grief in the community. She closed by asking that if anybody had seen anything at all, they contact the nearest RCMP detachment, or call their toll-free anonymous tips line. The recording ended, and the room began to clear.

"There will be only one eyewitness to this accident," Randall told Dion. "Maybe he or she will come forward. Otherwise, all we can hope for is a tipster."

"There'll be evidence of some kind," Dion said. "There always is."

Randall wasn't so sure. "Monty says it's not looking good. No witnesses, and so far, no calling card, either. They're still looking, and maybe something will be pulled from the body, he says. But none of the usual car bits and pieces on the road."

Dion was nodding too, but absently. Mention of Montgomery reminded him of last night's party and Azrael's awful farewell. He had passed Montgomery in the hall in the morning, and the corporal had smiled at him in his usual friendly way, which meant at least Tori's wrath hadn't bled, much. Still, he was uneasy.

Fishing for clues, he said, "How was the party after I left?"

"Kind of humdrum, actually," Randall said. "You left just before Tori arrived, and after that it went kind of sideways. She was snippy with everyone. Monty, I hate to say it, drank *way* too much, and he was all over her, and she didn't like it. Who would? Fascinating as it all was, I didn't stay long. May I ask why you're smiling?"

Dion was smiling because now he knew he wasn't the only one Tori had been snippy with. "I thought it was me," he said. He went on to tell Randall of meeting Tori on his way out, her wanting him to stay, his insisting on leaving, and her firing insults at him as he left the deck. "Everything looks worse at night," he said, and busied himself making a few last briefing notes.

Randall had slouched back in her chair. "I wouldn't take it personally," she said. "Tori's always coiling up tight till something gives; then she springs, and it can be messy. You learn a lot about people in hockey. Hockey's like a mini war, and she's not a good warrior. She's a really nice person, unless she gets bored, or loses at something, or sees someone prettier than her. Myself being no threat in the prettiness department, she likes me a lot. But we'll never be friends. She digs karaoke bars and bikers. Me, I'm happy flopping out on my sofa and studying. A good police periodical, mellow music, cup of cocoa. That's my heaven. But in Tori's mind, if you're not having the absolute most fun physically possible, you might as well be dead. *Carpe diem*, eh."

She might have gone on talking, but she noticed the wall clock and leaped to her feet. "Sam Stirling's touching down. I'm going to be there when he arrives. It's one way of jamming your foot in the door, you know. Be there, even if they don't want you there. *Always* be there."

Dion couldn't recall who Sam Stirling was, but wasn't about to say so.

"Ben's brother," Randall reminded him.

He clapped his notebook shut with a sigh and stuck it in his pocket. He and Randall left the room together.

"I wonder why Tori would be so vicious to you, though," Randall said. "I mean, what could you have done to —" she stopped both talking and walking.

Dion turned to look at her. "What?"

But she wouldn't share whatever it was. "Going this way," she said, pointing. "See you later."

Dion made his way to the general-duties pit, wondering what had given her pause. Had the same ridiculous thought crossed her mind as his? It had to do with the flash of anxiety on Montgomery's face as he answered his cell, and Tori's jumpy anger, which seemed to peak as Dion had looked toward the alley, and a young girl struck by a speeding car and left to die.

He gazed down the hallway, and in his mind's eye saw trouble taking shape. Michelin Montgomery's involvement in the hit-and-run investigation could be a problem, if there was anything to his speculations. But no chance. It was a mad idea, to be dropped cold, and he did so. He only hoped Jackie would do the same.

* * *

Leith stood to greet Sam Stirling, escorted in by Jackie Randall. The man was a labourer, grubbily dressed, hair chaotic after his long and complicated journey. Charter plane from Swift Current to Medicine Hat, he told Leith. Air Canada from Medicine Hat to Richmond. Shuttle line from airport to SeaBus terminal, SeaBus across the inlet, and finally cab to this address. Now he was here, the last place on earth he wanted to be, and he only wanted to get on with it.

Leith commiserated. He knew all about prairie travel routes, being from North Battleford. Their roots gave them something to talk about as they made their way to an interview room. Once there the small talk ended. They took seats, and he had to explain the procedure of trying to identify a body that was possibly unidentifiable. He went into some of the circumstances around the finding of the body, the where and the when, but not the how. He didn't describe the duffel bag or the extent of physical damage inflicted on Ben. He warned Sam that death had occurred some time ago, in the summer, and the body was badly decomposed.

"Yeah, I know," Sam said. "I've been told."

Leith produced the computer reconstructions of the dead man's face. Sam studied them at length, with a worried expression, and finally pushed them back across the table, shaking his head. "That ain't him."

"Well, like I say," Leith said. "These are only approximations composed by a computer."

"Yeah, but he never had that goofy haircut."

Leith reminded Sam that hair grew and hair could be cut. "Have another look. Take your time."

Sam looked at the prints again with a squint. "Yeah, okay. Maybe."

Leith next went to the photographs, again warning in advance that they weren't a pleasant sight, that there would be little left of the brother Sam had known.

Even with the advance warning, Sam gave a violent start. "Holy Christ."

It took a minute of staring at the portrait of the corpse before his eyes adjusted, it seemed, and he could look at the image objectively. He nodded, and his answer took Leith by surprise. "Yeah. Definitely. That's fucking Ben, all right."

Sam Stirling sat back, drawing breath. His eyes shone as the reality sank in, and he summed up his feelings with one all-purpose profanity: "*Fuck.*"

* * *

"So assuming Sam's right, we have a name for our victim," Leith told Monty. "But a lot of good it does us. Sam doesn't know anything about Ben's life since he took off. I've got a couple of names, though, kids Ben used to hang out with in Swift Current, who might be able to give us some insight —"

"Whoa, whoa," Monty said, hands up. "Didn't you get my memo?"

They were standing at Monty's desk at the quieter end of the GIS room.

"No," Leith said. "What memo?"

"The memo saying I'm no longer lead on Greer." Monty unwrapped a granola bar, took a bite, munched.

Greer had become the short name for the John Doe — now Ben Stirling — homicide file.

"You're not?" Leith said. "Why? They put you on something bigger?"

"Not bigger," Monty said, cheek bulged with granola. "Smaller. Literally. Breanna Ferris."

"You're taking on the hit and run?"

"Our leader has spoken. She wants it resolved fast, so I'm on it full-time, which means Greer is all yours. Have fun."

Sixteen

BITTEN

DION WAS BACK ON DAYS, which meant he got off work at 7:00 p.m., when much of the world was still awake. Off duty now, he sat dressed for winter chill on a bench overlooking the waters. There was no rain, but the threat of it spread in a drifting smudge across the horizon. Otherwise the skies were a murky golden grey as far as the eyes could see, lighting up the ships and barges with orange hues. Quite spectacular, actually.

He had lived by these waters all his life, but no longer felt part of the scenery. Coming back from the north, he had found the waters repelled him, to the point that he would avoid the harbour altogether. Which wasn't easy to do in a harbourside city.

What was that way of dealing with phobia? Immersion. Desensitization. Face the devil until it no longer scares you. This past summer, some off-duty shenanigans had immersed him in the ocean in a serious way. Was he better or worse for the dousing? Desensitized, empowered, no longer afraid of the devil?

No. But by degrees, he was getting better. He would never swim again, that was for sure, but he would keep up the good work, come down here whenever it was practical and contemplate the waves.

He was losing himself in the view and not thinking much about anything when a passerby stopped close enough to make him look up. She said, "Oh, hello!"

Her face took a moment to crystallize into a name. Farah Jordan, the Greek Taverna chef, in a long, woolly green coat, her cheeks and nose pinkened by the sea breeze. He moved over so she could sit down, and she did, and they smiled at each other in a friendly way. "Not at work?" he asked, a dumb question he wished he could un-ask.

If she thought it was dumb, she didn't let on. "Oh, we're closed today. Death in the family." She waved a hand at him not to worry about condolences. "Owner's mother. It was expected. And nobody liked her, anyway."

"So you have the night off." He left the words un-loaded, trying to avoid a replay of his clumsy attempts at the Taverna.

"Yes," she said. "And as usual, I'm working so hard at enjoying my time off that I'm not enjoying myself much."

He nodded, and together they looked out at the choppy waters, the gloriously lit barges, the Vancouver skyline. "Something weird happened," she said.

Over the years he had come to learn that one man's weird is another's mundane. He waited for her to finish the thought.

"Somebody's been in my house."

A trespass was not mundane. He looked at her searchingly. "You were broken into? Stuff's missing?"

"No, no. Just, you know, you get a feeling."

Dion did not know how you could get a feeling your space had been invaded, and she may have read the doubt on his face. "It's hard to explain," she said. "I suppose I could show you. If you have a few minutes."

* * *

She led him through the back, to show him the door that might have been breached. The lock mechanism was a joke. He showed her how useless it was by breaking in, twice, without tools. "This really needs replacing," he said, rattling the offending lock hasp.

"A lot of things around here need replacing," she admitted.

"But it doesn't look like it's been tampered with. You were going to show me some evidence of a break-in."

"It's not really evidence. Just things shifted about."

"Where?"

In the kitchen, she pointed at the cutting board, the knife block. They seemed to have been moved, she said — just slightly. He studied the knife block minutely, and asked if there were other possible points of entry — a window left unlocked, for instance.

"No. But I might have left the back door unlatched last week, actually."

"Might have?"

"Did." She ruffled her hair. "Look, I'm sorry. I shouldn't have bothered you with all this."

"Well, I'm bothered. Have you seen the news? Do you know what happened next door?"

"I haven't been watching the news."

He stared at her, searching for the lie. "Not at all? A man was murdered. His body was found in the crawl space. Leaving your door unlocked is insane. Don't do it."

She nodded, either chastened or pretending to be. "I won't."

He folded his arms and gazed at her. "Anything else you feel has been touched?"

"Hmm, no," she said.

He didn't believe her. "Tell me."

"Maybe my clothes …"

"In your bedroom?" He was appalled. "Show me."

Upstairs, her bedroom was cozily set up, a ceiling slanting over a queen-sized bed, colourful wall hangings that Farah told him she got from Peru. White cotton curtains over the window, a wind chime made of seashells — classic hippy junk — hanging in a corner. In spite of the daylight, the room was dim, so Farah turned on a lamp and pointed out a dark wooden set of drawers, glossy and antique-looking. "It's my very favourite piece of furniture, and I always shut the drawers tight. You know, out of respect. One day I came in, and the top drawer was just a quarter inch out. Again, about a week ago. I can't tell you what day, exactly. It didn't stand out to me, until all these little pieces kind of came together."

"The contents of the drawer?"

"Bras and underwear," she said.

He grimaced. "Were any missing?"

"No. And I don't know if they were touched, either. It's just a jumble."

"This is serious," he told her. "Unlatched door, knives, underwear. What?"

Instead of looking alarmed, as she damned well should be, she was smiling. "Don't worry, Calvin. Is it Calvin or Cal?"

"Cal."

"It's really all in my head, Cal. And I feel so bad for getting you out here and making you all anxious on my behalf. Are you able to stay for dinner? I'm making paella."

He stayed for dinner, helped her drink a bottle of wine, and they talked. Talk was easy with Farah. Just like on the night she had brought him in from the rain, she made him feel welcome. She made him feel he could say anything.

When was the last time he had talked about Looch to anyone? Never. He even told her about his tenth-floor apartment, and his goal of getting back there one day. He even talked about the disappearing memories he held of his mother. She, in turn, told him about hers.

They had moved to the living room, and instead of dessert, she brought out a bottle of Japanese whiskey.

"I can't," he told her. "I'm driving."

"No, you're not," she said.

The inference took a moment to sink in. He tried not to sound defensive. "You told me you were out of the dating game."

"I am. Doesn't mean we can't hang out and talk. Unless that's not cool with you."

Only talk, then. Still, his choices were to extend the evening, drinking Japanese whiskey in the company of the beautiful Farah Jordan, or go home to his apartment alone. There really was no contest.

* * *

Because her father's furniture was, in her words, about as comfortable as sitting on rhinos, they sat on her bed instead, listened to music, had a drink, and let the conversation flow. They talked about what they wanted in life. "Enduring true love," she said. "It's not as impossible as it sounds." And her previous relationships. "Such nice guys, but we never seemed to last a year. Probably my fault."

"I doubt that," he said.

She asked about his relationships, and he mentioned Kate, their on-and-off life together that had ended with the crash.

"If not for the crash, would you still be with her?" Farah asked.

There was no simple answer to that one. He had not been wholly faithful to Kate, and if she had returned the favour, it had just been payback. He twisted his mouth and tried not to look miserable. "Probably not."

"Relationships take work, forgiveness, and renewal," Farah said.

She was right about that, but when it came to Kate, his chances at renewal were long gone — let alone forgiveness.

* * *

Night fell, and Farah asked if the dead man next door had a name. Dion said the man had been identified, but at this point he wasn't free to share any of that info.

She asked nothing further. There had been nothing wrong with her inquiry — it was only natural for her to want to know — but it did snag at his conscience, for a couple of reasons.

Ben Stirling's name had not been released to the public yet, and in some complicated mental process, he believed she knew that. Which meant she had seen the bit in the news. Which meant she had lied to him.

On the other hand, he didn't quite trust his mental processes these days. Especially now, with a few drams of really excellent whiskey in his system.

Still, it mattered.

Farah got ready for bed as if he and she had been married for years. She crawled under her duvet, and though he offered to sleep on the sofa downstairs, she told him to join her.

"You trust me?"

"Of course."

He stripped to undershorts and T-shirt and lay down next to her. She seemed pleased, like they were two kids having a pajama party. It was strange, exasperating, funny, and in some way, exciting. The first one-night stand he'd had in a while without sex being the objective.

Without sex, period. Heads on pillows, their conversation began to break apart, to come and go in sleepy waves. But that was okay. It would pick up again tomorrow.

He lay on his side of the bed and watched her eyes close, and wondered if this pajama party was a test that she wanted him to pass. He could pass the damn test, he thought. She was worth it. Not a problem. Passing her damn test was worlds better than being sent home to his drab apartment, alone.

Only when she was sound asleep did he begin to worry about the practicality of this relationship. Himself a cop, hitched up with a slightly mad hippy? Would it really work?

Over the curve of her shoulder he noticed the window, a midnight-blue rectangle. Gauze curtains swirled gently; the sash was open a crack for ventilation. In watching the curtains breathe, he was reminded of the house across the road.

Careful not to wake her, he crossed the room and leaned a shoulder against the window moulding. He stared outward and down. There was the darkened road between Farah's and the Greer house. He could see into its yard at the back.

His snag of doubts began to multiply.

He had searched his memory and confirmed it: on the night the body was found in the crawl space, he had asked Farah if she had observed anything across the way. He had been specific about it. She hadn't said yes or no, but deflected the question. Twice.

He should have circled back, pressed her on it, or at least made note to alert his superiors of an evasive witness. Instead he had gone and slept with her — in a way.

He turned and stared down at her. She lay on her side, her dark-gold hair flowing onto the pillow, and just like that, she had gone from his future life partner to a blinking hazard sign.

What had he done? Why was he always sabotaging himself?

His worries left him feeling grimy, and he went for a shower down the hall, scrubbing himself down with a bar of soap shaped and scented like a slice of watermelon. The fruity scent and the pulse of water relaxed him. He was being childish. Had to stop overthinking everything.

Refreshed and in a more positive frame of mind, he pulled on shorts and T-shirt and walked down the upstairs hallway, exploring rooms. Inside one he found what was probably her deceased father's furniture, humped together and shrouded by white sheets. Across the hall was a linen closet smelling faintly of mothballs. Another door led up to an attic, and the stairs were steep and narrow. The door at the top was shut tight, and he could see nothing inside of interest except some scuff marks in the dust that looked quite fresh. He would have to ask her about that.

Coming back down from the attic, he saw there was one last door at the far end of the hall, also closed, also unlocked. He pushed it open, glanced inside, and froze.

A beast stared back at him through the confusing criss-cross of moonlight — a monster wolf — poised for attack, eyes glittering, hackles raised, fangs bared in a silent growl.

He pulled the door shut fast and stepped backwards. He held his breath, listening for the scrabble of claws on linoleum, the impact shudders against the wood. Instead he heard only the rasp of his own breath as he exhaled.

He swore at himself and again pushed the door open. This time he reached in and patted down the wall, searching for a light switch. The toggle was dead. With no electric light to guide him, he crossed through patches of moonlight and shadow. He dropped into a kneel on the cold floor before the animal to inspect its bright yellow eyes. He touched its fur, black and silver. He placed his palm on its snarling muzzle, ran his knuckles over the taut black lips. With a sudden dousing of loneliness, he pressed a fingertip against the point of one sharp fang, testing for bite.

* * *

Over the breakfast table he asked Farah about the wolf — and the various pelts, horns, weasels, ptarmigans, leghold traps, and firearms he had found stored in the dark little room upstairs. Especially the firearms.

Her father had been a hunter, she told him. Big game. Went up north a lot, killing everything that moved. Brought home their bodily remains out of reverence, she said, out of love, to immortalize them in all their nobility. "Wouldn't you want to be stuffed and put on display in reverence to your nobility once you'd been murdered, Cal?" she asked, making her views on trophy hunting blazingly clear.

She added that her father had not been on any major hunts in the last few years of his life, then went on to describe the wolf upstairs, which her father had bagged without a licence. In self-defence, she recalled him explaining to her.

The animal had been a mature male timber wolf — maybe the leader of the pack, who knew? She even gave Dion the coordinates from which the wolf had been taken, as her father had logged it. She described the nature of the wolf's habitat, its crags, valleys, plateaus, and open skies. She told him about the society of wolves: hierarchy within the pack, fidelities between mates, cub-raising, their omnivorous diet, their rituals, all interesting stuff he hadn't known before, but probably would if he watched more nature programs. She also told him of the consequences of the death of the leader of the pack, which led, with precision, to a question — what did he think about hunting as sport?

"I really don't," he said.

"You don't have an opinion one way or another? You don't care?"

He said nothing, and he could almost feel the ground between them splitting — which was great, just what he wanted. Why exactly finding the wolf last night had put an end to his daydreams about this relationship, he wasn't sure. But it had. She said, "Have you ever heard wolf song? I mean, probably not out in the wilderness, city boy that you are, but have you ever sat down and listened to a good recording? It's amazing, Cal. It's a dirge from another world."

She stood to go find the CD to play it for him. When she returned, he told her he wasn't interested right now. She laid it down and told him to keep it; maybe he would be curious some other day. He looked at the CD lying on the table in its case, the beautiful black-furred wolf face on its cover. He asked her if the two hunting rifles he had found in the room upstairs were registered.

She seemed surprised by the question, and told him of course they were, yes. Registered to her dad, not to her. Weren't licences grandfathered, or something? Anyway, nobody had ever talked to her about it.

He told her even if the registry hadn't followed up, she should have. It was up to her to ensure the guns were either documented or disposed of safely, and if she wanted to keep them, they had to be secured in a gun locker. "It's the law," he said.

"Okay, sure. Will do."

"I'd look into that this morning," he told her.

"Yes, all right," she said, tilting slightly to stare at him.

To avoid her eyes, he focused on the breakfast she had taken such pains to prepare for him. He had a plan — eat, say thank you, and leave. And this mistake he would not repeat.

Seventeen

SACRILEGE

LEITH WAS IN SERGEANT Mike Bosko's office. Bosko was often away, on a non-stop schedule, but when he was here, he made up for it, talking to everyone in his easygoing way and getting his unit back in shape with peculiar efficiency.

At this moment he appeared to have all the time in the world, though his wall calendar was all scribbled in like mad art. Leith sat across from him. They were doing the chit-chat thing, reminiscing about the Hazelton case, the snow, those mountains, that bunch of tough-spined locals who had made their job so difficult. Bosko asked how Leith's house hunting was going, then about his caseload, how it was holding up. Too heavy, too light?

"Pretty good," Leith said. "My priority is Ben Stirling, now that Monty's focused on Breanna Ferris. We're pretty sure we know where the duffel bag used to contain his body was bought from — an army surplus store on Kingsway in Vancouver. But all leads from there have been dead ends. Lot of tips coming in on Stirling, but they're all pretty wacky. We seem to have a werewolf in the neighbourhood, which is keeping us busy. We're working to keep it in hand."

"I've seen the wolf reference come up a few times," Bosko said. "Could be the real thing?"

"No. The only Wolf Pack I'm aware of around here is the junior hockey club."

Leith's phone rang. On the line was Doug Paley, saying he had a report in from Lynn Valley. "Kind of vague, but sounds like an assault," Paley said. "Two women. This being from up the valley, I'd say it's your problem, not mine."

"Got any specifics?"

"Yeah, I do," Paley said, and he sounded pleased. "Whatever this thing was, it howled."

* * *

The complainants Leith found himself questioning an hour later were two middle-aged sisters, Sabrina and Evelyn, who had been *accosted* while walking on the path that ran alongside Lynn Valley Road, close to the Baden-Powell trail. It was just getting dusk, they told him. They were still excited and spoke over one another to tell the story, standing in Sabrina's living room. Or not exactly accosted, they corrected each other, but definitely they were stalked.

Sabrina told of how she and Evelyn had been taking cover from the drizzle under the tree canopy, waiting while Ev's mini pinscher did his thing, and the two women had been startled by a sudden, violent rustling in the bushes just a stone's throw away. They had stood stock-still, listening. The dog leaped into Ev's arms and continued to yap at the bushes from the safety of her embrace.

Sabrina described how she and Ev had decided to walk briskly back toward the street, but to their horror, the thing had followed, skirting the path, keeping to the underbrush. They kept their eyes trained on the disturbed foliage marking the snaking line of the creature's progress, and just before they broke into a panicked run, Sabrina had caught a glimpse of the thing: a large, dark, semi-upright creature. Definitely a biped.

"A man?" Leith asked.

"Not a man," Sabrina said. "It's face was long, like this. Like a horse, sort of. But pointier."

She patted her chest as she finished her wine. Her husband Tom stood by, also with a glass of wine. He looked intrigued, but not what Leith would call worried.

"And then we made it to the street," Evelyn said. "And we heard it behind us. It *howled.*"

She shuddered. Tom grinned. Leith watched Tom and wondered if this was an in-house prank. If so, it wasn't funny. He asked the women about the howl, if it sounded like a human or an animal. Evelyn said it sounded like an abomination. Like a human abomination or an animal abomination, he asked, trying to narrow it down. She didn't know.

"And for one godawful minute I thought it was running after us," Sabrina went on, massaging the ribs over her heart.

"Man, did we run," Evelyn added.

These were two well-rounded women in their mid-fif-
ties who didn't look like born-again joggers. Something
had spurred them on, then. "But it didn't run after you?"
Leith asked.

"I guess not. Well, we didn't exactly look back to find
out, did we, Sab? But we're here, and we're alive. I guess
it stayed put."

"I think the lamplight scared it off," Sabrina said.

Evelyn agreed. "Definitely, it didn't like the light."

* * *

Leith phoned Bosko, who was at home now, and asked
for permission to set up two-point surveillance of the
woods. Couple of vans, Leith suggested. He'd place
them around the Headwaters, not on the park road itself, but near its entrance. Whoever was causing the dis-
turbances would avoid the main connectors and come
and go through ancillary paths — despite the brambles.
Whoever it was, they weren't afraid of the cold and the
wet, and they weren't afraid of getting scratched.

Audiovisual monitoring, he recommended to Bosko.
Amplified listening, infrared photography. "Because no
doubt about it, we've got someone hanging around in
there, and he's demented, and we'd better find him soon,
whether it's related to Ben Stirling's death or not. Before
someone gets hurt."

Bosko didn't quibble, but gave the nod to the request,
with signed authorization to follow.

* * *

The spell-checker was slowing down Dion's several reports, always correcting him. Sometimes he had to look up sound-alikes to get it right. Like *stationary.* He liked to blame his lousy spelling on brain damage, but in fact reading and writing had never been strengths of his. These days, though, getting it right seemed to matter. When Jackie Randall approached, he ducked his head to his computer and pretended he was too busy to talk. Hopefully she would take her crazy notions elsewhere.

Randall sat on the edge of his desk and leaned toward him, saying, "Excuse me, partner. Could you lend an ear?"

He sat back in his chair and lent her his ear.

"This is going to sound kind of odd," she said. "But I wanted to ask you about Monty's party."

Just as he'd feared. She hadn't dropped the idea, then. She was going to run with it. "Got to make it quick," he said. "I'm signing off." He shut down the computer to prove it and stood up, pushing his chair back in his cramped workstation. Tired, sore, all he wanted was a shower in the change room and a swift, uncomplicated departure. Instead he was forced to stand and wait for Randall's odd question.

She said, "How about we talk at Denny's?"

Denny's was at the other end of the main drag, a gruelling drive, if traffic was bad.

"How about we talk at Rainey's?" Dion said. Rainey's was nearby, a popular hangout for the younger police officers getting off shift. Not that he felt young. His voice was coming out like gravel and his neck ached.

"Denny's is more private," Randall said.

"All right. Whatever. I have to change first."

"No problem."

Forty minutes later they were in a booth at Denny's, ordering coffee. The place was near empty, just themselves and a few late diners sitting alone. Dion asked for decaf, hoping to avoid another sleepless night. Randall's civilian clothes looked dowdy, but her face glowed, scrubbed and healthy. Once they had coffee in front of them, she said, "First off, it's about Tori, so you'll appreciate why I wanted to meet off-site."

Dion stirred half a sugar into his cup.

"You told me you'd encountered her as you were leaving their house on Halloween, and about how hostile she was, but you kind of skimmed over the details. I wonder if you could go over it again for me, verbatim-like, exactly what happened."

"Verbatim-like," Dion said, heavily. "Why?"

"I'll tell you why, but I have a feeling, by the way you've been avoiding me lately, that we're *ad idem*, and you don't like it. I don't blame you. I don't like it, either, but that's not going to make it go away, is it? I'll recap. Stop me if I'm wrong. As I recall it, you're standing on the back porch. She appears in the floodlight. You give her a scare just by standing there, and she nearly bites your head off for it. What exactly does she say?"

Randall had a notebook out, but he told her no way was she going to take this down. She pulled a face that said, *Hey man, no problem*, and put the book away.

"She asked why I was standing there in the dark, if I was trying to scare her to death. Along those lines."

"And you replied?"

"I said I was just leaving."

"And she wanted you to go back into the house with her, is that right?"

"She did try to get me to stay."

"How exactly did she do that? What did she do and say?"

"She took my hand and tried to lead me in. Teased me. Playing the seductress. I can't remember what she said. Said she was afraid of Monty because he'd been drinking. I didn't believe it."

"She had ulterior motives," Randall suggested.

Dion glowered at her zeal. "Maybe."

"Was she drunk? Could you tell?"

"I didn't think she was drunk."

"Couldn't smell anything on her? How about her eyes? Did she look stoned?"

"No."

"Still, she was hyped up, acting strange. Shouldn't have been driving, should she?" Randall said.

"Probably not."

"D'you recall how Monty took a call from her before she arrived? How concerned he looked?"

"I don't remember him looking concerned."

"I do," she said. "Carry on. You insisted on leaving, and she yelled something rude down at you. What did she yell?"

"She called me a queer."

"Why?"

"I don't know. Maybe it was my sweater."

Randall ignored his joke. She was a bloodhound, nose to the ground. "Then what happened?"

"Then I left. She shouted at me that I didn't know where I was going, that I was heading in the wrong direction. Something like that. She called me a blind sonovabitch."

"So now you're a queer blind sonovabitch. Were you going the wrong direction?"

"I just stopped to look at the sky, the fireworks."

"And that bothered her?"

"I guess so. I had activated the floodlights as I headed down the stairs."

Randall seemed pleased. "That sounds like a non sequitur, but it isn't. You know exactly where this is going. What did you see straight ahead of you?"

"Path. Lawn. Fence. Back alley." He sighed. "Car."

"Right. Her car. It was parked there, wasn't it?"

"Can't say it was hers, but there was a car there," he said. He could say so with confidence because in the early morning hours that followed the discovery of Breanna Ferris's body, he had lain awake and worked on reconstructing the memory until he could almost see it. The car was pale and could have been an Acura. It had been parked in the backyard, away in the shadows, just an object, a paler glob against the darkness. Almost subliminal in nature, almost not there.

"What kind of car did you see?" Randall asked.

"I don't know. A compact. I couldn't tell the colour. Maybe white."

He was hardly touching his decaf, so far, and it was losing steam. He pushed the cup aside.

Randall said, "So she parked her car in the back alley, that's almost for sure. Seems a little strange. It would be a long walk in those heels of hers."

"The street was quite packed in front. Their garage is full of boxes. Van was in the carport. She didn't have a choice."

"There was lots of space further down. It would have been easier to walk that distance than negotiate that pathway out back. And there's something else. Tori would want to burst through the front door, not slink in through the kitchen. More bang for her buck."

Dion was still trying to reason a way out of this unpalatable theory. "How about this," he said. "Halloween, lots of cars and chaos. She's got a nice car, and she wants to keep it that way."

"It's an older basic-model Acura," Randall said. "I checked. Not exactly a showpiece."

He winced at her. "No, but it's fairly nice. So she parks out back so it won't get dinged by bad drivers or scratched by kids. And even though she was coming up the back path, she might have been intending to walk around the side and come in through the front door, until she saw me."

Randall considered his argument. Out the window, a couple walked by holding hands. Dion watched them go and thought about Farah, all the things he and she had talked about, how she made him feel. Already he was having second thoughts about his second thoughts. His departure had been curt but not final. In fact her last words were, "Give me a call when you're over yourself."

A little cryptic, but promising.

"It's time we made a plan," Randall was saying. "Start documenting this. If it goes somewhere, we want to have a paper trail. I want to start by taking your statement. While it's all fresh in your mind."

"No," he said, pulling change from his pocket and laying it on the table. "It's campfire stories, and you're a camper. I'm going home." He stood up and pulled on his coat.

She followed his rising with her eyes, and he saw her glint of derision. For his cowardice, he supposed. She said, "I'm just thinking it's funny how Corporal Montgomery jumped on that hit-and-run file. And then not only that, but made sure he'd be the lead investigator."

Dion paused in his coat fastening and glanced at her. This was news to him. She didn't look like she was kidding.

"At least that's what I understood," she qualified. "And did you notice how tense he's been lately? Isn't that kind of funny, too?"

It wasn't funny at all. It was an insinuation against a man who didn't deserve it. He said good night to Randall and left her to her sacrilegious thoughts.

Eighteen

A LITTLE PSYCHO

IN THE EARLY EVENING, Leith was at his desk when Dion showed up at the threshold of the GIS office. He came over and took the visitor's chair. He was in full active uniform, except for the cap, and with his pink cheeks, sweat-spiked hair, and put-upon expression, he looked like a police officer who had spent the last hour chasing down trouble.

Leith waited for him to broach whatever he was here to broach. When it didn't happen, he said, "Busy day?"

Dion sucked a barked knuckle and nodded.

"There's something you wanted?" Leith said.

"I was told to see you."

Now Leith recalled the semi-official instructions, Bosko's casual order: "Oh, Dave, let's try to bring Cal back into the fold."

Not a plan Leith agreed with much, or even trusted. Was this a genuine show of faith on Bosko's part, or was he still in the process of trap-setting? Leith sensed that whatever evidence Bosko had against Dion had fizzled, and his unofficial investigation was shutting down. But he didn't know, and not knowing left him on edge. One of these days he would corner Bosko and demand a definitive answer: is Cal still a suspect, or have we cleared him? So he could shut it down in his own mind.

"Right," he told Dion. "It seems we need extra hands, and I'm trying to get people going on some leads that are piling up. They're not what I'd call credible, but there's a lot of them. We've opened a separate file, not linked to Ben Stirling. I'm not even sure it's a GIS matter. The guys are calling it Code Werewolf. You can go ahead and laugh if you want. I'll send down the details."

"Sure thing," Dion said. He was up and heading off, but turned to ask how the hit and run was progressing, and who was in charge.

"Michelin Montgomery's got it well in hand," Leith told him.

Dion seemed taken aback by the news, and went on his way without another word. Strange.

* * *

With his new responsibilities in hand, Dion was learning that Leith was right, there were a lot of not-so-credible reports coming in from Lynn Valley since the discovery of Ben Stirling's body. Residents of the area were calling in with tips that ranged from suspicious-looking cats and dogs to UFOs. Surveillance had been set up at certain points along the road above the Headwaters, but hadn't produced any results yet.

Dion spent the day working with others on the list, making calls, following them up, checking them off. One report stood out more than the others, and he gave it a second read. Somebody's young son had overheard a classmate bragging that he personally knew a werewolf. After some time on the phone he had the classmate's info scribbled in his notebook. Troy Hamilton, ten years old, who lived on Dempsey, not far from the Greer crime scene. He advised his shift supervisor and went to check it out.

The door of the Dempsey house was opened by a woman covered in white powder. When Dion gave her the reason for his visit, that he wanted to talk to her son Troy, she invited him into the foyer and shouted at her husband to come and listen to this. Her husband was also dusted with white. Dion had interrupted them at a bad time, it seemed, and they were up to their ears in renovations. He apologized. The father went to fetch Troy.

The interview would have to take place in the dining room, Mrs. Hamilton said, leading the way. It was the only room not covered in drop cloths. Troy Hamilton was brought in, and to Dion he looked like a child genius from a Disney movie — serious, small-bodied, towheaded, wearing large glasses. He asked the parents to stay around for the interview, but they were eager to carry on with their work, if that was okay. He insisted that at least one of them remain in close proximity. In the end the mother agreed. She would be in the adjacent living room, patching drywall dings, where she could keep an eye and ear on the interview. Yes, she would pay attention, she promised.

Now, sitting kitty-corner at the table, Dion looked into the little boy's serious brown eyes and said, "Thanks for talking to me, Troy. I heard that you told a friend at school that you personally know a werewolf. Is that true?"

"Is what true?" Troy said.

In the living room, Mrs. Hamilton wasn't monitoring the interview as promised, but arguing with her husband about the colour of grout. When the debate ended, Dion carried on. "Is it true that you told a friend at school that you know a werewolf?"

"No, that's not true," Troy said.

"You never told anybody that you know a werewolf?"

"It's not true that he's a friend."

The interview went on in the same vein for a few minutes, until Dion scored a point and got the kid to admit he did know a werewolf. Yes, personally. But he refused to give up a name. Dion persisted, and only learned that Troy's favourite line was, "Not telling."

"Is he an adult werewolf, or a young one? Big, small? Your age, my age?"

"I'm not telling."

"You know that werewolves eat people, right?"

"I know that."

"This werewolf you know, does he eat people?"

"I'm not telling."

"He lives around here, though, does he?"

"I'm not telling."

"Why aren't you telling?"

"Because I'm sworn to not tell secrets."

"What would happen if you told his secret? Did he tell you what he'd do if you told?"

"No. He's my friend, and I don't believe in telling on friends."

"Oh, I see." In the other room the parents were talking over each other, about ceiling lights now, and insects. "I only want to talk to this guy," Dion said, "make sure he's not going around eating people in the middle of the night. That would be a bad thing, don't you think?"

"Depends on the people."

"What if he attacked your parents? You wouldn't want that, would you?"

Troy didn't answer, and his blank stare struck Dion as monstrous. The boy was a serial killer in the making. One day he would make the news.

"You understand some bad things are happening around here, don't you?"

"Like what?"

"People getting scared in the woods."

"Probably serves them right for going in the woods."

"Well, it's not a good thing, and we're thinking it might be a werewolf making all the trouble, or someone who's playing at being a werewolf, and so anybody answering to the name of werewolf we'd very much like to talk to. D'you understand me?"

Nothing.

Dion said, "Do you want to go for a ride in my police car? If your mom and dad say it's okay?"

"No," Troy said.

"Don't you believe in helping to stop crime?"

"No, and I don't believe in policemen."

Dion got mean. "Well, I don't believe in werewolves."

"I don't believe in you."

Dion stared across at the miniature psychopath and thought about the reward being offered for information leading to the capture of Ben Stirling's killer. But how to word it such that he wouldn't get in trouble? "There's a guy out there who's hurting people. We'll pay anyone who helps catch him. I think it's five thousand dollars. But only if we catch him."

Not an offer and non-specific. Nobody could fault him for that — he hoped.

Troy was interested. "You're going to arrest him?"

"Only if he's done something wrong."

"Mr. Glen," Troy said.

"Who's Mr. Glen?"

"Mr. Glen Oakley. Our janitor at school."

The boy would say nothing further.

Before Dion left the house he talked to the parents once more, hoping for some kind of confirmation. "Troy tells me he knows a werewolf."

Their flat expressions were a lot like Troy's, except they seemed to find it all quite funny.

"Do you have any idea who this werewolf might be?" he asked.

"There's no such thing as werewolves, last I heard," the father said.

"Maybe in his mind there is. You should be aware, he might be hanging around with a grown-up, somebody who could be dangerous. I'd keep an eye on him, if I were you. Is there anybody you know of who might fit that description, somebody in the neighbourhood he could be talking to?"

"No, of course not," the mother said.

"Do you know the janitor at Troy's school?"

They didn't. No, Troy never spoke of the janitor, or any janitor. Why?

He said, "I'm not accusing Troy of anything. I'm not accusing this man he knows, either. I just want to talk to him, make sure it's all fun and games."

Both parents shook their heads. Drywall dust floated around them like disintegrating halos.

"Your son could be at risk."

"But only on a full moon," the mother said. Like mother, like son. "I'm kidding," she told him, grinning. "Of course we'll keep an eye on him."

He had a final question, taking the janitor tipoff from a different angle: "Name Glen Oakley mean anything to you?"

Of course it didn't.

* * *

His car's computer told him where Glen Oakley lived. Not far away, in a condo in Deep Cove. Oakley was forty-seven years old and he had a record of fraud dating back a few years, something to do with the issuance of phony cheques. For his crimes he had received a fine and probation of two years.

At this point backup was unwarranted, as were silver bullets. Dion parked outside the condo, walked up to Oakley's front door, and pressed the buzzer. A tall man with salt and pepper hair opened up. He wore sweats and a baseball cap. His unfriendly expression maybe had to do with the game in the background playing loudly off the TV, or maybe it was the uniform he found himself looking at. Or both. Or neither.

"Glen Oakley?"

"Yes. What?"

Dion told him who he was and why he was here, investigating a disturbance in the neighbourhood. "And I was led to believe you might have some information. Mind if I step in?"

Oakley moved stiffly aside, but wouldn't allow entry beyond the entrance nook, so the interview had to take place between coats and shoes, as the TV blared in the background. "You know there've been reports of someone stalking passersby in and around the Mesachee Woods?" Dion opened.

"Yes, I know. It's on the news."

"Do you know a Troy Hamilton?"

"A what? No."

"He's a student at the school where you're employed as caretaker. Ten years old, about this tall, straight blond hair, glasses."

"I don't know. They all look the same to me. What about it?"

"You talk to the kids, tell them stories, get friendly with them?"

Oakley stared at him, said nothing.

Dion said, "Telling the kids you're a werewolf, sir?" Blunt and flat. Shock tactics. He kept a steady eye on Oakley, Oakley kept a steady eye on him, and the moment stretched.

"What did you say?" Oakley said. "I'm a what?"

"Did you tell Troy Hamilton you're a werewolf? Did you tell *anyone* you're a werewolf?"

"What's this all about? Is this a joke?"

"Maybe you were just kidding around, getting into the Halloween spirit?"

"I don't *kid around*. I learned a long time ago that kidding around does not pay. You got ID?"

Dion got out his ID with photo and regimental number. Oakley made a show of memorizing it.

"There's somebody going around in the woods dressed as an animal, howling like a wolf, and scaring people," Dion told him. "I was given your name, so I'm just following up. May I have a brief look around?"

Oakley raised his voice. "For *what*?"

"Only evidence relevant to the allegation," Dion said. *Fun fur*.

"Look around," Oakley said. He flung a hand toward the interior of his home. "Be my guest. What a load of bullshit."

Dion found nothing incriminating anywhere in the man's small and tidy condo. He considered having the janitor's room at the school also searched, but decided not to waste any more time on this particular red herring. Oakley was too perfectly surprised by the accusation to be a werewolf. In fact, Oakley was just a name picked out of a hat, and Troy Hamilton was a stinking little cheat who could learn a thing or two about honesty and respect.

He still believed the kid harboured a secret, a name which could potentially bring this nuisance file to a fast close. The problem was, ten-year-olds couldn't legally be picked up by the lapels and shaken. He would hand the information back to his supervisor, and from there it could be decided what to do with Troy. Get tough with the parents, fan out their inquiries, or put surveillance on the boy, if that's what it took.

Back in the coat nook, Dion apologized to Oakley for the intrusion. He received no forgiveness. He left the condo and the door slammed behind him, and whoever was prowling the thickets of the North Shore under heavy winter skies continued to roam free.

Nineteen

SUMFIN' WEIRD

THE OFFICE WAS COMING alive with fresh workers setting up for a new day. Leith had arrived early. He was in the lunchroom, taking the opportunity to write a letter home to his parents in North Battleford. JD Temple sat down across from him and said, "This just in."

Leith looked up from an incredibly unbeautifully constructed sentence. "Huh?"

"Fingerprints off the Greer house." JD was craning to see what he was writing. "Two good sets. One's got a name attached. Seems we've got us a suspect."

Leith showed her the letter so she could stop rubbernecking. "My folks don't believe in email. What's our suspect's name?"

"Jagmohan Battar, or Joey. Better yet, we have an address on him, and he's not going anywhere fast. He's doing time in Mission for B & E, and we've got clearance to talk to him."

"Meet you in the foyer at seven twenty," Leith said, nose back in his letter.

At his desk ten minutes later, he checked Google Maps and saw that Mission was not quite an hour's drive south. He gathered what he needed for the task, squinting irritably at the morning sun. It sat low on the horizon, entangled in clouds, but shining through the tinted windows hard enough to hurt the eyes.

He was finding fault with everything today, because his week had gone so badly. Mostly he found fault with real estate tycoons, all of them, because of the perfect house that got away. It had happened just last night. He and Alison met their agent at yet another property, and for the first time, liked what they saw. It was perfect in its imperfection, not far from the hum of bridge traffic, a bungalow in a not-great area. It was small, rundown, and in need of a new roof — so marvellously dilapidated that he and Alison had gotten their hopes up.

The vendors had been present, which was kind of odd; they were a husband and wife going over some details of the listing with their own realtor, while their kids hung around the backyard looking bored. It was probably an estate sale, Leith thought. That might work in their favour, he thought, with his great flare for naivety. Maybe they'd want to dump it at the first offer, fast.

The vendors stayed out on the back deck while Leith and Alison looked around. They agreed they should offer above asking, and while Alison remained out back in the cold sunshine, Leith and his agent did up the paperwork in the kitchen. No subject-to's, no inspection. Termites or sinkholes — fine, bring them on.

But of course it wasn't to be. As he and Alison departed the property, another vehicle pulled up, much snazzier than theirs, and the individuals who stepped out screamed *speculation*. They were going to up the offer, buy the shack, rip it down, build a skinny-ass yuppie condo, and resell at a massive profit. That's what.

It was time to shake the disappointment and move on. This was a brand-new day, and he would just have to make it a better one. He was reaching to activate the voicemail option on his telephone console when the thing warbled at him, its answer-me-now light flickering urgently.

"Damn you," he told it, and picked up. "Leith."

"Yeah, hi," the voice said. It was the croak of an older male, somebody patched through by the receptionist, for some reason, without introduction. That or a wrong number.

"Yes, sir?" Leith asked, sharp as a slap, patience not his strong suit.

"M'name's Starkey," the voice said.

"This is Constable Dave Leith, Mr. Starkey. Can I help you?"

"They call me Starboy." He sounded inebriated — or maybe just uncertain, like someone who didn't have much experience with phones. "The lady said it's you working on this fing out here, is that the truth?"

"What thing is that, sir?"

"The strange goings-on here in Lynn Valley."

Leith puffed out a breath. More tips from the twilight zone. "Yes, that would be me."

"Ah, good. 'Cause I seen fings."

Because life was short and seemed to be getting shorter every day, Leith felt almost too rebellious to pick up a pen. But he grabbed a new BIC from the supply in his desk drawer, removed the plastic lid with his molars and spat it into the wastebasket, punched his notebook open to a clean page, and prepared to take down the caller's hot tip. "What have you seen?"

"Wild dogs," Starboy said. "Two of 'em."

"Uh-huh. Where did you see these dogs?"

"Run right through my yard, sir. Yesterday. Not like your regular dogs. Vicious-like. I locked my doors."

Normally dogs off leash would be a case for the animal control people. But this case wasn't normal, and if the dogs were vicious ... "Where do you live?"

Starboy gave his address and said, "I'm not worried for myself so much, but there's lots o' little kids round here."

Leith jotted down the address. He suspected Starboy was only worried about Starboy; something in the wheedling voice said so. But big mean dogs running loose was definitely a matter of concern, under the circumstances. He looked at his watch. "So what did these dogs look like?"

"Because I seen on the TV that it's dogs what killed that guy at the old Harmon house, right? And then I got that notice in my door saying to report any unusual sort of stuff with animals, and stuff. So I figured —"

"And I appreciate your call. What did these dogs look like?"

"One was kind of dark yellowish. It looked like a shepherd or sumfin', but hairier. The other was smaller, whitish, with brown spots. Or tan spots. Maybe some of each."

Leith's pen lost interest. He slapped his notebook shut and said, "And what did these dogs do, exactly, that said they were vicious?"

"Not vicious as such. They run through my yard and went out across the road."

"Okay. Well —"

"Sumfin' weird about 'em, though," Starboy went on. "Like, I dunno, they were their own bosses or sumfin', if you know what I mean. Possessed or sumfin.'"

"Uh-huh," Leith said. "Okay. Thank you, sir. I'll put this in the file and —"

"And there's sumfin' else, sir, that's very fishy."

"Okay."

"We got a suspicious-looking van parked down this way, with I think some people inside. I couldn't tell too good 'cause the windows are all shiny-like."

"Yes, thank you. We're aware of that van. It's nothing to worry about."

"You want me to keep an eye on it for you, report any suspicious stuff?"

"No." Leith thought about telling the old guy the truth. With the cat out of the bag, it hardly mattered, and it might put the man's mind at ease. "I don't want you going around telling anyone, but for your own information, that's our surveillance van."

"Our what?"

"Surveillance van, sir. We're keeping an eye on the forest."

"Oh, for the wolves, you mean?"

"Yes, wolves, dogs, anything. We've got it covered. So thanks for calling —"

The man stuck in another question, fast. "So you'll be out to look at my yard, then?"

"I doubt that'll be necessary. But thanks for the descriptions. It's on file now, and I'm sure it'll be helpful."

"Because —" the voice said, but Leith's receiver was hitting its cradle.

His brand-new day had already dimmed. He looked up to see Cal Dion heading this way with a manila envelope. "One of the vans got a shot," he said and handed the envelope over.

Leith activated the voice mail on his desk phone, in case Starboy tried again, and extracted a report from the envelope. He read over the first line or two. "Well, I'll be skewered." More than a shot, the document told him. A series, captured last night on an SD card, now loaded onto a flash drive, ready for viewing.

Leith's wristwatch was telling him JD would be waiting in the foyer by now, and it was time to get on the road. But a few minutes late wouldn't hurt, and he beckoned to Dion. "Let's take a look."

They took the elevator downstairs. Leith received the flash drive from the exhibit custodian and took it into the adjacent viewing room, sat at the monitor, and activated the USB. The photos popped up. Dion pulled up a chair to join Leith in scanning through the images.

They were disappointing. Lots of them, burst mode, all unclear. Definitely a figure, but low resolution, impossible to make out its features. Leith chose the best shot and enlarged it on the screen. "Hold on a minute," he said. "Looks like ... well, damned if it's not Keith Richards!"

"'Scuse me," Dion said, taking control of the mouse. He leaned forward, reducing and enlarging the shot until he had the face centred on the monitor. The time-stamp in the lower corner showed 02:32:51. The face in the shot was not much more than a study in smeared contrasts — blobs of shadow where the eyes should be, the vague definition of a cheekbone, a grey smudge of mouth. Long dark hair, dark clothes, dark surroundings, a gleam of light silhouetting the craggy facial structure.

Leith tried the joke again. "Keith Richards, didn't I say so?"

"No, I know who it is," Dion said. He had leaned forward to spread his hand on the monitor glass, as though to stop the image from fleeing. "He's a prep cook. Works at the Greek Taverna." He screwed his eyes shut, then popped them open again, the excitement on his face illuminated by the monitor. "Steve! I think. Never got his last name. Lives in Lynn Valley. Carpools —"

He stopped cold and looked at Leith beside him.

"Carpools?"

"With one of the witnesses," Dion said.

He was hiding something now. Too innocent, too casual.

"Not a witness, actually," he qualified. "But that's how he came up, through canvassing."

Leith waited for the most important part, the name of the non-witness, and when it didn't come fast enough, he snapped, "*Well*?"

"Jordan, Farah. It happens she works with this man. Steve. I think it's Steve. I was in there, the restaurant, and she was there, too, she's a cook, a chef actually, at the Greek Taverna, and she pointed him out to me."

"Why did she do that? Did she suspect him of something?"

"She carpools with him."

"Which you've said. So she was just pointing out and naming people she carpools with, is that how it went?"

"It came out in small talk."

"You're sure that's him."

Dion had another look at the screen and was less thrilled by the image. "I'm not sure. I was certain it was him, at first glance, but now … I don't know."

Leith sighed and once again checked the time, which wasn't standing still for him. "Let's try and get some details," he said, shutting down the computer. "Go and charm this carpoolee's full name and address out of Ms. Jordan, then. I'm off to Mission to see a Mr. Battar. See you later."

* * *

Dion was worrying about the assignment he had just brought upon himself. If he hadn't blurted out about the carpooler, which led inevitably to Farah, but had simply written up a report, chances were he could have glossed over the details, and he wouldn't be here now, tasked with having to contact her.

Yes, he wanted to contact her again, but not like this, and not yet.

He still blamed the wolf. He had overreacted to the animal standing in the shadows of that storage room — well, not standing, but crouched in an attack stance so realistic it had frozen his blood, a stark reminder of life's perils.

Farah's passion for wolves worried him, too, and the fact that she hadn't gotten rid of her father's guns was the last straw. But firearms infractions were a mistake many in her position could easily make. He shouldn't have panicked. He should have been nicer about it all. Should have explained what was wrong instead of shutting her out.

It didn't have to be the end. In fact, calling her about the employee would be a good excuse to talk. He would start out with an apology, ask to come over. Maybe if he brought flowers, she would lay her palm against his face, as she had that night, as if touch was an important part of understanding something, as if he was worth trying to understand. But whether she forgave him or not, it was time to stop dithering. He had to ask the question about the prep cook. He took phone in hand, pulled in a deep breath, and thumbed out the number.

But he didn't reach her, so had to leave a message.

He expected she would get back to him shortly. Oddly enough, though, she didn't.

Twenty

CHILL

DION STOOD IN THE detachment's high-traffic main corridor, mission unaccomplished. He had tried calling Farah several times, both her home and work numbers. Next he would have to go to the Taverna itself, or call the owner, make inquiries about an employee named Steve. Except now he had his heart set on talking to Farah directly. Talking to Farah had become imperative.

He was still standing undecided in the corridor when the phone on his belt chirped. It wasn't Farah returning his calls, but Jackie Randall, a voice he had begun to dread. She was off duty, but hard at work, as always. She asked how he was. He said he was fine. She asked if he could meet her at the MacKay Creek Greenbelt, through which Sunset Boulevard ran, when he was free. Say in half an hour?

The Breanna Ferris hit-and-run scene. Had she found something?

"Why?" Probably she was just being dramatic, pitching her cause. She'd make him stand by the shrine of flowers, where he would feel the full impact of the child's death. Staff walked by on either side, himself an island in a stream, talking on the phone to a potential whistleblower. "It's your case, not mine," he said. "I'm not making any claims. I didn't see anything."

"You saw everything except the hit itself," Randall said. "You're what I would call the prime witness."

"Your prime witness is Michelin Montgomery. Ask him."

"You know I can't do that, Cal."

He moved aside, not to be jostled. "If you're going to investigate, make it official. Open a file and subpoena me. Whatever you want. Or send it to the top and let the white shirts deal with it." Though that would lead to an internal investigation by the last official body on the planet he wanted to face. "Just don't drag me into it, not like this."

"Meet me at the site. I won't drag you into it any further than I have to. Really, I just need a sounding board at this point. Think about it. Looking at the big picture, you don't actually have much of a choice. You're like the eyewitness to an MVA, legally bound to remain on the scene. Cal? You there?"

"Fuck," he said.

On Sunset, at the mouth of the greenbelt, he pulled his cruiser behind what had to be Jackie Randall's car, a shiny black Volkswagen Golf with a small Bart Simpson doll suction-cupped to its rear window. He left his vehicle and walked ahead to the Golf. Inside, the blurry figure of Randall gestured that he should sit next to her in the passenger seat.

"Hello there," she said, as he pulled the door shut. Off duty, with her rosy cheeks and wire-rimmed glasses, she looked deceptively harmless.

The engine idled, windshield wipers slapping, radio tuned to CBC. The woodsy section where Breanna had been struck was ahead of them, out of sight behind trees. The road was narrow there, nowhere to safely pull over, but Dion had driven past earlier. He had seen the crime scene tape was gone now, and in its place was a cross and a garland of weatherproof faux flowers, mostly pink. Flowers and cross had seemed to glow in the half light as he had driven past at a slow thirty klicks.

"I'm putting myself back at the scene," Randall told him. She was looking ahead to the dark, winding road, connecting with the dead. "Halloween night. I've been rereading all the reports. I did up a timeline there, too, if you want to take a look." She indicated a notebook wedged between seat and console, a cheap, well-worn school tablet with buff cover. Dion made no move to pick it up. Didn't need to.

"It was a cold night," Randall said. "But not frosty. Raining, but only lightly. The road's unlit. Traffic would have been light, almost non-existent, this time of year, that time of night. Right?"

Some vehicles had passed them as they sat, but only a few. This wasn't an artery to anywhere. Dion agreed that traffic on Halloween night at that hour would have been almost non-existent.

Randall had her radio playing quietly, an orchestral piece of noise that sounded like Tori's whatsit — the multi-faceted, incredibly complex whatsit. Gershwin. The skies were bruised with the purples of dusk. Randall gestured at the roadway as a car flashed past. "Did you see what he was doing? How do you slow them down?"

Dion had not come here to talk about traffic control. Nor to lend encouragement to Randall's conspiracy theories. Just the opposite. "Tori was in Richmond," he said. "Going home to Seymour Heights. She wouldn't be anywhere near here. It's not even close to her route."

Randall nodded. "I realize that. But I'll tell you something now, as my partner. Tori likes her pot, and I know for a fact she's tried a toot or two."

"How do you know? Are you tooting and toking along with her?"

"Hell, no. But she told me so."

"Why would she tell you so?"

"Like I said, we were classmates. We were like this." She twined two fingers, symbolizing inseparable love.

"I thought you went to school and played some hockey together," Dion said. "You never said you were best friends forever."

Randall ruffled her ginger hair and glared at him, and though Dion would never admit it to anyone, he thought she was prettier by far than Monty's fashion model fiancée. "Would you just listen?" she said. "I'm talking big picture here, relationships, habits, secrets. Does Monty know about his angel's bad habits, d'you think?"

"How could I possibly know?"

"I doubt it. Oh, and she also loves fast cars and driving. Throw that in the pot. And here's my personal opinion, for what it's worth. And it's worth quite a bit, because I know her pretty good. Like I said, in hockey, you get to know your teammates. Especially after the game, when everyone's had too much to drink and speaks their mind. You know what I mean?"

Dion had played beer league baseball. He knew what she meant.

She said, "I think Tori didn't want to go home to that party that night. It's more Monty's crowd than hers. Too many grey hairs."

"Tori's got nothing against grey hair. In fact, she digs grey hair. She's marrying a guy twice her age."

"I'm getting to that. Just between you and me, Tori made a mistake. She might have found Monty exciting at first, him being a decorated cop and a globetrotter, all that. But familiarity breeds contempt. He's just another guy, warts and all, and he's at least one generation too old for her. And if he found out she likes to smoke it up, he would put a stop to it."

"It's no longer the worst crime in the books."

"But it's still hugely immoral, in some spheres. Then there's Tori's insatiable need to be idolized. However much Monty adores her, he's also got an all-consuming career, which means she's not his be all and end all. All this adds up to regret on her end. Maybe she's wondering how to tell him the engagement is off. Maybe that night she took a detour to think it over. Right?"

Dion burst out laughing at Randall's growing list of maybes. "You know what I think?" he said. "You should find another hobby."

"Yes, I will," she snapped. "As soon as I take a look at Tori's car."

"And how are you going to arrange that?"

"I'll figure something out."

"Don't. There's no proof, because it didn't happen. And even if there was any, it'll be gone by now. All you'll do is trash your own career. Believe me."

They both watched the road, silent now. "There'll be a dent at least, and you know it," she said. "I swung by their house a couple times, hoping to find the car out and viewable, but of course it isn't. It's been either re-moved or locked up in the garage. In fact I'll bet my right arm the dent's already been fixed. Under the table, of course. No records. Amazing, though, what can be dug up. Nothing is really deleted, these days."

Dion crossed his arms. Randall relaxed sideways in her driver's seat, observing him as he observed the world through the windshield. He pictured her car and his as they stood currently, pulled over facing the road where a white crucifix with pink weatherproof flowers stood spiked in the grass. If Montgomery drove by right now — unlikely as that might be — he would see them here, recognize the cars, figure it out for himself.

Or maybe he already had it figured out. It seemed his friendliness had dimmed over the last couple of days. Still all smiles, still effusive, showing his teeth when passing in the halls. But it wasn't the same. There was a distance to him that hadn't been there before.

"So," Randall said. "What next? Am I on my own, or do I have your support?"

"I'll sleep on it."

"You know what they say about cold trails."

"I know what they say," he said.

"You think I'm crazy, but don't brush me off. I have a strong, strong feeling about this. We can't have cops covering up crimes. It's just the worst. Don't you agree?"

She was asking the wrong person. If she only knew how wrong. He kept his bitter reply to himself. *Yes, we're the worst.*

After a beat, she said, "I'm going to go find out what's with her car, even if it means confronting Tori. What d'you think? Will I find anything?"

A slight child like Breanna, hit at the very end of a long, screeching skid, low velocity by the time car and body made contact … Dion was afraid the dent may not be obvious, or even visible. A recently replaced hood or fender would be more telling than anything, and Randall was right, forensics would be able to say if repairs had been done, even if the records were buried miles deep. Probably for just that reason the dent would not be fixed, but covered for with some impossible-to-disprove explanation.

Still, if forensics ever got the case in their hands, if it ever went that far, the secret could be out — and what a mess it would be. Hit and run was a serious crime, but a cover-up by an RCMP member was unforgiveable.

He could laugh at Jackie all he wanted, but it didn't stop him from wondering if she was right. What if she was, and what if by some miracle she managed to prove it? Montgomery's career would be over.

But she wouldn't prove it. All she would accomplish was a stirring up of trouble for all involved, including himself. Definitive proof — no. There would be an investigation, suspicion, backlash, dropped charges, and heads would roll.

"Find something?" he said. "Oh, I'm sure you will."

Twenty-One

CREVASSE

Where have I gone wrong? The harder I seek the door, the further out of reach it becomes. I can see in the dark, but my daytime vision is weakening. I am getting heavier, not lighter. The boots aren't working.

STEFANO HAD BEGGED OFF sick, and he wasn't faking it. A body could take only so much battering from within, the endless push and pull, the shifting of atoms. Midmorning, and he was in the Headwaters park, on the far side of the river from the Mesachee. He was not on the network of trails, but deep in the thorny region above where most humans ventured. Fog hung in the treetops, and the world through his eyeholes appeared shadowy, cold, and pungent. Not that he could smell it — all he got when he sniffed was the synthetic interior of the mask. Paint, glue, polyester, and on top of that, his own unpleasant breath. He was sweaty, but the cold seeped through his fur and long johns and left him shivering.

Unbearable. He unzipped his throat and pushed back his head. It flopped heavily between his shoulder blades and dragged the front of the bodice up, cinching his groin and almost throttling him. He tugged the fur back into place.

Stefano was trying to get back to the higher reaches of the mountain, but they seemed impossibly far. He hadn't made it to the top in years. The first time was a few months after Anastasia's fall. He had been fourteen, and wanting to be dead. The accident had changed everything. Destroyed a happy family and put his little sister, math whiz and future concert pianist, into the darkest place imaginable, with no way out. And all because she had hopped and skipped after him in his explorations of the exciting wilds behind their new home. Down into the forest, following intriguing paths, climbing the rocks along the creek, the two of them leaping barefoot from surface to surface — he could still feel the heat on the soles of his feet — but Anastasia ...

Clambering after him, trying to keep up. He had turned to laugh at her struggles and watched her lose her footing, like a glitch in a film, the splice between that life and this, and disappear between boulders.

There had been a few numb months, but life went on. At fourteen he had been more agile. He had made it up beyond the treeline, trying to get lost. He lay on lichen-spattered rock and let the wind sweep over him. Even under the spell of his death wish it had been a beautiful world, and *he* was beautiful, his legs like springs, arms like pistons. As he had climbed into the higher elevations, he had found hope.

But he hadn't managed to get lost, then or ever. There was always the return, back to the house where the music was always playing. Bleak music, his parents' way of dealing with sorrow. They made him take piano lessons for a while, though they knew he wasn't the gifted one. After that, there was high school to get through, then trade school, then work, or recovering from work, or doing chores, or keeping an eye on Anastasia whenever his parents had to go out.

Poor Anastasia. More than once he had tried to wheel her down the road, out to the woods, where he would leave her to the elements. Because if *he* was uncomfortable in his cage, what must *she* be going through in hers? A fate beyond cruel.

Even in this he failed. It was too far, too difficult, and each time he had been forced to turn around and wheel her back to their Dempsey Road prison.

He stood in the wet, grabbing undergrowth, his shaggy legs shaking. How he loved and despised this park. He sometimes wondered if he had caught something from it, maybe on that day he lay on the rock and got aroused by the pressure on his crotch. He had tried to fuck the mountain, and now the mountain was fucking him. Something had crawled inside and was turning him into something … alien.

He looked downhill, and his stomach groaned. Should have brought a sandwich.

He thought about the contents of his fridge: bread and ham. With a shout of disgust, he turned and started back down, passing the spot where last month he had spied the intruder. There had been something so blithely content about the man in his bright-red jacket jaunting by that Stefano had wanted to jump out from where he hid and attack.

That was the first time his mind had gone scarlet. He had looped around, following the red jacket through the gloom. He had kept to the sides of the path — not always easy — until Red Jacket quickened its pace, broke into a jog, and finally dropped its gear and ran, no longer blithe, no longer content.

Stefano had run, too, or done his best to run in the boots.

Even with the boots buckling noisily with each stride, he had felt the power of that moment. Stretched to his full potential, free of weak shins and drippy sinuses and pocked skin, he had chased down his prey, and for a little while, he had become a child of the forest, had finally found his purpose.

More recently was the failure — one he wished to forget — with the two women on the path and their yappy dog. When they had turned and stared toward him, he lost courage and fell to a crouch in the bushes. When they ran off, he feared they would bring vigilantes, so he had hidden deep within the forest.

When he felt it was safe, he had stashed the skin and gone home, just as he was going home now, disappointed and unfulfilled.

He crossed the river upstream from the bridge, then made his way to the parking lot, cutting up through the Mesachee and into the suburbs. The road was all woods on this side, all houses on that, but he knew where to emerge undetected. As always, before re-emergence in human form, he packed his face, hide, and rubber boots in their sack and stuffed the sack into the hole formed by rocks that he had discovered some time ago, hidden by bracken. Back in running shoes, he was now on the asphalt and walking casually, a man out for a stroll on this pleasant November day.

A kid jingled by on his bicycle. A fat man on a ladder was doing something to his eaves. Stefano came to Chef's house and saw that her car was not in the driveway. He felt closer than ever to Chef, now that he had been in her house, but he had also become more realistic about their relationship. She would likely be alarmed by his presence, and may fight back. Possibly she was stronger than she looked. How to subdue a person, and keep them from panicking, so they would listen, and understand? He had left her house that day, knowing he wasn't ready yet. He needed to prepare.

Around the side of the house, he unzipped his jeans and sprayed the wooden siding.

Then he left out the back and walked along the road back to Dempsey, passing the house where his little friend Troy lived. Finally he was back home, padding in socks down the hall. From his sister's room came the gasping of her machines, and from his parents' room only silence.

Downstairs was nothing but his own walled-off suite, Paul's workshop, and the great hulking furnace that roared intermittently. There were also shelves with boxes of Christmas decorations and other artefacts from better days. Stefano expected nobody down here, as always, so was startled when he reached the bottom of the steps to find an intruder at the back of the basement.

The man stood still as a coat rack in the shadows by the storage shelves, tall and skinny, glasses and nose picked out by the scant light of the bulb above. It was Paul. Paul and Stefano looked at each other across the distance.

"Oh, Stefano. I'm looking for my hip waders. Have you seen them? They were in here." He pointed to a large cardboard box on the spiderwebbed storage shelf.

"No."

"How odd."

Stefano slipped into his den, closed the door, and listened. He heard nothing and guessed that Paul was gone, back upstairs to Colette.

The drapes were shut and his room was dark as night. Stefano undressed before the full-length mirror and confirmed what he could feel pushing and pulling inside. The unnatural strands of muscle were filling in his rickety frame, drawing him out longer and leaner. His mouth opened wide, stretching till the skin of his cheeks burned.

He ate in front of the TV with remote control in hand. He settled on a documentary about the aerospace industry and watched blindly while his jaws ripped and chewed. The day was young. Later, maybe, he would change skins and go further up the shaded paths. Stretch into the changes, tear up the miles. If only he had more time. Impossible, though, because he needed to work. He needed the money.

Or did he?

Huddled on the floor, bathed in the flashing TV's strobe and licking his lips free of ham brine, he grinned as it occurred to him where to go next — and what to be.

Twenty-Two

GUNNER

DION TRIED TO REACH Farah again, and again he was frustrated. He phoned the restaurant and was told she was not in quite yet, as she had some kind of appointment. He left a message for her to call him as soon as she was available, giving his cellphone number, the direct line to his office, and the detachment's main line for good measure. The girl taking the message said she thought it kind of sweet, all these numbers he was giving her, but it wasn't.

He was worried. Farah didn't get it. She lived across the road from a horrific murder scene, but hadn't seemed in any rush to upgrade her locks, as he had strongly recommended.

Now a man shaped like a wolf was creeping about the surrounding woods. The next time he talked to her, he would give her a bit of a lecture about safety — if it wasn't too late — and responsibility, and the unwritten law about returning calls.

He was trying to focus on paperwork when she did just that — called. Over an hour had passed since he had given her up for dead, so he counted to three before speaking. On the count of three he said in his calmest, deepest voice, "I've been trying to reach you."

"Sorry," she said. "I got your messages, and I meant to get back to you, but didn't realize it was an emergency till just now."

"I don't blame you for avoiding me. I was a jerk."

"That's your job, isn't it? No hard feelings. What's up?"

She sounded as level as ever. A little rushed, but not angry, or even irritated. There was a great deal of background noise behind her, shouting and banging pots, and something pinged. Dion was pleased about the *no hard feelings*. "It's this case I'm working on," he told her. "I have a couple of questions. You seem to be in a public place. Is the line secure?"

"Secure?"

"Anybody listening in?"

"No, nobody's listening in. You're perfectly secure."

"It's about Steve," Dion said, ignoring the light mockery. "The guy you carpool with. He's come up in our inquiries — nothing to worry about, but I need his last name."

"Steve? You mean Stefano?"

"If you wouldn't mind keeping this to yourself," he added.

"Why do you want to know? He's not in trouble, is he?"

"No. General inquiries. I can tell you more later, but for now, just give me his name, if you could. And keep it to yourself that I've been asking about him."

"All right," she said. "It's Boone. Stefano Boone."

"B-O-O-N?" he said.

"B-O-O-N-E," she said.

* * *

After some system-generated delay, Leith and JD sat facing twenty-two-year-old Jagmohan "Joey" Battar, deep
within the walls of the Mission penitentiary. Battar sat
in the dingiest green interview room, wearing the dingiest orange prisoner's coveralls, with nothing but the
dingiest grey future ahead of him, but he was a pleas-
ant-faced young man. He should have been out and
about, enjoying the world with friends, not locked up
for the foreseeable future.

What a waste, Leith thought. He introduced himself
and JD, then sketched in the background of why he was
here, looking into a serious crime out in Lynn Valley on
the North Shore. Battar said, "I figured you're here about
a serious crime 'cause you're from GIS, which is like the
homicide squad, right?"

"Something like that. Where have you been living the
last few years, Joey? You seem to be off the radar as far
as fixed addresses."

"I travel. Stanley Park sometimes, in the summers.
Burnaby Lake. West Point Grey once, believe it or not."
He couldn't remember where he had lived this past
summer, so. Leith asked if he had ever spent time in
Lynn Valley.

Nope, he'd never heard of the place.

Leith told him that was strange, as his fingerprints
had been found all over a derelict house in the very heart

of Lynn Valley. Battar said it must have been someone with identical fingerprints to his own. Leith told him fingerprints are unique, no two people's are identical.

Battar wanted proof of that theory. "Unless you check everyone, you can't say that for sure. It's like snowflakes. Who's going to go around checking every snowflake to see if they're the same or different? Right?"

A lot of time was wasted arguing the point, but Battar finally conceded that he *had* spent a few days with a friend in a place on the North Shore. He refused to give the friend's name, as friends don't rat out friends. It's the code.

Now they were arguing about codes of honour and how far they could be pushed, another argument Battar was doomed to lose. "You win," he said. "You a smoker?"

Leith said he was a smoker who was seriously trying to quit. Battar said he would help him quit by bumming a cigarette off him, for later. Leith gave him the whole pack.

"I'll just stick one in my mouth, like," Battar said. He sucked on the scent of his unlit smoke for a while, then finally went about breaking the code and ratting on his friend. "This buddy of mine was kind of a crook, to tell the truth. He'd go out in the daytime — best time for it, he says — and burgle places. It's all hearsay, though, because I never do that stuff myself."

"That's why you're in here, I thought. Partaking in B and Es with friends."

"Which is a misunderstanding. I fell in with the wrong crowd. I was set up to take the fall. The judge didn't believe it, is why I'm here."

Leith brought the discussion back to the matter at hand. "I need the name of your friend in Lynn Valley,

Joe. I wouldn't worry about getting him in trouble. He's beyond that."

He showed Battar the old school photo of Ben Stirling — a handsome, but glum-eyed young man — supplied by Ben's older brother. Battar said, "That doesn't look like him, but that's him. That's Gunner."

"Gunner — that's his nickname? What happened to him?"

Battar relaxed, now that he accepted he wasn't the target of this investigation, and turned out to be quite a talker. "I don't know what happened to Gunner. We parted ways at some point, back in that heat spell. Haven't seen him since."

He described meeting Gunner in Vancouver across from the old CP building. That was back in the spring. "He'd just got off the bus, was selling something, I can't remember what, small but hi-tech, and we got talking, and later bunked down together — not in that way, just friends. And later he invited me out to his place in whatever that was you said —"

"Lynn Valley."

"Big old house he found in a walkabout. We lived there all of August, but you can't make a living over there. Just doesn't pay to be homeless in North Van. You stick out too much, so you have to lie low. Better off in Vancouver, where you got more options. And if you're thinking Gunner's a criminal, he's not. He wasn't going to do B and Es forever. He had plans, was going to start a business. With global warming, there's this specialized kind of landscaping he read up on that uses very little water. He says it's going to become really big, and he's going to be the first in the city to offer it. He just had to build up some capital to get started. He was going to hire me, too, and we'd work together, was the plan."

Battar stared sadly at his unlit cigarette. "Gunner's a smart guy, but heavy into the dope. Sometimes smart people can't handle how smart they are and need the uppers and downers to kind of take the edge off."

Battar the psychoanalyst. "I see what you're saying," Leith said.

"So we only stayed in that house there, him and me and his girl, for hardly even that month. Too hot."

Girl. Leith thought about the fake-gold bracelet, a dime a dozen, found on a windowsill in the Greer house.

Battar said, "It was just a few days after Aphid left that we kind of broke up the scene. Gunner had kept telling her to go back to her parents because she was really young, and this wasn't a good life for her. She didn't want to go. It was like telling a dog, go home, go home, and it keeps following you around. But when she finally took off — that was around welfare day in August — he was really watery about losing her, and it wasn't the same after that. He left a few days after she did. I hope he went home, too. He has a brother somewhere."

Another pause.

"After Gunner didn't come back, I packed up and left myself. That place is creepy enough even when you're not alone."

"Gunner's girl?" JD asked. "You said *Aphid*?"

"Aphid," Battar told her. "Like the bug."

"How do you spell that?"

"A-F-F-I-D, I guess. Like the bug."

"Last name?"

"Hell if I know."

"Tell us what you know about Aphid," Leith said.

"She was his girl, about this high." Battar indicated about five feet off the ground. "She didn't talk much. She'd run away from home, is all I know about her."

Leith could get no more details about Aphid except hair colour — kind of like milky tea.

Battar asked Leith what it was Gunner had done to cause all these GIS questions. Leith told Battar that Gunner was dead.

Battar put down his damp cigarette and was silent. He asked how Gunner had died, and Leith told him that was exactly what he was trying to find out.

Leith asked Battar for a complete list of Gunner's friends. Battar said there were none, except himself and Aphid. Oh, except for the lady.

"Lady?"

"Yeah, man." Battar became more animated as he reminisced. "She walked right in and scared me and Gunner half to death. But turned out she was cool. Invited us over and fed us. Great food, nice place. And awesome soap. Fruity, eh?"

Twenty-Three

FEVER

JOEY BATTAR WAS TURNING OUT to be a treasure trove of new leads, and Leith thought it wise to just nod encouragement, prompting only when necessary, while JD quietly jotted notes. Right now a prompt was needed, as Battar seemed to have fallen into a deep reverie.

"Tell us about the lady, Joe."

"She showed up pretty soon after Aphid disappeared, and good timing, too, because Gunner was in a mood. Depressed. He needed a break. And a bath. He cared about Aphid in a big way."

"And so this lady came over. And what's her name?"

Battar shook his head. "I was laced that night, man, complete Nirvana. So it's all a bit of a dream state, to tell the truth."

Fabulous, Leith thought.

"What's kind of funny," Battar went on, "is a couple nights before she walked in, Gunner went over and ripped her place while she was out — I only found this out later — bagged a bunch of jewellery and stereo equipment. So then holy shit, when she just walked into our place and came up the stairs, we're like, yikes, what's up here, man? And she found us in the closet and she goes, 'Give me my stuff back, like, *now.*'"

Leith was glad his digital recorder was taking this all down, as JD seemed to have stopped taking notes. Like himself, she was too busy not believing her ears.

Battar said, "So I guess this is a first for Gunner, being told to give stuff back. Pretty quick he goes into his hidey-hole under the floorboards there" — the hidey-hole the team had discovered under the claw marks, Leith supposed, nothing inside but dead bee-tles — "and he gets the stuff out and gives it back to her, and me and him are both, like, wondering what she's going to do about it, if she's already called the cops and they've got the place surrounded, or what. But nope, apparently not. This lady just takes her jewellery and goes through it, checking for something in particular, which she finds. A ring, or something. She says none of it would score us any cash, anyway. Sentimental value, she says. And all the while I'm thinking, lady, there's two of us and one of you here. You should be a little more, if nothing else, respectful. Better yet, scared shitless. I sure would be. But anyways, far as I remember, then she says we can keep the amp and mini CD player, but she'll take the jewellery. And she wants her speakers."

JD seemed to have stopped writing altogether.

Battar continued, "She probably wasn't too wor-ried because we were both skin and bones by then and couldn't take her on even if we wanted to. Actually, she seemed more worried about *us* than herself or the crap Gunner took. She asked how long we'd been there, and how long we planned to stay, and if we were okay. She was talking about shelters, I think, trying to get us out of there and somewhere safe."

Some kind of do-gooder, Leith thought. Looking for converts.

"After getting scared so bad, I had to light up another one. Meanwhile she and Gunner sat down there on the floor and got talking, and then next thing you know, she's saying we should go over to her place, get cleaned up and have something to eat!"

Battar shook his head, amazed at his own memories. "So we did. Went over, and me and Gunner each had a shower. I was still pretty sure it was a trap, and she'd have the cops waiting for us when we came out. But at one point when you're really hungry, you don't care. I, for one, didn't. We went downstairs and, man oh man, the supper she had laid out for us, wow. I thought, maybe she's poisoned it in revenge for taking her stuff, but so what? That's how good it was. So good. Then I think the two of them went on talking."

"About what?"

"No clue. Boring metaphysical garbage. So I just got into the cake. It has apricots and rum, she says, and it was literally the best dessert I have ever tasted."

Again Leith asked for the lady's name, or a description. Unfortunately Battar seemed to have been so focused on food, drink, soap, and marijuana that he could recall little else. Leith asked where the lady lived.

"Oh, somewhere around," Battar said.

It was all he could say. Leith thought maybe if they took the kid to the Greer house, it would refresh his memory. "What about it?" he asked.

"Much as I'd like a field trip with you guys, I can guarantee it wouldn't help. We had just scored some Colombian Gold, very rich, very deep, and I was on a magic carpet ride all the way that night."

"Nothing else you remember?" JD asked, as if asking one more time would help.

It didn't. Except he did recall there was a cat.

"What colour?"

Battar said the cat was purple, for all he knew. Same with the lady.

"Put yourself back in the house you shared with Gunner," Leith said, "when she first walked in and scared you, and you were in the closet. Think hard and tell me what you see. What did she look like?"

Battar said he must have been hallucinating, because he thought she had hair over her face. Black hair. He didn't know her age, height, weight, ethnicity. Nothing.

A lady with black hair hanging over her face sounded a lot like a horror movie Leith had seen with Alison not too long ago. But probably Battar was right, it was just a clash of drugs and fear. He asked what happened after the great meal.

"I don't know. I must have passed out. But him and her went upstairs and had sex all night long."

"How do you know that?" Leith asked.

"'Cause he told me so."

Battar's next memory was waking up the next day back home in the Greer house — and Gunner's transmogrification. "That experience, it changed him. No more drugs, no more stealing. He was going to go straight, get an education, maybe meet somebody nice like her, have some kids. Then, you know, get a dog to protect those kids, and all that. He meant it, too. But it wasn't going to happen, man. It's too high of a hill to climb, for people like us."

Leith asked him if he or Gunner had seen the lady again. Battar hadn't, and he didn't think Gunner had either. In fact it might have been only a day or two later Gunner up and disappeared, leaving all his skunk and Chinese cooking wine behind.

"Didn't you wonder what had happened to him?"

"Not really. We were both ready to split. He just did it first."

Leith asked Battar if he had taken Gunner's belongings when he'd left the Greer house for the last time.

Battar returned Leith's gaze with a touch of indignation. "It's not a big deal, taking from a guy who steals, right? And possession is, like, five tenths of the law."

He'd gotten the expression almost right, meaningless as it was. Really, it was a shame he hadn't gone to school and become a lawyer. Leith asked if he still had any of those belongings. Battar said there was nothing to take but some clothes, sleeping gear, Aphid's bag of cosmetics, and Gunner's leather jacket. Oh, and the amp. He'd taken all of it. He had no idea where the clothes and other stuff were, but the amp and leather jacket had disappeared at his last billet.

No doubt about it, Joey Battar was a suspect in the murder of Ben Stirling, and he would be stuck on the board and analyzed at length. But he wasn't the killer, nor even an accomplice. Leith could tell by the vibes JD was giving off that she thought the same.

He thanked Battar for his help. He wished him better paths for the future and encouraged him to use his time in clink to study, as he had good brains and should be using them. Then he and JD left Mission in the rear-view mirror.

JD said, "Bag of cosmetics, huh? What young girl would leave that behind? I think we better put Aphid on the board next to her boyfriend."

The mention of a cosmetic bag hadn't stood out to Leith as anything special. Now that JD had put it to words, it glared. Not only significant, but ominous. "Damn, JD," he said, "I wish you weren't so smart."

* * *

Leith looked into the takeout bag that held his late lunch, and for the umpteenth time that day said, "Damn." He had forgotten to ask the girl behind the counter for the all-important takeout ketchup. He set down the burger as Dion came along. In a good mood, it seemed, which was nice for a change.

"Have a moment?" Dion asked. "Oh, you're having dinner."

"That's okay. Have a seat."

Dion removed his police cap, finger-combed his hair, and sat. "I got the prep cook's name for you," he

said. "Stefano Boone. I thought I could grab his address off the system, but can't find him, so I'll make
more enquiries through his employer. In checking
the directory I saw there's a *Paul* Boone on Dempsey,
and — hang on," he said, startled by his own words.
"Whoa! Dempsey."

He spent the next moment or so flipping back
through his notebook.

Leith unwrapped the burger and took a bite. Tasty as
cardboard.

"Troy Hamilton! He's on Dempsey Street, too. That's
just around the corner from Paul Boone."

"Who's Troy Hamilton?"

"Ten-year-old witness I interviewed, claims he
knows a werewolf. He disclosed the name of his school's
janitor. I eliminated that individual pretty quick. It's all
in my report. But …"

"But what?"

"But Troy Hamilton is on the same block as Paul
Boone," Dion repeated. "I'll track down Stefano Boone
and let you know. If he's also at this address, there might
be a connection."

"Okay, good," Leith said. He wasn't sure if the news
flash was pivotal to anything. If it was just more werewolf nonsense, he wasn't too interested. He waited for
Dion to leave so he could get back to his unpalatable
meal in peace.

"Who's Jagmohan Battar?" Dion asked, still sitting,
his eye on Leith's monitor.

Leith gave up waiting and took another bite. His
mouth full, he told Dion about Battar, the fingerprint

leaver at the Greer house from whom he'd just taken a statement. This was the statement.

"Oh." Dion seemed torn between interest and indifference. But Bosko's efforts to bring him back into the fold seemed to be working, and interest was winning out.

"Go ahead and read it, if you want."

"It looks lengthy."

"Incredibly lengthy and incredibly interesting."

Leith washed down the burger with takeout coffee, and Dion settled in to read Battar's statement, transcribed from audio by staffers on an expedited request. He seemed to be an overly careful reader, so Leith left him to it and went for a walk. Stretch the legs and try to ease the gut cramp that always came from cardboard burgers eaten too fast. Would he ever learn?

* * *

Moments after Leith had vacated the desk, Dion was ready to quit reading the long document on the computer screen. It was an interview of an inmate, a Jagmohan Battar, also known as Joey, and nothing he read so far seemed terrifically of interest, contrary to Leith's claim. Yet like any narrative, it pulled him along, enough that he switched chairs for a more direct view. He took the mouse and scrolled through the bullshit about fingerprints and DNA. At some point through the interview it appeared Battar had a cigarette in his mouth, which seemed to loosen his tongue.

Dion skimmed through more chatter, past some discussion about insects — aphids? — until it got interesting again. Mention of an intruder, a strange lady who had come over one day to retrieve her stolen belongings.

When Battar began his description of the lady, Dion tensed. By the end of the description his mouth had fallen open. He went back and reread the section carefully, looking for something, anything, to tell him the lady described was not who he thought she was. The black hair over the face reference could just be a stoner's bad tripping, but also a combination of confusion, darkness, and the woman's dusky skin.

The conversation around proximity gave him more hope. Farah's house was right across the road, so wouldn't Battar have said so, how close it was?

But again, Battar's sense of time was obliterated by whatever he was on.

No, it was definitely — almost definitely — Farah. When he got to the part where she took Gunner to bed, his heart was pounding and his armpits were slick.

He didn't finish the interview, but left the desk as he caught sight of Leith returning. He made his way back to the second floor, via not the elevator, but the more private stairwell, where he could sit and bury his head in his arms.

The door opened above with a faint squeal and thumped shut. Somebody was in the stairwell with him. He waited for the noisy descent of heavy boots, and instead, heard not much more than a whisper of motion.

JD Temple stepped down a few risers to stare into his face. "What's the matter?"

"Nothing," he told her, straightening his back. He was just a man out for a walk, taking a rest, nothing wrong with that.

JD's dark-brown hair was chopped short and spikey, bangs too high. She wore no makeup or jewellery. Her scarred mouth gave her a look of contempt, but he knew her well enough to see that even without the scar, she was sneering at him.

"What d'you mean nothing?" she said. "You look like your puppy just got run over."

"I'm fine. Just taking a break. You can go now."

She gave a who-cares shrug and started down the stairs. "Just taking a break in a stairwell with wet, blood-shot eyes — okay, whatever. Power to you."

"Bit of hay fever," he called at her back.

"In November, right, I totally believe you."

She said no more, but carried on downstairs, swift and silent. The moment he heard the fire door click shut below, he rose, dusted off his pants, and got on with what he had to do.

Twenty-Four

PAINT AND GLUE

STEFANO SAT SEWING and worrying. He had been aware for days that the authorities were looking for him, and he knew why. It was because of Red Jacket. He had chased it down the mountain, and now the police were looking for the beast that had done the chasing.

In fact they had come to the house last week, and he had heard them upstairs, talking to Paul and Colette in the open doorway. He had heard questions and warnings, not quite audible, and Paul and Colette mumbling answers and promises. But he hadn't been worried then.

The news Troy had brought over yesterday was what alarmed him. A policeman had been to Troy's house, had sat him down and asked a lot of questions about Stefano. The policeman didn't seem to know Stefano's name, however.

"And I didn't tell him," Troy had said, proudly. "Even though he said I could have five thousand dollars."

"Good for you." Stefano had patted Troy on the head. "Thank you. You're a good friend." He had gone upstairs to find a reward for the child, a handful of mints from the candy bowl and a loonie off Colette's dresser. He had padded back down and given them to Troy. Then, oddly shy about it, he had shown Troy the new, improved ceremonial costume.

Troy's jaw dropped as he admired the wolfskin. Stefano had stood smiling. The child sucked mints and asked a lot of questions about turning into a wolf, what it was like, whether it hurt. The process was so personal, so close, so *large*, that Stefano had stuttered badly trying to put it to words, and as he listened to himself speak, a switch in his mind flicked, revealing a horrible, frightening truth. It was like he had opened his eyes to find himself standing on the brink of a bottomless chasm, looking down. For a moment, he had realized that he was mad.

He had flicked the switch off, fast, and told Troy to get on home before his parents got worried. Troy had left the usual way, stepping up onto a kitchen chair to reach the foundation ledge, then through the window that opened out onto lawn and a row of cedar shrubs.

The night had helped wash away much of Stefano's anxiety. He sat on the floor now, hand-stitching and rocking. Without a name, the police would never track him down. He would just have to use extra caution when venturing forth. He would keep to the underbrush, eyes wide open. He wouldn't attack anyone else. He didn't need to, now that he had a higher goal.

But to achieve that goal, he had to get this done. The fur was draped across his lap, nothing to finish but one last paw. The paws were time-consuming, but easy. A comforting job.

The head had been completed for some time now. It sat staring at him eyelessly from across the room. It had been the biggest challenge, of course, but worth it. Far better than its predecessor, the boxy contraption now crushed and stuck so unceremoniously in the waste bin.

For the teeth he had used a yellowish modelling compound, baked solid. A bit of a disaster there, when Colette had come home from grocery shopping sooner than expected and found the teeth on the cookie sheet. But she hadn't asked him about it.

Attaching the teeth had been a job, too — varnished, semi-matte, hinged with wire. He had sewn them with heavy-duty nylon thread in place in the mask's gaping mouth hole, rigged with hardwood rods as stiffeners.

Stefano, have you seen my ebony dowels?

Last week, when Stefano had tried it on for the first time before the mirror, he had been shocked. With face painted black, snout strapped on, ears sewn erect to his balaclava, a strip of fur in between, he had stared at his reflection, and tears had sprung to his eyes. But he had braced himself and looked again, and decided it wasn't so bad.

This was no Halloween costume. He was not trying to fool himself or anyone else into believing it was his true skin. The robe was a representation of what he was becoming, a tool to facilitate the rites of passage. When night set in, and he had sunk into the shadows of the forest, as he wrote in his diary, the false skin would melt off the contours of his human body, and those contours would melt away with the costume until he ran free, strong, and wild, sliding through the forest like a rippling river of muscle and teeth, seeking sustenance. He had seen them on TV, wolves chasing caribou through winter-white fields. Hunter racing prey, neck and neck, the wolf gaining, passing, whipping around and making the leap to bring the larger animal crashing into the snow.

It was so clean and mechanically pure.

Chef would come easily, once he had taught himself the ropes. But he needed a training ground. He would start out smaller.

A tapping noise distracted him.

He looked toward the high windows that ran the length of his basement suite and saw his little friend Troy was back, crouched down on the walkway outside, looking in. Troy grinned and waved.

Twenty-Five

CONFESSION IN BLUE

FARAH BEGAN TO SAY HELLO with her usual warmth, but paused when she saw the look on Dion's face. "What's the matter?"

He stood on her porch with a cold wind punching at his back. "I'm not sure. That's why I'm here. To find out."

She moved aside, door wide open. "Come in, would you?"

He entered the house, but kept his jacket on. "Upstairs," he said.

She followed him up to her bedroom, her bedroom window, where he placed an arm around her shoulder and drew her close, so their lines of vision could run parallel. He pointed across to the dark Greer house, its upstairs window reflecting moonlight. "You never looked over there? Never saw a thing? That's what you said. Isn't that what you told me, when I was canvassing the neighbourhood?"

She moved away from him, not liking his attitude. She stood staring at him, more concerned than angry. "What happened? What's going on?"

He crossed his arms. "Were you burglarized this summer?"

"Burglarized?"

He saw false surprise on her face, and he knew he had her nailed.

There was no mistake. She *had* been burglarized this summer. By a flea-infested petty criminal and drug addict named Ben Stirling, whom she had then bathed, fed, and slept with, for some unfathomable reason, and who had a day or so afterward disappeared, only to turn up dead and decomposing some months later — all of which, yes, caused him some fucking concern.

"Burglarized," he repeated coldly.

She lifted her chin at him. She knew the game was up, and now he foresaw the rest of it, like a fast-forward preview of disaster. She was going to confess to the murder, and his relationship with her — so what that it was some kind of twisted platonic mad scientist hippy experiment — would take him and his career crashing down. So what if she had started out as a minor witness? Turned out he, once a rising star of a detective, had not only failed to recognize the killer, but dated her.

"Yes," she said, and even though he had come charging over here knowing the truth, he was shocked by the confession. "Last summer I happened to meet the two drifters who stayed in that house. Joey and Gunner. Or Ben Stirling, as I now know. Yes, they broke into my house and took some of my things. It was a pathetic bunch of loot, Cal. One broken CD player, some pewter costume jewellery, a handful of parking meter money, and a diamond ring that my mother had inherited from her mother. They were tiny diamonds. I'm sure in the industry they call it 'crush.' If lucky, they might have gotten a hundred bucks out of the whole sting. Anyway, I asked for the jewellery back, and they gave it to me. They were shaking in their boots. Should I have turned them in? Of course. I was going to. For their own sakes, if nobody else's."

"But you didn't."

"No."

He waited for her damn good reason why she hadn't reported that there were two squatters living next door who had stolen from her, and would go on stealing in and around the neighbourhood until they escalated to home invasions and somebody got hurt or killed. Which quite possibly somebody did, that being one of the burglars himself.

"Why don't you sit down," Farah said.

"I'm not interested in sitting down."

So she explained to him, standing. "I talked to him, to Gunner. About his situation, why he steals, how to get off that track, how to take on the system and use it for what it's worth. You know, how to eke out a living, crimelessly, which isn't as easy as those of us with privilege seem to think. Do you think my reporting him, and a bunch of cops descending on him out of the blue and throwing him in a paddy wagon, would really help?"

"That's what bunches of cops are here for, to arrest criminals and protect people like you. You want to rewrite the law of the land? Maybe exempt everyone who's a nice guy, but just a little misguided?"

"Oh, Cal," she said. "Where's your empathy? Have you never done anything wrong in your life?"

"I'm not talking to you," he told her. "I'm taking you in."

"It's easy to judge if you weren't there. You're looking at this like it's one of your typed-up reports. Gunner had never been in trouble with the law before. He stole because he didn't know how else to feed himself."

"Or his drug habit."

"He had a plan. It was elaborate, and it was sound. What he needed was the benefit of the doubt, and I gave it to him."

"You should have turned him in, Farah. You should have let the courts decide what benefit to give him. It's a civilized country. We don't cut off people's hands."

Dion was hot under the collar, but Farah was cool, and she was managing to keep the conversation level. As if from a separate self, he watched her with awe.

"Of course not," she said. "But we don't listen very well. I listened to him. I decided to give him a chance. We talked over the game plan and agreed to meet again. It didn't happen, and now I know he's dead, and I feel terrible about it. But that night, right or wrong, I didn't have the heart to throw those kids away."

"So you slept with them instead."

"What?" she cried, for the first time raising her voice. "No, I did not! Where do you get that bullshit from? Jesus!"

Dion made a noise of disgust, though he was no longer sure about his last accusation, almost convinced by her reaction. But it didn't matter. Whether or not she had slept with the vagabonds was moot. He looked at her squarely, himself the cool one now, and said, "I'm going to have to get your full statement. You know that? You know you're a prime suspect?"

Her eyes flew open wide. "What?"

"Yes," he said, with dark satisfaction. "You screwed up, Farah. If you had been up-front with me, we wouldn't be in this fix. Fact is, I can't even take your statement, because I screwed up too, by getting involved with you, which means you'll have to tell it all to someone else. Probably David Leith, who isn't half as nice as I am. And about a hundred times smarter."

"Oh, calm down," she snapped. "I didn't kill Gunner. How ridiculous."

They were staring at each other, and already she was back in control, more baffled than afraid. More curious than angry.

He gave up the contest and paced the length of the bedroom, fretting to himself. Farah seated herself on the bed, one knee slung over the other, to watch him pace. He stopped in front of her. "You'll have to tell them all about us. It'll come out one way or another. It has to."

"Us?" she said. "What *us*?"

"Doesn't matter how far we didn't go," he snarled. "We still had a relationship that went out of bounds. But that's my problem, not yours. I'll get in shit for it, but so what? They can't demote me any further."

"Wow," she said. "This is the happiest I've seen you. You really like being unhappy, don't you? If it comes to it, I'll tell them that we met and got talking, and I invited you over for dinner, and that's as far as it went. I can't be-lieve you'd get in trouble for some dinner conversation."

"The kind of trouble I get in depends on the kind of trouble you get in." He spelled it out for her. "*Cops don't mess with witnesses*. It can get a whole case thrown out. Follow me?"

She changed the subject. "You were going to tell me what Stefano has done."

"That was before you became my prime suspect," he said, through his teeth.

"Pretend for a moment I'm not. What did Stefano do?"

It took him a moment to remember why he cared about Stefano Boone, and when he remembered that particular line of inquiry, he almost let out a bitter laugh. "To your knowledge, is Stefano Boone a werewolf?"

Damp with anger, he waited for the absurd answer to his absurd question.

She said, "I don't believe Stefano is a werewolf. As far as I know, he's just a prep cook. Why? No, hold that thought. I'll be right back."

She left the room and he heard her step swiftly down the stairs. He sat on the bed and waited, looking at the narrow window with its great view of the murder house across the road. A minute later she came padding back in, probably with her father's loaded Winchester in hand, cocked to kill. When he glanced over he saw that all she held was a tumbler of something that looked like Scotch.

"This one's special," she said, and handed him the glass. "I bought it to have on hand for your rare inter-ludes of niceness."

He had come here with accusations of murder and immoral conduct, and in turn she treated him with sympathy and Scotch. He took the glass and studied it minutely, looking for powder sediment at its base. She was beside him on the bed. She rubbed his back gently, like he was a child with the flu, not a grown man going through a personal hell.

Liquor laced with strychnine, then. He threw it back like medicine. The only effect, a moment later, was a migrating warmth and a slight easing of the knot in his stomach.

"I think we should sleep on it," Farah said, her hand still on his back. He couldn't look at her any longer. He didn't have the nerve. He knew now that her plan was not poison, but seduction. She would knife him as he slept, leave his body in somebody else's crawl space, blame it on the wolves. Probably get away with it, too.

"I think that's a bad idea," he told her. He took her hand, as they sat side by side. "I'm going to have to take you in, right now, and get it all on the record. There's no other way."

"Okay," she said. "Whatever you'd like."

She leaned to kiss him, chastely, on the cheek.

* * *

Leith was minding Izzy, as Alison was out. He watched the child play and thought it was scary, how much he loved her.

He tried to imagine: what if she turned fifteen and decided to call herself Aphid and run away with a reprobate who burgled houses for a living? He tried to imagine the distance coming between them. How could he survive the hurt?

His phone rang, not the work jangle, but the personal *bling-bling*. He dug it out of his pocket, Izzy under his arm like a giggling sack of potatoes, and checked the number on display. Not a number he recognized, and he was struck with anxiety. Bad news was always out there, just waiting to pounce.

"Hello," he said. "Dave Leith."

"This is Patricia Klugman," said a tense voice. "We met last week. You put an offer on our little teardown on Delbruck. I realize there's been a delay, but there was some business we had to take care of. There's no time limit on your offer, I see, which is kind of unusual. I haven't heard from you, so I imagine you've made other arrangements."

So this was a different kind of bad news, from the vendor of that perfect house he had bid on so pompously. She sounded unhappy, and he wondered what he had messed up for her. "No, but anyway. What's up?"

He could hear rustling, then something clicking, then a flaring sound he recognized — a lighter combusting. She was firing up a cigarette. That's how much she hated him: she had to pause mid-conversation and suck up some smoke. He had probably jeopardized that deal with the zillionaire. He couldn't imagine how, but this conversation was clearly heading toward a lawsuit.

"We've accepted your offer," she said, and sucked, and blew. "If you're still interested, that is."

"Excuse me?"

Silence, then he heard her speak away from the phone to somebody. He wasn't sure, but he thought she had just referred to him, Leith, as a genius. Then she was back, apologizing for the delay. Not that he was hearing so well. This was news he couldn't quite process. She said, "You want the house, it's yours."

They discussed further details and set up a time to meet.

He disconnected, stunned, as another call came in. Corporal Paley had just spoken to Cal Dion, who claimed to have a witness that Leith would want to interview, and it better be ASAP.

Twenty-Six

MERCY

LEITH HAD TO WAIT a few minutes for the apparently critical witness to arrive. And that was her, he supposed, being marched toward him in the company of Constable Dion. Dion was off duty, judging by the casual clothes, but there was nothing casual about his expression. The woman at his side was a dark-skinned woman around thirty years old.

Some instinct told Leith this was Joey Battar's mystery woman, the one who had walked into the Greer house to set Ben Stirling on a more virtuous path.

With no evidence whatsoever, why did he think it was her? Because Dion had her in custody. Say no more.

Dion had directed the woman to go sit in the waiting area just outside the GIS office, and now he carried on to Leith's desk alone. He began to rattle off the details. "I've brought in Farah Jordan, from Lynn Valley. She's the witness I was questioning about the prep cook, Stefano Boone —"

"Slower," Leith said.

Dion took a chair and started over. "Farah Jordan is the chef at the Greek Taverna, where Stefano Boone is a prep cook. She drives him to and from work. I told you about that, the carpooler."

"Right," Leith said. The conversation was almost lost in the shuffle of his mind, but he recalled Dion recognizing a face in the surveillance van shots.

"After reading Jagmohan Battar's statement, it occurred to me Jordan fits the description of the B and E victim he was talking about, so I asked her about that, too. She admits she'd been at the Greer house and had met Ben Stirling. She only knew him as Gunner. I stopped asking questions right away and brought her in."

"Okay," Leith said.

Dion sped up again to finish his report. "She says she felt sorry for Stirling and Battar, and invited them over to her house across the road. She says she has no knowledge of what happened to them after that. Like I said, I didn't inquire further. I knew you'd want to get a warned statement from her soon as possible."

Leith nodded. "I'll do that," he said. "Soon as you tell me what's really going on here. You planning to do that anytime soon?"

"What's really going on," Dion said stiffly, "is it came out in canvassing that Jordan works at the Greek Taverna. That's a restaurant I go to sometimes, so when I was down there for dinner, we got talking, and it came up in conversation that she carpools with the prep cook. She pointed him out to me, which is how I later identified him in the surveillance shots. Just a string of coincidences, really."

You're a string of coincidences, Leith nearly said. He crossed his arms.

"I didn't consider Jordan integral to the investigation in any way," Dion continued, "so when she invited me over for dinner, I said sure. Nothing wrong with that. Later it turned out that things kind of linked up, so I told you right away."

In a nutshell, Leith decided, the cop was dating the suspect. But it was true that the connections might be tenuous, at best. The prep cook named Boone could be a case of mistaken identity. But even if he *was* lurking in the night and scaring people, that was weird, but not necessarily criminal. *Yet.*

More damning was Ms. Jordan fraternizing with the victim of a gruesome murder, then not divulging this most important information to authorities. But that could be merely an unwillingness to get involved, which definitely did happen amongst the less conscientious citizens of the world.

"Okay, then," he said. He rose and gathered his file folder. "Take her downstairs, set up the video, and let's get on with it."

* * *

Leith did the talking, and he allowed Dion to sit in. He allowed it because it helped him assess this relationship, which may or may not matter somewhere down the road. Jordan came across to him as a woman with nothing to hide. She described her meeting with the boys in the Greer house, and the pity she had taken on them. Fed and bathed them, like some kind of angel of mercy. She had a different name for what she had done — being human.

Looking Leith in the eyes, she apologized sincerely for not reporting to the police upon learning the identity of the dead man. As soon as she saw the composite drawing from the online news — that had been quite a few days after the police — well, Constable Dion, in fact — had first spoken to her, she realized it was Gunner. But by then she was afraid to get involved, and she didn't think her input would be helpful, anyway. Even with those hours she had spent with the men, she really knew little about them. Again, she was dreadfully sorry.

Leith saw Farah Jordan as a flower child — or flower woman. Still, he wasn't convinced of her innocence. After half a lifetime spent on the force, listening to the stories of frauds, thugs, sociopaths, commanding officers, and administrators, he didn't take anything or anyone at face value, ever. Not until he had pressed whatever they had to say through the fine-meshed sieve of doubt.

Could he charge her with something? Probably. Would he? Probably not. He asked her about the girl known only as Aphid. Jordan said she had never counted how many people were in the house, those few times she had seen flickering shadows over there. She had thought they were kids exploring, that's all, and hadn't given it much thought, until some things went missing.

Leith closed down the interview with an announcement of the time being 0136 hours.

As Dion shut off the tape recorder and applied himself to his notes, Leith told Ms. Jordan that he would like her to submit fingerprint impressions to help eliminate the un-knowns found at the crime scene. She said yes, of course, not a problem at all, and accompanied him down the hall.

As they waited in the privacy of the fingerprint station, he asked how she would describe her relationship with Constable Dion.

"A good friend," Ms. Jordan said, with that earnest warmth that could bake bread, if she turned it up high enough.

"It's not a crime if you got romantically involved," Leith told her, not adding that it sure as hell did complicate things, though. It showed a kind of deviousness on her part, one he had to take seriously, since it begged the question: had she gotten involved with the cop for her own nefarious reasons?

But this was all background building at this point, a fishing expedition, and he made sure to speak to her in a chummy, rapport-building way. "Seems to me good friendship takes time to develop. Romance is more of a brush fire. Just saying, in looking at the timeframe of how long you two have known each other, I have to wonder."

She smiled. "A brush fire. Nicely put. Poetic!"

He returned her smile.

"Cal is such a great guy," she said. "How could I not like him instantly?"

"But he's also a police officer, one who would've been interested that you knew the murder victim. Why didn't you tell him?"

"As I said, I didn't think my evidence would advance your investigation in any way. And also, I guess, I didn't want to spoil our friendship."

"Your *good* friendship."

"Yes," she said. "*Good* friendship. Which I'm sure is quite finished by now. Was it wrong of him to be pleasant to me, to come over for dinner, chat? Is he not allowed to have a personal life outside the force?"

"Of course he is. But if he questioned you, even if nothing came of it, he shouldn't be getting personal with you, not until the case closes. That's all."

"I know, and he told me exactly that. He feels so bad about it. But I don't see why. We had one dinner together. Mostly we talked about food."

Her eyes could not just bake bread, but light candles. Of all the liars Leith had interviewed over the years, this young woman took the prize.

Following the fingerprinting procedure, he thanked her, warned her to remain contactable at all times, received her solemn promise to do so, and saw her out the door. When she was gone he returned to the interview room, where Dion was still seated, no longer adding to his notes, but drawing what looked like a mean-faced daisy in the margin.

"Nice woman," Leith said.

"She is," Dion said. "Not too bright, though, sleeping with strangers."

Leith sat and faced him, and the interview was now between themselves. "And the strangers aren't too bright themselves, are they, Cal?"

Maybe Dion got the direct hit, or maybe not, but he agreed wholeheartedly that any stranger who slept with Ms. Jordan was not too bright. "You think she's involved in Stirling's death?" he asked, finally looking up.

The real question being, *How deep in it am I?*

Leith shook his head. "I don't think so. And even if she was, you're right, you couldn't have known. Still, you should have kept your distance. And it's got to end now."

"I know that."

"Don't worry about it. You brought her in soon as you learned of her involvement, and that's all that matters now. Got it?"

"Yes, sir. Thank you," Dion said, before closing up and leaving the room.

The *sir* was new. Leith saw it as just another way of putting distance between them.

* * *

On his way to the parkade, something pinged in Dion's mind, a task or errand he had forgotten to take care of. It was important, maybe critical, but what was it? He tried to count back through his thoughts and locate the buzzing fly, but it eluded him.

What was he forgetting? He would go back through his notes and search, but the chances were slim that he had written it down.

"Write *everything* down," he scolded himself, as he made his way to the stairs. He passed a group of constables on graveyard, and they were watching him. "And stop talking to yourself," he added, as the fire door closed.

In the dark cavern which was the car park, he beeped his Honda Civic open and dropped into the driver's seat. Where was he going? He couldn't even remember that. He ran his hands over his face and skull, and he could almost feel it caving in, bone and brain tissue. Whatever glue they had used to put him together was breaking down. He had another assessment coming up in two weeks — and the tests were getting harder.

He had two weeks to answer one scary question. Fail or quit?

Or to put it another way — quit or fail?

Twenty-Seven

DEMONS

THE NIGHTMARE ALWAYS took place on a straight, woodsy road. Dion was driving. Though the day was bright, the car's interior was dark. Looch Ferraro was in the passenger seat, staring ahead in silence. There was always someone in the back, and the moment of terror would come as the thing leaned forward to speak, never showing its features, a paleness looming forward in the rear-view mirror.

The dream came often, and Dion felt if he tried hard enough, he could take charge, one of these nights, and stay in the moment. He would not wake up, not look away. He would name the back-seat passenger, and in that way kill the dream.

He tried now, and it was painful. He looked at his friend beside him. "Looch?"

Looch didn't speak, but the demon in the back seat did, in a glassy shout. "*Brooke is here!*"

Dion shouted, too. He had flipped over and slammed the blankets with his arm. The demon was gone, his heart was racing, and he was looking at dust motes twirling in a stream of shuttered sunlight. *Brooke?* Brooke was Looch's long-time girlfriend. Dion had left town without saying goodbye, or better yet, *Sorry for killing the love of your life.* Just bang, gone, and there he'd been, up to his knees in the northern snow.

His cellphone rang. This being his day off, he considered letting voice mail kick in. On the third ring he rolled off the mattress and fought with the pile of clothes on the floor, untangled his trousers, located the phone and answered just in time. "Yes?"

The clock radio said 6:45.

"'Morning." Leith's voice was glum in his ear. "It's going to be another of those days. What's this memo about Troy Hamilton?"

"What memo?"

"The memo you left me."

Dion looked at the window, the haziest glow shining through the plastic slats. Morning had broken some time ago. He couldn't recall any memo.

"Jesus," Leith said, correctly interpreting his silence. "Want me to read it to you?"

"I'm just trying to remember —"

"It says, 'Troy Hamilton, brackets, ten, says he knows werewolf,' and you give a bunch of details I can't read. 'Hamilton,' something about three houses, 'Stefano Boone,' S slash B, follow-up.'"

Dion now recalled what he had been trying so hard to remember last night. So he *had* taken steps — at least left a memo. That he couldn't remember leaving the memo, let alone writing it, wasn't good. "What part don't you understand?" he said. "Troy Hamilton lives three houses away from Stefano Boone, and it should be followed up."

"Yes, I got that. We spoke about it earlier, and you were making inquiries. Thing is, Stefano Boone is nowhere to be found, and neither is Troy. The kid's mother just called. Says she looked in his room this morning to roust him out of bed for school, and he's a no-show. His coat and boots are gone. She doesn't know how long he's been missing. She's worried, but says it's probably nothing. Apparently he's gone AWOL before."

"And Boone?"

"We went to pick him up for questioning this morning. He's not home. Nobody's home. Doesn't mean much. For all we know they've all gone to Disneyland."

"Disneyland ..."

"Anyway," Leith said, "I thought you might know something more, but you don't, so that's fine. See you later."

"Wait!" The fuzziness of sleep had vanished, and Dion was sitting on the edge of his bed, putting the pieces together. "You'll put out a search for the Hamilton kid, right? Because maybe it's nothing, but with Boone gone, too, there could be something going on here."

There *was* something going on. The truth was gathering overhead like a storm cloud, and his own act of leaving a memo instead of taking immediate action now struck him as gross negligence. "I'd start with the park. Right? The Headwaters. You'll do that?"

"I'll put the word out."

The promise sounded genuine, but not sharp enough. It lacked urgency. Dion stood up to make himself clear. "No, don't just put the word out. Make sure it happens. I'll come in and assist."

"No need. Stick to your schedule, unless you're advised otherwise. I'll talk to Monty about setting up a search. Thank you." Leith hung up.

Dion got dressed for the long, cold day ahead and left his apartment.

* * *

Surprisingly, he found a search was getting underway when he arrived. He was told if he hurried, he could catch a ride in one of the two SUVs headed out to the Lynn Valley Headwaters.

He jumped into the back of the Chev driven by Corporal Montgomery and found himself sitting next to Jackie Randall. She was dressed like him, in a hastily thrown together outfit of jeans, solid muck-proof boots, sweater, and lightweight RCMP jacket. She told him she too was pulling extra duty. "This is a big one in my career," she told him. "Chasing demons."

Dion wasn't feeling up to returning her grin. If the Hamilton kid was dead because of his own inability to foresee this happening, the day was going to end in tears.

Up front, Montgomery was in conversation with other members. He sounded cheerful. His mood had improved since Halloween, and he seemed to have bounced back from whatever had been bothering him, which was probably that thing called *overwork*. Would Randall notice? Would she take it as a good indication that her suspicions were unfounded, and lay off her private investigation?

Dion hoped she would. She had not called him with updates lately, nor stopped him in the hallway demanding his help. Maybe she had taken his advice and dropped it — or lost interest, or faith, or found herself busy enough with real-life responsibilities.

They were on Mountain Highway now, no lights or siren, doing the limit. Dion wished they would spike it, *move*, but his worry didn't seem contagious. One of the men in the front seat was asking Montgomery if a wedding date had been picked yet, and where was the ol' stress level at. Next to Dion, Jackie Randall leaned forward to hear. Dion did, too.

"No date yet," Montgomery told his colleague. "Stress level: zero for me, eleven for Tori. You know girls, every eyelash has to be perfect." He raised his voice to carry. "And by the way, everyone in this vehicle is on the guest list."

Most of the crew hooted. Dion caught Montgomery's eyes in the mirror, a flash of blue. The eyes weren't looking at him so much as seeking out the person beside him, Jackie Randall, who had just snorted. "Ugh," she said. "Does that mean I have to dust off one of my two dresses?"

Arriving at the Lynn Headwaters, the same park where Aldobrandino Rosetti had met his end and where two boys had spotted a werewolf, Montgomery pulled the SUV in near several other police vehicles. Members gathered around Montgomery as he flattened a map on the hood of a cruiser and set out search zones with a highlighter. Dion looked for Leith within the group, but didn't see him. He and Randall were assigned a swatch of paths lower in the Mesachee that followed Lynn Creek.

"It's not the wedding day that's stressed her out," Randall said, as she stood with Dion, waiting for final instructions. "It's that moment she can't backspace out of existence. The Halloween joyride from hell. But I'm not so sure it was a joyride. I've found out something that's *very* interesting."

She hadn't given up, then.

"You've been prying?"

"I wanted to give it one more try. I drove by, but again, no sign of her car. I was going to keep going, but she popped out the front door, dressed for running. She saw me and flagged me down, and I had no choice but stop. She asked what I was doing there. I told her I was here to see Monty about something. She didn't believe me, so I skipped ahead to Plan B and told her what I think happened."

Dion winced. Montgomery was out of earshot, but he lowered his voice. "You're in for it, Jackie. Tori would have told him you were out there harassing her."

"Or not. At the end of our conversation, she said she wasn't going to pester him with this bullshit. I still thought she would for sure, but in fact, I don't think she has. At least, he doesn't seem to be bothered and is just as nice to me as ever."

"Let's hope it stays that way. What happened next?"

"After yelling at me for a while, she opened the garage and showed me the car."

The garage had been stacked with boxes and sports gear when Dion had been at the house. So between then and now, the couple had cleared it out and parked the Acura in there instead. But there was nothing sinister about that. It was just the natural progression of re-arrangement as two people settled into their new place.

"Tori's car has a few dings and scratches, for sure," Randall went on. "That plastic strip under the front is cracked, and there's a dent on the rear left quarter. But there's also a faint indentation on the nose, left front."

Dion raised his brows. A front left indentation was what the traffic analyst predicted, following the Sunset Boulevard set of indicia.

"I pointed it out to her," Randall said. "Asked her again if she had hit a trick-or-treater on Halloween. She denied it. My ears are still ringing. So I said to her, if you didn't hit the kid, then of course you won't mind me hauling this off to the shop for a forensic examination, right, just to rule you out completely? And she called me a crazy bitch and kicked me off the property — I'm talking a literal kick, but luckily I dodged it. Anyway, I guess we're on to Plan C."

Dion didn't want to hear what Plan C was, and he didn't have to, as Randall was looking down the parking lot, frowning. "What's that?"

The day was dark, the area blurred by a low mist, but Dion recognized the figure that seemed to be inching toward them. "Ray Starkey."

"A friend?"

Hardly. Starkey was the old guy who had come along to ask questions as Dion had stood with Montgomery outside the Greer house. Starkey had pointed out his own place for them, a little green-roofed house down the block. He had also told Montgomery about some kind of super-wolves lurking around the neighbourhood, and had cast accusatory stares at Dion, as if he were one of them.

The little figure gathered form as it moved closer through the mist.

"You look spooked," Randall said. "Who is he?"

"I'm not spooked," Dion lied. Starkey passed them, hunched and slow moving. He proceeded through the group of men and women in their bushwhacking clothes, straight to Corporal Montgomery's side. Montgomery looked around and down, and Randall and Dion moved closer to hear what Starkey was saying.

"'Scuse me, sir. What's happening here, mind me asking?"

Dion saw recognition in Montgomery's eyes, followed by irritation. Unlike that day outside the Greer house, he was multi-tasking now, and not up for a PR chat. "A child's gone missing," he told Starkey, and huffed out a breath as he looked around his crew, asking who had that photo of the missing boy. He was handed a copy and showed it to Starkey. "Troy Hamilton. Ten years old. Know him?"

"No, sir," Starkey said. "Don't know the boy."

"Right. Well, we're going to be searching the woods hereabouts, so if you don't mind —"

"It's the wolfs, hey?" Starkey said.

"There he goes again," Dion said. Arms crossed, he smiled down at Randall.

"We don't know what it is," Montgomery said. He turned to carry on where he'd left off, addressing the team, but was tapped on the arm.

"Except they're not wolfs," Starkey said. He dropped his voice so low that Dion had to step closer to hear. "I know what it is what's doing it."

Montgomery raised his voice, punching up the pace. "Yes? What's *doing* it, sir?"

Everyone was watching the old man now. If nothing else, he was a good storyteller. "It's nothing you can catch by the tail." He gazed around himself at the men and women of the search party and spoke up for all to hear. "It's nothing you can look in the eye, and nothing you can name. It's not wolfs as such. It's evil spirits, is what it is, and listen to me good, you boys go into them woods, you're not coming out alive."

Beside Dion, Jackie Randall murmured, "O-*kay*, get out the butterfly nets."

Some in the team worked at not snickering, but Montgomery stood deadpan. He said, "I'll tell you what, sir. Spirits or no spirits, we've got a job to do here. But later today, when he has a moment, this nice young man over here" — he indicated Dion — "will come by your place and get a full and proper statement from you. Just give him your address before you leave. Okay? Thank you, sir."

Either Montgomery had not noticed Starkey's anti-Dion attitude at their earlier encounter, or he had made the assignment as a bad joke. Starkey was looking as alarmed as Dion was feeling. Randall had been paying attention to all the actions and reactions, and said, "You two have some kind of history, do you?"

"There's something about me he doesn't like. Don't ask what. I didn't do anything to him. I didn't even speak to him."

"Maybe you're an evil spirit."

The secretive murmuring between Starkey and Montgomery was taking too long, and Montgomery seemed to age a few years as impatience wormed across his brow, his smile lines furrowing the wrong way. But he gave Starkey a last word, which seemed to satisfy the little messenger of bad tidings, who turned and went shuffling away down the road, shoulders pulled together, avoiding Dion like a pollutant.

Dion watched him shrink back into the shadows, toward the long road that would take him back to town.

"He thinks you're First Nations," Montgomery called out, grinning. "Said he's got nothing against 'Indians,' but he'd rather deal with a white man. Like me. I told him you're whiter than he is, but he didn't believe me."

Dion wasn't sure of his lineage mix. He had dark eyes that in the mirror sometimes looked roundish, and other times almond-shaped, depending on how mean he was feeling. These days it was mostly almond, which gave him an aboriginal or Asian look. Some research would end the mystery. Maybe someday.

"What did you say that put the big smile on his face?" he asked Montgomery.

"You're off the hook, Cal. I spared him having to deal with you. Said I'd stop by his place after we're done here, chat about wolves and Windigos to his heart's content." Montgomery turned to address the team with some last instructions. Police dogs would be called in next, along with extra crews of volunteers, but they might be a while, so for now they were on their own. He gave a double clap of the hands and told them to go get the kid, double quick. "Let's save our volunteers the trouble and get this done before they can even get their boots on."

Unlikely, knowing the size of the forest, Dion thought. He and Randall left the parking area and headed up toward the Mesachee. Once on the narrow, brushy lower path, they walked single file, keeping their eyes to left and right for evidence of recent passage. They called out Troy's name as they went, or used sticks to bat aside foliage, sending flocks of sparrows into the sky. The underbrush was thick and wet, so if the boy lay hidden too far off the path, dead or alive, he would be hard to spot — maybe impossible.

Whenever a side path accessed the rushing waters of Lynn Creek, they climbed down to explore its rocky beach. Randall's stick upturned a dead cat, eye sockets writhing with bugs. "Look at this," she said. "All that life, all that fierce beauty, reduced to this. You, me, all of us. It's going to come. Do you ever get scared when you look down the tunnel of time?"

"Never," Dion said, and looked away from the maggots.

"Me neither," Randall said.

The path ascended, and they stood to rest on crude wooden steps built by bicycle outlaws, looking down on the far side of the river, a reservoir of fog. "You were going to tell me you found out something interesting," Dion said. "You said *very*."

"Curious, are you? What happened to your hear no evil, see no evil policy?"

"Just spit it out."

"Linnae Avenue," she said.

"What about it?"

"Know where it is?"

He didn't, and was losing patience. He was opening his mouth to say, *What about it?* when Randall pointed along the river and up the bank. "What's that there? There, see? The black thing."

Dion saw what appeared to be the mouth of a small cave, some three feet in diameter and shrouded by bushes.

Randall cleaned her glasses and had another look. "An intergalactic wormhole?"

"Or a culvert."

"Let's take a look."

They descended the stairs, made their way to the river, bushwhacked and splashed their way along the rocky shore to the area of the cave-like opening, and found themselves looking up at an old metal culvert leading under one of the Mesachee paths. It sat on a natural shelf above, and water dribbled from its lip into the scrub below.

Randall had been faster than Dion, scrambling up the rocks, stretching to get a look inside. She called into the tunnel, "Troy? Are you in there?"

Nothing but her question bouncing around with a metallic ring.

"Can you see to the other end?" Dion asked.

She was too short. She lifted her light and peeked. "There's some branches or something in the middle. Oh, wait. Something moved. Hell, it's dark. I can't —"

They both heard something within the tunnel shifting. Rats?

Dion climbed up past Randall and used his own flashlight to pick through the flotsam. "Troy? It's Constable Dion. Remember, we talked the other day? Are you in there? It's safe to come out now."

From the pile of debris a pale little face popped into the flashlight beam and stared back at him.

Twenty-Eight

SPIRAL

A MUDDY AND BEDRAGGLED Troy Hamilton crawled on hands and knees to the culvert's opening, and with a bit of prompting, dropped into Dion's arms.

He responded only with head shakes and nods to Dion's questions, "How are you? Are you hurt?" He seemed to have no broken bones, no deep wounds, but there were at least a few scratches. Some on his hands and legs, maybe from climbing and scrambling, and some purple markings about the face and throat. He had only socks on his feet, and his glasses were missing. His clothes were soaked and smelled of urine. He was shivering violently, and wouldn't or couldn't speak.

Randall was on her radio, notifying Montgomery. Dion gathered Troy close in his arms. Fighting not to land in the sludge himself, he made his way down to the river with the kid clinging to his neck like a scared chimp. The climb was long and awkward, the kid heavier than he looked, and

Dion not as fit as he had once been. But he made it to the river, then up one trail, and down another, and finally to the parking lot, with Randall following close behind.

Montgomery and many of the crew were by the cars to meet them. An ambulance had been called, Montgomery said. And grateful parents were on their way. The team had been advised to stop searching for the kid, to muster at the culvert and start searching for evidence. "Fabulous job," he said to Randall, as Dion tried to unlatch the boy's arms from around his neck. "Great work, you two."

Troy had stopped shivering, but was refusing to let go, be set down, stand on his own two feet. Montgomery smiled at the clinging boy. "Mom and Dad are on their way over, Troy, my man. How are ya feeling? Little cold, huh?"

Dion dearly wished Troy would loosen his stranglehold, which was doing just that, strangling him.

Montgomery had answered a radio call and was now back with news. "Gotta go. They've found something upslope in the Mesachee, just up from the famous Rock. Ident's heading up there." He tried to catch Troy's eyes one last time. "You'll be fine, kiddo. Everything's okay now. Good man."

Troy turned away from the grin and buried his face harder in Dion's shoulder.

Montgomery left to escort newly arrived Ident members to the find, showering compliments as he went. "Good work, guys. Proud of you all."

The ambulance arrived. A sedan pulled in sharply, and Troy's parents arrived to pitch in and save Dion

CREEP

from strangulation. Reasoning didn't work, and neither did bribery. Finally they resorted to physical force, and with a cry of protest, Troy came unglued. He was removed to the rear of the ambulance to be checked for visible damage, taking the crowd with him, and Dion was free to walk about the parking lot, shaking his limbs and catching his breath.

Boy, ambulance attendant, one parent, and a team member disappeared into the ambulance. The doors swung shut, and off they went. The sedan driven by Troy's other parent scudded out after it, the team dispersed to their duties, and the parking lot was left all but empty under cloudy afternoon skies.

"What do we do now?" Randall asked.

"I guess we wait."

"Heroes of the day, and this is the gratitude we get."

They leaned against the SUV and looked at the wet wilderness. Randall tried to strike up her interrupted conversation about the Tori intrigue, but Dion told her he was too tired to talk about it. Hold the thought. All he wanted right now was silence.

Randall was more or less silent for fifteen minutes, until Montgomery returned from the Mesachee Woods, snapping his fingers, *time to go*. They all climbed into the Suburban. Montgomery drove, Dion by the passenger window, stinking like culvert sludge and piss, and Randall sat in the middle.

"What did the team find up there?" she asked Montgomery, as he steered out of the park.

If Montgomery knew Randall was hot on his tail, Dion observed, he was doing a good job of not letting on. Maybe Tori had meant it when she told Randall she wasn't going to bother her fiancé with all this bullshit.

"So far, a pair of child-sized spectacles, child-sized running shoes, and blood," Montgomery told her. "Not a lot of blood, but some."

Randall showed Dion a snapshot she had taken on her phone, a muddy and exasperated hero with a muddy and frightened rescuee wrapped around his neck. "Hard to say who's the more traumatized, hey?"

Dion took the phone from her, as if for a closer look, and touched the little garbage-can icon. The image was gone, and he handed the phone back.

"Hey!" she cried, hitting him. "That was going on my Twitter feed."

"No, it sure as hell wasn't."

Of course it wasn't, and Randall knew it, but she punched him again, anyway. Then she suggested they all go for drinks to celebrate today's win.

Dion smiled. Even caked in sludge, he felt, if not great, then better. He hadn't raised the alarm as fast as he would have liked, but he had raised it in time. Troy was alive and seemed not badly damaged, at least physically. Yet whatever had happened to him up there in the Mesachee Woods, the effects would run deep. It was a tempered triumph, at best. "All I want to do right now," he said, "is get into a hot shower."

He got his wish at the detachment, standing under the streaming water. The heat eased the knots in his shoulders, but not in his gut. He couldn't shake the feeling of guilt, which was not good. In his job, shaking guilt was a survival skill.

Before the crash he had been good at letting it all slide off. He'd been resilient. Whatever the fuck-ups of the day, he would party hearty at night and get on with life.

Must get back into the routine. Do his best, and stop worrying about every damn thing.

While he stood towel-drying his hair before the change room mirrors, Montgomery showed up and leaned against the wall. In the mirror he looked like a schoolyard bully about to pick a fight.

Dion watched him, wondering if this was the coming fallout from Randall's bullheaded inquiries.

"You're kind of a marvel, you know," Montgomery said. "You put a name on our werewolf, you pushed the search, and you found the kid. Who needs a full team when you've got Cal Dion on the case? I think if you play your cards right, you'll be back in GIS in no time." He was smiling. Not a bully, then, but an advocate.

"Any advice on playing my cards right?"

Montgomery's brows went up. "I'm so glad you asked. You want advice, you've come to the right guy." He doled out the advice as Dion pulled on his spare clothes. "It's not enough to be smart. You've got to project your smartness. Be confident, brilliant. Open your mouth more. Make yourself heard. You're too quiet, and that's what I keep hearing from your superiors. You're not a team player. You don't give anything away, and that makes people nervous."

They were kind words, but not the concrete help Dion would have been looking for, if he had been looking for help — which he wasn't. He had asked to be polite. Or maybe it was to get a better idea of what Montgomery was up to. Whether he liked it or not, Dion was becoming Jackie Randall's sidekick.

He nodded agreeably as he combed his damp hair.

"You also need someone on your side, someone with clout," Montgomery said. He curled a bicep. "That's me. Lucky for you, I'm your biggest fan, and I'm friendly with those who can make or break your career. Now, finish your preening and let's go talk to young Troy Hamilton. It's more your case than anyone's, seems to me, so I'm putting you in charge of asking the questions. And besides, the kid is, well, *attached* to you."

Dion recalled his last interview with Troy, the little psychopath's artful dodging and stonewalling. "I'd rather just listen in, if it's all right."

Montgomery flung out exasperated hands. "Didn't I just mention playing your cards? And what I mean by that is, play 'em. I don't want to alarm you, constable, but you've got a hell of a lot of people to impress, so you better start bedazzling. I can help you along, but I'm only going to back a winner. Get me?" He shadow boxed, a one-two punch.

The punch came too close to Dion's head, and he ducked aside, but laughing. In the spirit of renewal, he grabbed the cologne he packed in his kit but rarely used and misted himself lightly, eying Montgomery in the mirror. "You're still working on Breanna Ferris? Is that going anywhere?"

"Yes, to the first question, not far, to the second," Montgomery said. "What's that stuff?"

Dion showed him the bottle of Body Shop cologne.

"Nice." Montgomery winked and turned to leave. "A helluva lot better than what you had all over you before. Eau de latrine. Phew."

* * *

In the case room — on a case some called Operation Werewolf — Dion waited with the others for Troy Hamilton to be examined and handed over for questioning. Leith was present, and the head of the unit, Sergeant Mike Bosko, arrived for an update. Bosko the bear, taller than anyone else in the room, and looking younger than ever with the wire-rimmed glasses he usually wore absent for some reason from his heavy, pale face.

In some ways, Bosko was everything Dion wanted to be. Bosko was smart. He seemed to know something about everything. He retained facts. He had a cool, inquiring mind. He was effortlessly diplomatic. He was perceptive, analytical, unworried, and unhurried. In short, Dion's diametric opposite.

In a different world, he mused, he would probably like Bosko.

He watched Bosko conferring with Leith and Montgomery, and stood back, not yet part of the discussion. He wondered if Montgomery would actually pass on those glowing commendations, as promised. Maybe he was about to do that now.

As if on cue, Montgomery nodded at him to come over, join the discussion. Dion made himself taller and walked over. He smiled at his superiors. Bosko was smiling, too, as was Montgomery. Even Leith looked pleased. It was a smile-fest, for sure.

"So, I hear you're the one who found the boy," Bosko said.

"Constable Randall spotted the culvert," Dion told him. "Troy might have recognized my voice because I talked to him a couple days ago. It's the familiarity, I think, that got him out of hiding."

"Well, we're all impressed."

"Thank you, sir!"

Bosko gave him a playful salute, told Montgomery to keep him posted, then was off, chatting with some of the other members briefly before leaving the room.

Montgomery and Leith spent some time congratulating Dion now, and talking about his future. Leith agreed that Dion should conduct the interview of the Hamilton boy, and yes, should also be back upstairs with the detectives, and Leith would do his bit to try to make it happen. Dion thanked him. Montgomery entertained Leith with a description of Troy throttling Dion, and the full-team effort to pull the kid loose. Dion described his fear of imminent death as Troy's arms tightened.

All three men were laughing by the end of the story. The Farah Jordan fiasco seemed to be forgotten and forgiven. A nice little vignette of team spirit, in Dion's mind. A great act by all.

* * *

Across at the hospital, a uniformed member stood posted outside Troy's ICU room. "Keeping my eye out for stray wolves," he joked.

Within the room, Troy's parents sat in armchairs, reading magazines. Young Troy sat in bed, wearing pajamas and what must be his spare set of eyeglasses. Even cleaned up, he looked wet and ruffled and bewildered, though the doctor had assessed him as "ready to talk."

Dion didn't think the boy looked ready for anything, but Montgomery sat on the edge of the bed and told Troy what a soldier he was, and what a hero he would be if he could say what had happened to him today. Could he do that?

Troy nodded at Montgomery, but was gazing past him at his rescuer. Montgomery changed places with Dion and let him do the talking.

Dion didn't need to break the ice much. After saying, "Hi, Troy, you look great," Troy launched right into it, in breathless, broken snatches. "Stefano, he — he turned in — into a — a wo — a wo — a wolf, and he, he b-bit me."

Evidence backed up the claim. With the mud washed off, the cuts and bruises were standing out startlingly clear on the boy's pale skin.

"Where did he bite you?" Dion said.

Troy showed him the underbelly of his arm, the skin abraded, the soft tissue purple with ruptured vessels. The incision pattern did resemble a human bite mark, open-mouthed and vicious, but it fell short of an actual tear or gouge.

"He never did anything like that before?"

Troy shook his head.

"Tell me what happened, right from the start."

At the end of the hour, Dion's notes, verbatim except for the stuttering, read, in part, "I went in his window, and he said we would go for a walk, and we went in the woods. He pushed me down and he kept hitting me on the ground, and I hit my head on the rocks, and it hurt. He kept pushing me on the ground, and he tried to eat me. And I hit him, and he had a nosebleed. And he went away."

The lumps and bruises on Troy's head were not serious looking. Concussion had been ruled out. His coat had been unzipped and his shoes had come off, but the rest of his clothing seemed intact. He made no allusion to sexual interference, nor had any evidence of it been found on physical examination.

The attack had been brutal, but on Dion's scale of viciousness, aside from the bite mark, he would call it more in the *buffeting* range.

At the end of the interview, he asked Troy how Stefano had turned into a wolf, and Troy told him that Stefano wore a wolf suit, but he really *had* become a wolf. It wasn't just a mask.

Perceptive assessment from a child, Dion thought. He asked Troy where Stefano was now, and Troy said he didn't know. When he ran out of questions, Dion finished with one last comment, for Troy's ears only, though everyone in the room would hear it. "I'm sorry this happened to you."

"It's okay," Troy said.

Calmly spoken. Maybe it was just a side effect of shock, but the boy seemed markedly different from how he'd been in that frustrating interview in his home on

Dempsey. Elevated, even, as he made the effort to release Dion from guilt with a gesture, a hand lifted like Jesus, and his parting words: "It's not your fault. Really."

* * *

Leith was telling JD about his amazing luck as they waited by Monty's desk for him to finish a call. "The house isn't an estate sale," he told her. "It belongs to Pat Klugman's mother, Wilma, who's not dead like I thought she was."

"Good news for Wilma," JD said.

"Right. She's still alive, but had to move into a nursing home, and Pat and her husband were tasked with selling the property. The day we viewed it they had brought their kids along. Alison was out back and found the daughter, she's about fifteen, sulking on the steps, and got talking with her. That was Wilma's granddaughter."

"Is this going to be an incredibly long story with no twist?" JD asked.

"It's got a twist," Leith promised, but he got the message and cut to the chase. "It turns out grandmother and granddaughter are close, and they both love the house. They wanted someone in there who wouldn't tear it down. At least that's what Alison got from her conversation. The rest is just guesswork, but we think the granddaughter put the bug in her grandmother's ear that we should get the place, and since it's Wilma's decision, that's exactly what happened. And here I am, a happy homeowner."

"Wow, it's like a fairy tale," JD said. "As someone looking forward to a future of studio flats and ever-rising rents, I'm happy for you. I hope you put an inspection clause in the contract?"

Leith shrugged. "Don't need to. I was in construction before joining up. I can fix anything. Just need a pile of nails and a jumbo box of Band-Aids. You're going to help me paint, though, right?"

JD sniffed, but didn't say no, and that, Leith thought, was progress.

Monty was done with his call. "Am I going crazy," he said, "Or is our main suspect an honest-to-god werewolf?"

The search was now on for Troy Hamilton's attacker, starting from the culvert and radiating outward. Police dogs and Ident specialists were fanned through the woods, and members cruised the streets or hiked the trails of Lynn Valley, eyeing everybody and asking questions.

JD answered Montgomery's flip question with a sharp reply. "Our main suspect is Stefano Boone, who's come to believe he's a wolf, and desperately needs psychiatric attention, is what."

"I'm not so sure of that," Monty said. "If Stefano Boone killed our crawl space victim, he was definitely in wolf form when he did it. Ben Stirling was chewed up by some pretty nasty wolf-sized incisors."

"Actually," Leith said, "Stirling was mauled by a large dog, probably while he was alive. A whole set of experts said so. In which case, his death may well have nothing to do with Stefano Boone. Let's keep that in mind."

A toolmark specialist, a forensic odontologist, a veterinarian, and others had weighed in on the damages to Ben Stirling — the gouges, streaking tears, torn scalp, nicks and grooves — and concluded they were the bite and claw marks of a large dog. A dog had *not* sawn off the arm, however.

Monty took the rebuffs with a shoot-me shrug.

"I think what we're looking at is a burglary gone wrong. Large dogs are often sentries, and sentries and burglars don't mix, do they?" JD said.

Leith nodded. "Right. Say Stirling was breaking into a property on which some sort of illegal activity was underway. There's a dog on duty, and with or without its owner's consent, the dog kills Stirling. Now there's a mess that has to be cleaned up."

"And they can't report it, because they're meth cooks, or processing hot cars, or whatever," JD agreed. "Which probably means it happened in the industrial zone. Or elsewhere."

Monty suggested Surrey, his old turf. "Wide-open spaces, plenty of hideaways, strained police resources: the land of opportunity."

Leith was thinking of Cloverdale, contained within Surrey — a great place for an off-duty cop to hide a body. But that was another case and another worry. He stood by the map on the wall, found Lynn Valley, and placed his thumb on it. "So how does his body end up in the crawl space of the house he's illegally occupying? Maybe he's got connections with that lab or chop shop. Works there, knows the owner, got on their bad side, owes them money. Maybe it wasn't a run-in with a dog. Maybe the dog was told to attack. But one way or another, his killer is intimate enough with him to know where he lives."

Had they written off Ben's friend, roomie, and accomplice, young Joe Battar, too soon? Leith wondered. He told the others of his concern. "If Battar was working with Ben, not just living with him, he might be the link between the house and the murder. Time to dig into his soul a little deeper."

"Waste of time," JD said. "Battar's soul is an open book. He's harmless."

She was probably right, Leith realized. But right now, the harmless soul was the best lead they had.

* * *

Having changed into joggers and kangaroo jacket, a baseball cap shading his eyes, Dion sat at his desk in the detachment, twisting a paperclip into a spiral. He wondered if Farah Jordan had ever owned a dog, or had access to one. She wouldn't have the strength to haul a man's body to the Greer house, up over the fence, and then drag it under, in his estimation. But she could have had help. A boyfriend, maybe. Seemed she wasn't too particular about the kind of men she picked up.

He had been given the rest of the day off, having strained his shoulder in carrying the boy from the culvert. A minor physical strain that was nothing, really, except a good excuse to sit and twist paperclips. He thought of his jolly little meeting with Montgomery and Leith, them both laying it on thick, telling him what a great job he'd done, how he'd go places — Leith putting on an act for Montgomery, and Montgomery — maybe —

putting on an act for Dion, and Dion just doing his best not to be a defeatist.

He pulled on his jacket and left the detachment. There was something he had been meaning to take care of for the longest time, an exorcism of sorts, and since he had the day off, he might as well do it now. The trick was to just get in the car and barrel out there. Don't overthink it, don't fret, just go.

Once he was on the scene, far out there in Cloverdale, where his life had swerved so badly off course, he would finally know what to do with what was left of himself.

Twenty-Nine

SHUDDER

NOVEMBER WAS A GREAT month for rain on the Lower Mainland. It came down hard now, and already it was diluting Dion's plan. What kind of a plan was it, anyway? Go to the scene of the crash that had taken so much from him, stand there and, what? Talk to Looch? In this kind of downpour, even communications with the dead would be washed away in streams of mud.

Don't think. Just go.

The Ironworkers Memorial Bridge crossed the Burrard Inlet, then the thoroughfare dipped into a tunnel and became Highway 1, broadening into an eight-lane river of traffic as the city fell away behind him. He drove the limit in the gloom until conditions forced him to slow. It was the rain, buckets of it coming down, competing with the windshield wipers, messing with visibility. He was driving slower than the traffic around him, he realized. Dangerously slow. Finally he rolled to a stop on the shoulder with the hazards flashing.

It was a typhoon. He folded his arms over the steering wheel to wait it out. The other drivers caromed past on their daily commute, home to Surrey, Abbotsford, Chilliwack. The engine idled and the wipers whined and slapped, fighting off the flood. Blurry, clear, blurry, clear.

He had come out this way in the summer and found the intersection where Looch had died. But finding the crash site hadn't been his objective. He was trying to work backwards and find the gravel pit, where he would try to figure out if the body was still there or not. However unwise it may have been, it was something he had to do. He had found the accident scene and the pit itself. He had stood and looked around, but couldn't recall where the body lay. The place looked undisturbed, though, and he felt assured that the dead man, Stouffer, still rotted underfoot. Strange, because it was a shallow grave, temporary. He and Looch would have put Stouffer elsewhere, and a whole lot deeper, if they hadn't been seen by the girl with pink hair. Like an evil sprite, she had led them on a chase, straight into the path of a speeding Camaro.

The story would have turned out so differently, if not for the girl. Looch would still be alive. He would be here to share the burden, help figure it out, make it go away.

It wasn't going away. Sitting in his car in the rain, Dion wondered if the body had been found. But if it had, it would have been identified. The name Stouffer would have hit the news, and Dion would have known. On the other hand, maybe even if the body was found, even if the name was mentioned, the story could have faded so fast that he hadn't caught wind of it. A low-life was dead, a murder unsolved. Happened a lot in the Lower Mainland.

But then IHIT would have looked at the timeline, the proximity, considered all the unanswered questions surrounding Dion's crash, linked him with the body in the gravel pit, and come knocking on his door. Or maybe it was a work in progress.

It didn't matter. He was out here not to worry about his past crimes, but to visit the place where Looch had died. It seemed the best place to say goodbye, and ask for some advice while he was at it.

Except the rain wasn't going to let him get there. He was pulled over, miles from his destination, too cowed by the thundering of water on metal to carry on. He watched the river of headlights and taillights. He saw lights in the sky, a chopper passing overhead, and it struck him then that he was being watched, no longer in the abstract sense, but literally. Drones, agents, tracking devices. They had their methods.

His dashboard looked untampered with, but so what? Easy enough to plant something, have him monitored. If that's what they were doing, then they knew where he was right now, and they were wondering what he was up to. Or maybe they were well aware of what he had done, and were just waiting for him to prove it.

The eye in the sky belonged to Mike Bosko, he was sure of it. Experimentally, he drew a sharp, loud breath. He laid a hand on his chest. His heart was pounding hard. Were they graphing that out, too, tracking his emotions? He squeezed his eyes shut.

On the seat beside him his cellphone tweedled, making him jump. He watched it tweedle into silence. The second time it rang he lifted it to his ear. "Dion."

"Cal, it's Jackie," said the voice. "I'm glad I caught you. I just wanted to know if you're okay."

"I'm okay," he said, and presto, his anxieties sprouted another tentacle. Was Randall after him, too? The whole hit-and-run scenario could have been concocted. A trust builder, a scam. A Mr. Big scenario in reverse. "Why wouldn't I be?"

"Well, lookit. It seems to me I've put you in an awkward spot, and you're obviously conflicted. So I want you to know, you've done nothing wrong. It wasn't your theory, it was mine. All you did was answer my questions, right? I'm going to leave you out of it, from now on. Consider yourself untangled."

He gaped at the highway. There was a question he had been saving up for their next meeting. Linnae Avenue. But if she was shutting him out, it no longer mattered.

She went on in her usual snappy way. "And you're right. I'm putting it to bed on my end, too. If anything, I'll hand my notes over to Internal. I just wanted to give you the heads up, my friend, in case I do that, and in case they want to get in touch with you about it. Otherwise, there's just no proof, and I'm not going to waste any more time on it. Sorry I dragged you into it. I owe you a drink, okay?"

Her rapid-fire voice was annoying, but good, too, pulling him out of what felt like a bad dream and back into a less silly reality. The enemy fire strafing his car was just another full-blown west coast downpour, and Mike Bosko had better things to do than monitor anybody's heartbeat. The hit and run was real, Breanna Ferris was dead, and if Randall wanted to drop the conspiracy theory, he was more than happy to give it his stamp of approval.

"Good," he said. "But since you did confront Tori, we should meet and talk over how to deal with any possible flak. Don't hand it to Internal until we talk it over. We could do that now, except I'm in the middle of something here."

Technically, it wasn't a lie. With no breaks in the traffic, trucks and cars were thrumming by with a wet hiss, rocking his car on its shocks. Definitely in the middle of something. He said, "Denny's, in a couple hours?"

She surprised him then with, "Probably not necessary at this point. I've got it well in hand."

"I think it is necessary," he said. "We can't leave it hanging. I'm part of this whole thing. You saw to that, right? We need to debrief."

A slight hesitation on her end, and he had the sudden, sinking feeling that between this morning and now, something had gone off the rails.

"Yes, all right," she said. Not with her usual zeal.

"What's happening, Jackie?"

"What's happening is what I said is happening. But you're right, we should meet. Denny's, in two hours, say six thirty. That works for me. Bye."

There it was again, a different ring to her voice. She was lying to him.

"Wait," he said. "Linnae." It was something he wanted to nail down, before it got lost again in his own mind. "You said it's interesting, so what about it?"

"It's not interesting at all. It was me, a camper, making up campfire stories, like you said. Just another false lead. Anyway, see you soon."

He ended the call, signalled, waited for a gap in traffic, and pulled into the frantic rush of the slow lane, worrying. He would have to drive several kilometres south before an off-ramp would get him turned back homeward. Visiting Looch would just have to wait for another day.

* * *

From his apartment, Dion phoned the detachment to check on the progress of the Stefano Boone manhunt. Doug Paley told him that the wolf was still at large, but evidence — blood spatter left like bread crumbs — had guided them up a barely traversable trail that linked the Mesachee with the residential plateau above. A quick connection for Boone between home and forest. Not an easy trail, unless you're a wolf.

Also, there had been a sighting of a wild-eyed young man dressed in black fur, crouched at the curb near Dempsey. So the search was off the park for now and focusing on the area of Boone's home. There was no answer at his parents' house, where he lived in the basement. No answer from his cellphone, or from his parents' landline either. No vehicle sat in the driveway. Failing that, Paley told him, a search of the Headwaters park would get underway.

Dion had doubts. "All nine thousand acres?"

"If that's what it takes. I'll tell you what Ident found at the scene of the crime, though. Kind of fun. Tiny tufts of black fur snagged in the brambles. A whole series of them. Not biological fur — synthetic. We've got the bastard's polymeric DNA."

"Montgomery said there was blood at the scene, as well. It probably wasn't Troy's, as he didn't seem badly cut, so the attacker was wounded?"

"If so, not badly. It was a spattering, a drop pattern," Paley said. "A cut or a nosebleed — who knows. Nice that he left a calling card, anyhow. By the way, I see you wormed your way back into GIS. Congratulations."

"I'm a marvel. Just ask Corporal Montgomery."

Paley laughed and hung up.

At 6:00 p.m., Dion was at Denny's, half an hour early. He tried Jackie Randall's cellphone to let her know he was here, to see if she could move the meeting up, but her phone went to voice mail.

He sighed and settled in to kill time, lulled by the drifty music, MacArthur Park melting in the dark. Halfway through his decaf and still ahead of schedule, he called her again. This time she answered on the fourth ring, saying, "Hello," breathlessly. "Hoo," she said. "Steep." She didn't sound like she was sitting in her car, on her way to meet him, but like she was engaged in blood-pumping exercise.

"Jackie?" he said. "I know it's only six fifteen, but I'm sitting here —"

She cut him off, saying, "Sorry, Cal. Miscalculated. I'll be a little late. Make it seven?"

"Frankly, no." He looked down the length of the restaurant to its exit. "I'll tell you what. You call me when you're free, and we'll meet wherever is handy. Jackie? Hello?"

Silence. She had hung up, without apology or explanation. That wasn't like her. And where the hell was she? *Steep.* He frowned out the window. The tone of voice she used with him was always slightly jokey, whatever they were talking about. The few words she had huffed at him just now were far from amused. She sounded … irked?

He tried her number again. Got her answering service.

She was climbing a steep trail. Where else but at the Headwaters? She was a good climber, and it would take quite an incline to make her puff like that. That could explain the call cutting out. She hadn't hung up, but stepped out of range. That could be the Mesachee, where the signal was iffy.

She must have been dispatched to the scene. Maybe the werewolf had been found, and he, Dion, was being left out of the loop. Irritated, he paid for his coffee, got into his car, and drove.

But a dispatch wasn't the answer either, he saw as he approached the park gates. There was no evidence of a police presence in the park, now that the crime scene had been processed and Stefano had been tracked back to civilization. No cops, no hikers, nobody.

Just one car. At the end of the parking lot, nearest the footbridge, Dion found a single vehicle, the familiar black Volkswagen Golf, gleaming in the last throes of the late afternoon's rainstorm. He pulled in close behind the car and stared through the windshield at its backside, its witty bumper stickers, its Bart Simpson doll suckered to its rear window.

He walked over to peer into the interior of the Golf. It was locked up, cold and empty. Had she crossed the footbridge to the main park, or struck up the outlaw bike trails of the Mesachee? Her aborted message didn't give enough clues.

He again tried her cell number, with no luck. He crossed the footbridge, stood where the trail forked, and shouted her name into the darkness. Then he backtracked and got his flashlight from his car, as darkness was filtering in. The culvert area made more sense. He walked along the road to the unofficial, unendorsed path that would lead up to the Mesachee. Not along the creek, but up.

Steep.

The attack on Troy had happened somewhere above the culvert, but he didn't know exactly where. Montgomery had said it was above the Rock. Possibly that's where she was headed. Should he call the office? Maybe someone there had a clue of what was going on.

But nobody would know, because if this were official, she wouldn't be alone and probably wouldn't have brought her private vehicle. There was something off about the whole thing. He hesitated a moment longer, then began to climb the Mesachee trails, pondering as he went.

Randall had been given the rest of the day off, as he had. She should be home catching up on her R and R, not following up leads on her own. What troubled him was that Randall seemed cannier than most, and it followed that if she had taken the trouble to come out here, there must be something worth coming out for. But why hadn't she simply told him on the phone what her plans were? Maybe she had meant to before the line cut out.

Flashlight beam leading the way, he headed up the path, squinting against sporadic hits of rain that came battering down from the evergreen canopy. At every bend, he expected to see her, or hear her, or get some useful clue. But nothing. For a third time he stopped, breathing hard, surrounded by the same crushing darkness, and knew there was no going back. He cupped his mouth and called out her name once more, and again the only reply was pattering water and the jostling of branches.

Cell service up here was too spotty to be trusted, and after the next bend he really should head back, call the office from the parking lot, alert them that there may be an issue. Instead he pressed on, reached the Rock, kept going. The path branched, leaving him at a standstill in the night forest. It was a frightening place, but for a change worry trumped fear.

He was puzzled, too. The path had not branched like this that time he was here with Montgomery and the boys on their bicycles. He shone his flashlight along the two forks and realized one was the actual trail, the other just an old creek bed, transformed by rain into a muddy slough.

He was turning to retreat when a noise stopped him. It was a dull and distant, a thud, not solid, not liquid — maybe an axe striking wood? It came from somewhere up the slough, how far he couldn't say. Light shut off, he walked cautiously up toward the source of the sound.

The wind had picked up, grown frantic. The bushes rushed and settled, rushed and settled, and as he made his way quietly forward, something — man or animal — rose and fled, shuddering the thickets. Dion shouted, "Hey!" and levelled his flashlight beam, catching only a choppy glimpse of the individual. Afterward, he could only say it ran upright but stooped, that it was gasping and staggering and seemed desperate to get away.

His pursuit ended in a clumsy slither as another turbulence in the brush distracted him, too close for comfort, a thrashing followed by an awful moan — it sounded human — then silence. He stepped backwards, once, twice, and crouched. He aimed his flashlight toward the source of the thrashing, now only leaves playing in the wind.

Nothing lunged. The moaning had stopped, and he could hear distorted breathing, louder than his own gasps. This was a burbling and harsh whine that he recognized from his attendances at car wrecks and assaults over the years. It was the sound of someone drowning in their own blood. He moved forward, scanning his light about until it blazed over an object jerking in the bracken, the foot-end of a stout leg in jeans and a hiking boot. He reached down and grasped the leg, following it upward through leaves and stalks that bristled with thorns, tearing at his skin.

It was Randall, lying face up and convulsing. Dion dropped into a kneel beside her, shining his light over her injuries. Her mouth was a gaping hole, sucking in air and exhaling pink bubbles. Her eyes were open wide.

"Jackie," he said. His hand hovered over her face, afraid to touch her. He wanted to help, but didn't know how. He saw splintered bone jutting from the flesh at her temples, and semicircular gouges at her throat that only partially registered in his mind. He grasped her by the jacket to pull her out into the narrow clearing formed by the creek bed — but remembered injured people are not to be moved.

She stared up at him as he stood above her. He had his phone out, looking for service. He found a single bar and made the call, fingers slippery with blood and rain. Dispatch finally picked up, and he asked for help, lots of it. He knelt at Randall's side then, his hand against the undamaged side of her face, looking into her wild eyes, telling her, "Hang on, Jackie. Help's on the way." Then he watched her die.

Thirty

HORRIDUS

THE HOUSE IN LYNN VALLEY that Leith and JD were called out to as darkness fell was the same one Leith had been keeping tabs on over the last day and a half — the Dempsey home, where Stefano Boone lived with his parents. It sat on a bit of a rise, with a well-kept lawn, cedar shrubs along both sides. No vehicle in the driveway, no signs of violence on its exterior.

The violence was all on the inside. Classical music was playing, and apparently nobody here was sure if the CD should be left spinning or turned off. Leith turned it off.

The female was still alive — the news had come over the radio as JD pulled in — but the male was dead. Leith and JD arrived in time to see the woman being lifted to a gurney. She had been found in what appeared to be a modest library, or lounge, with comfortable plush chairs and every inch of wall taken up by loaded bookshelves and framed photographs. The nubby carpet was littered with glass, the woman groaning and barely conscious.

She was breathing, Leith saw. One of her eyes was open, but probably not seeing anything, and the other swollen shut. Her face was covered in blood, and her nose looked broken, though it was hard to say, as an oxygen mask had just been strapped on. The paramedics were asking her questions and receiving no response. She was carted out, leaving Leith to stare at the large picture frame on the wall above where she had been found. The glass in the frame was smashed and bloody, much like the victim's face.

JD had disappeared. An Ident member stood nearby, getting pictures. She aimed at the damaged frame. Leith watched her, a photographer taking photographs of a photograph. The poster behind the shards was a depiction of a birthday celebration, with a man in what Leith imagined was Victorian garb leaned to slice into a fancy cake, while a group of women looked on.

JD returned, tagging him on the arm. "Dave, this way."

They walked down the hall to another bedroom, this one rigged with medical equipment, so much chrome and plastic that it looked like a homemade ICU. Leith took in a scene as sad as the one in the library. A lanky, grey-haired man, similar in age to the injured woman, was down on the floor, seemingly toppled over from a frozen cringe. Broken and bloody, eyes open. His button-up shirt was yanked out of order and his throat was discoloured. JD pointed out gouges on the throat — not from teeth, but fingernails — suggesting he had been throttled. Unlike the woman, who could hopefully be saved, the man was dead.

"This is his bedroom?" Leith asked. It didn't seem right. The man was fully dressed and looked bony, but fit. He didn't seem to be an invalid who needed hoisting in and out of this heavy-duty hospital bed.

JD shook her head. "This must be the daughter's room. I talked to the neighbours. They don't know much about the Boones, except they're a retired couple with two grown children. One is a girl; she was in some kind of accident and is bedridden. The son would be our missing Stefano. Tall, dark young man who comes and goes. Unfriendly. The whole family is quite insular, by the sounds of it. They have a van. Neighbour has observed the parents packing the girl inside from time to time and driving off."

Leith left JD and went to explore the lower level of the house. Downstairs, he'd been told, was the werewolf's lair. Low ceiling, simple floor plan, windows along the street-facing wall covered in drapes. The suite was dark, messy, and fairly smelly, too. The dampish odour of young male bedding and clothes that could use a good laundering. An ordinary space, except that around the perimeter stood large canvas paintings, stacked three or four deep. Not facing outward on display, but turned to the wall like punished children. Creepy paintings, Leith saw when he tilted one back to see. Mostly black.

In the fridge he found very little. A carton of milk and a few packets of greyish, raw stewing beef, the shrink-wrap glaring with red discount stickers.

The question of who had attacked the Boones was not much of a mystery. The pressing question was where Stefano Boone was now. And the van. And, most urgent of all, Stefano's bedridden sister.

Leith's phone buzzed. *What now?* he thought. *Tell me it's not more hell-raising.*

* * *

A posse came to meet Dion partway up the trail in the Mesachee Woods. Among them were a dishevelled Mike Bosko, who rarely came out to crime scenes; Michelin Montgomery; JD Temple; and now Dave Leith was here, asking Dion if he was okay. Others he recognized, but couldn't name. The alarm was out, and the troops would be tripled through the coming night, the park cordoned off tight to catch whoever had attacked Jackie Randall.

Which wasn't going to happen. Dion was sure the killer was long gone — he had either climbed up to Lynn Valley Road, or gone down across the river. As Dion had mentioned to Doug Paley, on that side of the river were thousands of acres for a person to hide in, if he had the means. If he didn't, he wouldn't survive the week.

But the endgame was not Dion's problem. For now, his job was simple — keep his wits together, lead the way to Randall, and describe to the team what had happened.

She lay as he had left her, stone still now. Not a flutter. He stared down at her face — what had been her face — upturned and illuminated by Leith's strong flashlight beam. Leith seemed to be lead investigator, keeping to the front of the line, deciding how close they should get to the body, and asking the questions.

The Mesachee was no longer a lonely place, as constables made their way up the trails, loaded with portable lights and search gear. Leith and Montgomery were discussing Randall as if she was just another case. Bosko was trying to make phone calls. The lights were set up, and the woods became as bright as midday, a confusion of glare and tree shadow, a flickering of rain and foot traffic. Dion heard himself describing the call from Jackie, how the call had ended abruptly, then his coming out to find her. A dull thud, someone crashing away through the underbrush. Done with the narrative, he was now asked more questions, but he wasn't following it much. He was looking for a place to sit down, because his legs felt about ready to buckle. Somebody told him it was time to go. That was Leith. Montgomery was beckoning.

The parking lot was busy now with vehicles and other members. It looked like a movie set to Dion. The way he was feeling, maybe it was. "I'm okay to drive," he told Montgomery.

"That's not going to happen," Montgomery replied, and explained why. Right now, Dion was not only a witness, but a living exhibit, and like any exhibit, there was the matter of continuity to consider. They were to return to the detachment together, where Dion would be checked over by a physician —

"I'm fine! They're just scratches."

"You're not fine," Montgomery said. He loomed at Dion, placing a firm hand on his shoulder and directing him away from his Honda, which he was grabbing on to like a life raft. "You're not thinking straight, and who would be? Come on."

"I'm a suspect? You think I killed Jackie?"

True, he wasn't thinking straight, and he felt he was about to fall apart, like a child, melt down and wail — until he was distracted from his own state by what he saw in Montgomery's pale-blue eyes. They were glittering with tears.

Or was it the rain that was sleeting down and covering *everything* in tears? Men, women, vehicles, bushes and trees. The entire park was crying. Montgomery released him and stepped away. Dion tugged his baseball cap brim lower and followed the corporal to the unmarked SUV.

* * *

To Leith, the night turned into a kind of a déjà vu of his brief stint in the Hazeltons, up in the northern half of the province. It was the similar confluence of wild nature, black night beaten away by halogen beams, miscellaneous equipment noise, and the hubbub of investigators. But most of all, it was being with Mike Bosko in such an unlikely setting. Different, though. Up in the Hazeltons the complication had been the bitter cold and the mid-winter snow. Here it was the sogginess and the unfriendly underbrush, skunk cabbage turning to mush, ooze punctured by the stems of plants that turned to spikes in winter's death. He could hear blasphemies from every quarter as team members fought with nature. Then a yell of, "*Fucking hell, something bit me!*"

Leith saw Bosko glance toward the source of the shout, as if enlightened. "Looks like he's discovered a rare patch of *Oplopanax horridus*. Devil's club. Known to ward off evil."

"And detectives," JD said.

Bosko nodded, but absently. "Some local hikers tell me devil's club has not been seen in this park in recent years. Forestry confirms it. But it seems we're proving them wrong. Rosetti's patch, and now this."

Rosetti's patch? Who or what the hell was that? Bosko was often baffling to Leith. "I don't understand. Why would you be asking Forestry about a plant you've only just noticed?"

Bosko turned to look at him, brows up. "I forgot, you're not on that detail, Dave. I'm sorry. Let me fill you in."

Yes, do.

"Aldobrandino Rosetti is the hiker who had a coronary a few weeks ago," Bosko told him. "Hiking down the Headwaters trails. His was not considered a suspicious death, but once the werewolf sightings started coming in, you recall, we decided his case should be looked into a little further. His wife handed over his belongings. Amongst them was a camera."

Now Leith did recall that unlikely tangent, the hiker named Rosetti, his snapshots downloaded and scrutinized for clues. "I thought that went nowhere."

"Yes and no. We were able to backtrack through his day somewhat, though ultimately, like you say, it went nowhere. The last shots were of interest, though, and I did notice the late-season devil's club. I checked into its prevalence in the park, and learned that it's considered extinct. So I've got some people out there seeing if they can locate the patch depicted in the photographs, which will pinpoint, possibly, what happened to Rosetti."

Good thing Mike Bosko knows his botany, Leith thought. But what a waste of manpower, especially now that the Jackie Randall crime scene was going to provide all the evidence they would need when it came to bagging this menace. "Bit of a long shot," he remarked.

Bosko didn't deny it.

"Wasn't Jackie Randall first on scene at Rosetti's death?" JD said.

"Randall and Dion," Bosko confirmed.

More uneasy Hazelton connections for Leith. Himself, Bosko, Dion — just another kind of haunting. He looked around at the dark woods, and his skin prickled. Something lived here, and it was watching them. Accompanied by Bosko, he trudged up the trail and looked at the big-leafed plant that had spiked one of the constables into shouting the F-word. Bosko lifted an aging yellowish leaf to show the still virile thorns running along its underside and bristling off thick stalks.

"Good thing it's rare," Leith said.

"You should see it in its prime."

Bosko said good night and left the team to their work. Leith and JD stayed. Jackie Randall's body remained for now, a part of the crime scene, being examined, photographed, measured in every way possible. Leith saw a flurry of activity a stone's throw uphill. Deep in the bushes, something had been found by the dogs. Some minutes later, an Ident member brought the prize down to show off. A twenty-four-inch pry-bar, imprinted with the word *Roughneck*.

"Hasn't been there long," she told Leith and JD. "And look."

As she turned it to the light, they saw a mash of blood and debris on the heavy end of the thing. "Pry bar, the standard burglar's tool kit, right?" Leith said.

"Bit hefty," JD said. "But maybe."

"And there's footprints," the Ident member told them. "They're partials, but collaged together, just eyeballing it, I think they're about size twelve. Probably running shoes. Tread's indistinct, too wet up there, but we'll see what we can do."

Leith said, "From what I know of Boone, he's taller than average. He'd be at least a twelve."

"There's also fibres," the Ident added.

"More fur? Where?"

"Not fur. Fibres." Ident people weren't fond of imprecision. "Close to where the body lay, snagged in the thorns. It's a dark spun poly of some kind."

She took her pry bar off to bag and label.

"There's something else they found in the area of Troy Hamilton's attack that you aren't aware of," JD told Leith. "In the bushes near the culvert. Werewolf puke. It contained synthetic fibres and fine, blond human hair. The synthetic's probably his own, and the hair is yet to be determined, but a good match to Troy Hamilton. Troy was lucky. Looks like he was just the appetizer, and not even a tasty one."

Leith had seen something on Jackie Randall's neck that looked like it might be a bite mark. Torn, frenzied. A swift progression up from the relatively tentative chomp on Troy's arm, a chomp that had been followed — as he now knew — by vomit. The predator was learning fast, and building a stomach for human flesh. What if Dion hadn't interrupted the attack? What would have been left of Jackie Randall then? Stripped bone?

He thought of the community at large, kids running around the neighbourhood. He told JD — a trite observation — "We've got to get this guy, and soon."

Not a guy, he thought. A skinwalker. It was a word he had overheard Bosko using sometime this night, talking to the coroner's assistant about transformation, archetypes, mythology. He thought about the figure Dion had described, just a blot against the blacker blackness, fleeing away into the night. Stefano Boone was mutating; look at his attacks on Troy, his parents, Randall. Then there was his sister, Anastasia, missing. Leith's hope for her safe recovery was thin at best.

He drew in his shoulders, chiding himself for letting the forest get to him. There was nothing more supernatural than delusion happening here. A young man with a hate-on for the world had flipped out, not for the first time, and not for the last.

Of course there was another possibility to keep in mind: Boone was *not* the killer. But how likely was that?

Leith was cold and tired. He wished he could stay and assist in the tracking of Boone, but he needed sleep. By the way JD was yawning, she did, too. They left the scene and parted ways in the parking lot. He drove home, and it only came to him when he was in bed next to Alison, when the lights were out, when she had fallen back asleep, and the noises began their usual creep through walls and joists, that awful word Bosko had thrown out so matter-of-factly: *skinwalker.*

Thirty-One

PUSH

THEY WERE DONE AT LAST, at least for now. Dion had been photographed in the chilly medical exam room. The scratches on his arms were documented, just in case they turned out to be defensive wounds, say, inflicted by Jackie Randall as she fought him off. The clothes he wore were taken, bagged, and labelled. Or *seized*, was the word.

The physical exam — with a GIS constable named Frye looking on — was thorough. The doctor had asked questions, looked into Dion's eyes, and swabbed blood off his hands and face, scratches that only now were starting to sting and throb. One slash on his neck got a few stitches. He couldn't remember getting slashed on the neck. The underbrush must have been pricklier than he realized.

He watched the bloody swabs being placed into tubes and labelled for the lab. Next came a saliva swab, also tubed. Finally the doctor toured around Dion's mouth with a scope, asked how he was feeling emotionally, then folded the scope away and prescribed painkillers.

Wearing borrowed clothes, as he had no spares left in his locker, Dion was next questioned by Montgomery. Montgomery audiotaped the statement, but deemed videotape unnecessary. Constable Frye sat in.

Montgomery asked Dion what he was doing up in the Mesachee tonight.

Dion said it all again, but with a slight difference. Now he had the complication of Randall's private investigation to worry about, not least because the subject of her investigation was doing the questioning, and he had to watch his words.

"I was going to meet Jackie at Denny's. She didn't show up, so I phoned her. We talked briefly. She wanted to postpone the meeting. Then she either disconnected or cut out. She might have walked out of range. It sounded like she was walking, and she mentioned it was steep. I thought she might be calling from the park, something to do with the Troy Hamilton case, so I went out to look for her. I didn't think she was in trouble. Didn't sound like it, on the phone."

"Weren't you both off duty? Is there some reason for all this running around meeting each other?"

"She liked to talk over cases. So do I. We get along. Got along."

"Nothing wrong with that," Montgomery said. "She was a good cop. Damn shame." No trace of tears in his clear-blue eyes now, and probably there never had been.

Surprisingly, Montgomery didn't pursue the fairly unorthodox unofficial talking-over of cases between two off-duty members, or try to explore whether Dion was responsible, even indirectly, for Randall's death. The interview had no teeth, and was over within the hour. Maybe it was just a warm-up, but to Dion it felt more like a brush-off.

At the end of the day, nothing was said about detention in barracks, so he returned to his apartment and bolted the door. He downed painkillers and a sleeping tablet on top of it, and some non-prescribed Scotch — to hell with the warnings on the pill bottles — but still couldn't sleep. His thoughts kept turning over everything Randall had ever said about her hit-and-run investigation, how she began it and how she ended it. He had no doubt she would come to him in his dreams, burbling blood, but unless ghosts were real, she wouldn't be able to finish the thought.

He grabbed his laptop to watch the news, but instead pulled up a map and located Linnae Avenue. He had an idea it was down below Keith Road, but it wasn't. It was just northeast of where Breanna had been killed, and not so far away.

* * *

In the morning, after a restless sleep, he was back in the hot seat. This time it was two internal investigations detectives, a man and a woman, with questions for him. The man was named Miles, super friendly, and the woman was named Morrison, super attentive.

The interview was hellish from the start. They jumped topics often to rattle him. Their background investigation had been thorough, and they were curious about many things. His relationship with Jackie Randall, and with the witness, Jordan. They wanted to know about the head injuries he had suffered last year, how he was feeling these days. He said he was doing well. Yes, in spite of some disciplinary issues this year.

The questions switched back to Jackie Randall and the discussions he'd had with her lately, as he had mentioned to Corporal Montgomery last night. Which cases, exactly, had they discussed?

"Breanna Ferris, for one," he said. "Hit and runs. She hasn't been on the job so long, and it's new to her, these things — DUIs, and speeders in the area, the inability to enforce the laws, kids getting killed, what should be done about it."

"So your get-togethers were, what, some kind of venting? Did you consider yourself a friend, a counsellor, to Jackie?"

Before the crash Dion had been an excellent liar. After the crash, not so much. Now he could feel his body language giving himself away. He wasn't sure how straight to sit, how much eye contact to maintain. When to smile, when to frown.

"No," he said. "Nothing like that. Just …"

He closed his mouth and looked down at the table, his body language flashing fear, no doubt. He had just recalled Randall's notebook, the little buff-coloured school tablet jammed between the seat and the console of her vehicle. Had the investigators found it, and was his own name embedded in there somewhere?

He expected it to come out now, slammed down in front of him, but it didn't happen. His hands found each other and clasped on the tabletop, their knuckles whitening. Miles asked him about the car crash in Cloverdale, what he remembered of the moments leading up to it.

Dion gritted his teeth. Anybody who had read his file, as these two would certainly have done, would know he claimed to remember nothing on the day of the crash, or the days leading up to it. They would know all this. Miles was just pushing buttons. "How does my crash relate to Randall's death?"

Miles's index finger pressed out three spots on the tabletop to enumerate how, and he was no longer being super friendly. "I'm interested in Jackie Randall, you, and where you're coming from these days. That's all."

Dion unclasped his hands and punched them into his trouser pockets. He tried to sound calm, but instead sounded like a shaky detainee. "Frankly, I don't think about it much. Better to move forward, right?"

"Of course," Miles said. He took Dion back to the snowy Hazeltons and some bad choices he had made up there. Then back again to the Cloverdale car crash and Luciano Ferraro's death. Then back to Jackie Randall, then a further switchback to Farah Jordan, and just when Dion was ready to bury his head in his arms on the table and sob, their questions ended.

He sat back in a relaxed pose, timed his breathing in and out, and waited to be released.

Morrison leaned toward him and softly asked, "Why do you get so angry when we talk about the crash?"

"I'm not *angry*!" he said.

They let it be the last word. The interview was over.

* * *

Still angry, he went to see Mike Bosko, but was told Bosko was out for lunch.

Down the street at Rainey's, he found the sergeant sitting alone in a booth, reading something on his phone and eating a croissant sandwich. Bosko looked at him with no show of surprise and gestured at the seat across from him. "Good. You got my message. You kind of jumped the gun; I think I said three o'clock in my office, but that's fine. Thanks for coming."

Dion sat across from him. "What message?"

"To come and see me in my office at three o'clock," Bosko said, with a slight edge. "But no worries. A wire must have crossed. Can I buy you a sandwich, coffee, anything?"

"No, thanks."

Croissant flakes littered Bosko's shirt front. He brushed at them, but missed a few. His tie was a dull, solid rose, not snugged too well against his collar. His longish fair hair was untidily ruffled, and there was a faded phone number in ballpoint on his palm. "I understand you've been talking to the internal investigations gang," he said. "How did it go?"

"I've been suspended with pay," Dion said, almost hovering in indignation. "They seem to think I killed Jackie."

Bosko's eyes were impossible to read behind the sheen of his glasses. "Did you?"

"No, I did *not*."

"Then don't worry about it," Bosko said, adding, "Don't forget to breathe."

Dion sucked in air. "I'm not worried about it. I've got bigger things to worry about. Like why I'm here at all, in North Vancouver, when I'm *dysfunctional*. You know I'm not fit for the job. Everybody knows. Everyone's wondering why I'm still coming to work every day. They look at me, not just Internal, but everybody. Why don't you tell me why I'm here?" He lifted his face and waited. Whatever the answer was, it was bound to change his life, and he wanted to face the changes squarely.

But Bosko had taken another bite of his sandwich, and his mouth was full. After munching for a bit, he put it down, cleaned his mouth with a serviette, and said, "When I was in New Hazelton, Serious Crimes down here in North Van was kind of scattering to the winds, and we needed to build it back up. You made yourself noticed, I'll put it that way. I wanted you here, and I got you here, and that's about all there is to it. You seem to want to shoot yourself in the foot. I'm hoping you'll smarten up soon and come back to my section, in a more rooted kind of way. Stick around for a change."

"How about Luciano Ferraro?"

Bosko straightened his spine, though not in a startled way. "What about him?"

"Is that why I'm really here? Looch was a friend of mine. He was supposed to have died in a car crash, with me in the driver's seat, but I've yet to see the proof. I've seen a tombstone with his name on it. That's not proof. They say he's cremated, but nobody wants to show me the death certificate. I got posted up north, where I didn't do so well, then you come along and get me back here like some kind of promotion — which nobody believes, especially me. I can't help thinking there's a connection."

He stopped and listened to a replay of what he had just said. Put into words, the connection seemed to lose its glue. He dragged a hand down his face.

Bosko said, "I have to say, your logic eludes me. Look, maybe just keep in mind one thing, Cal. You are *not* the centre of the universe, as you seem to think. It's okay, we all slip into that groove. Just think before you make your next move. And keep your guns holstered. A'right?"

Dion opened his mouth, but Bosko raised his salad fork to interrupt him. "That includes speaking your mind."

For nearly a minute, they sat in silence. Bosko went back to his food and reading. Dion said, "What did you want to see me about at three o'clock? Might as well deal with it now."

Phone and croissant went down. "Mostly I wanted to find out how you're faring. Also how your meeting went, but you've coloured it in for me fairly well. I do strongly suggest counselling, though I hear you've turned it down. After what you went through yesterday, it's almost a given it would be a good idea. You don't have to say anything now," he said, pre-empting an objection. "Just think about it and let me know."

Dion walked back to the detachment in the rain, thinking over the counselling suggestion. Everybody was urging him into it as a matter of course, because a cop doesn't come across his fellow officer in the way he had come across Jackie and then carry on with life as usual. Morrison and Miles had made the same suggestion, off the record, and Dion had taken it as a threat instead of concern for his well-being.

Smarten up, Bosko said. Maybe it was time to start doing that. But counselling was not what he needed to come to terms with what happened to Jackie, and neither was a leave of absence. The only therapy he needed was to help catch her killer.

Thirty-Two

INCOMMUNICADO

A THOUGHT CAME TO DION as he stood looking up at his detachment — the madman Ray Starkey's prophetic words, "You boys go into them woods, you're not coming out alive." Well, not quite prophetic, because most of the boys who had gone in there *had* come out alive, and Randall, the only one who hadn't, wasn't a boy. Still, Starkey might know something about Boone that could be useful, and he should be paid a visit. Not by Dion himself, because he was suspended, but somebody on the case.

A voice behind him startled him from his thoughts. "What's up? You casing the joint, boyo?"

It was Corporal Doug Paley. He wore a dollar store transparent raincoat over his suit, hood up, no umbrella. He didn't stop to get an answer, but kept on his way to wherever he was going. Dion called out to stop him. "Doug! Who's lead on the Randall case now?"

Paley stopped and squinted back at him. "Why? You're incommunicado, right?"

"There's something I have to report."

Paley had moved back into speaking range. "Monty's in charge, but he's in meetings. What've you got?"

"There's this guy, kind of a crackpot, out in Lynn Valley, Ray Starkey. When we were searching for Troy Hamilton, he showed up with a tip."

"A tip, yeah. So let's hear it."

A city bus charged noisily by, drowning Dion's words.

Paley asked for a repeat, and spun his fat fingers, telling him to get on with it.

"He told us the thing we're hunting isn't human," Dion said, knowing Paley would turn it into a joke. "He said it's an evil spirit."

Paley's eyes twinkled. "An evil spirit, eh? Did he give you a name to plug into the database?"

"What he said was we won't come out of the woods alive. Montgomery laughed him off. Everyone did. So did I. But that was before Randall was butchered. Somebody should follow up. Maybe Montgomery's got it covered already, I don't know, but I want to remind him about it, in case it slipped his mind."

Paley looked down the street, as if lunch was calling to him, then back at Dion. "I'll pass it on for you," he promised. "Now go do the incommunicado shuffle. Christ, it's cold, though, isn't it?" He flapped his plastic-coated arms. "I feel like a dick in a condom."

Dion went on his way, back to the underground parkade. He sat in his car, but didn't start the engine. Montgomery had been Randall's case, and now that she was dead, she was Montgomery's case. He thought of the hit-and-run intrigue and its great honking lack of proof. In spite of everything she'd said, and in spite of appearances, he believed Montgomery knew that Randall suspected Tori. If so, was Dion also on Montgomery's radar? Was Montgomery trying to buy him off with compliments, offering fast-tracking back to GIS?

But there he was, falling into the trap again. Randall was simply wrong, and she had known it. That explained her change in attitude. Her clues, such as Linnae, hadn't panned out. Maybe she was embarrassed by the whole thing. Even possible she had no intention of passing her notes on to Internal, and was just going to let it all blow away.

Or maybe it was just the opposite, and she had found out something she wasn't willing to share with him.

The November chill grew chillier in his vehicle. He made up his mind, left his car, and went upstairs to GIS, where he was told Montgomery was in a meeting and couldn't see him right now. He went in anyway. Montgomery stood at his desk, occupied with both a phone call and several members asking him questions. Dion waited until the team dispersed and the phone was put away. Montgomery stared across at him. "You're not supposed to be here, Constable. What's the problem?"

"I'm not staying. I just wanted to check with you on something, about Jackie. It's important."

Montgomery sank into his chair and leaned sideways to wait. He looked colourless today, chin like silver sandpaper, bloodshot eyes. "Go ahead. I'm listening."

Dion remained on his feet, ready to say what he had to say, then go. "Ray Starkey — have you gone to check out what he had to say?"

"What, the old guy and his flying saucers? No, actually I think I wilfully forgot. Why?"

"Did you get his address? Aren't you going to send someone out there, at least, get his statement?"

"None of the above," Montgomery said and made a shooing motion.

Dion said, "Jackie Randall was there at the park. She heard what Starkey had to say. Maybe she wanted to follow up with him, do it on her own. She was like that, right?"

"Yes, thank you, I'll make a note of that."

"If you logged his info into the file, she could have got it from there, but if you didn't, she could only have got it from you or me. She didn't get it from me, so I'm wondering if she came to you, asking about him."

"She didn't. Mystery solved," Montgomery said. "There's nothing to follow up, but thank you for bringing it to my attention."

"Regardless, Starkey might have info about Stefano Boone, where to find him. Also, Jackie could have run into him on the street. He seems to be out and about a lot. Maybe they got talking, and whatever he had to say sent her up the Mesachee. I just think you have to cover the possibilities."

Montgomery reached for a pen and jotted a note, a scribble that looked to Dion destined for the trash bin. "All right, then." He tossed aside the pen and placed the note on a stack of documents on his desk. "Done deal, I'll go see him, *ASAP*. Now, sorry to kick you out, but I'm kicking you out."

"When's 'ASAP'? I think it's pretty important, considering what we've got here. So if I were you —"

"Well, you're not me, are you?" Montgomery was on his feet. "The case is in good hands, trust me. I've made a note to go see Mr. Starkey, and even though I really don't need to spend the night listening to werewolf stories from half-baked —"

"But you have to agree with me, there could be something there. Starkey said if we go into the woods, we die. Randall went into the woods, and she died. He may be a lunatic, but on the other hand, sometimes it's the lunatics —"

"All right!" Montgomery shouted. He slapped both hands on his desk, startling Dion and everyone else within earshot. "All right, I hear you," he said, more quietly. "Now, as I recall, you're suspended until further notice, so go on home and do whatever you do when you're suspended, and let me take care of business on this end. *Comprende?*"

Dion did comprende, but didn't move.

Montgomery had lowered his head as well as his voice. "My hands are a tad full right now. Do you know Boone went on a killing spree? He didn't stop at Jackie. He wiped out his entire family. Do you know that?"

Dion didn't know that.

"So excuse me if your point of focus seems a little, I don't know, *trite*. We've got all the bases covered. Believe me. We do." He finished with a more aggressive *get-lost* motion, both hands flapping at air.

"I need to get some commitment from you on this," Dion insisted.

"You're in no position to get anything from me, Cal."

"I think I am. And if you're not going out there, I intend to check it out myself."

Montgomery pinkened, then seemed to calm himself. He held up a hand, *stop*. He gestured politely toward the exit. "Come along with me for a moment." He led the way out the fire door, up the stairs, down a short corridor, and around a bend, into one of the less-used men's rooms. The door self-closed behind them and Montgomery became a stranger, advancing on Dion in two fast strides, ending just short of a body-slam. "Listen, you fuck," he bellowed. "I'm not sure what kind of leverage you think you have on me, but get this straight. I loved Jackie Randall as a fellow officer. I'm sorry she's dead, but she was barking mad. She had nothing on Tori, and in case you plan on continuing this little *mission* of hers, which I have this uneasy feeling you intend to do, don't even start. Because I'm onto you, constable."

Behind Dion was a cold white ceramic wall, and a hand dryer. The hand dryer banged into his back.

Montgomery was still raging at him. "I told you I could make your life easier, but maybe you don't realize just how fucking *hard* I can make it. I can *sink* you. So stay away from Tori, stay away from me, keep your paranoid delusions to yourself, and maybe, just maybe, we'll get along until I can get transferred out of this shithole you call home."

"What paranoid delusions should I keep to myself?" Dion said.

Montgomery shoved him and began to swear.

Dion's boot soles skidded. He tried to right himself and bring his fists up in self-defence, but was grabbed by the jacket front and given another bone-jarring slam against tile. The words leaving the corporal's mouth were filthy and savage. Dion shot back words of his own, just as crude, as he twisted free of Montgomery's grip.

They stood apart, glaring. Montgomery lifted a warning finger for his last word. "You're on shaky ground. You're not liked around here, you're not trusted, and it would take nothing for me to give you the big push. I've made notes about your conduct, and they're sealed in my safety deposit box with instructions to my solicitor. Now, if I get any grief from you, you're going down with me. Understand?" He repeated it in a roar. "Do you understand me?"

"I understand you," Dion said. And with a rush of amazement, he thought he really did.

Thirty-Three

WOLF TRAP

THE ROOM WAS SMALL AND DARK, populated with dead animals, loops of rope, black steel contraptions. A wolf crouched as if about to spring, but it never would. Stefano sat in a tight corner next to the mounted corpse, his wolf head unclipped and thrown aside, arms hugging his knees. In light of what he had found here, he wondered if Chef was not the good person he thought she was.

Wolf-killing bitch.

His face was dirty, dusty, and tear-streaked. His hands ached as if every tendon had snapped. He was trapped in this half life, not wolf, not human. He had caused such mayhem, but accomplished nothing. Couldn't even deal with small prey, barely more than a squirrel. Clamping his teeth into Troy's flesh had not subdued the boy, but made him thrash frantically.

The experience of the bite was the most shocking surprise to Stefano. It had been horrid. The flesh felt soft yet gristly under his molars, nothing like what he expected.

What had he expected? Boiled ham? No. Caribou flesh ripping away in his jaws, that's what, delicious and bloody. He had released, gagging, and Troy went running and tumbling downslope like a small crashing avalanche. Stefano had thrown up. The strain of heaving set off a nosebleed. He had climbed up to the street, not taking the time to stash the skin. Knelt at the curb, shivering, polluted, and for the first time in his adult life, he had let go and cried. A car zipped past, faces staring out at him. He had half staggered, half crawled down the block to the house of Paul and Colette, where he had surprised Colette down in his room, his own private space, looking through his things.

He hadn't wanted to kill Colette. Why had she chosen that moment to come down? Was she looking for the rent he wouldn't be able to pay this month, or ever again?

No, she was talking about the teeth in her oven, staring at his skin, asking what was going on. Why had she decided to look at his paintings now, this worst night of his life? And why had she chosen that moment, after all these years, to tell him what she thought of his art, raising her voice to call it odd and disturbing.

Odd.

Disturbing.

He had chased her upstairs and cornered her in the library where she and Paul spent their days, reading and listening to music, surrounded by photographs of Anastasia before the accident, Anastasia smiling and bowing, Anastasia in chiffon, sitting at her piano, posing with her tiny violin. Really, the peak of perfection would have been to crush Colette's nose against one of those hallowed Anastasia pictures, but due to time and space, it didn't work out that way, and instead he had pushed her face into Sergei Rachmaninoff and family, asking her in his half-human shout if this was Odd and Disturbing, too?

Paul rushed to her rescue, stronger and livelier than Stefano had ever seen him, pelting Stefano with objects, paperweights and tea mugs, books and lamps, a water jug, which shattered on the hardwood floor, followed by smaller missiles — a cellphone, pens and pencils.

Stefano had taken refuge in Anastasia's room. Paul followed, and there they had fought to the death, as Anastasia in her machines stared on.

Finally there was Anastasia to set free, and the effort had almost finished him off.

It seemed so long ago. Now he was at the only place in the world he thought would be safe, Chef's house, where he found the back door shabbily locked. A forceful shove with his shoulder and he was in.

He had been waiting for a long time. He wished she would come home. He was cold and uncomfortable. His fur was matted and damp, soggy in the hindquarters from his struggle with Anastasia and the long trek home. Above all, he was thirsty. The thirst had begun as discomfort, but now he could think of nothing else. His tongue scraped at the roof of his mouth, his saliva too thick to swallow. It was not human blood he thirsted for, nor caribou, nor even water. What he wanted was orange juice. OJ by the gallon.

When he could take it no longer, he rose to his feet. He was shaky in the knees, his limbs stiffened from too long spent in a fetal curl. He shuffled out of the room, touching walls. "Got to get something to drink," he told the dusty animals as he left them behind. He bit and pulled off one front paw, then the other, let them fall, and sidled toward the stairs leading down to the main floor.

He was standing in the unlit kitchen, preoccupied with the contents of her fridge, hand on the handle of a large glass juice jug, when she approached, moving silently on stockinged feet from the front foyer. They both yelped, and their words tangled.

"Stefano —"

"Sorry, I'm sorry, I —"

"— what are you —"

"I'm sorry." The juice jug was in his hand, shaking. "I was just g-getting a drink."

"Yes," Chef said softly. "I see that."

* * *

"I was *so* thirsty," he told her. Inside the jug he held, the juice was making waves like a restless sea.

"Here. Let me get you a glass."

She put a tall tumbler on the counter next to him. He filled it, spilling some in his anticipation. She told him to sit at the table, calm down. He did as she said. As he gulped the juice down, she placed a kettle on the burner and offered food as well. He sat in silence and watched while she opened a tin of tuna. She brought lettuce from the fridge, but put it back again when he insisted he didn't eat vegetables.

When he was fed, when they both had tea in front of them, Chef finally spoke. She asked him what was happening, why he hadn't come to work, and whether he was all right.

"I'm not all right," he said quietly. "I have a terrible problem."

"Yes, Stefano? Tell me about it."

"First, I want you to have this," he said. He unzipped his fur, and from the inner pocket brought out a small satin-clad diary bought in Chinatown for a few dollars. Brilliant turquoise with vinyl corners. He pushed the book across to her. "It really says it all."

She picked it up and studied it, respectfully. "Thank you."

"You're welcome," he said. "I won't stay long, because I think it's happening, I can feel it, and you're not safe around me. I've always wanted you for my own," he said, and quickly lifted a hand to reassure her, as she looked alarmed. "I won't hurt you. I wanted to say thank you, actually, I mean for hiring me, and giving me rides back and forth, and all that. I don't think I have long to live."

She was looking at the fur of his arms resting on the table, his hands clasped, white knuckled but still. She reached out and placed her palm on his knot of twined fingers. "Why do you say you don't have long to live, Stefano? What's the matter?"

The touch made his heart ache, and he was weeping again. "It's difficult to explain," he whispered. "But you see, I'm no longer of this race. I never was, entirely. But I — I'm having problems transitioning. I mean, I get to this point ..." He paused, closed his eyes, and tried to find the words. He realized this was the first real conversation he had had with her, one where he was doing the talking. He forced himself to push on. "Maybe that's a good thing, because a full and complete transformation would set me free at last, but at what cost to mankind?"

Odd, how good he felt. How could he have ever considered harming Chef, who was the kindest person he had ever met?

"It's a difficult world, Stefano. Jobs are scarce and the cost of living is ridiculous, especially for young men like you. But you're not an animal. You're a very nice man, and a fine cook. You have a real flair for food. I've noticed that. I think you'll do well in the industry. In fact, if you want, I could help you —"

Her dreadful words were sinking in, and he stood to silence her, raising his voice and thumping his own chest. "I am not a cook!" he shouted. "I don't belong here. I'm not one of you. Your only chance ..." he could hardly talk now, sobbing between words, "... is to evict me from this world. You have to *kill* me. If you don't, I will bring a terror upon you that you can't even begin to imagine. Stop me, before I do it again. I don't need a job. I need a bullet between my eyes. I need *peace*."

Chef had stopped sipping her tea. "You must be tired, Stefano."

"I am. I'm very tired."

"Would you like to lie down?"

"I would like to die."

"I understand. But maybe that's because you're so tired. Things can seem awfully bleak when you need your sleep. We'll try to work it out once you've rested some, all right?"

He went with her up to her bedroom. He had prowled through it on that earlier occasion, but had never been led in like this, like a guest. He looked around with a new, cleaner interest. She said he should maybe take off the fur, and he did, explaining as he did that it was only a tool of transition. "But it must be hard for you to understand what I'm talking about."

"A little," she admitted.

Under the fur he wore his long johns, embarrassed that they were inside out, grubby, and too small, but Chef made him feel like they were perfectly appropriate. She gave him an oversized bathrobe to use, and she folded up his wet skin in a corner of the room.

Warm in the soft terry cloth robe, he gazed at her as she fussed about. She set his tea on a small table, provided a box of Kleenex, and asked if there was anything else he wanted. She was beautiful. Kind. He would lay down his soul for her. "I'd really like to sleep with you," he said.

"But you also really need your rest," she said, plumping a pillow. "Lie down, and later, we'll talk some more. I'm here for you, Stefano. Believe it or not, every problem can be whittled down to a manageable size."

He looked down at her cloud-like bedding. "I prefer to sleep on the floor."

"Whatever you like, Stef."

He lay on his side on the rug next to her bed, and only now realized how desperately tired he was. He closed his eyes and barely registered that she was covering him with a blanket, turning off the light, closing the door.

Only then he recalled the dead wolf in the room down the hall, and his eyes flew open in the darkness.

Thirty-Four

BOXER

MONTGOMERY'S NASTINESS continued to reverberate in Dion's mind, but he wasn't going to deal with it now. His best revenge at the moment was to go see Starkey himself. If Starkey had any valuable information to share, nobody was going to get a medal for the breakthrough except himself.

His cellphone buzzed as he made his way through the detachment parkade to his car, and he answered as he walked. It was Farah, speaking in such a low voice that he had to strain to hear. By the sounds of it, she wanted to engage him in one of her strange discussions, which he was really in no mood for at the moment.

"Speak up," he said.

"I said I'm glad I caught you, because I have a bit of a situation."

More situations, he thought. "I'm busy," he told her.

"Well, but this is —"

"Call you later," he said, and disconnected.

He drove through town too aggressively. He should have known better. Kate had once tried telling him about the concept of karma, and he had tried listening. It had to do with personal responsibility, cause and effect, and then something about vibrations. In the simplest terms, a person's inner peace and harmony bring a return of good luck, health, and prosperity, while ugly feelings attract an ugly fate.

Karma caught up with him on his way to Lynn Valley, at a busy intersection. It was partly his fault for crossing on an orange light, but mostly the right-turning Corolla's for presupposing he wouldn't. There was a thud, a crunch, a scattering of plastic bits. Dion swore loudly as his vehicle settled into place. He could see the Corolla man doing the same. He pulled over and heard something scrape the asphalt. Driving for any distance didn't look promising.

He and the Corolla man got out and inspected their vehicles. The Corolla was only scuffed, but Dion's right front quarter panel was hanging like a broken wing. They exchanged registration information, along with some advice on how to drive, and within minutes were parting ways.

Dion pulled into the nearest collision shop, which happened to sit just off the intersection. He parked in an open bay and went to speak to the receptionist. He was told to wait a minute. He sat in the chilly foyer and used his cellphone to call the ICBC claim line. It was a protracted call, most of it spent on hold, listening to patchy Muzak. He then had to deal with the body shop mechanic and the necessary paperwork. By the time he was seated in his courtesy car, an older model dung-brown Impala, it was early evening.

He took a moment to familiarize himself with the car's retro control panel, another moment to remember his mission, and another to work up the enthusiasm to proceed with it.

His mission carried him uphill to Lynn Valley, the little green-roofed house on Kilmer that had been pointed out to him by the leery character named Ray Starkey.

The house he had seen only from a distance turned out to be a neatly kept stucco structure on a good-sized lot, surrounded by fat, erratically pruned boxwood hedges. A small blue Mazda pickup sat in the driveway. No visible house number that he could see. He parked his courtesy car at the curb, walked through the gate and up the cement walkway, stepped up onto the porch, and rang the doorbell.

The door opened just wide enough for a face to peer out. The face was knobby and corrugated, an alarmed Ray Starkey.

Dion introduced himself and showed his ID through the narrow opening. "I just have a few questions for you, Mr. Starkey. Have a moment?"

"I'm kinda doing my dishes." Starkey raised a sudsy scrub brush. "Maybe you could come back later?"

"The dishes can't wait?"

"Well, see, the water's hot, and if I don't do 'em now —"

"How long, then? Ten minutes? I'll wait in my car."

The door seemed about to snap shut, but instead creaked open. Starkey was in well-worn cargo pants, a sweater, and slippers. "Forget the dishes," he said with a sigh. "Come in."

Dion walked into the house, told not to worry about his boots. He found the furnishings spare and utilitarian, the air stale and sad. The living room doubled as a dining room, with its aluminum-rimmed table from another era and lone matching chair. A series of pictures on the wall drew his attention — old photographs and framed newspaper clippings. All the clippings were boxing related. He went for a closer look.

"That's me," Starkey said, having followed at a safe distance. "Top-of-class welterweight out east when I was young. Knocked a lotta guys flat in my time. Starboy, they called me."

Dion read a few headlines, but mostly he looked for likenesses in the yellowing halftone clippings of a handsome fighter sparring for the camera, or holding up a trophy; black eye, big grin.

"This is me, too," Starkey said pointing out another. "That was a bad one. Blood all over, eh? Boxing ain't what it used to be." He bobbed his head like a sinewy little bird, ready to flap off at any sudden move. "All commercialized, all regulated, eh? Old days it was straightforward, put on the gloves, knock 'em dead. Ever enjoy the sport yourself?"

"No, I don't know much about it." Dion could see nothing of the young boxer in the weathered face beside him now. "I have to tell you, Ray, I'm just following up on something you said to members down at the park yesterday. You don't have to help me out, but I'd appreciate if you would. The force would appreciate it. You understand all that?"

Starkey's head responded confusingly, up and down, side to side. "Yessir, I get it, sure."

Dion indicated the frames on the wall. "Is that what you've done all your life? Boxed?"

"That, and odd jobs around. Dockyards. Slaughter-house. Lotta warehousing."

"Retired?"

"Yessir. Took my early with disability at fifty-five. Legs hurt me. Worked at 'K' Line here on the North Shore for twenty-two odd years, so the pension's pretty damn good."

"Dock work?"

"S'right. Freight and forklifts and whatnot."

Dion knew Starkey also had a criminal record to stick on his résumé, because he had checked on PRIME-BC. Six counts of possession of stolen property and one assault charge. But it was old stuff, all of it, probably as old as the newspaper clippings on the wall. He decided to clear one matter off the table, first thing. "You have something against First Nations people, Mr. Starkey?"

Starkey looked shocked. "Me? No."

"You told Corporal Montgomery you'd rather talk to a white man. I'm just wondering why."

"Oh, nothing personal, not at all." Starkey's hands were up, like he was being prodded with a loaded gun instead of an inquiring glance. "Honest, I got nothing but respect for the local Natives. I got original Native art up on my walls in the kitchen. I bought it on the Island. You want to see?"

"I've seen it," Dion said. A dreamcatcher hung in the window over the kitchen sink, dyed feathers and plastic beads. "If it's not personal, what is it? Why are you afraid?"

Starkey's grin was sheepish and fawning. Maybe he more socially inept than racist. "You people have powers," he was saying. "Mystic powers. That's all."

Dion said nothing.

"Which tribe is you from?" Starkey asked.

"Coastal," Dion said, fudging it. If Starkey wanted to believe he had mystic powers, let him. Awe could be useful. He went on with the reason for his visit. He didn't have a photograph of Jackie Randall to show his witness, so he described her as best he could — height, weight, hair colour. He asked Starkey if he had seen anyone of that name or that description in the last couple of days. More specifically, yesterday afternoon.

Starkey hadn't.

"You came along when we were searching for a missing boy. You spoke to Corporal Montgomery. He told you he was going to come and see you, didn't he?"

"He said he would. I waited. He didn't show up."

"This woman, Jackie Randall, was there in the search party. You don't remember seeing her then, or anytime afterward?"

"No, sir."

Dion next asked about Stefano Boone. Starkey didn't know the man. Or anyone matching his description? No.

Coming out here had been a fruitless exercise, then. Dion had bothered a lot of people, wrecked his car, and blown two hours for nothing. He wouldn't get a medal, and wouldn't be rubbing anything in Montgomery's face. But what he had succeeded at was covering the bases, and he had no regrets.

He thanked Starkey, and on the way to the door said, "You warned us about going into the woods. You said there were evil spirits. Can you explain what you mean by that? You're saying there's 'natives' in there?"

They were in the hallway neat as a barracks. Starkey hesitated. "See, I'd rather not talk about it, that's all."

Dion watched Starkey, seeing an oddball strength in the man. And buried in his attitude was a warning, but a warning for whom, against what?

"You don't want to talk to me because I'm First Nations?"

"No, sir, that's not it at all."

"You seemed to think it was important when you talked to Corporal Montgomery yesterday. So what's changed?"

He could almost see Starkey's brain at work behind his anxious, watery eyes. Finally Starkey gave a nod of resignation. "Best to get it done with, sir, but honest to God, it's like you cops don't take me serious. I tried. I honestly tried."

"I take you seriously."

"When Officer Montgomery didn't come by last day, I was going to call up the number I got on the fridge. But I figured he thinks I'm just an old kook."

"I'm here. I'm listening. Go ahead and tell me what you wanted to tell Corporal Montgomery."

Starkey remained edgy, doubtful, yet keen.

"I'll pass it on to him," Dion told him. "Promise."

"But it's kind of in the basement."

"What's in the basement?"

"The fing, what I was wanting to show Officer Montgomery."

"What thing? What's in the basement that you wanted to show him? Describe it for me, would you?"

Starkey hunched his shoulders. "Don't really know what it is, sir."

"Something to do with the evil spirits in the woods?"

The old face lifted and the eyes brightened. "Yes. I'd say so, yessir. I don't know what the heck it is. I found it. It's like this, oh, I don't know what you'd call it, all engraved-like."

"You found it? Where?"

"Yessir, in the orchard."

"What orchard? You mean the house on Greer? The old Harmon place?"

"Yessir."

Dion stared at him. "When did you go to the orchard and find this thing?"

"Oh, after all the fuss died down, last week."

"Why? Why were you in the orchard? And how did you get in?"

"Curiosity killed the cat, sir."

Dion wasn't sure who the cat was in this case, himself or Starkey. He crossed his arms.

"I seen fings over there," Starkey said. "I know I should of stayed away from there, but I couldn't help it. It's like it was calling me."

"How did you get in? It's locked up." But no longer guarded.

"It was open, sir."

Open? Somebody had left it unsecured?

"Can you show me what you found, then?"

Starkey rubbed his grizzled chin. His eyes were swimmy, and whatever he had stashed in the basement,

Dion thought, was either fantasy or breaking news. Whatever it was, he wanted to see it and bag it — or, more likely, humour the man and be gone.

Starkey had grown moody, but he shrugged and turned away, leading Dion into a shadowy nook at the end of the kitchen. He drew back a heavy-duty barrel bolt and opened a solid wood door, stepped onto what looked like a landing perched over darkness, and flicked a switch. There came an electric buzzing sound, but not much light from below.

Starkey grunted and proceeded down steep wooden stairs, grumbling insults at fixtures and salesmen. "Them fluorescents take forever to kick in, faulty starters, every last one of 'em. Thirty-nine ninety-five, one-year warranty. Ought to take 'em back and shove 'em down their throats, is what I ought to do."

Dion brandished his penlight and followed the man down the stairs.

"There, on the table at the back," Starkey said, when they were both standing on the concrete floor. He was pointing to the far end of the dim basement. "Hang on a sec, here." He cast his eyes about, found a broomstick, and used it to bang the faulty fluorescents strung above.

Dion shone his beam toward an object at the back of the basement. Something on top of a workbench. It was a human head, severed and toppled sideways. He blinked at the object, then turned to Starkey and found the man still busy cursing and poking at the lights with his broomstick.

"Mr. Starkey," Dion interrupted. "What's on your workbench?"

"The friggin' fing from the orchard," Starkey said shortly. "Hang on. I gotta get the ladder. Tubes must be loose. Don't you go back there till we got some light going. It ain't safe."

"Wait, stay where you are," Dion ordered. He narrowed his eyes through the shadows at the object on the workbench. Could it be? He took a few steps forward, light beam casting its pale glow, until he was sure. The object on the workbench was no human head. It was a small, shrivelled pumpkin.

A jack-o-lantern.

And somebody was making a fool of him.

He was turning to confront Starkey about this poorest of jokes when he heard the click. It came from somewhere above, like a latch catching, and with a curse he realized his mistake. He knew the precise moment he had made it, too — looking away from his host and stepping toward the lure. Brilliant.

"Starkey!" he shouted, in the deepest voice he possessed. The barely heard response, through chipboard, underlay, flooring, and carpet, was a shrill laugh of triumph.

All ambient light from above was gone. The closed door would be locked — of course it would be.

He climbed the stairs and rattled the knob, shoved, banged on the wood with the side of his fist. He shouted Starkey's name. He heard silence.

The two faulty fluorescents buzzed and glimmered on the basement ceiling, casting only scant light on his dungeon. He walked back down the stairs, found the best strategic corner to stand in, pulled his cellphone from his jacket, and checked its juice level.

It didn't look good, and he knew why. His extended call to ICBC. Plus he hadn't been able to charge it in the courtesy car, because he had forgotten to take his charger. And compounding the problem, the phone had been acting up since a bad fall on his bathroom tiles. Brain injured, like himself. In the last few days it had been draining faster than normal, so much so that he had downloaded an app that would warn him when it was running low.

Fortunately it hadn't beeped at him yet. He would just have to be economical.

Calling David Leith would be faster than calling 911, he decided. Leith would take the info and act on it, no questions asked.

Not knowing Leith's extension, he called the detachment. Val the receptionist picked up. He told her to patch him through to Leith, and fast, as his phone battery was low. He added it was an emergency, and hoped she had caught those last few words before rerouting his call.

He was on hold and already regretted not calling 911. Still not in the red, though. Plenty of time. His low-battery app beeped a warning.

"*What?*" he asked it.

Val came on the line before he could disconnect and go the 911 route, saying Leith was out on a call, but she was connecting him to Corporal Wallace. Chris Wallace happened to be the foggiest member in general duties. Dion shouted, "*No!* Not —"

"Wallace."

Dion outlined the situation to the corporal, then got to what mattered, fast. "I'm at Kilmer Road in Lynn Valley. I don't have the exact —"

"You're *what*?" Wallace said.

Dion felt like a car short of fuel, on a road between two gas stations — not sure whether to go forward or turn back. He decided to go forward, and repeated himself to Wallace. "In Ray Starkey's house, on Kilmer Road in Lynn Valley, locked in his basement. I think he's still upstairs, and I don't know if he's armed, or what he's up to. Kilmer. Within eyeshot of the Greer house. Like I said, I can't give you the exact —"

"Cromwell?"

The warning beeped again.

"What?"

"You said Cromwell Street?"

Where did Cromwell come from? And how could the battery be draining so fast?

"Kilmer. *Kilmer*. Kilo India Lima — just send out a car —"

Beep.

"— and they can pull his address. White bungalow, green roof, mid block, close to the Headwaters road. Silent approach, 'cause I don't know what this guy is —"

"Just let me get a pen here," Wallace said, and Dion's phone died.

Thirty-Five

SOS

FARAH JORDAN DIDN'T SEEM to realize how serious the situation was. When she'd made the call, she had been told in no uncertain terms by dispatch to clear the scene and stay away till further notice. Her idea of clearing the scene seemed to be reversing her little white car down to the end of her driveway, switching it off, and waiting there, ignoring the gloved gestures of the ERT guys.

Bulked out in bulletproof like the rest of the team, Leith was tasked with getting rid of her. Keeping an eye on the house, he more or less sidestepped to the driver's window and rapped on the glass. Ms. Jordan stared out at him angrily, no trace of flower child in her now. He waved at her impatiently to start her car and back out further, make herself scarce. *That way, that way.*

She pulled a face that said he was full of shit, started up her car, and backed slowly out. She didn't roll off down the block as far as he was trying to indicate was appropriate — out of bullet range, in fact — but reparked close enough that she could keep an eye on her front door.

He had no time for her snit. Let her sit there in the line of fire. He watched the house instead, listened to communications, and waited. As it turned out, there was no gunfire, no military manoeuvres. Not even a shout or a scuffle, and scant minutes after the ERT had entered the house, they emerged with their prisoner between them in handcuffs.

Stefano Boone was a tall, skinny individual with a hawkish nose, fierce eyes, sallow skin, and scraggly black hair. He was wearing a woman's robe over some kind of PJs. He was barefoot, lifting his soles gingerly over the cold, rubbly concrete as he was led down to the vehicles.

Leith monitored the arrest, listened as the man's rights were read out, and instructed members on the plan. The killer was loaded into the car, no resistance, not a word said. He glanced up only once, staring past Leith, down the driveway, at the little white Rabbit parked too close to the action.

With the prisoner off-site and the house cleared of threats, Leith walked down to Jordan's car and asked her — again with hand gestures — to roll down her fucking window.

It was one of the old-fashioned crank windows. Jordan was smudging tears away with her knuckles as she cranked, and Leith felt bad for his impatience. He toned down what he'd had every intention of saying, and said instead, "We'll need to search your house, right now. Is that all right, ma'am? For anything Boone might have left behind."

"I understand."

"And I'll need to get your statement."

"Yes, of course."

She led the way through the front door and into a living room. She took the middle seat on a lumpy old sofa. Leith's options were a heavy-duty recliner, a straight-backed wooden chair, or his feet. He chose the wooden chair and busied himself preparing interview equipment. Pen, pad, digital recorder.

Upstairs the team tromped about. He could hear odd words, muffled laughter. Jordan heard it, too. She grimaced and said, "He's obviously very disturbed. As I told your receptionist, you didn't need to send in the SWAT team. I told her he's not only unarmed, but fast asleep. I should have done what I thought in the first place. Let him get his sleep then bring him in myself."

Leith's response was explosively short and snappy, but he kept it to himself. In silence he tested his pocket recorder for sound pickup.

"I mean, he thinks he's dangerous, but he isn't. He thinks he's a wolf," she said.

"Yes," Leith said, softly. Ms. Jordan didn't know what Stefano Boone had done to his family, to Constable Randall, to a defenseless child. He couldn't blame her for not knowing, and would just have to grin and bear through her misplaced sympathies.

The recorder seemed to be working fine, so he read in the time and date. But Ms. Jordan halted him, something to say. He flicked off the recorder to hear her out.

She held a small book on her lap. It might have been a Bible, except it was brilliant turquoise. She stroked its surface as she spoke. "I don't follow the news as much as I should, so I might have missed something. I've been warned about someone lurking in the woods, possibly dressed as a wolf, so obviously when Stefano showed up in my kitchen dressed as a wolf, I clued in and reported him. Which again, I wish I had gone about differently. But is there something else? He seemed to imply he had done something bad. Is this connected to the death of Ben Stirling?"

Bad, he thought. "We can talk about it later," he said. "For now I need you to answer my questions."

"All right."

The recorder was on again. Leith got through the preliminaries, then asked her how Boone had come to be in her house.

"Probably through the back door," she said. "I've been meaning to replace the lock. He was just seeking refuge with someone he knows. We know each other. But you're aware of that, aren't you, that Stefano and I both work at the Greek Taverna?"

"Yes, I'm aware of that."

"I think he trusts me. Or *trusted* me. I doubt he'll trust anybody now, though," she said, biting her lip reflectively. "Poor Stef," she added.

Grin and bear it. "Just go through tonight's events for me in your own words. In as much detail as you can recall, then I'll have some questions for you. Just start from the beginning, please."

She opened her mouth to begin, but Leith's cellphone trilled in his pocket, almost knocking off his mantle of forced patience. He took the call briskly. "Leith."

"Chris Wallace," the caller said. Wallace sounded doubtful, as if puzzled by its own name. "Do you have a minute?"

Wallace's story was he had just received a call from Cal Dion, who was complaining of, what? Being locked in a basement somewhere in Lynn Valley?

Wallace was oblique at the best of times, but he was outdoing himself here, trying to describe what had to be some kind of miscommunication. Leith apologized to Jordan. He took the call out to the hallway, then apologized to Wallace and asked for a repeat.

"He called, like I say, just minutes ago. Isn't he suspended?"

"He called and said what?"

"I'm not sure. He was babbling. Going around in circles. Seemed excited. And then he just hung up on me."

Babbling and excitable wasn't the Dion that Leith knew — but he didn't know Dion all that well. "And he was babbling about being locked in a basement?"

"Yes, in Lynn Valley. On Cromwell Street."

Leith closed an eye and failed to locate a Cromwell in his sketchy mental map of the area.

Wallace continued, "He gave me a name, and I thought I had it written down, but I — hang on, I have it here on my — no, I don't. But if you give me a moment. Oh, yes, I've got it here. Is that an S or a B? Must be a B. Barkley. Yes, Ray Barkley."

Leith gripped the phone under his chin to jot the information into his notebook. *Ray Barkley, Cromwell St.* "And then he hung up on you, sir?"

"Hung up cold," Wallace said. "I think I offended him."

Leith apologized again to Farah Jordan, telling her something had come up and he would have to finish this conversation later. If he couldn't return in person to get her statement, he would send someone in his place.

Outside, he dropped into the driver's seat of his Crown Vic on the now quiet avenue and tried calling Dion's cellphone. It went to voice mail. He then logged in to the onboard computer and worked at finding a Ray Barkley in the area.

There was no Ray Barkley in Lynn Valley, and neither was there a Cromwell Street. There was a Barkley Street in Port Alberni, and a Cromwell Road in Victoria, and plenty of people named Barkley everywhere, as well as plenty of Rays, but no Ray Barkleys — or anything close — in this area, which was all that mattered.

He tried Dion's number again. It went to voice mail, and Leith was left where he had started fifteen minutes ago, sitting in a parked car outside Farah Jordan's house with a cry for help he couldn't answer. Cal Dion was lost — sucked into the cracks of Wallace error.

He dispatched two cars to look for any sign of Dion or his vehicle in Lynn Valley — a fairly new dark-blue Honda Civic, neatnik owned and driven. No, he could give no coordinates besides Lynn Valley, but would provide updates soon as they came in.

He called the detachment and spoke to the operator who had patched Dion through to Wallace. She told him that Dion had tried to contact him, Leith, and had been transferred to Wallace as an alternative. Dion was in a hurry because his phone was low on battery, and though she wouldn't call his demeanour babbling or panicked, he did sound stressed. She also suggested Leith try server disk array.

"Try who?" he asked.

Telephone monitoring records, she told him. "It's all recorded. Right?"

He told her to, yes, please, track down that call for him. Val said she couldn't do it herself, but would contact the technical department.

As Leith waited for the IT people to find the recording, he looked up Dion's car registration on the database. Then he contacted the two patrols en route to Lynn Valley with his instructions narrowed down, to grid search for Dion's Civic — HVK 995 — keeping eyes out not only for his car, but anything out of whack in the neighbourhood.

He placed another call to Chris Wallace. He asked the corporal to scour both his memory and notes for any more particulars on Dion's SOS, as the name Ray Barkley and the address Cromwell Street seemed be incorrect.

Wallace took offence and said any errors must have originated from Dion's side of the conversation.

It didn't matter. The techies would locate that recorded call soon enough, and hopefully therein the answer would lie. Leith set down the receiver and once again looked over his map of Lynn Valley, scanning for street names that audibly resembled Cromwell. Or, failing that, *remotely* resembled Cromwell.

Constable Lil Hart called to say she had spotted only one blue Honda Civic parked in someone's driveway, but this Honda was dirty and plastered with decals. It also had a different plate.

"Want us to check anyway?" she asked. "Licence plates can be switched."

"But dirt and decals?" Leith said. "Forget it. Just keep looking. Thanks."

A man from IT called to tell Leith he had located no call from Dion, but he had discovered an hour of silence overlaid with odd noises. It happens from time to time, the IT guy said. It's called system failure.

Leith knew it was something more sinister. It was called Cal's luck.

Thirty-Six

GLITTER

WITH THE DIMMING RAY of his penlight sweeping floor and walls, Dion explored the basement from
corner to corner. In the process he discovered what
looked like a spattering of old blood dried to black in a
nook behind a laundry tub, and more on the adjacent
wall. But it didn't matter right now. It was nothing but
a waste of battery power.

The basement was twenty feet by forty, with a ten-foot
ceiling. Near empty, with all the clutter of storage boxes
and old automobile tires and whatnot stashed in one corner. Under the stairs he found a pantry of sorts. There were
jars of homemade jam, bags of potatoes growing pale arms,
onions sprouting tails through mesh. And at the back, one
workbench with no work on or around it except for one ob-
noxious jack-o-lantern, badly carved and caving into itself.

Some carpentry tools were scattered about. He
looked them over with interest. Having no firearm, he
equipped himself with the best weapons he could find in

the collection: a fully loaded manual staple gun, which he test fired at a wooden support post; a large flathead screwdriver; and a small, blunt hatchet that couldn't do much damage to lumber, but would easily knock a little shit like Starkey on his ass.

Potential escape routes: nothing but the door at the top of the stairs and a tiny window high on one cement wall. He discovered how solid the door was by driving his body weight against it. Didn't even quiver. Smashing the dull blade of the hatchet against the wood only nicked the surface.

The second option, the basement window, was far too small for him to crawl through. He stood on a rickety kitchen chair and smashed the glass out, anyway. He shouted through the jagged opening, "Hey! Help! Anybody out there?" The only response was a keening of November wind, then the frenzied yapping of a neighbourhood dog somewhere beyond his view.

The barking gave him an idea. He scribbled a note, then whistled out the window in an encouraging way, hoping that a dog would come running. He would attach the note to the animal's collar, shoo it off, sit tight, and wait for the owner to find it.

But even if his plan had any brains, the bylaws kept dogs from running free these days, and after whistling his lips numb for two minutes, note in hand, no dog came running. There was some reply, though. A whistle. No, not a whistle, but a high, wavering cry. He stood on the chair and listened.

It was the wail of a child coming from within the house. He looked up and around, cupping his ear, but the sound had faded. He called out to the child, but received no answer.

He picked up the meanest shard of glass he could find from the broken window and added it to his arsenal. He stepped off the chair and stood collecting his thoughts.

"Wallace got the message," he told himself. "Help is on its way."

He didn't believe himself, because too much time had passed, and Wallace was Wallace. He had transposed enough letters that the search would circle the block for weeks. He kicked the rickety chair across the basement.

Daylight was dimming, but he was reserving his flashlight for the worst-case scenario — being trapped here all night long. As darkness flooded the basement, so did the cold. Hardly an hour had gone by, and he was shivering, bewildered, and now hungry.

Still not worried, though. He had worked out in his head why he was here. He had fed Starkey's assumption that he was First Nations, and Starkey, who was clearly paranoid and a complete mental turnip, had locked the enemy in his basement. It was a case of self-defence, and Starkey would now call 911 and get the cops over to deal with the problem.

What a laugh they all would have when the door flew open.

There had been nothing but silence from above, but now came a distant thump. Dion bounded up the stairs to the landing and banged at the door with his fist. He stood with hands and forehead against the door and tried to hear what was going on. Sounds of movement in the house, distant footsteps. No voices. He shouted

Starkey's name, then a list of Criminal Code sections the man could be charged under, along with minimum sentences, if he didn't open up right now.

Nothing.

He was getting scared. He tramped back down and stood in the centre of the basement, armed with nothing but a crappy collection of carpentry tools and some broken glass. A sound or motion caught his attention, and he looked up. From between the joists came a faint glow. He walked closer and shone his light up at a three-inch hole bored through the wood, a spot he would have tried hacking open with his hatchet, if he had noticed it sooner.

The light blotted out and Dion jumped back in surprise as an eye appeared.

A human eye, staring down at him as he stared up. Starkey.

He shouted at the eye, "Open the door, Starkey, before you're in this so deep you'll never get out. I'm a police officer. Doesn't matter I'm off duty. The consequences are going to be just as bad — worse — if you don't cut the crap and let me out of here."

The answer was odd. "You want light?"

"What?"

"Light. Little flood lamp under the stairs."

The spying eye disappeared. With a soft thud, the hole went dark.

In the makeshift pantry, along with potatoes and onions, Dion found a dust-encrusted flood lamp wrapped in its cord. He felt better now. Starkey didn't want to harm him, it seemed, offering the comfort of illumination while they waited for the cops to show up. Illumination would be welcome. He plugged it in on the workbench and it flared to life, stabbing his eyes, bright-lighting at least one third of the dungeon and spreading a muted glow into the corners.

He then wasted more minutes up on the rickety chair, hacking at the floorboards around the hole — floorboards that weren't half so flimsy as they appeared — until a new set of sounds from above distracted him from his work. He stood still, breathing hard. A series of taps, like beads spilling across linoleum, but in a steady rhythm, not random. And moving.

Claws.

Police dogs? No, there were no businesslike voices or thudding police boots. Just the swift clacking of a single animal. Heavy but energetic, moving from here to there overhead. Something wrong with the picture. He remained standing on his chair, hatchet in hand, heart pounding. He heard a fumbling, and then a faint whoosh with a squeal as the door at the top of the stairs eased open.

Open!

He left his chair and lunged, but skidded to a stop as he saw what was happening.

Now he got it. The pieces snapped together. He had been given a cellmate.

The door was closed again and locked, and his cellmate sat on the cramped landing at the top of the stairs: a big squat dog in dark silhouette against the paler planes of the door.

The dog remained facing away from him, interested only in the door that had just closed on its nose. It growled at the door. Tried whining. Scratched at the door's base impatiently, first with one paw, then with both.

The door didn't open, and the dog began to look around for other options. Dion dropped into a careful crouch and picked up the hatchet. The dog's bulky head swung to sniff the air, catching the scent of something exciting — human fear.

Some dogs took fear as a sign to protect, but this was not that kind of dog. This was the attacking kind. Dion took another step back as the animal's wide-set eyes glittered to and fro in the darkness. They fixed on him, and stayed. The dog flattened its small ears against its skull. It drew back black lips to bare its teeth, made a purring noise. Not a purr, but a moan of loathing.

"God," Dion said.

Thirty-Seven

DOG FOOD

LEITH LEFT THE CANVASSING of Lynn Valley to others and worked on backtracking through Dion's difficult day.

The day started with a grilling by internal investigations. The meeting ended in suspension, pending further investigation. Then Dion had met briefly with Mike Bosko at Rainey's, where — as Bosko summarized it — Dion was told he'd better keep his cool and behave.

Leaving Rainey's, Dion had spoken to Doug Paley on the street outside the detachment. This Leith knew because a fellow GIS officer had seen the two talking in the pouring rain, and it hadn't looked like a friendly chat. Leith tried Paley's number and it went to voice mail, which seemed to be the theme of the day.

More digging revealed that Dion had dropped into the detachment for another short and heated conversation, this time with Corporal Montgomery — according to eyewitnesses — before completing his vanishing act.

Leith needed to talk to Montgomery and find out more about that conversation, but Montgomery seemed to be away from his desk and not answering his calls. Leith left yet another voice mail, again underlining the urgency of a fast reply.

He then revisited Mike Bosko's office to hammer down more details on the conversation at Rainey's. Bosko agreed that Cal was upset by the end of it.

"And no mention of what he had planned for the rest of the day?"

"I'm afraid not. Sorry, Dave. Keep me apprised."

Doug Paley returned Leith's call, apparently from his home, asking what was up. Leith told him about Dion's disappearance. Paley wasn't one to fret much, but he was fretting now. "I'll come in. Be there in ten."

"But first, tell me what he talked to you about on the street this morning. I'm trying to figure out every move he made today."

"He was standing in the rain looking like a lost tourist, so I asked what he was up to. He wanted to know who was lead on the Randall homicide. I told him Monty, and he gave me a message to pass on to him about some crackpot in Lynn Valley. This crackpot had a tip about evil spirits, and he wanted me to remind Monty to follow up. I didn't do it, Dave. I didn't take him seriously, and I forgot. "

"A crackpot. Did you get name, address, anything?"

"Now, what the hell was that fucking name?"

"Ray Barkley, or thereabouts?" Leith said, and the name Ray Barkley rang a distant bell in his own mind. Just couldn't quite pin it down. "Cromwell Street?"

"No, nothing like that."

A stretch of silence on the line, and Leith could hear that Paley was on the move, boots crunching on gravel. He heard a car door beep open. "For some reason I'm thinking Hutch," Paley said. The door thumped shut, an engine fired up. "But that can't be right. Ask Monty. He'd know."

"I'm trying," Leith said. "Thanks."

Montgomery finally got back to Leith, saying he was on his way in. "Is there a problem?"

"A big one. I told you this is important. I almost code-redded you."

"Sorry, Dave. Can't talk now, but let's meet at my desk in two minutes, is that cool?"

It wasn't cool, and it was more like eight minutes before Montgomery showed up, sat at his desk, and popped the lid off his Starbucks coffee. "Whew, what a crazy day. What's happening? Your message said something about Dion? He's missing, you say?"

"Yes, and it could be serious," Leith said, because Montgomery was grinning. Leith had run down enough false alarms to know that, at the end of the day, grinning could be in order. But not right now, with Cal at the wrong end of that alarm. "He was in here earlier, talking to you, and I need to know what he said. Doug says it was about a crackpot in Lynn Valley. Mean anything to you?"

"Crackpot," Montgomery said, thinking hard. "Sure! The old guy who approached us when we were mustering at the base of the Mesachee. You weren't there. Actually that's the second time I met him. Much like the first time, he rambled about wolves and evil spirits in the woods. Cal came in this afternoon saying it should be followed up. I begged to differ. He left. You're thinking he went out there on his own?"

"I don't know what to think right now," Leith said. "You have a name for this guy? Dion mentioned a name to Wallace, Ray Barkley. He gave a different name to Doug, but Doug can't remember. He thought it was maybe Hutch. He said you'd know what it was."

"Let me go through my notes," Montgomery said. "Might as well have a seat, Dave. Note taking was never my strong point. Nor is a tidy desk."

Leith took a chair and said nothing, hoping his silence and firmly crossed arms spoke louder than words.

Monty shuffled through papers. He said, "I have to tell you, I like Cal, but the guy's not firing on all cylinders. The accident, I guess — well, you've seen it. He drifts. I don't suggest he hears voices, but, well, I know paranoia when I see it. I sometimes think he's fixated on me, for some reason."

Leith cut in, because Monty's uncalled-for psych assessment was not only annoying, but also slowing down the search. "Let's just get that name."

Monty flipped back through his notebook, and at last put his finger on an entry. "Starkey, Ray. Now, why didn't I write down his address?"

Starkey, not Starsky *and Hutch*, Leith thought. Damn Doug Paley and his fucked-up memory palace. Then it pinged — the gravel-voiced man who had called with a hot tip just the other day. If Wallace had got the name just a degree closer, he would have twigged. "No address? How about a phone number?"

Monty snapped his fingers. "I know why I didn't write it down. Because I knew where he lived. He pointed it out to us. Green roof. Cal was there, so he'd know as well."

Leith cut the conversation short, leaving his chair spinning on its casters. He had the tipster's address and phone number in his notebook, somewhere, but there was a quicker solution. He crossed the floor to his own station and seized the phone directory, leafed through it still standing, and found the name listed. He tore the page out clean and was out the door, gathering backup as he left.

* * *

Dion had abandoned the hatchet, grabbing instead the rickety kitchen chair. It was working so far, and he was keeping the animal at bay, lion-tamer style, but it wouldn't last. The dog was a perpetual motion machine, a dedicated ball of muscles, and Dion was only a badly maintained man, already weakening under the assault. Dripping sweat, tripping in the lamplight, shouting in fright.

He was exhausted, and the monster was just warming up.

The dog's strategy was simple: *hit, hit, hit,* and never relent till the prey is on its knees. Once on its knees, latch onto an artery and shred. Dion knew that to fall would be the end of him. He had to stay focused and upright. He had to keep out of corners. An object or wall met his heel, and in knee-jerk reaction, he gave a samurai yell and danced forward with his lion-tamer chair. The bluff worked until the dog caught the rhythm of the dance and came looping around, aiming for a rear attack.

Dion synchronized his turns with the dog's circling, keeping his back covered, but the plan was unsustainable. He needed to up the tempo, spin on his heel. He had just enough strength to pull it off, and the chair legs smacked the dog with force, catching it in mid-lunge. The dog flopped to the ground with a grunt. One of the chair legs had snapped off and flown wide. The others dangled loose. Dion stopped spinning in one direction and unwound dizzily. He steadied out, trying to catch a breath before the animal could rebound. He watched the dog find its footing, shake out the blur of impact, reconnoitre.

Dion threw aside his broken chair. The dog lowered its breast to cement as though to rest, and was silent. But it wasn't resting. Its silence was scarier than its noise. Dion grabbed the hatchet off the floor.

"Aim for the eyes," he muttered, dry-mouthed. *Bash out its brains.*

The dog scrabbled its hind legs on the cement and launched, and this time Dion stayed to meet it, hatchet hooked back over his shoulder like a baseball bat aiming for a home-run shot.

The moment stretched, and he was playing softball on the detachment's co-ed team at Kinsmen Park, more a social event than a sport, but there were points to be won, and he would swing the bat like everyone else, hitting it square occasionally, and when the ball sailed in an arc, he would sprint through the dust like his life depended on it.

Strange how it all merged, sun and fun with a basement from hell, so when the dog sprang for him, he swung with all the home-run force he could muster. His arms jolted as metal made contact with flesh, and he was still drawing parallels. Was it just the act of swinging the bat, or was it his heart slamming in the socked-in summer heat? It was Looch Ferraro shouting encouragements, and it was David Leith grabbing him and dragging him backwards as the dog spun around for the last attack.

It was all things at once. The world whirled, and he backed against Leith with the man's arm outstretched across him, pointing at the dog as if conducting a lesson on danger. *That's the enemy, this is the cannon, here's what you do.* He watched the cannon in Leith's fist kick hard, the explosion like applause from the bleachers. He wasn't sure where he was supposed to turn next, as Looch and sunshine disappeared, but it didn't matter, because Leith led the way, pulling him out of a collapse and away from the dog yelping about on cold cement, all the way to the staircase, where he was released like baggage.

He sat on the wooden step, drenched and shuddering, and it had nothing to do with baseball or the summer's heat. He was back in a dungeon in Lynn Valley — and now that his body was given free rein to hurt, it hurt like daggers.

* * *

Relieved of Dion's weight, Leith turned to his final task. "Jesus Christ." The newscasts would focus on this, like it was all that mattered. The force would get flooded with complaints, maybe even death threats. He drew his shoulders up and walked back to the dog, and for a moment watched it writhe on the floor, slithering about in its own blood, fatally wounded. Whatever anybody said, however noble it was in its heart, the animal had been unloved from the time it was taken from its mother, born and bred to go down fighting, with or without cause.

Like there wasn't enough bad shit in this world.

Doing himself and Dion and everyone else a favour, not least the dog in its pain, Leith aimed low and plugged a final bullet into the creature's solid skull.

Two members clattered down to the stairs. The junior constable only stared at the dead dog on the floor, and the senior told Leith, "Something upstairs you gotta see, Dave."

"Now?"

"*Right* now."

Thirty-Eight

CHOKE

SHE WAS MAYBE IN HER MIDTEENS, the skinny girl found in the closet in Starkey's bedroom. She lay in a nest of damp, putrid bedding. Nobody wanted to move her until the paramedics showed up. The member who had summoned Leith upstairs now pointed out that the small closet door was rigged with a sliding lock latch, but as found, the bolt had not been shot. Maybe because it wasn't needed; the prisoner was too weak to flee.

Leith glanced at the latch mechanism and saw it was fairly new, cheap-looking; a nickel-plated, hardware-store kind of device. The scars to the wood looked fresh. The room was fairly shipshape. Unremarkable, except for the lock on the closet door and, next to the neatly made single bed, as pointed out to Leith, a three-inch-diameter hole in the floor.

The hole looked historical, for an old vent pipe, possibly. Large enough to drop an apple through. Hunkering down, Leith peered through the hole and got a surprisingly good view of a swath of the basement below.

The paramedics arrived to remove the girl, and the shifting of body and bedding released a reek of mould, sour milk, stale urine. The girl looked parched and greasy. Her hair was the colour of milky tea. They had found Aphid.

* * *

In the morning the girl was responding to stimuli, though not communicating. JD had found an official name for her. She had taken what little data she had for the captive — approximate age, general description — and with much tracking through computer systems, provincially, then nationally, then internationally, she had linked her with a fifteen-year-old possible runaway from Seattle, missing for over a year. April Quail.

Dental records and an exchange of photographs between agencies confirmed her identity. Her parents were informed, and they made arrangements to come and collect their daughter — once she had woken from her fugue and given a statement.

On the second day her parents sat with her, and her unresponsive body was introduced to liquids. In the evening she murmured a few words, and Leith expected her to soak up food like a sponge, but was told that wasn't to happen. Re-nourishment had to take place one sip at a time.

On the morning of the third day she uttered a few unintelligible words, and in the afternoon she gave her first coherent answer to Leith's questions, spoken in a reedy whisper: "I don't have to tell you any fucking thing."

Rescue a wildcat, and it might bite. Reactions to police intervention varied, in Leith's experience. He had received nice thank-you cards, and he had received gobs of spit. More spit than cards. So he wasn't surprised to be sworn at by this little bag of bones.

He left JD and others to give it their best shot, and spent his time at the detachment, building a case against Ray Starkey.

Starkey was responsible for Ben Stirling's death and disposal, and April Quail was going to prove it, once they had proved April Quail and Aphid were one and the same. Leith needed April to admit she was Aphid. He needed her testimony, because Ray Starkey wasn't talking. Starkey had listened to his lawyer and was sticking to his guns. Even with the blood in the basement that was going to prove Ben Stirling died down there, without a confession, there was nothing to tie the homeowner to culpable homicide beyond the shadow of a doubt.

On the evening of the third day Leith talked to Aphid about his own daughter, Isabelle, or Izzy, or Iz. "April is a pretty name," he said. "What do your friends call you?"

She told him her friends didn't call her anything, because she had no friends.

"Isn't Gunner a friend? What does he call you?"

She clammed up, but he had made progress. He texted JD to get over here right away. It was her turn to try. She had a way with the young and scared, and he bet she would succeed where he had failed. An hour later she proved him right.

* * *

With April Quail's damning statement in front of him, Ray Starkey confessed.

An all-or-nothing kind of accused, he went from saying nothing to answering anything Leith asked. He first described the hot day in August when a young lady had come ringing the doorbell.

"She wanted to use the phone, eh?" Starkey said. "But I know the trick. She's looking around, scoping the place for valuables. What was I to do? I invited her inside."

Leith could think of a few good alternatives to inviting a potential burglar into your home. He said, "Sure. And then what?"

"Girl was hungry. Homeless. Not well. I said she could stay, and I'd take care of her till she figured out what to do. She stayed."

Starkey seemed to half-believe his own story, but Leith continued to believe April's. As she told it, she had been scoping the joint for Gunner, eyeing the place for an easy hit. But she was a young and inexperienced burglar's assistant, and she had been offered cash in exchange for favours, and she had taken the lure, had followed her mark down the hall, towards the dim light of a bedroom, and from there straight to hell. Pepper spray, straight in the face, and next thing she knew she was locked in a closet.

Leith reminded Starkey of this radically different tale. Consent or pepper spray? Somebody here wasn't telling the truth.

A smarter prisoner might have tried to lie his way out of trouble, or at least develop a selective memory. But Starkey didn't seem to know what was in his own best interests. "Well, sir, that little girl had some learning to do," he stated. "You can't go robbing people and not pay for what you done. I told her me keeping her was a lot better'n what the cops would do to her."

"Uh-huh? So what was the long-term plan?"

"I treated her right. I gave her food, bathroom breaks. But figured she's got to promise to smarten up and go straight. I told her so. She wouldn't promise, so I said I'd have to turn her in. But still, I wanted to give her a chance, y'know."

According to April, there was no such wheeling and dealing. Just a lot of yelling and swearing and name calling, on both sides. When she came to, tied up and locked in a closet, the old bastard just called her a whore and a thief — through the closet door — and wouldn't let her out.

There was no sexual assault, and yes, in the beginning he had fed her and let her go to the washroom. He wasn't that bright, she could tell, and she expected she might even have escaped. But then the event happened. The horror. The night she had heard Ben. That was maybe four days after her capture. He had come to save her, she was sure of it. He was somewhere in the house, down below, screaming. Horrible, terrible screams that shredded her heart. In the silence that followed she knew Ben was dead. She had given up then. The days dragged by, countless days, and she felt herself fading. Without Ben, she didn't want to live. Thanks for nothing.

What if Dion hadn't come along and saved the day? April would have faded to nothing. She would have vanished without a trace, or ended up an unsolved mystery, down in another dark hole, just like her boyfriend.

Leith's belief, based on the scraps of information he'd gotten from various sources, was that Ben Stirling, a.k.a. Gunner, had tried to shoo April back to a better life, so when she had disappeared, he had at first thought she had done just that, shooed off. But Gunner had his doubts, had wondered about certain houses his girlfriend had been casing out for him, had worried something had happened to her. He had gone to find her, and died trying.

Starkey was not going to admit that he had meant to let the girl die. Technically, maybe he really hadn't. But it didn't matter, Leith knew. They were far from done talking. Next up was the death of Ben Stirling, and by the end of the night, the indictment against Ray Starkey was going to be long enough to choke him.

Thirty-Nine

GOREOPHILE

FACE TO FACE, SPEAKING ACROSS a table about Ben Stirling's brutal death, Starkey struck Leith as callous, but apologetic. Fearful of the consequences, but without the faintest appreciation of the intrinsic rightness or wrongness of his acts. Leith was no psychologist, but he had his own ideas about what drove the man to lock people up and watch them die — an evil twist on voyeurism.

To any healthy mind, there could be nothing sexually stimulating about watching a girl waste away to nothing, or seeing a man ripped to pieces, but maybe in Starkey's atrophied mind, the suffering of others brought back enough sensation to qualify as an actual turn-on.

That was Leith's theory, anyway. Starkey's explanation was less colourful: he was only protecting his property. He hadn't meant for anybody to die. He only put the dog down there to make sure the native kid didn't escape, and when the savaging started, it was too late to do anything but watch.

It took some back and forthing for Leith to realize the "native kid" in Starkey's mind was Ben Stirling. Starkey explained that he knew the man was native because he had seen him on the street, sneaking in and out of the old Harmon house. Leith wondered if Stirling's faux hawk haircut, depicted in his autopsy photographs, had confused the killer, for in fact, there was not a drop of Indigenous blood in Ben Stirling. According to his brother, Sam, he and Ben were of Ukrainian descent.

With some prompting, Starkey admitted he had watched the kid die. He couldn't explain why. To find out what happened next, he supposed.

That was summertime, only a few days after he had locked the girl in his closet so he could figure out what to do with her. He had come home after a bit of shopping to see a man at the back of the house flitting across the hall. Likewise, the man must have heard his return and hid in the basement. Starkey had run over and shut the basement door. Had some scrap lumber handy, and went about hammering boards in place to keep the thief secured.

He had meant to call the cops right off, he explained, but then got a better idea. "Buddy of mine I used to work with, Duggy Vahn, he had to go off to the States quite sudden because of a death in the family, and he wanted me to look after his pup for him while he was gone. What I had to do is go out to his place in Blueridge once a day, feed 'im, change his water, all that. Dog lives in the backyard, runs on a wire, all in chain-link. Pixie's his name. Duggy loves that pup. But always keeps him hungry. Makes him a better watchdog that way."

Leith sat marvelling as the story flipped on its axis. In the space of one breath, Starkey had gone from righteous homeowner making a citizen's arrest to a premeditating monster, and without any manoeuvres on Leith's part. Arms crossed, he waited for the man to finish nailing his own coffin shut.

So with the burglar locked in the basement, Starkey went on, he had gone and fetched Pixie from Blueridge, a pretty quick trip. Pixie was a good dog, but he could be snappy, and as a rule wore a muzzle in public. With the dog heeled at his feet, Starkey pried the boards away from the basement door, moving fast, worried that the native kid would burst out on him. But the kid stayed down below and kept quiet, probably thinking it was the police coming, probably busy inventing excuses for his trespassing. Starkey ushered the unmuzzled Pixie through and boarded the door up again. When he heard the shouts that soon became screams, he had squinted down that hole in his bedroom to watch Pixie cornering the burglar, grabbing hold.

"Not a pretty picture," Leith suggested.

Starkey seemed to shudder at his memory of the deed, while taking no blame for it. "He screamed so loud," he said. "Like a broad in one of those horror movies. The girl was screaming, too. Between the two of 'em I thought they'd wake the whole neighbourhood. "

"So why did you figure it was better setting a dog on the boy than calling the cops?"

The answer was prompt. "'Cause you call the cops, he just does six months, gets out again, robs someone else. Maybe somebody'd get hurt. This is better."

"What's better?"

Pause. Starkey was looking at him across the table, eye to eye, not sure what part of *this is better* Leith didn't get. "Well, getting rid of 'im."

"Getting rid of?"

"Like, put 'im down." Starkey grinned nervously. "Bad dogs get put down, right?"

Leith persisted. He needed Starkey to state his intentions, not in coy euphemisms, but plain English. For the record. "What d'you mean, Ray, *put him down*? I don't understand. Down on the ground?"

Starkey drew a finger across his own throat.

Which looked great on video, the classic *execute* hand signal, but Leith wanted it in words. "Huh?"

"Better to just have 'im dead." Starkey lowered his voice, as if slipping his words under the table. Maybe he didn't realize that the softest sigh was being digitally captured, that every whisper would be amplified to the jury, and in their deliberations, that jury could replay it all to their hearts' content.

"Better to have who dead?"

Starkey worked to hide his surprise at how dense this policeman sitting across the table was. "The kid, like I said. The kid what tried to rob me. Y'know."

Leith was satisfied with the admission and moved on. "Okay. So then what?"

Then Starkey had let Pixie back upstairs, fed the animal, and taken her back to Blueridge. Then went across to Vancouver, up Kingsway, to an army surplus store and purchased an old duffel bag. Paid with cash. Returned home and went downstairs. Considered dismembering the body for ease of transportation, and managed to saw through an arm. But it was too tough, so he'd opted for the wrap-it-up and take-it-all-in-one-piece route. Got the corpse into the bag, which was sonovabitch difficult. He had used a rope and pulley set-up to get the duffel bag upstairs, then left it on the back porch for a bit.

Then the cleaning up all the next day, mopping down the cement, the walls. Found one of the kid's shoes lying in a corner and threw it out with the trash.

Took a day or two to work up the energy to deal with the body. Plan one was truck it to the dump, but then he thought better of it, because if the remains were discovered too quick the employees there might remember him. In the end he had loaded it onto his dolly — really took the wind out of him — and onto the back of his Datsun, and gone out looking for a place to drop it. He knew the perfect spot, too. The very house the kid was hiding out in, which he knew for a fact sat boarded up and empty.

"How did you get in?" Leith asked. "The gate was chained and padlocked."

"Gate was chained and padlocked, but I had the key."

"How'd you get the key?"

Starkey explained. Two summers ago he had borrowed bolt cutters from Duggy and gotten rid of the old padlock on the back gate of the Harmon house. Replaced it with his own, so he could get in and out as he wished. "Wasn't harming nobody. Just hated to see 'em go to waste."

"See what go to waste?"

"Them crab apples growing in the yard there. For jelly."

Starkey had dollied the body through the gate, in a

sweat about getting caught, but wasn't caught, and up to the rear of the house, with plans of just leaving the bag tucked there, hidden from view.

The crawl space was another epiphany. He saw the gap in the foundations and thought, *Better yet* ...

But it had been a helluva job again, worse than anything so far, dragging the body through the hole, a real tight squeeze, and along the sand in the dank underbelly of the house, and he wouldn't do it again, hell no, not if you paid him.

"Not nice places at the best of times, crawl spaces," Leith commiserated.

"And I got this rheumatism, makes it tough." Starkey showed off his stiff, curled hands.

"How did you manage?"

"Stuck a stick through that duffle bag handle, the one on the end, grabbed the stick with my arms like this, and inched ass-backwards. Hard on my knees, too. But, no shit, it was a real good hiding spot."

"Sure."

Sandwiches arrived, and Starkey helped himself. The food in his belly energized him, and he went on to describe the months of fear that followed his delivery of the corpse to the crawl space.

It had started with the howlings. He heard them all the way down the block. They came from the mouth of the dead boy under the house. "I wasn't so scared of 'em till after that," he told Leith. "But I shoulda thought of it, eh? Shoulda been more careful. They turn into animals after they die. They come looking for you, if you do 'em wrong, even if you're doing right, protecting your own property. They don't have that same respect for property like you and me have."

"You think the burglar was coming back for you? In animal form?"

"No, sir. Dead is dead. And me, I'm not superstitious or nothing. But you start to hear howlings in the woods what sound, y'know, half human-like, you get to thinking maybe there's something in 'em Windigo stories, right? You lock your doors, but they walk right through 'em."

Leith noticed that Starkey was watching the grey wall to his left. He seemed to see something forming there, and whatever he was seeing worried him enough to bring beads of sweat to his temples.

* * *

Long after midnight, Leith sat at his desk typing up his report. He was at the part about probable cause to enter the premises, which had not been much more than a patchy SOS from Cal Dion. He reflected as his index fingers sought and plunked out the keys that, like all such reports, it was about nine-tenths information for the purposes of prosecution, and one-tenth covering his own ass. Which meant in his job, he was always about one-tenth afraid, not of the enemy out there, but of his own matrix. Which was sad, but probably necessary. It was called law and order.

Covering his ass, he made it clear in his report that upon arrival at Starkey's house last week, the front door had been unlocked. He had knocked — loudly — and gotten no reply, and quite frankly, he hadn't waited long before bursting in, flanked by his team, to catch Starkey scuttling out of the bedroom.

Leith's final questioning of Starkey about that night's events, the unlawful confinement and attempted murder of Constable Dion, was short and unsatisfying. On this topic, Starkey seemed to grow foggy, like a man of limited vocabulary trying to describe a complex dream.

Starkey did admit he had locked the basement door knowing the police officer was down there. He had gone to Blueridge to pick up Pixie, telling Duggy Vahn he just felt like taking the animal for a walk. He had returned home, unmuzzled Pixie, and locked him in the basement with his prisoner. He had not, at any point after that, unlocked the door, nor made any effort to help the police officer.

Why? was the question he couldn't answer, except to say this visitor was an "Indian" too, and not a real police officer, and a threat to his well-being.

He would not admit that he had watched the dog attack through the hole in the floor, or that he wanted the cop dead. But again, Leith didn't need any further admissions to wrap up his report to Crown counsel with confidence. He closed the interview, and the twisted little soul was processed and housed, pending remand. If he didn't end up in a psych ward, he would spend the rest of his years in jail.

Finished with his report, Leith proofed it and filed it, then sat thinking. Deep in the oil pits of Starkey's heart, his motivations had been pure sadism. Because what else was there? Sometime between the murder of Stirling and the attempted murder of an RCMP member,

Starkey had gone out and purchased a heavy-duty barrel lock set and attached it purposely to the door leading down to his basement.

Not strange in and of itself, since a man who has been burgled once might naturally become more security conscious. Except Starkey's basement had no real access to the outside, so a lock could serve only one purpose.

Besides, weren't locks futile against werewolves and Windigos, which passed through doors and walls, if Starkey could be believed?

No, what they had arrested was an opportunistic serial killer in the making, Leith believed, and the basement was his trap. It was just a damn good thing someone qualified had stumbled into it before anyone else did. If qualified was the word.

Forty

DEVIL'S CLUB

IN THE PASSING DAYS, Dion had no graceful chance to thank David Leith for saving his life. The problem was mostly schedule related, because of shift work. If Leith wasn't at work or asleep, then Dion was asleep or else stuck in one room or another at the detachment, giving a statement or filing forms.

Week's end brought one last meeting. This one had the smell of an intervention, and was supposedly off the record, informal, just a chat in an upstairs boardroom. He felt unusually chipper as he entered the meeting. Maybe because he'd had some days to make peace with the end of his career.

He walked in, said hello to everyone, poured himself a cup of coffee, and took his chair.

There were no documents in front of those present, only cups. It was a large room for a party of four, himself facing Inspector Theresa Stein and Sergeant Mike Bosko, with Michelin Montgomery to his right.

He and Montgomery were cool but polite to one another. On his way in today, Dion had decided that if he found himself going down, he would try to bring Montgomery with him. But he realized it wouldn't work. He had no proof. All he would do was embarrass himself and give everyone else a bunch of free entertainment. He would have to keep the hit-and-run issue, along with the assault in the men's room, to himself.

Montgomery seemed happy to let it lie, too.

The meeting promised to be brief, and started on a positive note. Dion was commended for his initiative, and the end result of saving April Quail, as well as bringing Ben Stirling's killer to justice. He remembered to sit up straight and respond with short and civil answers. When he couldn't come up with an answer fast enough, he played for time by sipping coffee and looking thoughtful.

Where exactly did things go wrong? Later he tried to trace his steps back to the point where he could have kept his mouth shut. Probably it was his answers to the general question about the wisdom of going off on his own while suspended.

He described, with maybe too much specificity, why he needed to see Ray Starkey, how he had tried to alert others to his suspicions, and how some had stonewalled him. Going on to say, "Stonewalled is an understatement," was the point at which he strayed from his plan, and looking meaningfully at Montgomery didn't help.

Montgomery's friendly blue eyes widened in surprise, and Theresa Stein asked what he meant by that.

"What I mean is Corporal Montgomery not only wouldn't go see Ray Starkey, after I told him how important it was, about five times —"

"And where do you get that?" Montgomery interrupted. "Didn't I tell you I would? I made a note, and I told you I'd go check it out."

"You made it clear you'd go later, not right away — if at all."

"You mean I should have stood up and gone charging out there, bugles blasting?" Montgomery looked both injured and amused.

"Yes, I mean stand up and charge out there —" Dion said, and the next bit in retrospect should have been reworded — "bugles fucking blasting."

Theresa Stein told him to lower his voice and watch his language, but it was too late. The blood pressure was up, the argument in full swing, Dion and Montgomery facing off. "If you'd been listening," Montgomery exclaimed, "you would have heard me say I would send a member out shortly."

"You didn't say that. You said you believed it was a waste of time, called it werewolf stories, and then threatened me."

"*What?*"

Stein said, "Calvin —"

"This man doesn't just want me gone from here," Dion told her. "He wants me dead."

"Which brings me spot on to something I want to talk to you about," she said, "namely Samantha Kerr. She's a new counsellor over at the medical building. I hear she's very good."

"Which is exactly what he wants," Dion told her, slapping the table top. "He wants you to think I'm unfit, because I'd been talking to Jackie Randall. Why does that matter? Because she was digging into his handling of the hit-and-run case, which he didn't like. That's why he wants me blacklisted."

"And dead," Stein reminded him. "You know, it seems to me Corporal Montgomery has shown more concern for your welfare lately than anyone else around here. He's championed your cause, in fact has done a much better job of it than you have. But he's also worried about your state of mind — and I'm beginning to see his point. You'd better think hard before you go throwing allegations around, especially in a forum like this."

"I did think hard! I defended him. I told Jackie she was wrong, even when I thought she was right, and in the end, she agreed. She was going to either hand it to Internal or drop it. Probably drop it. I was only too happy to do the same. But ask me again what I think."

"Sit down, Cal," Bosko said.

Dion hadn't realized he had risen, but he wasn't done yet. "Not only that, I want full access to Jackie Randall's file. Before he goes and tampers with that, too."

"Sit down," Bosko said again, louder.

Dion sat back down in his chair as belligerently as he knew how. "And by the way, does a man concerned about your welfare march you up to the john, shove you against the wall, and tell you he's collected evidence that's going to ruin you? Is that what an innocent man does, or is that someone with something to hide?"

"Holy Toledo, where did *that* come from?" Montgomery remarked.

"Are you saying that never happened?" Dion asked him. To everyone else he said, "You want me to tell you the bottom line? Because I'm ready if you are."

"Is this about Tori's supposed involvement in the hit and run?" Montgomery asked.

He said it openly, without hesitation or concern. Dion stared at him. He saw sympathy radiating back at him, and not much else. Now he understood the game plan. Montgomery had pre-empted the attack. Not just let the cat out of the bag, but fed it. Stein and Bosko seemed to know the punchline. They had known all along. That's what this meeting was all about, silencing the dead whistleblower and finding out where the live one stood on the issue.

He picked up his coffee cup. He thought about that buff-coloured school tablet again, full of possibly coded notes that only he could cast light on. What about Linnae Avenue? In the end, Jackie had written it off as a dead end, but she hadn't convinced him. Then there was his own idea about checking cell records, pinpointing Tori's phone call to Montgomery on Halloween night. None of it was going to be looked into now.

He re-centred himself and pitched it one last time at Stein and Bosko. "I should work on Jackie Randall's murder file. I have a perspective that you're going to need."

Stein stood, straightening her suit skirt. "This is where I hand it over to Mike and Corporal Montgomery. Outline your ideas to them. All right? And don't forget Samantha Kerr, Calvin. It's no longer optional, by the way. See you all later."

Stein left the room. Bosko's cellphone had buzzed, meanwhile. He was on his feet, making a hand signal at Montgomery, *Carry on without me*, and now he was gone, too, and like a cruel joke, Dion and Montgomery were left to sort things out on their own.

* * *

The Boones's wheelchair-equipped, teal-blue Sienna van had been found. Leith and JD drove up to Lynn Valley to take a look at the evidence *in situ*. It sat off a rarely used lower-park service road, driven into a sludgy spur and abandoned. The wheelchair was still inside.

The mystery of Anastasia Boone's disappearance was solved two days later. She lay stretched out supine within a gulley, fairly high in the park and off the beaten track. Two officers in search of Rosetti's devil's club patch — as seen in his final photographs — found not only the patch, but the young girl. Like the van, she was shrouded in foliage, canopied by the big spiky leaves that were withering to gold in the frigid November air.

She wore a nightgown, soaking wet and plastered to her skin. Her eyes were somewhat open, her dark hair rayed out neatly, and a small bouquet of dollar store flowers lay on her chest. The coroner suggested cause of death was suffocation. If not for the late-season insects visibly mining her body for nutrients, Leith thought, she could have been the flawlessly beautiful subject of a romantic painting.

"Imagine carrying her all this way," JD said. "Must have been nighttime, or someone would have seen him."

Leith nodded with a sigh, and looked around. He wouldn't express it to JD, but once again he could feel the spirit of the place, in a most visceral way. The breeze up here was biting, the red cedars massive. And there was the hush. Even with everyone standing around and the pockets of conversation, the silence was overwhelming.

If his own limited imagination was affected like this, sensing some higher power resident in these trees, imagine the sway it would have over a mind on the edge of madness.

Forty-One

LINNAE

LEITH SAT IN MIKE BOSKO'S OFFICE, called in to talk about nothing more controversial than workload and rotas — or so it seemed. At the end, however, Bosko placed a folder on his desk, removed a document, and passed it across. "On an unrelated matter, take a look at this, Dave."

A set of photocopies. Scribbles, handwritten letters, numbers. Mostly numbers. "Is this supposed to mean something to me?" Leith asked.

"Probably not. It's from a notebook that was in a box of documents recovered from Jackie Randall's apartment. It seems to be related to the Breanna Ferris hit and run, but I could be wrong."

"Hmm."

"I'd kind of like to know what Randall was up to," Bosko said. "Especially in light of this." He next placed a mini recorder on the desk. "Have a listen and see what you think. No, not here. Take it with you. Just keep it to yourself for now. Okay? Thanks."

The meeting was over. Leith picked up the recorder and went to his desk to listen. It seemed Bosko had recorded a conference of some kind. Dion was there, being commended, then questioned, and sounding like humble pie. And though the conference started off low-key and friendly, the key changed fairly fast. With Dion in there, how could it not?

* * *

Dion sat in the lunchroom, eating and thinking. The conversation between himself and Corporal Montgomery in the meeting room the other day, once everyone else had left, had been surprisingly productive. A great weight had been lifted off his shoulders, by the end of it.

"Look, I'm sorry," Montgomery had told him. "I was under a lot of stress. Tori told me Jackie had come around, accusing her of things — running over Breanna Ferris on Halloween — and by implication, accusing me of trying to bury the case. Tori didn't want to tell me, so as not to upset me, but in the end she did. I was shocked. But I'm a civilized man. I knew I could talk to Jackie, off the record, and set her straight. But of course, I never got the chance. Why did I take it out on you? Jackie had just been brutally murdered, and so her accusations were left up in the air. You and Jackie seemed close, so I imagined you were going to take up where she left off. I should have just talked to you about it, instead of blowing up. Again, I'm really sorry. I don't usually lose my head like that."

His apology seemed genuine. His blue eyes were kinder than ever. Dion had taken the conversation home and mentally gone over his own suspicions, along with every interaction he had had with Jackie and every change he had witnessed in Montgomery's behaviour. What he was left with was no evidence, and a perfectly believable explanation from the man he had unfairly suspected.

Instinct, he thought with disgust. It was something he had, but something he could no longer trust. It wasn't instinct that had led him to Starkey's door, as people seemed to think when they clapped him on the back, telling him what a great sleuth he was. It was a fluke.

At the end of his detailed introspection, he had come to the conclusion that he had been right all along, that Tori had *not* been driving through Sunset Boulevard that night, and Montgomery had *not* covered up the crime.

In fact, the next time he had seen Montgomery in the hall, they had chatted in a friendly way. Even agreed to go grab a drink later. The end result was that the whole hit-and-run/cover-up thing was officially checked off in Dion's mind as so much premium-grade bullshit.

Now he was just waiting for the depression to lift. Why it was still hanging around, he didn't understand. Probably it was Jackie Randall's death by werewolf. Or maybe it was the one question he couldn't answer — why the hell had she been in the Mesachee alone that night?

Leith walked into the lunchroom with an armload of books. He got himself a coffee, came over, and said, "Mind if I sit?"

Dion smiled. "Please. I was waiting for a chance to thank you for saving my life."

"Hey, no problem."

"I would have been toast, for sure."

"Or a dog's breakfast," Leith said.

There was something different about him today, and it took Dion a moment to figure out what it was — reading glasses, gold-framed and smart-looking. "What are you studying there?"

Leith removed the glasses with a sigh. "Trusses, and what to do about them. The first thing I discover crawling up in the rafters is one whole section has to be replaced. But it was all on the disclosure form, and I opted out of an inspection, didn't I? It's nothing less than I expected."

"What trusses?" Dion said.

Leith told him about a house he had bought. Hadn't moved in yet, but he was getting prepped for some hard work.

"Cool," Dion said, and waited for Leith to open his truss book and get on with it.

But Leith was ignoring his manuals. He was slumped back in a casual way that rang alarm bells in Dion's mind. The slump was out of place, artificial. It was a means to an end.

"There's something I wanted to ask you about," Leith said. "In a meeting last week, I hear you had a few things to say about Michelin Montgomery."

Dion's appetite vanished, and he pushed aside the remains of his sandwich. "I did," he said. "But that's over. I apologized."

Leith ignored him. "You said Jackie Randall was digging into his handling of the Breanna Ferris case. You also said he assaulted you. He's already put it on the record that Jackie was accusing Tori of the hit and run.

He didn't tell us she was accusing him of covering it up. I want to go over all that with you, get your version, in full. I also want to know more about this assault."

"Forget about it. Jackie was a workaholic. If there wasn't enough crime in her life, she made stuff up. I fell for it myself, for a while. But for all her investigations, she didn't come up with a shred of proof. As for the assault, there wasn't one. It was a discussion. We sorted it out. It's history."

Leith sat looking at him cynically. "What you said in that meeting was he shoved you against the wall and told you he was collecting evidence that would destroy your career. You also accused him of wanting you dead."

"Blacklisted," Dion said.

"Dead, actually."

Dion could feel the heat rising to his face. His depression was back, arm in arm with its mates, fear and anger. "How do you know all this? Who recorded the meeting? And who gave you the recording?"

Leith pointed at Dion's plate. "Eat your sandwich."

"I'm not hungry."

"Then sign off. We're going for a drive."

* * *

They wore their warmest, most waterproof clothing for their climb in the Mesachee. The weather was too miserable for even the hardiest mountain bikers, and they found themselves alone in the park. They made it to the site where Jackie Randall had died, and Dion saw that it was unmarked now. Nothing to show for her passing in the midafternoon gloom but a lot of bruised and broken undergrowth.

Leith said, "The bite marks on her throat weren't clear, but they could be a match to the bite on Troy Hamilton's arm. Can't be disqualified, anyway." He showed Dion the stalk of a plant that had been apparently cut and removed. "There was blood on the thorns that matches Stefano Boone's blood type. DNA pending, but I'd put money on what the results will be. Also black synthetic fur, same as the tufts found in the Hamilton attack. Over there is where the crowbar was found."

Dion stared wherever Leith pointed and then, finally, into his eyes. "So you're saying Corporal Montgomery planted the blood and the fur? What about the bite mark?"

"He had the file. Had access to all the forensics, including photographs. It's not out of the question to fashion something out of wood, say, that would leave impressions to match Boone's."

"That's crazy."

Leith shrugged.

Dion turned over the concept in his mind. It was almost too wild to absorb. Not only wild, but crushingly sad. But it was a rush, too, in a way. Hadn't it been there in his brain all along, from the moment he'd found Jackie dying, like she was whispering in his ear? *Go get him, my friend.*

"Risky," he said. "What if Boone could prove he wasn't here at the time she died?"

Leith had an answer for that, too. "Boone was on the run. When found, he'd probably have a hard time proving where he was or wasn't. And if you hadn't come along when Jackie was still alive, say she was found a couple of days later, maybe longer — the time of death would've been hard to pinpoint with any accuracy. Right? You really fucked it up for him."

Dion squinted against a strange rain that seemed to hover rather than fall. "You're sure he did it. Why?"

"Tori's fender-bender, for one thing."

"Fender-bender?"

"She hit a lamppost in the Safeway parking lot. Tuesday. Had to get the front end replaced." Leith pulled out cigarettes and lit one.

"You can't smoke in the park."

"This is the Mesachee," Leith said. "It's Crown land. You can smoke on Crown land. I think." After a puff he said, "So there's the fender-bender. Probably it's more the way Monty hates you, though. You were stuck in Starkey's basement, and I was trying to figure out where you were, and he took his sweet time looking for the info I needed."

"He couldn't have known I was getting eaten alive by a dog."

"No. But he couldn't have known you weren't, either. It's just not right, is it?"

Dion thought about it, watching Leith smoke. He knew Leith was an addict, trying to quit. Dion smoked occasionally himself, but could take it or leave it. Looch had smoked notoriously. If the crash hadn't killed him, the cigarettes would have.

Leith caught his eye and offered the box. Dion declined and said, "So what, that Montgomery hates me? Doesn't mean much."

"Why would he hate you, if not 'cause you're treading on his plans?"

A bird flitted down and landed on a branch overlooking Jackie's deathbed. Dion thought about how far she might have gone in life, if given the chance. Commissioner, probably. "Any idea where Montgomery was at the time Jackie was attacked? Or where he says he was?"

"I know where he says he was," Leith answered, "because some of us were talking about it later, about where we were and what we were doing when we got the call. He was at home, Shop-Vaccing his van for an upcoming trip to the Island. He got the call about Jackie on his work phone — and so that will confirm he was where he claims he was — dropped everything and ran. It sounded natural enough when it came up in conversation. Now it reeks of setting up an alibi."

"If he says that's what he was doing, then he was," Dion said. "Those vacuums are loud. He'd have done it on the street, and the neighbours will confirm it. So he figured some way to get here and back, fast. Maybe even left the vac going. Got back in time to catch the call about Jackie."

"That's some distance to cover. He borrowed a car? Rented one under a false name?"

"Bicycle."

Leith finished his cigarette, then started up the track. "This way. Signs of passage. Careful."

Dion avoided a back-thwack of branches and followed him. Five minutes of climbing brought them to another point of interest. This was a path delineated through the underbrush, more sparse than it would be in summer, leading up and out of sight. Leith said, "It's the blood drop trail. You can't see any prints now, but there was evidence of bike treads and boots leading up and down from here. If you're fit, a fifteen-minute hike will get you up to Lynn Valley Road. A lot faster if you're good on a mountain bike."

"Does Stefano Boone have a mountain bike?"

"He doesn't have any kind of bike, that we could find."

Dion crouched to study the ground. "The path's been examined all the way up?"

"All tracks charted and photographed, and a few plaster moulds."

Dion fiddled with his phone, set the timer, then started on the path, scrambling up a muddy natural staircase of rocks and roots. Leith followed. When they stood on Lynn Valley Road, catching their breath, Dion read out his stopwatch results. "Eleven minutes."

Leith was still catching his breath, and said nothing.

The street was quiet, not a soul in sight, except in the distance, a figure cycled around a bend in the road and disappeared. Dion was revving with excitement by now. The case was shaping up. He said, "He set up his Shop-Vac scenario. He lured Jackie to a meet in the park, and jumped on his bike. It would have to be his mountain bike, to get down through the trails. He'd have a lot of options, cutting through from Seymour Heights to Lynn Valley. Finding Jackie and dealing with her, maybe add twenty minutes. It's possible."

"I'm hung up on Jackie. How did he lure her out here? Call her up, say, *Hey, I've got something to show you?* She wouldn't fall for anything like it. Meet in the woods with a man you're trying to destroy? Unlikely."

Dion thought it was more than unlikely — it was unthinkable. There had to be more to it, and he wondered aloud if Linnae Avenue could be the answer.

"Linnae Avenue, what's that?" Leith said.

As they returned to the Headwaters parking lot — it was even more difficult going down than up — Dion told Leith about the mysterious clue left behind by Jackie Randall.

Forty-Two

METAMORPHOSIS

LEITH WAS BACK TO BUSINESS as usual. He was kept in the loop, though, as the Integrated Homicide Investigation Team burrowed deeper into Montgomery's last days and nights. It was a detailed burrowing, carefully conducted so as not to tip him off.

IHIT kept Leith in the loop, and Leith in turn informed Dion. The Breanna Ferris and Troy Hamilton files were turned inside out. Monty's access to exhibits, every phone call, every text, every memo, was studied. Phone records from the night of the hit and run showed he had received a call from a number that didn't belong to Tori; it turned out to be a throwaway phone, a burner. The call had come within the time-of-death estimate in Breanna Ferris's autopsy report.

Monty's neighbours were interviewed. The time he was home, vacuuming out his van, and the times he could have slipped away were all nailed down. He would have had to take a different vehicle, since the van and Tori's Acura remained parked at the house at all times.

His window of opportunity seemed impossibly short, until IHIT members considered the man could have swapped bikes, relay fashion. The swifter street bike would have shaved minutes off the trip from Seymour Heights to the Mesachee. The mountain bike might have been stashed in advance, in the bushes at the top of the trail, used, dumped, and later retrieved when the coast was clear. It was another risk that Monty might not have taken, had he known he was going to be all but caught in the act.

With the means worked out, Leith expected the rest to fall quickly into place. He did not look forward to the arrest, and the inquiry to follow. It felt like fratricide.

The week after his confidential talk with Dion had been strange, in several ways. The weather was weird in the Lower Mainland. Not yet December, yet a great dump of snow had fallen, putting the city in a panic. Many Lower Mainlanders hardly knew what snow was, let alone how to drive in it. But just as weird, Monty surprised the crew by announcing he and Tori had gotten hitched. Under the radar, so to speak, a civil ceremony solemnized by a Justice of the Peace. No white-gowned, fun-filled affair complete with confetti, cake, and champagne. No speeches, no friends to cheer them on.

Monty claimed the reason was that his dad was terminally ill, and he and Tori wanted to tie the knot sooner than later. It would make Dad happy. "Makes me happy, too," he told his colleagues, as they doubtfully congratulated him.

"More like means he's scared," Leith told Dion in the lunchroom. "Wants to use the spousal privilege clause, limit what Tori has to say in court about what they're conspiring about. He's caught a whiff of the investigation. Life as he knows it is over."

Dion didn't look thrilled. He said if Montgomery was scared, then he was scared, too. Something was going to break. "When's the arrest?" he asked.

Double arrest. Tori was getting hauled in, as well.

"Probably tomorrow. I'll let you know."

* * *

Leith couldn't sleep, and it was Dion's prediction that something was going to break that kept him tossing. When he arrived at work, and Montgomery was absent, he fetched Dion away from his regular uniformed duties. "Just think it might be a good idea to go check it out," he said.

Out at the Montgomery home in Seymour Heights, Monty's van was not in the carport, and Tori's car was not in the open garage.

"They've made a run for it," Dion said. "Split up and dashed."

In the picture window of the home across the street, a woman stood looking out. Leith waved at her. She waved back. "Let's go talk to her," he said.

They crossed the street. Leith rang the bell and questioned the woman who opened the door. She told them she had seen Tori heading off for her usual morning run, down at the park. On further questioning, she said it was the Headwaters trails that Tori was doing these days. Yes, even in this weather. The Lynn Loop. Where Monty had gone off to, she couldn't say, but he left about half an hour after Tori, and seemed in a hurry.

"Which way did he go?" Leith asked.

She pointed.

Dion drove and Leith phoned his IHIT contact, letting them know what he was doing and where he was headed. In case there was trouble.

"Probably nothing," he told Dion.

But down at the Headwaters parking lot, Monty's van sat, still warm, right next to Tori's Acura, and suddenly Leith had the feeling it wasn't nothing after all. "What's Lynn Loop?"

"This way." Dion was already heading at a jog toward the footbridge. Leith followed, at less of a jog. Snow beautified the landscape. Whereas it had already melted to light skiffs in the city, it remained thick along Lynn Creek, and patchy up into the trees. He crossed the bridge and saw Dion was already up at the fork in the path, staring northward.

While scrambling up the Mesachee trail last week, Dion had griped to Leith about how out of shape he was. But he wasn't. Even loaded down with gun belt and its paraphernalia, he was fast on his feet. Leith was puffing down off the bridge and Dion was restlessly waiting, eager to get going. "Loop begins here," he called, pointing.

"Go on, I'll follow," Leith called back.

Dion took off at a jog again. Leith tried for a semi-jog, but when he saw Dion ahead break into a run, he did too, as fast as his legs would take him.

The Monty and Tori scuffle looked about as dirty as any street fight Leith had broken up in his career. The couple were off the boardwalk, whaling away in a swampy, snow-filled hollow. As Leith drew close he saw that Monty was clearly winning — an unfair fight, with his extra pounds and martial arts muscles, though his wife in her soggy spandex was fighting back for what she was worth. Leith caught up as Dion was dogpiling on top of both of them, trying to get Monty's arm back and locked. Monty was having too much fun trying to strangle Tori to heed Dion's shouts of warning, so Leith pitched in. Together they managed to separate husband and wife, and while Tori flipped like a landed fish, gasping for air, Montgomery turned on his heels to attack his attackers.

It was a scary metamorphosis. Monty was no longer a man coming at Leith, but a roaring mad dog, with bloodshot eyes popping, throat pulsing, mouth foaming. Tori had gotten her breath and crawled out of the way to collapse on the boardwalk. Monty took swings at Dion first, then Leith. Flying knuckles caught Leith on the cheek, knocking him off balance. Dion went for a rear-attack neck hold, but Monty leveraged out of it and judo-tripped him. Leith was getting up as Dion was going down. Dion lay winded in the snow, staring at the sky. Leith shouted out a warning as Monty lunged to give the downed man a head stomp, and Dion's arms crossed upward to deflect the boot. Not only deflect, but grab hold and twist. It was a good, full-body twist, and Monty tipped sideways. Dion scrambled to his feet and piled on Monty with Leith.

They worked together, fuelled by adrenaline. While Leith ground Monty's head into the bog, Dion got out handcuffs and applied them to their prisoner. A minute later Leith was reciting Monty's rights for him — silence and counsel, just like any other criminal. Two hours ahead of schedule, they had him bagged.

* * *

The newlyweds were gone. An ambulance had carted Tori away, and Monty was removed — still shouting death threats at anyone who looked at him — by IHIT members. Leith and Dion were obliged to stay in the sleety, overcast parking lot to meet the team, who would be coming in to gather evidence. In the interlude, Dion danced.

The dance was only a few seconds long, but wild — a wet, muddy man in uniform kicking about in a semicircle, arms out like little wings, and it reminded Leith of the moves he had seen at a powwow once — which made him wonder if maybe Starkey was right. He felt like joining in, frankly. It had been the most fun he'd had in a while, taking down Michelin Montgomery.

* * *

With stitches, bandages, bruised eyes, and puffy mouth, Tori insisted on placing a Japanese fan in front of her face as she told Leith and an IHIT officer the truth. Or, as she put it, "The truth, the whole truth, and nothing but the truth, so help me God. The Richmond shoot collapsed because one of the girls got something in her eye. Long story."

The modelling gig, Leith interpreted.

"Anyway, so I got off early and went to this guy's place I know. Yes, a guy, who happens to be married, and his wife happened to be out of town. I know her. She's a doll, but doesn't deserve him. People fall in love, things happen. The heart is a lonely hunter."

An affair.

"I didn't have a lot to drink — maybe one martini, and a lot of time in between sips, so don't blame what happened on that."

Bit late to check blood alcohol levels, Leith thought. But as soon as they got the boyfriend, they'd find out how many martinis she'd actually downed.

"I was fine," she said. "Yes, I realized how late it was, and I had to get to Monty's party, or he'd kill me, but I didn't speed. Your expert guy says I was doing seventy klicks? I find that hard to believe. I'm pretty sure I was doing forty. And the kid just zipped out in front of me, and in a curve, too. I hit the brakes, and I almost didn't hit her. It was just a light thump. I was pretty sure she'd be okay. I know I should have stopped, but I was really, really scared. I pulled over where it was safe to and called Monty. I used my other phone, my boyfriend phone, by mistake. But anyway. Monty said to call 911 and stay at the scene. I told him no way. It wasn't my fault, but can you imagine what even that kind of publicity would do to my brand?"

The shy-eyed, wildflowers-behind-the-back kind of brand, Leith guessed.

She continued, "I told Monty nobody saw it, there's no damage, the girl's fine, and I'm going home. He told me that if I didn't stay put and call 911, he'd call 911 for me, which would get me arrested. I told him if he did that, I'd tell everyone about his fetishes."

Oh lord, Leith thought. Tori seemed to be smiling behind her fan. But it wasn't a happy smile — more the *I'm dead, so I might as well enjoy it* variety.

"So he told me to get home quick, park in the back, and keep cool. No, actually he said, keep *fucking* cool. Then I found out the girl had died," she said. No longer smiling, Leith noticed. "I was like, no, this can't be happening. But Monty said don't worry, he'd take care of it. He didn't do such a good job, though, did he? Because next thing you know, Jackie's snooping around. She's always been a nosy piece of work, even in school. She told me she knew I hit that girl. She looked at the car and asked how I dented the front. I said it happened in a parking lot. Somebody must have dropped something on it. Then she said she knew I was up in that area on Halloween, because I was visiting my boyfriend. I have no idea how she knew that, because nobody in the world knows about it."

But we will soon enough, Leith thought.

"I told Monty about her visit. I mean, everything except what she said about my boyfriend. Monty went ballistic."

She took a break to sip her San Pellegrino — part of the confession negotiations — before getting onto the cold-blooded set-up and slaughter of Jackie Randall. "Monty was a beast to live with after that. He stayed up all night, then in the morning told me how we could make this disappear. It's the only way out, he said. And I'd either cooperate or spend my best years in jail, my choice. All I had to do was convince Jackie to come and meet me in the park. Since I'm a notorious fitness freak, it was easy. I'd tell her I'm checking out the bike trails at the Mesachee, to come meet me there, because I have something to tell her about the accident, and about Monty, too. Keep it vague, but tempting. And I'd only talk to her, nobody else. If she tried to get anybody else involved, I'd clam up. So that's what I did. Had a hell of a time finding a pay phone, but there's one in the mall. Then it took some convincing to get her to meet in the woods, but I told her it's hard to get away from Monty, and I had to talk to her in total privacy, so since I was going to be trying out the bike trails, it seemed like the best time and place to meet. She agreed."

She had put down her fan to grip her San Pellegrino, and Leith saw how badly disfigured her face was. He wondered if it would ever properly heal. She said, "Actually, I don't bike. But anyway. And as I told you, I had absolutely no idea he would hurt her, let alone kill her. I didn't know until I saw it on the news. I'd never have gone along with it if I knew. I liked Jackie."

Even if she was a nosy piece of work.

"I was fairly terrified of Monty by then. He's not talking much, and he's calling up city hall or whatever it is, booking a JP to marry us soon as possible. Creepy. So I don't have to testify against him, or something."

She next went on to explain how she and Monty had come to be fighting to the death on the Lynn Loop trail this morning. "I was heading out for my daily jog, and we got arguing about just about everything, especially Halloween, which caused all this. He was back to why was I on Sunset Boulevard that night, which is totally not on my way home from Richmond. I had told him I was going for a bit of a spin after the gig, before heading home. Taking the long way around, sort of. He believed it, or wanted to believe it. Because it's something I do. I like driving. But you know how it is when you're arguing; you start throwing dirt. He goes why would I go for a spin after driving in from Richmond — but with lots of bad words in between. So finally I admitted that I was seeing a guy, and I said he's young and handsome and I love him. Then I left. And I guess he came after me, with murder on his mind."

Leith asked her if her boyfriend lived on Linnae Avenue, by any chance?

"Goddamn, you detectives," she said, and her deformed mouth tried to grin. "Kevin Poon. He's a model, and I love him. We worked together in the summer. Swimsuits. That's another thing I told Jackie on the phone. Leave my boyfriend out of this."

Yeah, sorry, Leith thought. That's just not going to happen.

* * *

After Bosko was done congratulating Leith on a job well done, Leith felt it was a bad time to ask his wrecking-ball question. But it was now or never. "Why did you secretly tape that meeting? Are you still investigating Cal? Did your PI find something? I thought it was over."

Bosko was never ruffled by anything, and conflict only seemed to make him mellower. In his mellowest voice yet, he said, "I taped the meeting because every time Cal opens his mouth, something interesting comes out. No, my PI did not find anything, but yes, the file remains open."

"Why? If you have something on Dion, arrest him. Make him part of it. If you have nothing, leave him alone. I don't get this dicking around."

Bosko nodded. "I know what you're saying. But here's how it is. I frankly suspect him of a serious crime, and

I can't ignore that, can I? But I have nothing on him to, for instance, lay before IHIT. Zero. So I'm left in this dicking-around limbo, where I can only keep my eyes and ears open."

"I don't understand."

"It's a complicated path, and I *will* tell you about it, Dave. But not today."

"When? I'd like to know whether I can work with him or not. I'm not going to work with somebody today that I may be arresting tomorrow."

"Seems to me you've done just that," Bosko said mildly.

"That's different," Leith snapped.

Bosko seemed to mentally twiddle his thumbs for a minute, maybe weighing his words, or maybe thinking about dinner. Then he said, "I'll tell you this much that I know for sure. Somebody out there knows something. I'm just waiting for her to come out of the woodwork again, and tell me what I need to know."

A chill went through Leith's veins. "A witness?"

Bosko leaned back and nodded again, either regretting his news, or doing a good imitation of regret. "A witness, yes."

* * *

Farah opened the door, smiled at Dion, and welcomed him inside. "You've changed," she said.

He was surprised. "I have?"

"You've solidified."

He supposed it was his newfound conviction she was seeing. He was here to woo her, and fiercely. Grinning, he opened his arms, placed them around her waist, pulled her close. "I was hoping for more of that great whiskey."

She laughed, reached up to clasp her hands behind his head, completing the circle. "Is that right?"

"And paella."

"I don't have paella, but I will have a great stir-fry."

"And to apologize. I was a creep."

"You weren't a creep. You were afraid."

He kissed her on the side of her face. "Maybe. But I'm not anymore. Pour me a glass of the good stuff, and I'll tell you about my week. It was wild."

She poured him a glass of whiskey, and they talked, but the evening didn't progress as it had before. She didn't say as much, or as freely, or make him feel magically swept off his feet. As she prepared dinner, he asked her if his apology hadn't taken, or something. Or if she really wasn't up to cooking? He didn't want to impose. In fact, let him take her out for dinner.

"No, Cal," she said. She had come over to where he sat in the same kitchen chair he had occupied to interview her on that first night, which now seemed so long ago. She stood before him with arms draped around his shoulders in a loose capture. "I think you're hoping for something that's not going to happen."

He looked up at her. He had a strong idea of where this was going.

"Not because I wouldn't like it to happen," she said, "but because you're fooling yourself. You're so obviously in love with Kate that it's quite funny. And touching. And inspiring. I think you should go get her. That's what I think."

"Kate?" he said. He couldn't recall telling Farah about Kate, except in a roundabout way. He shouldn't have mentioned the ex. Should have just shut up about previous relationships. It made him look like a dud. A hopeless, loveless, unlovable dud. He backed away from Farah's arms. He said, "She's got a boyfriend, and unlike you and me, they're true love forever."

"I have a feeling they're not."

"How the hell could you know what Kate and Patrick are or are not?"

"Because you're so smart, and you think there's still a chance," she said, recapturing him.

"I don't."

"I can read between your lines," she said, touching the tip of his nose and grinning down at him, treating him like a child.

"You can't," he said, and tears filled his eyes.

She hugged him. She let him stay with her that night, no sex, barely any talking, and then it was over. In the morning she sent him on his way.

Forty-Three

WOLF

CHEF HAD WOUNDED STEFANO. He didn't even realize how deeply, until she told him, like a confession, through the grill, the thick glass. At the end of her confession, she apologized. "I had no other choice, Stef. You were in trouble, and you needed help. I just wanted you to be safe."

Wanting him to be safe, she had turned him in? How twisted was that logic?

He was now in a cage, and he had prowled its perimeters, looking for a crack, but there was no way out. He had slammed at the door till they came and restrained him, and that was the worst of all, being tied to the bed. They had drugged him, too. He knew it because his perceptions had warped. His only contact with the real world, the cries of his brothers, had faded to distorted yips and growls, and echoey bugle-like calls in mushy English.

He was confused, but enlightened, too. He knew things now. Never trust her again. Never open himself up.

She came to see him, not just once, but on many days. She was being nice to him.

She felt sorry for him. She talked in a matter-of-fact way to let him know he was a normal guy, just needed a bit of talking to. She told him his paintings were hot stuff. They were going viral.

Viral. He liked that word. It sounded like mayhem.

Along with his freedom, the pain of metamorphosis was also gone. This distressed him more than anything.

Did it mean …?

The loss of the pain he could blame on nobody but himself. Shouldn't have mentioned it to the staff here, the ache in his legs and buttocks. He had just wanted them to untie him, but instead they had run tests. Then called the pain *sciatica*, and said it was odd, because sciatica was an older person's condition. They had given him something for it, and now his human form was stabilized.

Stabilized. What a horror. It meant he was no longer leaving this body behind. He was trapped within.

He scratched his face till they restrained him again.

The restraints made him howl, so they upped the dosage.

By degrees, he was learning not to act out.

He huddled in his cage and was quiet.

But he had a plan.

He would be good. He would live in his quiet forest. He would stop complaining and banging and scratching, and then they would stop drugging him, and the steel in his fingers and thighs would harden. He would keep his mouth shut, lips tucked in to hide the teeth pushing through his gums.

And one day, because she was so nice, she would convince them. She would ask to take him outside for a walk, him being so good, so cured. That would be his chance, all he needed to find that door. His tormentors would remove the restraints and let him out of the cage. Chef would take him for a walk. And then, only then, he would attack — like never before.

ACKNOWLEDGEMENTS

Though *Creep* is not the first in the B.C. Blues Crime series, it's been in draft form for a few years. In fact it's the first work I shared with others — which was a very big deal. Those others were a warm-hearted crew of internet spirits from an online writing group called the Next Big Writer. We knew each other by screen name, and shared critiques. They were not only kind, but hugely constructive, and I've been looking forward to officially dedicating this book to them ever since.

Creep came out of cold storage last year, and I want to thank J.G. Toews — who is about to publish her first crime novel! — for being the first to read the revised version. Her advice and support carried me through some tough times.

Editors and critiquers David Warriner, Allister Thompson, and Catharine Chen whipped *Creep* into finished shape and gave some big-picture advice that I especially appreciate. And as always, the team at

Dundurn I work with — Michelle Melski, Kate Condon-Moriarty, and Jenny McWha — have been wonderfully patient and helpful.

I am also grateful to Irene Lau for her technical wizardry, friendship, and profound knowledge of whiskey. And finally thanks to my son for his (often) good-natured assistance with virtually anything.

* * *

A note about location: I have taken some liberties with the geography of North Vancouver; there is no Mesachee, and no spur of road called Greer with a creepy old house on it. Otherwise I have tried to be accurate.

Mystery and Crime Fiction
from Dundurn Press

Birder Murder Mysteries
by Steve Burrows
(Birding, British Coastal Town
Mysteries)
A Siege of Bitterns
A Pitying of Doves
A Cast of Falcons
A Shimmer of Hummingbirds
A Tiding of Magpies

Amanda Doucette Mysteries
by Barbara Fradkin
(PTSD, Cross-Canada Tour)
Fire in the Stars
The Trickster's Lullaby

B.C. Blues Crime Novels
by R.M. Greenaway
(British Columbia, Police
Procedural)
Cold Girl
Undertow
Creep

Stonechild & Rouleau Mysteries
by Brenda Chapman
(First Nations, Kingston,
Police Procedural)
Cold Mourning
Butterfly Kills
Tumbled Graves
Shallow End
Bleeding Darkness

Jenny Willson Mysteries
by Dave Butler
(Banff National Park,
Animal Poaching)
Full Curl

Falls Mysteries
by Jayne Barnard
(Rural Alberta, Female Sleuth)
When the Flood Falls

Foreign Affairs Mysteries
by Nick Wilkshire
(Global Crime Fiction, Humour)
Escape to Havana
The Moscow Code

Dan Sharp Mysteries
by Jeffrey Round
(LGBTQ, Toronto)
Lake on the Mountain
Pumpkin Eater
The Jade Butterfly
After the Horses
The God Game

Max O'Brien Mysteries
by Mario Bolduc
(Translation, Political Thriller,
Con Man)
The Kashmir Trap
The Roma Plot

Cullen and Cobb Mysteries
by David A. Poulsen
(Calgary, Private Investigators,
Organized Crime)
Serpents Rising
Dead Air
Last Song Sung

Strange Things Done
by Elle Wild
(Yukon, Dark Thriller)

Salvage
by Stephen Maher
(Nova Scotia, Fast-Paced Thriller)

Crang Mysteries
by Jack Batten
(Humour, Toronto)
Crang Plays the Ace
Straight No Chaser
Riviera Blues
Blood Count

Take Five
Keeper of the Flame
Booking In

Jack Taggart Mysteries
by Don Easton
(UNDERCOVER OPERATIONS)
Loose Ends
Above Ground
Angel in the Full Moon
Samurai Code
Dead Ends
Birds of a Feather
Corporate Asset
The Benefactor
Art and Murder
A Delicate Matter
Subverting Justice

Meg Harris Mysteries
by R.J. Harlick
(CANADIAN WILDERNESS FICTION,
FIRST NATIONS)
Death's Golden Whisper
Red Ice for a Shroud
The River Runs Orange
Arctic Blue Death
A Green Place for Dying
Silver Totem of Shame
A Cold White Fear
Purple Palette for Murder

Thaddeus Lewis Mysteries
by Janet Kellough
(PRE-CONFEDERATION CANADA)
On the Head of a Pin
Sowing Poison
47 Sorrows
The Burying Ground
Wishful Seeing

Cordi O'Callaghan Mysteries
by Suzanne F. Kingsmill
(ZOOLOGY, MENTAL ILLNESS)
Forever Dead
Innocent Murderer
Dying for Murder
Crazy Dead

Endgame
by Jeffrey Round
(MODERN RE-TELLING OF AGATHA
CHRISTIE, PUNK ROCK)

Inspector Green Mysteries
by Barbara Fradkin
(OTTAWA, POLICE PROCEDURAL)
Do or Die
Once Upon a Time
Mist Walker
Fifth Son
Honour Among Men
Dream Chasers
This Thing of Darkness
Beautiful Lie the Dead
The Whisper of Legends
None So Blind

Border City Blues
by Michael Januska
(PROHIBITION ERA WINDSOR)
Maiden Lane
Riverside Drive

Cornwall and Redfern Mysteries
by Gloria Ferris
(DARKLY COMIC, RURAL ONTARIO)
Corpse Flower
Shroud of Roses

TER 1/18